THE VENICE HOTEL

Tess Woods once had a simple life until her compulsion to write made-up stories complicated everything. She's now an award-winning and bestselling author of contemporary fiction.

Tess also works as a physiotherapist in private practice, and she shares a clinic and a home on the stunning Western Australian coast with her husband. She's the mother of two brilliant grown-up children and one grumpy grown-up cat. Tess's favourite thing to do is to curl up with a good book and a cup of tea, ignore the book, forget the tea and scroll on her phone instead. You can find her lurking on Instagram and Facebook or drop her a line at tess@tesswoods.com.au

THE VENICE HOTEL

TESS WOODS

PENGUIN BOOKS

UK | USA | Canada | Ireland | Australia
India | New Zealand | South Africa | China

Penguin Books is part of the Penguin Random House group of companies
whose addresses can be found at global.penguinrandomhouse.com

First published by Penguin Books, 2024

Copyright © Tess Woods, 2024

The moral right of the author has been asserted.

All rights reserved. No part of this publication may be reproduced, published, performed in public or communicated to the public in any form or by any means without prior written permission from Penguin Random House Australia Pty Ltd or its authorised licensees.

Bible verses from The Holy Bible, New International Version®, NIV® Copyright © 1973, 1978, 1984, 2011 by Biblica, Inc.® Used by permission. All rights reserved worldwide.
Cover photography by Panama/Adobe Stock, gammaphotostudio/Adobe Stock, alen_rush/Adobe Stock, Simona Sirio/Shutterstock, Stefanos Kyriazis/Shutterstock, Pierluigi.Palazzi/Shutterstock and Iofoto/Dreamstime
Inside cover images: front by Eky Studio/Shutterstock and back by Pegaz/Shutterstock
Internal illustrations by Marina/Adobe Stock
Cover design by Nikki Townsend Design © Penguin Random House Australia Pty Ltd
Author photo © Thomas Paul
Typeset in Adobe Garamond Pro by Midland Typesetters, Australia

Printed and bound in Australia by Griffin Press, an accredited
ISO AS/NZS 14001 Environmental Management Systems printer

 A catalogue record for this book is available from the National Library of Australia

ISBN 978 1 76134 440 4

penguin.com.au

We at Penguin Random House Australia acknowledge that Aboriginal and Torres Strait Islander peoples are the Traditional Custodians and the first storytellers of the lands on which we live and work. We honour Aboriginal and Torres Strait Islander peoples' continuous connection to Country, waters, skies and communities. We celebrate Aboriginal and Torres Strait Islander stories, traditions and living cultures; and we pay our respects to Elders past and present.

For all the daughters and the mothers, especially mine.

Prologue

She stood above him while the air left his body in a low, final exhale. She never considered herself to be a violent person; in fact, she prized her gentleness. It made her feel superior. But that moral high ground collapsed beneath her when he died.

Now she's been forced to rethink what she's capable of. Murder, apparently. This new understanding is an epiphany of sorts, one that's come to her on the twelfth day of Christmas. Because life's funny like that.

Would her actions be the same if she had her time over? Unquestionably. She'd gleefully watch the canals of Venice run red with his blood, over and over again.

That's who she is now.

On the
FIRST
DAY *of*
CHRISTMAS

Loretta

The woman is drowning. She stands tall inside a glass tank so narrow that her shoulders almost touch its sides. Her hair and dress are both long, flowing and white. Her bare feet are submerged in water and the hem of her flimsy dress swirls in it. Loretta has heard that the water is from the canal, but it's only a rumour. By the looks of it, though, she suspects it's true.

A small metal sign rests on the pavers in front of the tank. It bears a solitary word, engraved in a scrawling black font: '*affogando*'.

'What does affogando mean?' an American teenager, standing close to Loretta on the steps of the piazza, asks her mother. She mispronounces it.

'No idea.' The mother breathes steam.

Loretta clears her throat. 'It means "drowning". She is telling us she is drowning.'

'Ah,' the mother says. 'Aren't we all?'

The teenager turns her back to the performance artist and the Basilica di San Marco. She holds her phone up above her head, purses her swollen, glossed lips together and arches her thickly pencilled brows. Her mother copies the pose. The pouting duo are surrounded by grey: the grey stones of the ground and buildings and archways, the grey clouds above.

Alberto nudges Loretta in the ribs. 'Shall we take a photo too?' he says in Italian.

'What for?'

'I don't know, because it's Christmas. Why not?' He smiles.

She ignores the request, indicating with her chin at the artist. 'Look at her, she's freezing. Her hands are trembling.'

It's one of the coldest Christmas Days on record.

'She recognises you,' Alberto says.

Loretta knows this. She's always being recognised. She's been a cover model for *Vogue* and a guest on too many TV shows to name. But does the artist recognise her or *remember* her? That's what she really wants to know.

As she's considering this, Loretta's fingers glide across a short bristly hair on her neck. She curses inwardly. Even after she plucked half-a-dozen nuisance hairs in front of the magnified mirror on her dressing table early this morning, already here's a new one announcing itself, reminding her that she's old now. She pinches the hair between her thumb and index finger and gives it a few sharp tugs, but it remains stubbornly attached.

Alberto's loud breathing annoys her. Even here, in the crowded piazza, she can't escape the sound of his shallow, wheezy breaths. How she wishes he'd quit the cigarettes. She turns to look at him, standing a head shorter than her in his black bowler hat that hides his ever-growing bald patch, hands tucked deep into the pockets of his woollen trench. His face is tired, his skin blotched and yellowing.

He meets her eye. 'Andiamo, cara?' There's a warmth in the way he looks at her that softens her resentment.

'Let's go.' She hooks her arm into his.

The artist hasn't taken her eyes off Loretta, despite tourists milling about between them. Loretta gives her a small wave as she walks away. She thinks the woman returns her smile but she can't be certain.

The streets leading back to Hotel Il Cuore are heaving. The souvenir shops are packed with tourists admiring their colourful glass baubles, and the cafe crowds overflow to outdoors despite the cold. Christmas decorations strung high across the lanes form a canopy over Loretta and Alberto as they walk. The hanging lights get more extravagant each year. Every street is different.

'I wonder when the food writer will arrive,' Loretta says, more to herself than to Alberto.

'It's strange how she's turning up on Christmas Day,' he replies. 'On her own.'

'She's coming for work. Of course she's on her own.'

'It's not right. She should be with family at this time of year.'

'Some people don't think like that.'

'Not everyone is as lucky as we are.' Alberto pats her hand. 'We'll make her feel less lonely.'

'Why do you assume she's lonely?'

'She's travelling alone halfway across the world at Christmas. Of course she's lonely.'

Loretta doesn't argue.

A young tourist couple walks past them and the woman's expression changes to one of stupefied delight when she makes eye contact with Loretta. It's not often that Loretta leaves the hotel without her sunglasses on, but occasionally, on days like today, she longs to see the outside world not through a darkened lens.

'Oh my God, babe!' the woman squeals after they pass. 'I swear that was Signora Bianchi!'

Alberto and Loretta exchange a smile and keep walking. He sings 'Silent Night' and she listens.

Back at the hotel, Marina stands red-faced behind the reception desk.

Loretta hurries to her. 'Can I help?' She smiles at their new guests, the Dawsons, who stand on the opposite side of the desk.

'It would be good if *someone* helps.' The sweat drips from Signore Dawson's bushy white eyebrows onto his 'I love Venice' sweatshirt.

Loretta reaches for the remote control and resets the temperature in the foyer. Marina's overdone it with the heating.

'Signore Dawson was unhappy with Signore Giuseppe's singing on the gondola ride.' Marina's smile doesn't reach her eyes.

It's hard for Loretta not to snort.

'We paid a small fortune for that singer and all we got out of it is a thumping headache for my wife.' Signore Dawson's crossed arms rest on his belly.

'One minute please, signore. I'll be happy to assist.' Loretta takes off her coat and says quietly to Marina in Italian, 'Go, go. I can take over from here.'

'You haven't had your rest upstairs yet. I can handle it.' Marina twirls one of her long dark curls around her finger, a habit she's had since she was a small girl.

'The artist in the tank has arrived. Go and see before she freezes solid. I'll take care of this idiot.' She pushes Marina lightly in the back.

'Okay, grazie, Mamma.' Marina scoops up her jacket and bag and practically jogs across the carpeted lobby to the glass front doors.

Loretta reaches inside her turtleneck for the gold chain she wears. From it dangles a medallion of the Madonna cradling baby Jesus to her bosom. It was a gift from Nonna, given to her when she was nine years old, on the morning of her first Holy Communion.

'The Blessed Virgin always listens. She'll never fail you if you remember her. Do you hear me, Loretta? Promise me, you'll remember to pray.' Nonna gripped Loretta's shoulders with her knobbly fingers until she made the promise.

But Nonna was mistaken. The Blessed Virgin has failed Loretta many times since that day. Still, out of habit, she holds the pendant and silently prays. *Ave o Maria, piena di grazia—*

'Signora Bianchi? Signora Bianchi! You gonna help us out or not?' Signore Dawson's face is inches away from hers.

'Yes, of course, signore. I was only thinking of how to fix the problem. You see, this is the first complaint we have ever received about Signore Giuseppe. He is one of the most respected singers in all of San Marco.'

'The *best* singer,' Alberto interjects from behind her.

She gives him a pointed look. 'The kitchen bin needs emptying.'

Alberto laughs and disappears into the kitchen.

Turning back to the guests, Loretta lets go of the pendant. 'I will be sure to give the gondola company your feedback. In the meantime, because you booked the ride through us, I will arrange a full refund from the hotel for you immediately. Is this satisfactory?'

Signora Dawson, a short, thick woman with a close crop of white curls, who wears a matching 'I love Venice' sweatshirt, gives her husband a quick nod. She keeps her eyes downcast and her face is flushed. Loretta's struck by how startlingly blue Signora Dawson's eyeshadow is and how heavily it's caked on.

'Yes, yes, that'll do,' il signore says. 'And let the company know that for one of the *most respected* singers, I sing better in the shower.'

Loretta doubts this is true, but she nods. When the old couple leaves, she wakes the computer to search for their guest file.

'Che succede, Mamma?' Rocco appears from the kitchen, smiling. He's always smiling, Rocco. It's one of the things about her son she loves the most.

'I'm crediting an account for a hundred and seventy euro. Giuseppe's singing wasn't good enough for our guest, apparently.'

'L'Americano?'

'Who else?' She brings up the Dawsons' account.

'This morning at breakfast he complained his wife had a headache because the walls of the dining room are too pink.'

'I heard.' Loretta rolls her eyes. 'It seems like everything in San Marco gives that woman a headache. Take a small cheese plate to their room for me, will you? Tell them it's on the house, for Christmas. It might slow down the complaints.'

'Okay, and I won't hum anywhere near them, or he might request a refund for their entire stay here.'

'Yes, be careful.' She laughs.

She begrudgingly credits the Dawsons' account and then responds to two email enquiries. Alberto comes back from the kitchen and stands behind her. His breathing is louder and faster than normal, instantly irritating her.

'Listen to you.' She keeps her eyes on the screen. 'Keep on smoking, it's doing you good.'

'I don't feel good.'

'I was being sarcastic.'

'Loretta,' he pants, his voice strangled.

She whips her head around to see him leaning on the desk. His face is shiny with sweat. 'What is it? What's wrong?'

He gasps and shakes his head.

She clutches his arm. 'Tell me what's wrong!'

His knees buckle and he lands in a crumpled heap on the floor.

'Alberto!' she screams. 'Alberto!' She drops to her knees and turns him over onto his back. He's a dead weight; his eyes are shut. The loud breathing has come to a sudden stop.

Is he breathing at all? She can't tell. 'Rocco! Help!'

She grabs his flaccid arm and feels his wrist for a pulse. Is there one? She's not sure.

'Rocco!' she cries again.

Rocco comes running down the stairs. 'Papà!'

'Call the ambulance!' she shouts at him. 'Quick!'

Rocco lunges for the phone and hurriedly gives the operator their details.

Is he dead? Santa Maria, is he dead?

'Is he dead?' she yells at Rocco.

'I don't know, Mamma. I don't know.'

She looks over her shoulder towards the front door for Marina, willing her to come back.

A growing crowd of hotel guests gathers in the lobby.

Alberto doesn't move.

'Have you called an ambulance?' someone asks.

'Does anyone know first aid?' another says.

'Resuscitation!' Loretta shouts at them. 'Who knows how to do resuscitation?'

The guests shake their heads and mumble apologies.

'I'm going to resuscitate him,' she says to Rocco.

'Do you know how?'

'No.'

She tilts Alberto's head back, pulls opens his slack mouth and lowers her lips to his. He tastes of stale cigarettes. She breathes a ragged breath into his mouth as hard as she can and then again. How many breaths should she give him? She does it three more times.

'Compress his heart,' she orders Rocco.

Rocco moves around to Alberto's other side and with shaking hands he pushes over the centre of Alberto's chest. 'I don't know what I'm doing.' The tears pool behind his glasses.

'Keep going. A few more.' She takes a deep breath in and meets Alberto's lips again.

Together, she and Rocco cycle through the breaths and compressions. Alberto remains deathly still.

She's fast getting short of breath; her head starts to swim. *Don't stop*, she tells herself as the fatigue escalates. *Don't stop.*

'I'm a doctor.' A new hotel guest from this morning, a young Australian man, Signore Taylor, looms large above her. 'What happened?'

'I don't know. I don't know! He said he was unwell, then he collapsed.' She shuffles out of his way.

Signore Taylor kneels down next to her and leans his ear close to Alberto's mouth. 'You've called for the ambulance, yeah?'

'Yes.'

'Has he eaten anything he could be allergic to? Any alcohol or drugs?' He holds up Alberto's arm and feels for his pulse.

He asks his questions fast, so she answers fast. 'He is not allergic to anything, no. He had one glass of red wine with lunch. No drugs, never drugs.'

'Does he have a history of stroke or cardiac arrest?' he asks.
'No.'
'Any other medical conditions?'
'No.' She swallows. 'He smokes.'
'I can tell.' Signore Taylor lifts Alberto's eyelids one at a time and shines his phone torch in his eyes. Alberto's pupils are dilated. 'I'll do CPR until the ambulance arrives,' he says.
'You are a doctor?' She needs to hear him say it again.
'Neurosurgeon.'
Grazie a Dio.

The doctor immediately gives Alberto two short sharp breaths. She watches as her husband's chest rises and falls. Then the doctor presses firmly and with absolute confidence over Alberto's heart, many more times than Rocco did, before he gives him another two breaths and then repeats the compressions. He's calm and measured. This wonderful man, with the face of an angel, knows exactly what he's doing.

Rocco wraps his arm around Loretta, and they stay huddled on the floor as the doctor counts out loud once again to thirty, pushing down hard on Alberto's chest with each count.

Loretta stares at a stain on the carpet near Alberto's head.

Dio, I beg you to save my Alberto. Let me hear his laugh again. Let me hear him sing again. I promise I'll be good if you spare him. Alberto's smiling face on their wedding day flashes through her mind, how proud he was to be standing across from her at the altar.

She prays until the paisley patterns on the carpet begin to swirl and then she blinks. She looks up at the murmuring crowd and locks eyes briefly with the Signora Taylor, the doctor's young wife, who stands close by. The size of her, Gesù Cristo. What an odd couple they make, the husband looks like a runway model with his chiselled features. Even in her distress, Loretta can't help but notice how piercingly blue his eyes are.

'I think he's breathing.' The doctor places his ear close to Alberto's mouth again. 'Yep. He's breathing.'

'He will be okay?' Rocco touches Alberto's shoulder.

'I don't know. What's his name?'

'Alberto,' Rocco replies.

The doctor shakes Alberto roughly by the shoulders. 'Alberto! Can you hear me? Alberto! Wake up!'

Alberto's head lolls about.

'He's not waking up,' Loretta whispers to Rocco as the doctor shakes him again.

Then Alberto's wheeze is back. Loretta's never been so happy to hear it.

The next minutes pass in a blur. The paramedics arrive, pushing past the onlookers. They speak in English to the doctor, who wipes the sweat away from his forehead. He commands the room with his height and broad shoulders and his deep voice.

'You saved his life, dottore. Bravo.' The female paramedic, a petite brunette, bats her eyelids at him.

The paramedics test Alberto's blood pressure and oxygen levels. They shake him again. 'Alberto, wake up!'

He moans but his eyes stay closed as he breathes wheezy unsteady breaths.

'Signora, we're taking him to the hospital. There's only room for the patient on the boat,' the male paramedic tells her.

'I'll walk,' she replies.

Rocco helps Loretta to her feet and they hug tightly. He's still shaking and so is she.

Loretta turns to thank the doctor but he's nowhere to be seen.

A stretcher is brought in, and Alberto's loaded onto it and carried towards the back of the hotel, which opens onto the canal where the ambulance awaits. She squeezes Alberto's floppy hand as the paramedics roll away the stretcher. Does he know what's happening? Is he suffering?

She doesn't release his hand until she has to.

Once Alberto's taken away, some of the guests come forward and offer her and Rocco words of comfort. Rocco eases her through the crowd, shielding her.

It's only when the onlookers are behind them that Loretta sees the nun standing by herself, in front of the big Christmas tree in the centre of the lobby. The nun is dressed in a tan habit and black veil, a wisp of greyish-blonde hair escaping near her ear. She looks directly at Loretta, her head tilted sideways, a shy, almost questioning smile on her lips.

For a moment Loretta worries it isn't just Alberto whose heart will stop today. She holds her palm against the thudding in her chest and takes shaky steps towards the nun until there's almost no gap between them. She has to stop herself from reaching out to touch the other woman's face, to make sure she isn't an apparition. 'Flavia?' Loretta's voice is hoarse. 'Is it really you?'

'I haven't heard my birth name for decades.' Flavia's smile grows. 'Hello, Loretta. How are you?'

Loretta can't find the words to respond. Everything around her fades away. All she can see is Flavia.

'I haven't timed my arrival very well, have I? I'm sorry.' Flavia wrings her hands. 'Was that your husband? I hope he'll be okay.'

'What are you doing here?'

Flavia lets out a small laugh. It's been thirty-six years since Loretta last heard that laugh but it still has the same effect on her. 'Isn't it obvious?' Flavia says softly. 'I'm here for you.'

Loretta is unable to stop staring, bewitched by Flavia's hazel eyes, her full lips. Her beauty hasn't diminished even a tiny bit with age.

Rocco steps up next to them. 'Buon Natale, Suora.' He addresses Flavia with a respectful nod, before turning to Loretta. 'Mamma, do you need me to fetch you anything for the hospital?'

Her son's presence reminds Loretta of where she is, of whose *wife* she is. She's suddenly aware of herself swooning as if Alberto's life isn't hanging in the balance. Who knows if he's even still breathing.

'Bring me my handbag,' she tells Rocco. 'I need my phone too. And pack my glasses.'

When Rocco jogs away, she lifts her chin and looks Flavia in the eye. 'If you've come for me, you're late. Thirty-six years late.' She strides away from the nun.

'Loretta!' Flavia calls.

She stops but doesn't turn.

'I'm staying at San Zaccaria, at the rectory there.' Flavia's voice carries across the lobby.

Loretta continues towards the hotel entrance without a backwards glance. Outside, in the freezing Venetian air, she tucks her hand inside her top for the comfort of the medallion. It's true there have been many times Loretta has felt abandoned by the Blessed Virgin, but she fervently believes that Santa Maria won't fail her today. The Madonna has already shown herself by delivering the angel-faced doctor to save Alberto's life.

Loretta holds tightly onto the pendant and prays to the Blessed Virgin to follow through by making sure Alberto recovers well.

She walks quickly towards the hospital. It's only when her teeth start to chatter that she realises she left without her coat and without even waiting for Rocco to bring her handbag. She keeps walking regardless, away from the woman who abandoned her to the man she hopes won't.

Sophie

Sophie wonders if her guide is in training for a new season of *The Amazing Race*. The woman's so far ahead, Sophie could easily lose her in the crowd. 'Excuse me. Sorry,' she mutters every few seconds at the growing number of annoyed strangers she inadvertently hip and shoulders, desperately trying to keep up.

The guide, a stick insect in white leather pants and stiletto heels who didn't actually introduce herself when they met at Marco Polo Airport, reaches a set of stairs and mercifully stops to tap something into her phone. Sophie breaks into a jog to reach her. It's the fifth lot of stairs she's come up against since getting off the vaporetto. In her daydreams about the beautiful canals running through the city, she didn't factor in the need to get across those canals on footbridges, with all these bloody stairs. She's overheating even though it's freezing, and a rubber wheel on her luggage is already wonky, on its maiden voyage.

Also on their maiden voyage are the hot-pink ankle boots that she clicked once on Instagram last month, so they kept coming up in her feed eight times a day until she relented and bought them. They're now making both of her heels burn with what are sure to be blisters. They call it aggressive mimicry in the animal world, getting sucked in by a predator's looks only to have them kill you. Predator/ankle boots, same-same.

She's already walked past half-a-dozen boutiques in the last five minutes with loads of gorgeous boots in their windows that are most likely half the price of the death traps she has on. What idiot buys leather shoes *before* coming to Italy?

'Follow me, please.' The guide doesn't look at Sophie before taking off again at land-speed record pace. Sophie may as well be chasing the road runner, all the while dragging the dodgy wheeled luggage behind her. 'Here we are, signora.' The guide comes to a sudden stop again and waves a piece of paper under Sophie's nose. 'We are arrived at Hotel Il Cuore. Now, if you will sign here. Prego.'

Sophie signs the yellow slip. 'Thank you, I appreciate—' But the woman's already raced off, back towards the Grand Canal.

'Meep meep,' Sophie says under her breath. She should feel grateful that *Foodie* magazine arranged a guide to meet her at all. She would never in a million years have found the hotel on her own. They'd turned left and right more times than she could count to get to this street.

She takes a second to marvel at the frontage of the iconic Hotel Il Cuore, a three-storey building of bright blue stone that sparkles like a jewel among the red and cream buildings surrounding it, before she drags the luggage up the six steep steps to the entrance. She was shamed at Melbourne airport with a massive '*HEAVY*' sticker slapped onto the side of her case. When her shoulder almost dislocates lifting it onto the top step, she silently curses the Sophie of yesterday who packed just about everything she owns for this two-week trip because 'options'.

Panting, she leans her weight against the glass door leading into the lobby. Inside, Il Cuore is just as it appeared online – small, dated, charming, with plush patterned carpet, thick white pillars with fake plants snaking up them, elaborate chandeliers hanging from the centre of ceiling roses, a front desk of dark mahogany and, in the middle of the lobby, a Christmas tree so huge it practically swallows up the place.

'Buongiorno, signora. Merry Christmas! You are checking in?' An employee rushes towards Sophie from the far end of the foyer.

Ooh, hello. What do we have here? Tall, tick. Dark, tick. Handsome, TICK.

She smiles at him like she isn't a heaving sweaty mess. 'Hi! Yes, I'm checking in. My name's Sophie Black. The reservation might be under "Foodie Mag", or maybe "Foodie Enterprises"? Actually they probably just booked it under "Sophie Black". That's what they usually do. Just me confusing myself. And you. Ha!' *Stop talking.*

'Ah, you are the food writer! Allow me to take your suitcase, please. Prego, prego. Come, follow me. I am Rocco Bianchi, the son of Loretta Bianchi!' He walks with her to the reception desk, which has an elaborate garland sprinkled with fairy lights wrapped around it. 'Marina. Marina! La signora from Australia has arrived. Marina! Dove? Wait here, please, signora. Sit, sit.' He points to the velvet brocade couch near the desk. 'One moment, please.' He holds up a finger and runs off, disappearing beyond a swing door.

Do all Venetians run everywhere? Is that a thing here?

Sophie's phone vibrates in her pocket. It's a message from Bec.

You there yet?

How do you like bella Venezia?

Are you wading through water in gumboots?

Just got here!

No sign of the floods but it's icier than Nicole Kidman.

Off to Piazza San Marco for a proper sticky beak soon.

How's Christmas going?

Post-apocalyptic. Everyone's passed out in a food coma.

Let me know how you go tomorrow.

Can't wait to hear what you think of Signora Bianchi!

> I just met her son.
>
> Not too shabby!

Ooh, but does the man cook?

Rocco reappears with a woman trailing behind him who surely has to be his twin. Both tall and lanky, with huge brown eyes, high cheek bones and messy black curls – his short, hers falling over her shoulders. Both of them are bespectacled, Rocco in John Lennon–style wire frames and Marina in oversized, plastic red ones. They're both intimidatingly good-looking.

Rocco gestures at Marina with a flourish. 'Here she is. My sister!' It's as if he's presenting Sophie with a senior royal. *Bless.*

'Merry Christmas, signora. Has Rocco explained the situation to you?' Marina sits behind the desk. She's a significantly less hyped-up version of her brother.

Before Sophie can reply, Rocco says, 'A *very small* inconvenience only, signora.' He holds his thumb and index finger close together to show her just how small the inconvenience is. 'You see, today, our papà, he had a *very small* heart attack.'

What in the actual...? 'A heart attack? Oh my God! Is he okay?'

'Yes, grazie a Dio he was saved and now he is at the hospital,' Rocco replies. 'Everything is fine.'

'Everything is not *fine*.' Marina gives him a filthy look. 'Our father almost died today. He is stable *for now*, but he is in intensive care and the doctors say he needs an operation. We don't know what the next few days – or even weeks or months – will be like. Our mother is with him at the hospital, of course. She may not be able to work for some time. I am sorry, signora, but we must cancel your assignment.'

The air leaves Sophie's lungs. 'I see.'

'But Papà will be home soon and everything will be back to norm—' Rocco says.

'Everything will *not* be back to normal for a long time,' Marina interrupts. 'It is terrible timing, I know, but we cannot have a food writer in the kitchen when all this is happening.'

Fuck.

Rocco stares at the ground, his jaw set.

Marina sighs. 'My apologies, signora.'

Sophie quickly collects herself. 'Please don't worry, it's not a problem.'

'Thank you for understanding,' Marina says. 'Can I help you with flight arrangements back to Australia?'

Far out, lady, give me a minute. 'No, no, you've got enough on your plate. I'll sort myself out in the morning and be out of your hair as soon as I can, I promise.'

'You must be very tired after your long day of travel.' Marina smiles, liking Sophie more, it seems, now that she's agreed to bugger off home. 'Let us arrange a slice of fruitcake and a cup of tea to be brought up to you. Rocco will show you to your suite. Again, my apologies, signora.' Marina hands her a key card.

Rocco leads Sophie across the lobby, insisting on taking her luggage. Sophie hobbles behind him. The second she's alone, the predator boots are being kicked straight into the bin. Or maybe not – they're so pretty.

As soon as they're out of Marina's earshot, Rocco leans his head closer to Sophie's. 'Ignore what my sister said. Don't leave. Marina thinks she can convince our mamma not to work, but that will never happen. Stay and wait for Mamma to come back. She was looking forward to working with you.'

'Are you sure? I'm only supposed to be here for two weeks.'

'I spoke to her on the phone only a few minutes before you arrived, and she was trying to convince me to go to the hospital in her place so she can work this evening. Papà is driving her crazy there.' Rocco lets out a small laugh. 'It will not be long before she is back, I promise you.'

'Heart surgery's a big deal though. You might be underestimating things.'

'I know my parents. Papà will want to leave the hospital as soon as he can, and all Mamma will be thinking about is the restaurant. Our apartment is here inside the hotel, so we can all look after him. Please don't leave, signora. Stay.'

He smiles at her and she immediately decides to stay, because even if Signora Bianchi doesn't come back to work in time, who could say no to an Italian this cute who's asking this nicely?

'I guess I can wait it out for a bit, if my boss agrees, and see how things go with your parents.'

'Excellent! So you will not leave and you will stay, and when Mamma comes back, she will show you the best Venetian recipes for your magazine. Mamma is a wonderful cook. And she is the most wonderful person in the world. You will see!'

'I can't wait to meet her.' Sophie's thoughts flash quickly to her own mother and the four calls from her today she's let slide through to voicemail. She knows she should ring her back. If you don't return your mother's calls at Christmas, when do you?

They stop at the lift. She's only seen lifts like this, with an iron gate surrounding the door, in old movies. Rocco motions for her to step into it and then he follows her with the luggage, reaching across to manually close the gate and door.

'Your suite is on the first floor. We have given you our best room.' He smiles at her and her belly gives a little flip. 'Another reason you must stay is for the *Venice Rising* exhibition that started today,' he continues. 'There is art here from all over the world for twelve days until the festival for the Epiphany. It is a very important exhibition for climate action.' He swoops his arms in and out while he talks, like he's playing a piano accordion.

'Is that right? I'll have to look it up.'

They stand close enough to each other that she can smell the coffee on his breath. The lift rattles and shakes as it ascends for way longer than she imagines it could ever take to go up one floor. She studies Rocco's face the way she watches flight attendants during turbulence. He seems completely unfazed. By the time the lift finally stops with a thud, it might as well have reached the top floor of the Empire State Building.

'Prego.' He gestures for her to step out into a hallway, which is lined with pastel pink doors along both sides. Facing the lift at the end of a long-carpeted corridor, in a gilded gold frame, hangs an enormous portrait of the Pope.

'Pope!' she shouts, pointing, like she does when she sees cows from the car.

'Yes. Il Papa. You like him?'

'Ah, I'm not very religious.'

'You are the same as me. But my mamma'—he lets out a low whistle—'is very, very, *very* religious.'

Good to know. No Jesus jokes.

He unlocks the door to the furthest suite on the right and holds it wide open. 'This is your room. Welcome, signora.'

'Sophie.'

'Okay. I hope you enjoy your stay in this suite, Sophie.'

She takes in the pink and white vertical-striped wallpaper, the embroidered linen quilt on the brass bed, a cosy armchair in the corner and a white wooden chest, on which stands a vase of fresh pastel roses. It's the room of her childhood dreams. If it wasn't for the searing pain in her feet, she'd be tempted to give a little jump for joy.

Rocco walks to the window and pushes open the red shutters. The sheer curtains blow as a cool breeze sweeps in. 'It's cold, but come for just one second, Sophie. Come and listen.'

The booming operatic voices of the gondoliers singing in unison rise up from below. She crosses the room and leans over, looking down at the narrow canal. Two gondolas float by, one after the other. The gondoliers duck their heads as they pass under a footbridge. A little girl riding with her parents spots Sophie and Rocco and waves. Sophie waves back and Rocco blows the child a kiss, which makes her cover her smile with her hand before the gondola disappears around the corner.

Church bells begin to ring, loud and melodic.

'The bells from the tower in Piazza San Marco,' he explains. 'It is only now between Christmas and the Epiphany when the bells ring every hour. Usually it is only twice a day.'

'What a gorgeous noise!' Sophie exclaims.

The chiming bells sound like they're coming from next door, rather than blocks away.

He closes the shutters once the ringing stops. 'I will come back with a nice snack in two minutes, okay? I will knock on the door. When you hear the knock, you will know it's me, Rocco.' He adjusts his glasses on his nose.

Sophie looks at this sweet, sexy man with his black curls sticking out every which way, who carried her bags, led her to this little slice of heaven and is about to bring her treats to eat and drink, and she thinks she might have just fallen a smidgeon in love with him.

As soon as he leaves, her phone vibrates with an incoming call. Seeing that it's Penelope again, she lets it ring out. The Venice trip got her out of spending Christmas Day in her mother's depressing townhouse, eating Woolworths pudding, but she's going to have to talk to her eventually.

There's a knock at her door. It's Rocco, carrying a silver tray with a floral ceramic teapot and matching cup and saucer, and a side plate with two generous slices of a rich-looking fruit cake.

'Mamma's special marantega cake,' he announces proudly, as he walks inside and carefully lowers the tray onto the dresser. 'Mamma bakes a fresh marantega cake every day for the twelve days of Christmas. So today we enjoyed this first one. I hope you enjoy it too, Sophie.'

She breaks off a big piece with her fingers. It crumbles on her tongue, the flavours of fennel and apricot and raisins competing with each other. 'Mmm. Delicious.'

'You see? It's good, eh? Buon appetito.' He looks at his watch. 'I will see you in the restaurant at six for dinner, yes?'

'Will you be all right without Signora Bianchi?'

'Ah, so-so.' He talks with his hands. 'Our papà is also missing from the kitchen, of course. Our cousins Chiara and Salvatore have come from Padua to help us. They work here but today they were supposed to be on a break for Christmas.' He laughs. 'Anyway, now it is not so bad. Mamma prepared everything already this morning before poor Papà . . .' He stops and sighs. 'But tomorrow will be a different story. The tourists only come here to see Mamma and eat her food. I hope they are not very disappointed when Signora Bianchi is not there, and it is only her idioto son doing the cooking.'

'I'd be happy to help out,' Sophie says. 'I know my way around a kitchen.'

'That is very kind. But you are here to write a story about Mamma, not to be a kitchen worker.' He checks his watch again. 'Now, you rest. You have your nice tea before it gets cold, you eat some cake and at six o'clock come to the restaurant. I will save the best table for you.'

When he leaves, she opens the shutters once more and sits by the window with the steaming cup of tea warming her hands.

Alone with her thoughts, the sadness immediately swamps her. For the last month, ever since Sophie learned the truth about her mother, Penelope's words keep rushing back to torture her.

'It wasn't a heart attack, you know. It was me.'

Penelope had been drunk when she'd confessed after one of their regular mother–daughter Thursday night dinners. So drunk, in fact, that Sophie isn't sure her mother has any recollection of the words she'd spoken as she'd served up overcooked silverside and runny mashed potatoes. Penelope used to be a good cook once, the best cook. But those days are long gone.

The next afternoon Penelope had called her as though nothing had happened, as though she hadn't blown up Sophie's entire world with her revelation.

Sophie shakes her head as she remembers Penelope talking the next day about a new recipe she'd been testing out in the Thermomix. 'It even chops the onions for me, darl. Honestly, do get yourself one if you can.'

Stop talking about your Thermomix, you cold-blooded murderer! Sophie had wanted to scream down the phone.

The music from the gondoliers fills the air and Sophie sips her tea. She won't be able to avoid Penelope forever, but for now she's here, in this beautiful new city, far away from her.

She finishes the cake and then unpacks her bag. When the bells ring through the air signalling five o'clock, she slips her stockinged feet into less evil shoes, ties her hair up in a ponytail, grabs her key card and walks out of the suite.

In the hallway, she comes face to face once again with the freakishly large portrait of Pope Francis. He looks like he's hiding something.

Downstairs, at the end of the lobby, the concertina doors leading to the restaurant are wide open. Entering the restaurant is like stepping into a garden wonderland. The high glass ceiling gives the space an alfresco feel, but the strategically placed gas heaters keep the air toasty warm. More than a dozen clay pots that reach Sophie's hips hold six-foot-high ferns, which are lit up by thousands of fairy lights threaded through them. The ferns are interspersed among the twenty or so square tables that are topped with pink and white gingham tablecloths and vases of brightly coloured roses. It's no wonder this place is famous.

Sophie takes a moment to draw in all the beauty, then she exhales and pushes through the swing door labelled '*Staff Only*'.

The atmosphere in the expansive all-white kitchen is chaotic. Rocco and Marina, along with another man and woman who are also tall, lean, curly haired and insanely good-looking – who Sophie assumes are the cousins Rocco told her about – are all talking over each other, while a row of giant stainless steel pots bubble away on the stove. The massive marble island bench in the centre of the room is a crowded mess of cookware, tea towels, vegetables on chopping boards and dozens of palm-sized raw ravioli spread out over baking paper.

Nobody notices Sophie there.

'Hi!' she calls out.

They continue to talk in Italian with raised voices, all playing pretend piano accordions at each other.

'Hi there!' she says, louder this time, and everyone immediately stops and turns to stare at her.

'Signora, hello.' Marina frowns. 'Can I help you?'

'I'm here to say the same thing to you.' Sophie smiles. 'How can I help?'

'Sophie.' Rocco steps towards her, lifting his arms in greeting. His black shirt has large sweat patches in the armpits. 'You are too kind. I told you not to worry about us.'

'And I chose to ignore you. You've had an absolutely horrific day. I've had a rest and a delicious afternoon tea – thank you very much for that by the way – and I'm feeling totally rejuvenated.' She spots an apron hanging by the door. 'Now.' She slips the apron over her head and ties it around her waist. 'What can I do first?'

The smile that explodes on Rocco's gorgeous face melts her heart into a puddle.

Elena

Mamma clutches Elena's hand as if Elena might disappear if she let go. They're sitting together on the threadbare brown couch in Mamma and Papà's apartment with a neighbour squished in next to them.

Mamma stares at Elena. On the rare occasion they had video-chatted, Elena had manipulated the lighting to hide from Mamma how bad things had become. She'd also tried to hide as much of herself as she could behind Christian. He'd always been the one holding the phone. So the first time Mamma had really seen her in five years was when they'd turned up on her doorstep three hours ago.

'You've changed,' Mamma had gasped.

Elena hadn't replied. Instead, she'd thrown herself into Mamma's open arms and they haven't let go of each other since.

The apartment is bursting with family and friends who are meeting Christian for the first time, and also seeing what has become of Elena. She avoids their eyes and looks around the apartment instead. Not much has changed. The old television still sits on a faded wooden crate, a single row of thin green tinsel draped across it. The lace terylene curtains are yellower than she remembers, covering the only small window in the room, which overlooks the narrow street. Mamma's collection of decorated plates hang on either side of the window. Elena loves everything about this tiny, overcrowded space. She didn't realise how she much missed being here.

They'd arrived in Venice late this morning, a thirty-two-hour trip. Elena had been desperate to come straight here to see Mamma after checking in at Il Cuore, but Christian had needed to sleep. He'd completed his final exam only hours before they'd boarded the flight from Sydney, and he'd slept for four hours straight as soon as his head had hit the pillow. Elena had lain there, agitated, waiting for him wake up. In the end, it was Signora Bianchi's screaming for help from the lobby that had woken him. In minutes he'd dressed and was running down the stairs.

Elena had still been taking in the scene, hadn't even registered what was actually happening, when Christian had already jogged straight into the circle of people, elbowed them out of the way, rolled up his sleeves and launched into CPR on the old hotel owner.

Elena's known her husband for six years but today was the first time she'd witnessed him in action. Christian had stayed with Signore Bianchi until the paramedics had everything under control, then he'd snuck away, ushering Elena quickly out of the hotel before he could even be thanked. Neither of them has mentioned anything about it to anyone here now at Mamma's.

Elena's cousin, Marta, in an impossibly low-cut top, is pushing her breasts out so far towards Christian's face that Elena's surprised Marta's spine hasn't snapped in two. Christian's always had this effect on people. He's deep in conversation now with Padre Alessandro, who's come home all the way from the Vatican. Alessandro is a carbon copy of what he was like before Elena left for Sydney, around the same time he left for Rome. He's still roguishly handsome with blond hair that flops over his blue-grey eyes, looking more like a Scandinavian model than an Italian Catholic priest.

Alessandro sneaks glances at her while Christian talks to him. She can't bear the way everyone in here keeps doing that. How can she blame them? She'd stare too.

Elena lets the noise wash over her as she zones in on the Christmas tree. Sparsely decorated, it's shorter than hip height and shunted off in the far corner of the room, like a shy guest. Colourful unwrapped gifts are stacked around it.

A memory sweeps in of a Christmas Day when she was a child and her brother, Paolo, was alive, when their home was still a place of fun and laughter. Papà had built a go-kart using a fruit crate from his little greengrocer shop. She had sat between Paolo's legs and screamed with delight and terror, her hair flying in the wind, as Papà pushed them down the steep slope towards the piazza.

A thick layer of dust covers the floorboards around the tree. Of course Mamma hasn't had time to clean while caring for Papà by herself these last months. Elena's throat tightens. She squeezes Mamma's hand.

There's so much to say, but Papà has only been dead for four days and Elena can't find the words yet. She's still so raw in her grief, it's like her skin has shed. A thousand sharp needles prickle her body all over.

The small talk continues around her, without her. The female relatives bustle about, going back and forth between the kitchen and the lounge, as organised as an army of ants, loading the fridge and table with food for the funeral tomorrow, setting out the crockery and cutlery. Elena's offered to help but her aunts won't hear of it. 'Sit with Anna-Maria,' they say. 'She's been all alone.'

The meaning of their words is clear. *Your father was dying and you didn't come home.*

Elena doesn't need her aunts to make her feel guilty. She already couldn't feel worse about herself if she tried.

The playlist in her head is on a never-ending loop of guilt, regret, guilt, regret. Mamma had called her last month with the news that the treatment for Papà hadn't worked, the cancer had spread. 'They've given him a month, maybe two. It's everywhere now – his lungs, his liver, his spine. I'm struggling to look after him. He's so heavy, Elena. I have to lift him on and off the toilet on my own, shower him, dress him.' Mamma's voice broke.

'What about your sisters?' Elena asked. 'Can't they help?'

'They do help. They come when they can. But they have their own families. I need someone here all the time.' Mamma paused. 'Come home, Elena. We need you.'

But Elena didn't come home.

She shuts her eyes for a brief second and takes a breath.

The touch on her shoulder startles her.

'You okay, babe?' Christian's at her side.

'Yeah. Just tired.'

He strokes her hair. 'Tell me when you're ready to leave.'

'A bit longer yet.' She wants to escape the crowd, hide herself back in the hotel, but she isn't ready to let go of Mamma, who's aged decades in the five years since Elena's wedding in Sydney.

Mamma's once dark brown hair is now mostly grey, her face is deeply lined, she's lost weight and looks much older than fifty-two. The customary mourning black she's cloaked in ages her even more. A plain wool dress hangs off her, two sizes too big. She must have borrowed it from one of her sisters.

'Do we really have to wear black tomorrow, Zia?' Elena's cousin Portia calls out across the room to Mamma.

'Why are you asking her when I told you yes already?' Zia Romina answers her.

'Black's so morbid though,' Portia complains. 'It's supposed to be a celebration.'

'A celebration?' Zia Romina shouts. 'A celebration of what exactly? It's a funeral, not a carnival.'

'A celebration of Zio's life, Mamma!' Portia matches her mother's volume.

Zia Romina waves her arm in the air. 'What life? The poor man is dead at fifty-nine, God rest his soul.' She crosses herself.

'In England everyone dresses in bright colours now for funerals,' Portia persists.

'If you love England so much, go and live there!' Zia Romina is practically screeching now. 'See how you like it, cooking and cleaning for yourself.'

Christian catches Elena's eye and they exchange a quick smile. He doesn't speak Italian, but anyone could sense the vibe.

Portia thankfully lets it go after that and Elena resumes her close inspection of the lounge room furniture. Zoning out is the only thing that's keeping her together. If she lets herself think about how Papà is dead and how her life is a giant clusterfuck, she'll fall apart. And she can't allow herself do that. Today Mamma needs her, so Elena takes another deep breath and keeps smiling.

Zia Sonia, another of Mamma's sisters, approaches the couch with a silver tray. She bends down to offer Mamma a slice of her special torta dea marantega. It's tradition for Zia Sonia to bake a marantega cake big enough to feed the whole family every Christmas. Elena is struck by how profoundly her life has changed since she left Venice but everything here stays the same.

Mamma lets go of Elena's hand to take a piece of the fruit cake. Elena feels every set of eyes in the room on her as Zia Sonia holds the tray to her. She shakes her head, no.

Mamma cups Elena's cheek. 'How did this happen to you?' she whispers.

'Things got out of control,' Elena tells her truthfully. 'I won't stay this way, I promise.'

She looks up at Christian, who's now entertaining a group of her cousins with the true story of how close they came to missing their flight when the Uber they were in ran out of petrol.

I won't stay like this, Elena promises herself.

GAYLE

It's been a day of ups and downs. First there was the glass blowing on the island of Murano. Now that was something! The man doing the demonstration blew a glass horse in only a few minutes. And then he gave it to Gayle. The room was full of spectators. *Full!* And he chose her!

'I'd bet my last dollar it was because you were wearing the "I love Venice" sweatshirt,' Mike said on the windy vaporetto ride back to San Marco. 'I told you, didn't I? The locals like it when we do that.'

'And you were right as always, hon.'

After the excitement of the glass horse, there was the drama with the gondola ride.

'It wasn't so much that he couldn't sing that bothered me,' Mike complained to her afterwards, 'but I'd been looking forward to singing along with him.'

Mike said he'd imagined a selection of Sinatra or Elvis hits that he and the singer could have harmonised together, to the delight of people leaning from their balconies to listen as the gondola floated past. Gayle could have recorded it for him to put up on the blog. But of course he wasn't able to sing along when all the songs were in Italian.

'I reckon those Italians do it deliberately,' he fumed, 'so they can hog all the attention for themselves.'

Thankfully, Signora Bianchi absolutely insisted on refunding them the cost of the gondola ride. She even surprised them by sending that sweet bespectacled son of hers, Rocco, up to their room with a rather generous cheese platter. Like Mike always says, 'It pays to complain.'

If only they could have enjoyed the cheese. Instead, all hell broke loose with Signora Bianchi screaming downstairs like the place was on fire. They followed Rocco, of course, as he ran to see what the commotion was about. Other guests came out to join them, just about causing a stampede down to the lobby. Gayle held tightly onto the railing as people pushed past her on the stairs, taking them as fast as she could to keep up with Mike, who was quicker and fitter. She was positively panting by the time they reached the lobby.

And what should they find there other than Signore Bianchi, passed out cold on the floor, with his frantic wife beside him. Signora Bianchi looked right at her when she asked the crowd if anyone knew first aid and Gayle guiltily shook her head. All she could do was watch and wonder if the poor old fellow had gone and died on Christmas Day of all days.

Seeing Signore Bianchi in such a state made Gayle instinctively reach for Mike, needing reassurance that her own husband was upright and breathing.

If it wasn't for the wonderful young Australian doctor who appeared at just the right moment, goodness knows what would have become of Signore Bianchi. The (very handsome) doctor saved the old gentleman's life before their eyes. She and Mike joined the other guests in giving that fine doctor a hearty and well-deserved round of applause.

By the time they were back up in their suite, the cheese was crusty and warm from being near the bar heater, which put Mike in a mood again.

And then, just as Mike cleverly predicted she would be, Signora Bianchi was missing at dinner time, and they were served instead by the younger ones in the family, along with a new Australian waitress called Sophie. The staff were all helpful and friendly, Sophie especially so. You never would have guessed she was new. In fact, she told

Gayle she'd only just arrived a few hours earlier from Melbourne. The Australians truly saved the day at Il Cuore!

Sophie was so charming and confident, Gayle and Mike agreed it was as if she'd been working at the hotel for years. She was a very pretty young thing too, bouncy blonde curls in a high ponytail, big green eyes, bright red painted lips, and she was dressed beautifully in a fifties-style lilac floral dress with a big black belt, a pearl choker and patent black Mary Janes. There was something rather Old Hollywood about her.

But as lovely as Sophie was, the point was that it was Signora Bianchi they were here for, the only reason they chose to stay at Il Cuore. So despite the effort that Sophie and the younger Bianchis were putting into making it seem like everything was still well and good in the restaurant, Signora Bianchi's absence was acutely felt.

Gayle and Mike had arrived in Venice yesterday, and on their first evening eating at Il Cuore, Signora Bianchi had stopped by their table and chatted to Gayle for several minutes, had even posed for photos with her. When Gayle looked at the photo later, she wished she'd changed out of her sweatpants before dinner and worn a more supportive bra. She looked and felt every day of her seventy-five years. And Signora Bianchi, who was only nine years younger, was even more show-stoppingly beautiful in the flesh than she was in their photo together. Tall, willowy and fine boned, all the things Gayle wished she was. Signora Bianchi's olive skin glowed with radiant health, probably thanks to all the wonderful food she made (and maybe genetics too). Gayle had been so mesmerised by the famous cook that she'd struggled to finish her delicious dinner of braised beef medallions and roast root vegetables, her stomach full of butterflies.

Tonight though, the restaurant felt muted without Signora Bianchi flitting about between the tables, with something pleasant to say to everyone. They asked Rocco about Signore Bianchi and, as pleased as they were to hear that he was stable, Gayle and Mike came upstairs after dinner somewhat dispirited. It certainly wasn't the special Christmas dinner with Signora Bianchi at the helm that they'd dreamed about back home.

In the suite now, they sit together at the small table next to the bed, chairs pulled close to each other with the iPad propped up in front of them as they wait for the video chat with their children back home in Little Rock. Justin, their oldest, is due to do the calling.

'On the wrong side of fifty now, and still ain't ever been on time in his life.' Mike checks his watch. 'For Pete's sake, it's three minutes past now. I might call him and see what the hold-up is.'

'Give him another minute, hon.' The words have just left her mouth when Justin's name flashes up on the screen.

'Slide to answer,' Mike says, as he swipes his finger across the iPad.

Gayle's heart doubles in size when the screen lights up with the smiling faces of her children, grandchildren and even her little great-grandchildren, all crowded around each other, streaming in from three separate houses.

'Mom!'

'Heya, Pop!'

'Happy Christmas, Nanna and Gramps!'

'Say hello to Big Nanna, Amber.'

'Look, Joshy, can you see Gramps?'

'Merry Christmas, you guys, we miss you!'

Gayle's overwhelmed with them all greeting her at once and doesn't know who to talk to first, so she waves and blows kisses at the screen. It's the first time they've ever tried a group video call, and Gayle could just kiss Justin for his thoughtfulness in bringing them all together this way. She can't quite believe he's pulled it off and that here she is in Italy, looking at the faces of her loved ones in the US.

'Well, would you look at that,' Mike says, laughing. 'Ain't technology an amazing thing!'

Their children and grandchildren's smiles turn to frowns.

'We can't hear you, Pop!' Susan, their eldest daughter, says. She's sitting next to her husband, Hank, with Gayle's great-granddaughter

Elsie on her lap. Gayle's granddaughters and their husbands are crowded in behind them. Their whole family is in holiday sweaters, even baby Elsie. It's too adorable.

'What do you mean you can't hear me?' Mike raises his voice a few notches. 'What about now?'

Gayle winces at his volume. Everyone's still frowning and shaking their heads.

'You're on mute, Pop,' Elizabeth, their other daughter, says. She also has her husband, Derrick, next to her and their three boys and their wives are all there too.

'Can you hear me now?' Mike shouts even louder.

Elizabeth's two-year-old grandson, Hudson, reaches forward, touching the screen, pointing at Gayle. 'Big Nanna!'

Gayle touches the screen back at him.

Justin's son, Corey, says, 'Turn yourself off mute, Pop.'

Mike turns to Gayle. 'What does he mean, turn myself off mute?'

'Tap the microphone,' Justin says.

'What microphone?'

'Tap the screen first, Pop. You should see a microphone icon.'

'Ah, there it is.' Mike taps the icon of the microphone. 'Can you hear me now?' he bellows.

The children laugh and clap.

'How the heck are you two, anyhow? We miss you already.' Justin rubs the top of his head, where the hair's stopped growing. 'Tell us about Venice.'

Mike dives straight into the story about the flag-waving protestors in the small boats who tried to stop their cruise ship from docking yesterday. 'There we were, your mom and I, excited as anything to finally be arriving in Venice, when we're *attacked* by a gang of angry Italian hoodlums! Had to whisk your mom back inside to safety in case they threw a grenade or something up at the deck.'

Truth be told, it was hardly a gang, just three young men and one woman in a tiny boat solemnly waving a flag and looking entirely non-threatening. The protestors were hopelessly outsized by the big cruise ship as it came in to dock and had no choice but to get out of its way. Gayle smiles as Mike continues with his embellished version of the story.

'Made it just about impossible to disembark,' he complains. 'You should've heard them heckling us! I was in half a mind to sue.'

The 'heckling' was an Italian chant the protestors repeated from their little boat as the tourists walked out onto the esplanade, but they were so far away that the wind barely carried their voices.

The children have of course read this story in Mike's blog from last night, but they listen intently and make all the right noises. Gayle loves them for it.

'Why were they heckling you, Gramps?' Elizabeth's son, Elijah, asks. His neck tattoo of a snake is poking out from his collar. Gayle's trying hard to get used to it.

Mike shrugs. 'No idea. Just minding our own business, we were. Did nothing wrong! These Europeans are always getting their knickers in a twist about nothing.'

Elijah raises his pierced eyebrow. 'Gramps, that's a bit raci—'

'Why don't y'all open your presents like we planned?' Gayle says quickly. 'You got them there?'

Immediate chaos ensues as the gifts Gayle lovingly wrapped before she left are passed around the groups in the various houses. It gives her such joy to see their faces as they open them. Some were requested, like Corey's new car seat covers for his SUV, and others, such as the ceramic hair curlers for Justin's daughter, Jemima, are a surprise.

'Nanna! Just what I wanted!' Jemima squeals. 'How did you know?'

'I asked your mom.' Gayle beams at her daughter-in-law, Nicky.

'I love you, Nanna. Thank you.' Jemima blows kisses at the screen.

'Don't forget to thank Gramps, too,' Gayle says gently. 'He's the provider who made all these blessings possible.'

Shouts of 'Thank you, Pop!' and 'Thanks, Gramps!' are echoed all around.

'Nothing's too much for the Dawson clan,' Mike says proudly.

'How about a prayer, y'all?' Hank says and everyone bows their heads as he begins. 'Lord Jesus, our Christ and Saviour . . .'

Gayle's arms physically ache to be able to hug them all. This is the first Christmas that she doesn't have the family gathered around her in their home in Arkansas.

'What's Signora Bianchi like, Mom?' Susan asks after the prayer.

Before she can answer, Mike tells them all about the drama surrounding Signore Bianchi's heart attack. 'So the whole point of coming to Venice is gone now.'

'I still got to meet her though,' Gayle says. 'And she was just precious. Oh, and the forest restaurant – why, y'all, I think that's what Eden itself would be like!'

Gayle loves to watch *Cooking with Gina* on the television most afternoons. And Signora Bianchi is a regular guest on the show whenever Gina travels to Venice from her home in Bologna. Gayle's very taken with Signora Bianchi, even more than she's taken with Gina. So when Mike had surprised her with the vacation to San Marco, staying at Signora Bianchi's hotel no less, she was beyond grateful. The Big Italy Trip was timed so they'd be out of the country for Christmas. Mike knew how heartbroken Gayle would be without Noah at their Christmas table, so he came up with the Venice idea, bless him.

Except now, the whole idea of escaping to Italy to ease the heartache feels pointless. Christmas Day is almost over and she couldn't imagine her heart aching any more in Little Rock than it does right here in Venice. It's so sore it might just break in two. She has a splitting headache too. But then again, she always has a headache nowadays.

She doesn't like to complain because Mike's gone to such an effort to bring her here. So she smiles and waves and blows kisses to the children and grandchildren as the call comes to an end.

While Mike's hunting around for the iPad charger, Gayle's phone pings. It's a message from Elizabeth.

How are you really, Mom? You doing okay over there?

> I'm doing just fine, sugar.
> Missing y'all is all.

I miss Noah, Mom. It's not the same without him.

'Who's that you're talking to?' Mike asks.
'Only Lizzie.'

> I know, sugar.

> I miss him so much I could
> just about die.

'Lizzie? What does she want already? You just finished talking to her.'
'Nothing important, hon.'

Loretta

Alberto groans and flutters his eyelids open. Loretta flies out of her seat to be at his side.

He looks at her from under his heavy lids and smiles a weak smile. 'Loretta.' His voice is raspy. 'Ho sete.' *I'm thirsty.*

The nurse, a woman called Oriana, who looks young enough to still be in high school and has long peroxided hair pulled into a severe ponytail, is already standing on the other side of his bed, filling up his glass with water. 'Signore, are you comfortable?'

'What's this for?' He tugs irritably at the nasal prongs.

'Oxygen. Don't touch it,' Oriana replies as she checks his temperature. 'Are you comfortable?'

'No.'

'What's wrong?' Her baby face is full of concern.

'I want to go home.' He directs this at Loretta.

'Is there anything I can do to make you more comfortable?' Oriana rests her hand on his shoulder.

He coughs. 'Yes, let me go home.'

'I can't do that, signore. I'm paging Dottore Falcone to let him know you're awake again.'

Alberto waves his arms about. 'I already told the other doctor before, I'm not having any surgery.' He turns to Loretta. 'Tell them, cara. Tell them there's nothing wrong with me. I fainted, that's all.'

'Nothing wrong with you?' Loretta shakes her head. 'You nearly died today. Your heart stopped!'

The curtains are pulled open and the cardiologist who took over on the ward a few minutes ago, Luca Falcone, walks in. Luca is the son of one of Loretta's oldest friend's, Pia. She's known him since the day he was born.

'Buonasera, Zio, Zia.' He gives them a small smile and consults the clipboard at the foot of the bed. 'Zio, my colleagues tell me you're refusing to have the defibrillator inserted. Care to tell me why?'

'It's not natural having a machine in my heart. Besides, I'm fine now. Look at me, I've never been better. I can even sing, listen.' He breaks into the chorus of 'O Sole Mio' at full volume.

'*Shh.*' Loretta slaps his arm. 'You're in the intensive care unit. Cretino.'

'Just because you can sing doesn't mean you won't have another cardiac arrest,' Luca says.

'I don't want to end up like Alfonzo Buccaletti,' Alberto replies. 'He went to Milan and let the fanciest heart specialist in Italy operate on him, and what happened? Boom, dead! No, thank you, no boom dead for me.'

Luca pulls up a plastic chair and sits next to Loretta. The chair barely contains his long, athletic limbs; Luca is well over six foot tall. He's always been handsome, no less so now that he's middle-aged. His dark hair, just beginning to be speckled with grey, is held in a bun and he has a nicely cropped beard.

'I heard about Signore Buccaletti,' Luca says, 'but you're not in the same situation as he was. He was a very sick man needing extremely risky surgery – that's why he had to go to Milan. The surgery you need is simple. I've performed hundreds of them. And I'll tell you something. Considering you're a heavy smoker, your arteries are in surprisingly good shape. The only reason you had the cardiac arrest is because your heartbeat isn't well regulated. It beats too fast. If we put the defibrillator in, the problem's fixed. You'll live till you're a hundred – as long as you give up smoking.'

Alberto waves dismissively at him. 'My heart beat a bit too fast one time, so what? It won't happen again.'

'You're wrong,' Luca argues. 'It's very likely to happen again, and if you have another cardiac arrest you might not be so lucky next time.'

'Listen to Luca,' Loretta says. 'You need the operation, Alberto.'

Alberto juts his jaw out. 'No.'

She has to stop herself from slapping his arm again.

Luca turns to her. 'Have you tried to convince him, Zia?'

'I have.' She narrows her eyes at Alberto. 'And you just missed Rocco and Marina here. They both tried too. None of us can get it through his skull made of concrete.'

Luca stands. 'Give it some more thought, per favore. I'll come back to check on you soon.'

When Luca leaves, Oriana occupies herself with Alberto's bedside chart. Loretta's about to give Alberto a strong talking to, but he reaches out for her hand and clutches it tightly.

'I'm scared, Loretta,' he whispers.

Her anger at his stubbornness evaporates. He looks so small. 'What are you scared of?'

'Dying in the operation like Alfonzo.'

'But you heard what Luca said. It's different.'

'Still.'

'I'm more scared about losing you if you don't have it.'

'You won't lose me,' he says. 'Do you want me to sing again so you can see how strong I am now?'

'I beg you, no.'

He laughs and then lets out a long sigh and shuts his eyes, keeping them closed.

Soon he's breathing deeply and she's left alone with her thoughts. Shamefully, instead of those thoughts remaining on Alberto, she goes back to obsessing over Flavia, whose surprise reappearance has stolen her mind ever since she saw her standing in the lobby.

It's not that she doesn't love Alberto, it's just that he's no competition when it comes to her love for the nun.

Elena

'You know that old redneck American couple we saw when we were checking in? I bumped into them out in the hallway and the old fella does this big wave and he goes, "Hola, Doctor!"' Christian laughs as he walks into their suite. '"Hola!" So I wave back and say "Ni hao, sir." He didn't get it. They're in matching "I love Venice" tops.'

Elena laughs through her nose. 'I saw them rubbernecking when you were doing the CPR.'

Elena had stood watching, as helpless and useless as everyone around her, as Christian breathed life back into Signore Bianchi that afternoon. But she wasn't like the other hotel guests, morbidly fascinated without the emotional attachment. She loves the Bianchis. She's loved them for most of her life. Her brother, Paolo, played junior football for years with Rocco. They were like a second family to her growing up. The last time she saw any of them was at Paolo's funeral twelve years ago when she was sixteen.

Christian had chosen Hotel Il Cuore. She'd wanted somewhere closer to Mamma's apartment in the Jewish Quarter, but predictably, like most foreigners who know nothing of Venice, Christian was all about the San Marco location. He liked the sound of the forest-themed restaurant at Il Cuore with the glass dome ceiling and the draw card of the famous Signora Bianchi.

She hasn't told him she knows the Bianchis; she's relying on them not recognising her.

Christian walks over to where she's sitting on the bed and presents her with a white cloth napkin, folded over, concealing what's inside it. 'Remember Marina told us about the cakes they leave in the restaurant for the guests? Here, I went down and got you something.'

She opens the napkin and her stomach twists. 'Oh, a cannoli.'

'Chocolate custard filling. You told me it used to be your favourite when you were growing up, yeah?'

She nods, it's true. That's a whole lot of calories she'll be consuming if she agrees to eat it. She wants the cannoli though. Oh, how she wants it! But it wouldn't be without consequence. She'll have to atone for it, for days. Is it worth it? Saliva pools in her cheeks.

'Go on, Ellie,' Christian's tone is gentle. 'Just this once, babe.'

He didn't see her scoffing a slice of marantega cake earlier behind the closed bathroom door at her mother's apartment, or he wouldn't be saying 'just this once'.

She chews her lip. 'I should be watching what I eat.'

'It's been a hard day. You deserve it.'

It *has* been a hard day. She relents, taking a large mouthful. The pastry crumbles onto her chest. 'Mmm, so good. Thank you.'

The custard is deliciously lush. As soon as she's swallowed the last piece, the regret courses through her. It wasn't worth it.

Christian walks into the bathroom. 'Let's go for a walk before bed, babe,' he calls out. 'The installations for that climate art exhibit I was telling you about went up today. Some are supposed to light up after dark. Sounds pretty cool.'

'Christian, I'm exhausted. I don't want to go out again.'

Elena used to care about climate change. She was so passionate about it that her university major was Environmental Law. But now, the whole world could erupt into a giant fireball for all she cares. Her papà is dead and she didn't make it back in time. She waited for Christian to sit his final exam so they could come back to Venice together. And for that, she blames him.

She hears him gargle and spit in the bathroom before he calls out again, 'But it's Christmas, Ellie. Let's do something fun. The whole day's been so bloody depressing. Come on, put on your coat. It'll cheer you up.'

She knows she should do this for him, go on the stupid walk, look at the stupid art. It would make him happy, and he's been so good with her family today.

But with the death of her beloved papà, something in her has snapped. When she was packing for Venice; for the entirety of the flight; when she set foot on home soil; when she saw Mamma so broken, so scared; while she listened to Padre Alessandro discuss the order of the Mass – throughout all of it, her rage towards Christian grew bigger and deeper.

So rather than agreeing to go on the walk, she hears herself say, in a tone that's wholly unfamiliar to her, 'Nothing about today feels like Christmas. My father's *dead*. If you want to go look at art, go by yourself.'

Christian emerges from the bathroom holding a hand towel. There's toothpaste in the corners of his mouth. He uses the towel to wipe the froth from his lips and sits near her on the bed. He lifts a lock of hair off her forehead. 'Take a breath.'

'Sorry,' she whispers. 'I'm not myself at the moment.'

'Everything's going to be okay, babe,' he says softly.

'I know.' She sighs. 'I know.'

Gayle

Gayle and Mike are side by side, cosily tucked under the embroidered quilt on the big brass bed. Mike's busy writing the Christmas Day edition of the blog. It includes the stories of the glass horse in Murano, the terrible singing on the gondola that resulted in the gifted cheese platter, which was then interrupted by Signore Bianchi's heart attack, and the disappointing dinner minus Signora Bianchi afterwards, all of which he's already told the children about on their call. Gayle proofreads the blog, with little laughs of appreciation in the right places, and Mike hits the button to make it go live.

Once that's done, he fixes them cups of hot chocolate from the minibar.

'You spoil me, hon.' She pats his arm. 'Thank you.'

He climbs back into bed, turns on the TV and they settle into watching an old episode of *Antiques Roadshow*.

Part way through the episode comes a scream. They turn to each other with wide eyes.

'What was that?' Gayle whispers.

'Shh.' Mike puts a finger over his lips.

'Sounds like it was from inside the hotel.'

'Shh. I'm trying to listen.'

She clutches his arm. 'I think there's a lady in trouble. Should we do something?'

'Like what?'

'Like go out there and see what's going on.'

'We're in pyjamas, hon. We can't go out there dressed like this.'

Another scream, more desperate than the first.

This time, Gayle flies out of bed. 'Please, Mike, this sounds bad.'

'Okay, okay, don't get yourself all worked up.' He throws off the covers. 'You stay right there. I'll handle this.' He opens the door a tiny fraction and sticks his nose through the crack. Quickly he closes the door again. 'Nope, nothing out there.'

'Are you sure?'

'Yep. Must've been coming from somewhere else.'

She wrings her hands and says nothing for a few seconds but then the next scream comes and she just has to speak up. 'Hon, it sounds mighty close to be coming from somewhere else. I'm quite sure it's a lady screaming inside the hotel.'

'Well, we can't go banging on strangers' doors, now, can we? That's rude, that is, it being after nine and all.' He checks that their door is locked. 'Come back to bed.'

'I can't, I'm too nervous.' Gayle paces back and forth across the room.

'Nobody will hurt you while I'm here. Don't you worry about that.'

'It's not *me* I'm worried for.'

They wait a little longer, Mike leaning against the door, Gayle still pacing.

'Seems to have stopped,' he says after a while. 'You know, it might not have been a lady screaming at all. Might've been a rat screeching or something. Lotta vermin in Venice, the water brings them in. Know that for a fact.'

She doesn't answer.

'Come back to bed,' he says again, holding his hand out to her.

Gayle does as she's told.

Back in bed, Mike blows on his hot chocolate that's now cold. She blows on hers. He turns the volume of the TV up and they watch without speaking.

At one point, she's certain she hears another scream. She jumps, but when she asks Mike to go and check again, he assures her it's only the rats and he turns the TV up louder again. She hears nothing after that.

By the time the show is over, Mike's head has dropped down onto his chest and he's snoring. She gently rouses him and helps rearrange his pillows. He's fast asleep again seconds later.

Gayle stays sitting up. She knows what she heard, she knows it wasn't a rat. The guilt keeps her awake. If she was a braver person, she'd have stood up for the woman in danger. If she was a braver person, she'd have stood up for Noah.

She's been thinking about Noah all evening, missing him even more acutely after the call with her other children. How was Noah's Christmas? Did he miss them at all today? Did he even think about them? Is he happy? No, how could he be? How could anyone truly be happy when they're estranged from their family?

She's only had fleeting moments of happiness since he left. Being given the glass horse, for example – that was lovely, but she couldn't call herself *happy* as such. Happiness is something that eludes bad mothers, and rightly so.

She casts a glance at Mike, who's not plagued by guilt at all. Mike who's so sure of himself. She wishes she was the same.

They've been married over fifty-five years now, fifty-five faithful, fruitful years. And for every one of those years, they've honoured their covenant to each other and to the Lord, he as her headship, she as his helpmeet. Gayle has always known her place, known what the Bible asks of her – *wives submit yourselves to your own husbands* – and that's exactly what she's done, lovingly and willingly.

Then Noah, the youngest of their four children, forever her baby, even now as a middle-aged man, turned his back on them and left, never to be heard from again. Like the shepherd in the parable, Noah's the lost sheep Gayle worries most about, the one she's desperate to bring home. To do that, she has to challenge Mike. But in their faith, the husband's will is considered God's will. It's assumed that the husband is always right and that he shouldn't be questioned.

Lately there's been a gnawing thought inside Gayle that perhaps Mike could be wrong, that perhaps he *should* be questioned. As much as she's tried to push that ugly thought away, it's grown bigger and more invasive, like a cancer in her head.

Today, for example, she thought Mike was wrong about the gondola singer, who had quite a beautiful voice, actually. And he was definitely wrong about the screaming rat. If he's wrong about these things, couldn't he also be wrong about Noah?

She looks to the Lord for an answer, picking up the worn leather-bound Bible, always kept within arm's reach. She opens it to the start of Luke and immerses herself in the story of the nativity, in honour of the day of the Saviour's birth. The word of God indeed gives her the answer she's looking for, and she puts the Bible down with a new resolve.

Mary stood by her son from the moment of the immaculate conception until the very end. Gayle will take her lead from Mary and find the strength to do the same with her own son. Tomorrow she'll challenge Mike. Tomorrow she'll be the mother Noah deserves. Tomorrow Gayle will be brave.

Going against her husband makes her anxious enough that she has to tiptoe from bed and crouch over the toilet, where she brings up the hot chocolate, followed by the expensive seafood pasta dinner from the restaurant. What a waste of food, she thinks. Not only was Signora Bianchi not there to serve it, but now Gayle's gone and thrown it all up. A wasteful dinner, to be sure.

She rinses out her mouth, changes the incontinence pad and underwear she soaked through and crawls back into bed.

'Everything okay there, hon?' Mike stirs.

'Just needed to use the bathroom.'

'God bless,' he murmurs, already drifting off again.

She wipes her mouth with a trembling hand. 'God bless.'

SOPHIE

Sophie doesn't hear a single scream from the suite up the hallway. Her noise-cancelling earbuds are doing exactly what they promised, and all she hears are the dulcet voices of Oprah Winfrey and Nigella Lawson on the Christmas edition of Oprah's *Be You* podcast. It's not a podcast she subscribes to – Oprah's a bit rah-rah for her taste – but she likes to keep her finger on the pulse of what the celebrity chefs are up to.

Nigella's telling Oprah that her weight loss was thanks to 'being a little more choosy' but that she's always embraced her curves at every size. Sophie rolls her eyes. She thinks about how every episode of Nigella's TV show ends in the trademark sneaky late-night treats straight from the fridge. Everyone knows you don't get that thin raiding the fridge for chocolate mousse at midnight.

When Oprah launches into an ode to the fat women she admires, Sophie hits the stop button. She keeps the earbuds in and shuts her eyes, breathing in the silence.

She's made it, Christmas Day is almost over. The distraction of an international flight and settling into new accommodation has been a blessing. She should plan something similar for next year. But it's a whole year before she has to think about Christmas again and the horrors it brings to mind. What's important is that she's survived another Christmas Day. Surviving is what Sophie does best.

Right on cue, her phone vibrates with an email from her mother.

Sophie!

I've been trying you all day, darling.

Hope all is well? Is there phone reception in Venice?

Happy Christmas anyway. May the peace of the Lord be upon you, sweetheart.

I've sent you a little gift, I hope you get some use out of it!

Do give me a call when you can. I'll try you again in the morning.

Love,

Mum xx

She clicks on the attachment. It's a one-year membership to a diet app.

She punches out a reply to her mother, reads over it, then immediately deletes it. Instead she copies the link and texts it to David.

Sophie only talks with her brother over text messages once every couple of months or so, mainly to share memes. She sees him in person even less than that, although he and his wife, Courtney, only live an hour's drive away.

But it is Christmas Day, after all, so it's as good a day as any to send a text.

> Merry Christmas and all that.
>
> Behold, my present from our dearest mother . . .

Merry Christmas yourself.

Ha! Court got a virtual mosquito net
from Oxfam.

Sophie snorts.

> Poor Court. That's worse than mine.
>
> What'd you get?

One ticket to Bublé at Rod Laver Arena
in February.

Mum has the other ticket.

My Christmas present is being her
driver. Just call me David Uber.

D'Uber for short.

I prefer my rap name Lil Dube.

God I love you, you big dag, is what Sophie thinks. *Catch ya later,* is what she writes.

Still smiling, she opens up the document she started working on this evening, the feature about Il Cuore. She's got nothing more than the title, 'Il Cuore: A Canal-side Palate Paradise', and a whole heap of photos of the restaurant and kitchen she took this evening.

She clicks on a shot of Rocco grinning ear to ear as he carries a stack of empty glasses. She zooms in on him, closer and closer. The closer she zooms, the hotter that Italian man gets.

On the
SECOND
DAY *of*
CHRISTMAS

Loretta

Loretta's leg is going numb. She wriggles on the hard plastic chair to shake off the pins and needles. It's been one of the longest nights of her life, in the intensive care unit keeping company with Oriana, the nurse who also hasn't left Alberto's side, and Luca, who's been checking on him regularly.

Luca comes back in at just before six am and props himself against the foot of the bed. 'I'm going home to sleep. My colleagues will take good care of him, don't worry.'

'Thank you, Luca. God was smiling on us the day you were born. My Alberto's in safe hands with you.'

'That's if he ever agrees to let my hands near him.' He looks sideways at Alberto, who's breathing heavily in his sleep. 'I hope he changes his mind and consents to the surgery. I'm genuinely worried for him if he doesn't.'

'Oh, he'll consent. You leave that to me.'

'I didn't know Zio was so stubborn.'

'He's scared.'

'More scared than he is of dying?'

'What can I tell you?' She shrugs. 'The man's an idiot.'

Luca chuckles. 'You look tired, Zia. You should think about going home. You need to sleep.'

'Sleep? Ha! I have to work. I'm calling Marina to come sit in my place so I can go and cook.'

'You can't be serious. You're *working* today?'

People come from all over the world to eat at [...] [ti]mes they tell me they've been saving for years [to] dine at Il Cuore. I feel guilty enough about [... sai]d Alberto was stable. So it's safe to leave him [... isn'] t it?'

'[H]e's stable, yes, *for now*. But he had a resting heart rate of one seventy-five when he was brought in yesterday. I can't guarantee it won't go up again. And what about you? Excuse me for mentioning your age, but you're sixty-six years old. You have advanced arthritis, and it wasn't so long ago that you were admitted here yourself with dangerously high blood pressure. I haven't forgotten that, you know. Maybe what happened yesterday is a sign to slow down.'

'Slow down?' she scoffs. 'Are you mistaking me with someone else, dear Luca?'

He squats down in front of her and takes her hands in his. 'Zia, you know how much I love and respect you. But you going to work today is madness. Please go home and get some rest, then come back and convince your stubborn husband to let me save his life.'

'You don't need to worry about me. Ciao, Luca, ciao ciao.' She waves him away.

Once Luca's gone, she pulls her chair closer to Alberto's bedside. The room is separated from the others by a thin blue curtain that doesn't keep out the sound of a child crying and the stream of questions from his panicked mother to a nurse. Along with the incessant beeps of monitors, the phones and pagers ringing and the ambulance sirens, it's a wonder that Alberto's fallen asleep again.

Loretta picks up his hand and strokes the back of his knobbly fingers. Just about every joint in both of their hands is misshapen, swollen and red. She at least looks after her nails, but Alberto's are brittle and yellow.

Maybe Luca's right; maybe the time has come for Alberto to slow down. Alberto works as hard as she does, starting his day before sunrise to get ready for the market with Rocco, then being her right hand all day long. He cleans fish and trims meat, washes dishes, sets and clears the tables, arranges the flowers, looks after guests, serves, helps with laundry. There's nothing he doesn't do apart from the cooking. He's ten years older than her and he never complains. Now his body has complained for him.

Alberto opens his eyes and moans. 'Loretta? Are you still here?'

'Yes.'

'I dreamed you left.'

'I'm here.'

He squeezes her hand. 'Good. I was worried you'd gone to the restaurant.'

'I'm not going anywhere.'

He sighs. 'I want to go home.'

'I know you do. Luca just left. He's insisting you have surgery.'

'What does Luca know? He's barely out of nappies.'

'He's a forty-year-old man. One of the most celebrated surgeons in Italy. What are you talking about?'

'Keep your voice down, we're in a hospital,' he stage-whispers. 'Even after I have a heart attack, you still scold me.'

'I wouldn't be scolding if you had even an ounce of common sense.'

He gives her a sleepy smile. 'Give me a kiss, Loretta, go on.'

'With that breath? You're dreaming.'

'What else did Luca say, then? Tell me.'

'He said you have to quit smoking.'

He guffaws.

'I should try to set him up with Marina,' she says.

'You say this like the thought has just come to you, not like you've already tried and failed to force it eighty-five times already.' He yawns.

She ignores the jibe. 'The two of them make sense together.'

Luca's not only intelligent and handsome, he's also sweet natured, and it doesn't hurt that he's wealthy. He comes from a good Venetian family, he goes to church. What more could Marina ask for?

'He must have been lonely yesterday with the girls away at their mother's for Christmas.' Her lip curls whenever she speaks of Luca's ex-wife, Corrine, a French nurse who cheated on him with a man twice her age, when their girls were toddlers. A Bitcoin tycoon she met online apparently. Loretta has never trusted the French. 'I'll invite him to the restaurant. The more he visits, the more chance Marina has to see what she's miss—' She stops when she sees that Alberto's eyes are closed again.

He looks anxious even as he sleeps. It makes her heart ache.

She shuts her eyes too and the events of yesterday come rushing back to her. She remembers how only minutes before his cardiac arrest, Alberto had asked her for a photo of them together in the piazza and she'd refused. It scares her to think this might have been the last opportunity for them to ever have a photo, and instead of smiling for him, she'd rejected him.

Next time he asks, she'll say yes. Come to think of it, has she ever asked him to have a photo with her instead of the other way around? She can't remember a time when she did.

'I do you love, Alberto, I do,' she whispers.

She promises herself that when he's home and feeling well again, she'll pull out her phone and take a photo of him. For posterity.

Oriana leaves her station in the corner of the room and comes to Alberto's bed to check his drip. He stirs but doesn't open his eyes.

'They're organising his room on the ward now,' Oriana whispers. 'We should have it ready in an hour or so. If there's anything you'd like to bring for him from home, now's a good time to go.'

'Yes, okay. I'll go get his toothbrush and mouthwash, more for my sake than his.' Loretta's lower back cracks when she stands. 'If he wakes while I'm gone, will you tell him where I am?'

'I will.'

'And you have my number in case anything happens?'

'Yes, yes, go, signora. I'll look after him, I promise.'

Loretta kisses Alberto's forehead. 'I'll be back soon.'

He stays asleep.

The big Christmas tree at the entrance of the hospital makes her inexplicably sad. When she steps out of the hospital's front doors, the cold air coming off the canal slaps her in the face. She tightens her scarf and zips up the jacket Marina dropped off for her last night. It isn't often that she's outside this early, so she steals a glance at the dark blue water, waves gently lapping under the light of the moon that shines even as the sun rises.

The streets of San Marco are abandoned. Venice is slow to rise and early to bed, especially in winter, and Loretta likes being out in the city before the clatter of tourists on the streets. She walks quickly, her hands tucked into her jeans pockets and her breath warming the scarf, until she reaches the front steps of the hotel.

But she doesn't go inside. Instead, she finds herself continuing along narrow intercepting alleyways and across empty piazzas to San Zaccaria. The huge wooden doors of the church are closed but she knows they'll be unlocked. San Zaccaria never closes. Without letting herself think about what she's doing, she pushes the door open.

It's freezing inside the empty church despite the heaters glowing orange. Loretta crosses herself with holy water. She drops five euro into a rusted tin, lights a thin white candle for Alberto and slots it into position on the top row of a metal stand. By the end of the day, the entire stand will be filled with the hopeful prayers of others, but for now hers is the only intention, flickering golden on its own.

She walks up the centre aisle and genuflects next to a wooden pew close to the front of the church. She kneels on the padded kneeler, clasping her hands in prayer. Looking straight ahead past the altar, to the large painting of the Madonna resplendently swathed in robes and seated on a throne with the naked infant Jesus in her arms, Loretta whispers, 'Ave, o Maria, piena di grazia . . .'

Her heart skips a beat when the sacristy door creaks open. She stays focused on the painting of the Blessed Virgin. Footsteps approach. From the corner of her eye, she sees the nun walk past. The nun slides into the pew behind Loretta and sits close enough that Loretta can hear her breathing.

'You came.' Flavia's voice is quiet.

Loretta links her fingers tighter together. 'Don't ask me why I'm here, I couldn't tell you.'

'Because you want to see me as much as I want to see you.' There's a Roman accent in Flavia's speech.

'Why now?' Loretta struggles to keep her voice calm as her pain bubbles to the surface. 'Why, after all these years, have you come back now?'

'A young Venetian priest I work with at the Vatican was coming home to celebrate a funeral mass happening today. I liked the idea of having company for the journey.'

'In thirty-six years you haven't found someone to catch a train with?'

'I see you haven't lost your sharp tongue.' Flavia giggles and Loretta's heart squeezes at the sound of it.

Loretta continues facing the front of the church. Flavia's sweet floral perfume fills the air. It feels especially sinful that a nun can smell this good. Loretta breathes Flavia in, committing her scent to memory so she can go to the big farmacia next time she's in Milan and smell every perfume they have until she finds it.

'Is it Padre Alessandro you travelled with?' Loretta asks when she can find her voice again.

'Yes. You know him?'

'Everyone knows him. It's not often a priest from Venice is promoted to the Vatican.' Loretta pauses. 'Or a nun. Congratulations.'

'Thank you, cara.'

The easy way Flavia slips in the term of affection makes Loretta giddy. 'Whose funeral is it anyway?' she asks to keep the conversation in a safe space.

'Do you know Signore Zanetti?'

'Anna-Maria's husband?'

'I don't know the family. Alessandro said his name was Virgilio.'
Loretta chokes up. 'That's him. I hadn't heard. God rest his soul.'
'Amen.'

Loretta falls silent. *Poor Virgilio. Poor Anna-Maria.* She wonders if their daughter has returned for the funeral. She'd heard years ago that young Elena had moved to Australia, leaving her parents all alone.

After a minute or two, Flavia coughs. 'You became famous.'

'It was unintentional.'

'It made me so happy to see you on TV, I can't describe how much. I love that you still wear the black turtleneck and blue jeans. I don't know anyone else who can dress in her sixties the way she did in her twenties and look just as good. You're an icon.'

Loretta snorts.

'I save all the clips of you, you know,' Flavia continues. 'I watch them over and over. It comforts me – it's like you're with me.'

'Hmm. I haven't had anything of you to comfort me in decades. Not one thing.'

'I know. I never forgot you though, even before you were on TV. I missed you every day of every week of every month of every year.'

'That's quite the declaration, when you're the one who left,' Loretta reminds her.

Flavia sighs. 'Aren't you going to turn around so I can at least see your face?'

Slowly, Loretta pushes herself off her creaky knees and turns to face Flavia Castellani who, even at sixty-five and with her hair hiding beneath a veil, is still the most beautiful human she's ever laid eyes on.

Flavia smiles at her with closed lips and Loretta's heart thuds and thuds.

'Hi,' Flavia says.

'Hi.'

'You're as stunning as ever, Loretta. Even more so, if that's possible.'

'That's not true.' Loretta looks down.

'How's your husband? Recovering, I hope?'

'He is.' She picks at a piece of splintered wood on the pew.

'Are you happy?'

Loretta takes a deep breath. 'We've been together now for over half of my life. He's a good father to our children and a good partner for me with the hotel. And he loves me, so . . .' She lets the sentence fall.

'I was surprised to find out you got married and had children. I didn't see that coming.'

'*You* were surprised by *me*? You blindsided me! I gave you ten years of my life. Ten years, Flavia, and you abandoned me. What did you expect me to do?' Loretta bites her lip. 'My parents were desperate for me to marry. I was thirty when you left me with nothing. I told them I'd marry whoever they found for me.' She looks into Flavia's eyes. 'They found me Alberto.'

'You'll never know how sorry I am for the hurt I caused you. But I had to leave.'

'We both did what we had to do.' Loretta sniffs. 'I have to get back to the hospital. Alberto will be wondering where I am.'

'Let me walk you there. It's barely light outside; I'll keep you company.' Her gaze is intense.

Loretta looks away. 'That's not a good idea.'

Flavia touches her arm and it sends a shock of electricity all the way down to her fingers. 'Ciao, Flavia.' She edges out of the pew. 'Please tell Padre Alessandro to give the widow, Anna-Maria, my best. I don't see much of her these days. Have a safe trip back to Rome.'

'You're saying goodbye before we've even finished saying hello? Why?' Flavia's voice is hoarse.

'Because we made our choices a long time ago and we have to live with them.' Loretta hurries out of the cold church into the colder wind before Flavia can stop her.

She walks as fast as she can away from San Zaccaria, berating herself for her foolishness. What good did she think would come of going to the church? *Idiota*.

As she approaches the hotel, her breathing is still ragged, her heart is still galloping. She doesn't want her children to see her like this, so she walks on towards Piazza San Marco.

The artist is already standing in the tank, wearing the same white dress as yesterday. Two men walk away from her, carrying a long ladder between them. The artist's name is Magdalena Jansen. She's a big deal in performance art, likely even the biggest deal in the world. But nobody's there to watch her yet besides Loretta.

Magdalena sees her and there's a look of instant recognition in her eyes. Magdalena holds her palm up to the glass. She beckons to Loretta with a nod. Loretta takes slow steps towards her. She holds a shaky hand up to meet Magdalena's, the cold glass separating them. Their hands are almost identical in size, both with long fingers spread out. When Magdalena holds her stare, the tears Loretta's been holding on to escape. Magdalena doesn't look away.

More seconds pass and then Loretta takes her hand off the glass. 'Grazie,' she mouths.

The level of the water in the tank is higher than yesterday, now reaching Magdalena's knees, soaking more of the dress. It's only day two of the twelve-day exhibition.

Loretta turns away from Magdalena and walks with her head down to the hotel to collect her sick husband's belongings for hospital. Flavia is here, her darling Flavia, within agonisingly close reach. But Loretta's future with Alberto, loyal loving Alberto, may as well be set in stone like the stairs of Venice, there until the day they sink into the sea, paving the way to nowhere.

Affogando.

Sophie

Sophie wakes up smiling at the thought of the day ahead in the kitchen. Last night, the Bianchi siblings and their cousins were so grateful for her help that it was easy to convince them to let her do it again today. The best bit is that Rocco promised she'll get to do some cooking today.

But with an uncanny knack of ruining good moments, her mother strikes with a text message only seconds after Sophie's alarm goes off.

Hello again, darling!

Did you receive my email? Just wanted
to wish you luck on your first day with
Signora Bianchi.

Make good choices with all that
tempting Italian food, won't you?

What she wants to reply is:

> Good choices? How good have your
> choices been, Penelope?
>
> Fuck you.

What she does reply is:

> Thanks, Mum. Sorry I've been quiet,
> it's crazy busy here.
>
> Chat when I get home x

Next, she opens Twitter to check the Australian news. The images of the fires raging through the Eastern States are dystopian. The government is laughing off claims that the disaster could in any way be related to climate change.

That reminds her of the climate art exhibition Rocco had mentioned, so she looks up *Venice Rising* and clicks on a recent article.

> A showcase of international art will descend on Venice, Italy, on 25 December 2019 to bring attention to the rising water levels surrounding the city. Curator Franca Menori says of the inaugural event, 'Our goal is for the world to finally take notice of the tragedy of our sinking city.'
>
> Venice has just recorded its worst flooding in fifty years with water levels rising to almost two metres, causing millions of dollars' damage to Saint Mark's Basilica among other historical buildings, and forcing hundreds of local businesses to close.
>
> The Mayor of Venice, Luigi Brugnaro, proclaimed, 'Venice is on its knees. We need climate action now!'
>
> The governor of the Veneto region, Luca Zaia, echoed these sentiments, calling the floods 'an apocalyptic disaster'.
>
> If the rising water levels continue at the same rate, it's predicted that Venice will be uninhabitable within fifty years and completely underwater as early as 2100.
>
> A printable map of San Marco showing where to find the *Venice Rising* installations can be downloaded here.

Uninhabitable in fifty years! Is that true? Sophie googles it: it's true. How do Venetians deal with this knowledge without completely freaking out? And will an art exhibition actually change anything?

She follows the link to the map showing where the art installations are and takes a screen shot.

So, Australia burns while Venice sinks.

Her stomach growls, pulling her thoughts to more immediate matters than the future of the planet – breakfast. She climbs out from under the fluffy doona and opens the shutters, throwing light into the room. The air is icy when she leans out the window. A fading fog sits over the water of the canal and a solitary moored rowboat rocks in the breeze. There isn't a gondola or tourist to be seen. The cream stone building opposite is so close she feels as if she could lean over and touch it. She didn't appreciate yesterday just how narrow this canal is. How on earth do the gondoliers manage to steer around corners that tight?

She takes out her camera and snaps photos of the misty water before she nervously calls Bec. After working together for seven years, she knows her boss well enough to predict Bec won't be pleased with the situation of no Signora Bianchi in the restaurant. She does a little fist pump when Bec doesn't answer. She can tell her over text instead. Once that's done, she gets herself ready for the day and leaves the sanctity of her pretty pink room.

Her mother's *make good choices* message pops into her head again and she stomps down each step of the carpeted staircase. It doesn't matter how far away from home Sophie gets, Penelope somehow always finds a way to make her feel like crap.

When she reaches the hotel lobby, she takes a long, cleansing breath. Today she's working in the famous Il Cuore, with a side-serve of a hot Italian male. If that's not living the dream, she doesn't know what is. So she's determined to absolutely *not* let her mother ruin this for her.

Marina and Rocco told her to come to the kitchen at around nine, so she goes into the restaurant first, once again having her breath taken away by the gorgeous forest décor. Along the entire length of one pink-painted wall, a rustic wooden trestle table groans under the weight of fresh fruit, hard-boiled eggs, pancetta, whole loaves of bread, green olives, cherry tomatoes, a cheese board and at least three types of cakes and pastries, along with jugs of juice and a pot of coffee on the end.

'God, I love my job,' Sophie says under her breath as she makes a beeline for the coffee.

The small restaurant is packed with couples and families. Breakfast isn't open to the public; these people are all hotel guests. She's the only one dining alone.

She pulls out a chair at one of two vacant tables. An elderly American couple at the table next to her stand up to leave, clipping on their bum bags. They're in the same matching tops they were wearing last night when she served them dinner.

The man, who's a dead ringer for Santa with his big belly and bushy white beard, is also wearing a bright green sun visor, on an overcast winter's day, with a slogan on it that gives off 'Make America Great Again' vibes. The woman has a tight grey perm and a kind-looking round face with rosy cheeks. Her blue eye make-up is straight out of the 1980s.

Mrs Claus gives Sophie a friendly smile, with hot-pink lipstick stains on her teeth. 'You have a good day now, won't you, sugar?' she drawls in a thick southern accent. 'God bless you.'

As soon as the couple leaves, Marina rushes past and begins to quickly clear the table they vacated.

'Hi, Marina,' Sophie says. 'How's your dad going? Any news?'

Marina gives her a distracted look. 'Sorry? Yes?'

'Um, I was just asking how your dad's going.'

'He is okay, grazie a Dio.' The plates clatter as Marina hurriedly stacks them on top of each other.

Sophie puts her coffee cup down. 'Is everything okay? Do you need help back there now instead of at nine?'

'What? Oh, no, no, thank you, Sophie. All is well.' It's quite obvious that all is far from well by the manic way Marina manhandles the crockery. 'Are you sure you want to spend your day in the kitchen with us? We will manage on our own, no problems. You should go and explore the city while it is not raining.'

As Marina's talking, Rocco appears from the kitchen, tucking his tight-fitting shirt into his even tighter-fitting pants. When he catches Sophie's eye, a huge smile lights up his whole face. He pushes his glasses higher on his nose and gives her a jazz-hands wave.

'There's nowhere I'd rather be than in the kitchen with you guys,' Sophie replies to Marina.

'You are very kind, thank you.' Marina's tone softens a little. 'Make sure you eat first.'

Salvatore comes out and calls Rocco back into the kitchen.

Sophie helps herself to some eggs and bread. Once she's back at the table, her phone pings with a message from Bec.

What?? Signora Bianchi's husband had
a heart attack?

Why didn't you tell me this yesterday?

And why aren't you coming home?

WTF IS GOING ON OVER THERE?

                              Heya! Don't freak out, it's all good.

                                     Having brekkie now, so yummy!

                                 Just helping them out for a while.

                              The fires over there though. OMG!
                                                      Insane!

                                                         Stay safe x

Don't deflect!

I'm calling you.

A second later, Sophie's phone rings.

'Explain yourself!' Bec shouts.

'They're understaffed, so I offered to help out, that's all.' Before Bec can reply, Sophie says, 'I was thinking, even if Signora Bianchi doesn't come back to work while I'm here, the feature could be from a different perspective: what it's like to dive head-first into a busy Venetian restaurant. What do you think?' She bites her lip.

Bec's exhale is loud. 'The whole point of sending you over there was to feature Signora Bianchi. Now it's just you being a slave for these people. Have they even offered to pay you? Don't let them use you.'

'They didn't ask me to work, I volunteered! And I don't need them to pay me, I'm being paid by you. That is if it's still okay for me to stay on?'

Rocco comes out from the kitchen again with a fresh pot of coffee that he takes to the buffet table. He smiles and double-hand waves at her again like he's seeing her for the first time and he didn't do exactly that three minutes ago. She could eat this man with a spoon.

'Soph, you've never worked in a busy kitchen. You've only ever written about them,' Bec says, pulling her back into the conversation. 'You've no idea how hard this will be. Just come home for Christ's sake, it's Christmas!'

'Christmas was yesterday. Let me do this, please. I really think I could write a great feature. Otherwise I'll take annual leave and stay on here to help anyway.'

There's a long pause, then, 'Ugh, you're impossible. Fine, stay.'

Yes! 'You're the best, thank you! You won't regret it.'

'Hmm, that remains to be seen.'

When the call ends, Sophie scoops up her dirty crockery and cutlery as well as those from a nearby table on her way into the kitchen. There she's greeted by Rocco and his cousins like she's their long-lost relative who's just been freed after being held captive in someone's basement for the past seventeen years.

'Right, where do I start?' Sophie rubs her hands together.

'How neat is your handwriting?' Marina produces a piece of white chalk from her apron pocket. 'We all have terrible handwriting, but the daily menu needs to be written on the board. Papà usually writes it.'

'Easy done. My writing's so neat I could moonlight as a calligrapher.'

'You are saving the day already!' Rocco beams at her.

Marina leads her to a tiny office behind reception where she lays an A-frame blackboard sign flat. She hands Sophie a small piece of paper. On it is scribbled:

Signora Bianchi é via oggi, menù di Rocco Bianchi.

After travelling extensively over Italy for work, Sophie can read basic Italian. The note says, *Signora Bianchi is away today, menu by Rocco Bianchi.*

Underneath it, the menu reads:

Primo – Zuppa di fagioli

Secondo – Parmigiana di melanzane

Dolce – Tiramisù

Vino – Prosecco di villa Fresca

Sophie knows just about every Italian dish in existence and none of this menu features the traditional Venetian food Signora Bianchi is famous for.

As if reading her thoughts, Marina says, 'Today we cook what we found in the pantry. We did not have time for the market. So we have no fish, no meat. It's lucky we at least had leftover beans and eggplants to make the soup and parmigiana. Let's hope we don't receive bad reviews.'

'This all sounds delicious,' Sophie reassures her.

Sophie learned early on that the best Italian restaurants cater for the locals, so their menus are never in English. And the smaller the menu, the better the food.

Signora Bianchi has taken the limited menu idea a step further. The restaurant offers a single entrée, main and dessert at a set price that changes daily depending on the cost of the produce. The meal comes with a glass of Italian wine chosen to match the food. Il Cuore takes no reservations and opens strictly from six pm to eight pm on a first in, best dressed system.

Marina excuses herself and Sophie gets to work writing the menu, feeling the warm glow of being needed. It gives her a buzz to be writing on the same board that she's seen in countless Instagram photos. Would Sophie's mother think she's made a *good choice* in staying on at the hotel instead of coming home? She can guarantee the answer would be no. But Penelope Black is an addict who's ruined lives. She has no right to talk about good choices.

Elena

Elena wakes at a quarter to nine after another fitful night. As quietly as she can, she slides out of bed, then spends a solid half-hour attending to her face and neck, using a collection of concealers, foundation and powder.

She dresses head to toe in black: blazer, shirt, pencil skirt, opaque stockings and boots. Her straight dark hair is thin and limp; there's no improving it no matter how she tries with the GHDs and hairspray. She studies her reflection, thinking she might as well be interviewing for the role of an assistant to the Addams family.

She's putting on earrings when Christian comes into the bathroom and they make eye contact in the mirror. He looks at her with those deep blue eyes she once found so hard to resist.

'Ellie.' He stands behind her, leaning his head on hers. 'Big day today, babe. Will you be okay?'

She nods, knowing full well she won't be. Who's okay the day they bury their father?

They walk down the stairs, hand in hand, for breakfast.

Rocco's standing at the long buffet table, clearing the food away. His face breaks into an enormous smile when he sees Christian, and he quickly puts the bowls of pastries back onto the table. 'Ah, dottore, buongiorno! Buongiorno, signora.' His smile fades a little when he looks at her and he quickly returns his attention to Christian.

She's used to this kind of thing. It's why she hates dining in public, *hates it*. Will Rocco surreptitiously be watching to see what she eats? People always do.

'How's your dad?' Christian asks him.

'He is resting in hospital, grazie a Dio. Last night he was joking and laughing, like nothing was wrong. But I tell you something, dottore, when Mamma went to the bathroom he made me promise to look after her if anything happens to him. It is all an act how he pretends he is not scared, eh?' Rocco's hands fly around as he speaks, tugging at Elena's heart. She's missed being around Italians.

Rocco's face is a little lined now, but he's otherwise unchanged from when he played with Paolo in the North Italian Junior Football League. He still has the same messy curls and big warm smile, still hasn't grown into his long limbs, and he's as affable as he ever was.

He talks incredibly quickly in perfect English, even though his accent is thick. 'Maybe you prefer to eat somewhere else tonight, eh?' He laughs. 'I cannot guarantee the food, you know. I try, but I cannot guarantee. Ha, ha! Come sit, sit, prego. Take your time with breakfast. Please eat, enjoy. I put away the pancetta and bread already, but I go and get them. Now you eat and drink anything you like, eh? It is all free of charge for the rest of your stay with us.'

'Nah, Rocco, mate, you don't have to do—' Christian says.

Rocco holds his hands up. 'Dottore, please. My papà is alive today because of you. Of course you will not be giving us another cent.'

Rocco leaves them alone in the restaurant. Elena watches Christian eat with her eye on the clock.

Marina comes bustling in and gives them a cursory smile. Marina was so glamorous back when she was a high school senior, with her perfect features, long, jet black curls, supermodel body and a wardrobe to die for. She was always in high heels, even at the muddiest of football pitches. Pre-teen Elena was in awe of her.

Now Marina looks tired and sad. She's lost all traces of the sparkle of her youth. Perhaps it's worry over her sick father, but she also looked tired and sad when she checked them in and that was before

Signore Bianchi had the cardiac arrest. Maybe it's just the way she is these days. Even so, she remains breathtakingly beautiful. There's something regal about the way the Bianchi women carry themselves. Elena can't take her eyes off her.

Marina and Rocco must be thirty-five now, the same age Paolo would be. Her heart hurts.

Christian wipes his mouth with a linen napkin. 'Sure you don't want to eat anything, babe?'

'No, thanks, I'm good.'

They always play this game, the two of them, as if it's a casual question between husband and wife.

Upstairs she watches him change into his black Armani suit. He checks himself in the mirror for three seconds at most. Christian doesn't need a mirror to tell him he looks good.

'Let's go, babe.' He holds his hand out to her. 'I've got you.'

The walk to San Zaccaria isn't long, but her legs are so heavy it's as if she's dragging her feet through wet cement. The lanes are alive with holiday-makers, buzzing with post-Christmas cheer. The cocoon of grief surrounding her as she walks is a forcefield, blocking the joy on the streets from penetrating through to her. How dare everyone be so happy? Don't they know that the kindest, loveliest man in the whole world is dead? She hates every last person going about their life obliviously happy on this terrible day. It makes her irrationally angry to pass by people posing next to fountains, buying colourful marzipan treats, trying on Venetian masks. She has to stop herself from swearing at a couple with a pram who block her path.

True to his word though, Christian does have her. He leads her by the hand around the couple with the pram and on through the streets, expertly navigating their way through the festive crowds like he's lived here all his life.

When they reach the church, Mamma's already there waiting with some of the family who have come early, along with Padre Alessandro in his special purple funeral vestments. It's the first time

Elena's ever seen him dressed as an actual Catholic priest. It's as if he's cosplaying.

Mamma wears a black veil, hiding her hair and making her look even more the widow than she did yesterday. Her black woollen coat swamps her and her short boots hang loose around her bony ankles. Mamma's always been petite, but the grief has ravaged her; she's tiny now. Her pale cheeks are sunken and her beautiful brown eyes are blank. She's surrounded by people, but to Elena, she's never looked more alone.

When Mamma sees Elena, she rushes to her and they hold on to each other until they're led by Alessandro to a small room at the side of the church where Papà's closed casket awaits.

Alessandro indicates for Christian to leave with him. 'We will give you two some privacy to say goodbye,' he says gently.

But Elena can't say goodbye. She can't say anything. No words come from the emptiness inside her. So she rubs Mamma's back instead, staring into space as Mamma wails her final endearments to Papà, draping herself over the shiny wooden casket.

'I have no one now,' Mamma sobs.

'You have me, Mamma,' Elena says, her heart cracking. 'You still have me.'

Alessandro ducks his head in. 'We're ready.'

The funeral directors tread carefully around Mamma, like she's an explosive that might detonate. They give Mamma and Elena a travel packet of tissues each, a laughably inadequate amount to mop up the tears over the love of their lives. Elena has plenty more tissues in her handbag anyway.

Christian walks between her and Mamma. He gives Elena his hand to grip as they follow Papà's coffin down the aisle. Elena can't stop imagining Papà in there. Have his eyes dried out? Are his eyelids sunken? Are his lips and fingernails blue?

The choir is singing loudly, so very loudly. She wants to cover her ears. She avoids eye contact with everyone standing as they watch her enter. Christian leads her to the front of the church where there's a large portrait of Papà with his hair slicked back, his face cleanly shaven and looking so handsome in a suit and tie. He's smiling broadly in that photo and she remembers why.

It was her graduation day from university. He and Mamma scrimped and saved to make the trip to Sydney for it. She can almost feel Papà's strong arms around her, hear the pride in his voice as he pointed her out to strangers after the ceremony. 'My daughter, this one. Bachelor of Laws *with Distinction*. Very smart girl.'

Next to her in the pew, Mamma's knuckles are white from gripping her glass rosary beads. Her thumb continuously slides across her index finger. The only jewellery Mamma wears, her wedding band, sits loose on her ring finger. Elena rests her hand over Mamma's, but it doesn't stop her twitching.

The Mass begins and Alessandro's prayers wash over her. Christian steps up to the lectern for the Second Reading, from the Gospel of St John, which he executes flawlessly and with a depth and gravity befitting a grieving son-in-law.

Alessandro takes over again, reciting prayer after prayer. Elena dutifully repeats the responses that have been ingrained in her head since she was a child. Her teeth chatter from the cold or the grief, or both. The choir sings hymn after mournful hymn. The congregation chants and kneels and stands and sits. It's never-ending. Time has stood still in this freezing church on this freezing day.

Every time the young altar boy rings the bell, she jumps. It's as loud to her as a fire alarm. The smell of incense is thick and heavy and makes her feel sick.

'Lord, hear our prayer,' she mouths as her cousins, all obediently wearing black, line up at the altar, each given the task of saying a prayer of the faithful. They walk solemnly back to their seats afterwards, wiping their eyes and giving her and Mamma sorrowful smiles as they pass by. She feels a surge of love for them: Stella, Pietro, Tomaso, Lara, Giacomo, Marta, Portia, all so close growing up before becoming strangers to her once she moved away.

Then it's time for Alessandro to give the eulogy. With a quaver in his voice he tells the congregation, 'Virgilio Zanetti was like a father to me.'

Alessandro's words echo and bounce around her head as if he's shouting them from a mountain top and she's stuck deep in the valley. As soon as it's over she can't remember anything he said.

She lines up behind Mamma and accepts a wafer on her tongue that sticks to the roof of her mouth, and from the same chalice as the others, she drinks red wine that burns her throat.

When she kneels after receiving Holy Communion, no prayer comes to her. Instead, she stares at Papà's lonely coffin and at his beautiful smiling face behind it and she repeats the same three words in her head over and over: *Mi dispiace, Papà. I'm sorry.*

Finally, the Mass is over.

It's a short walk to the cemetery, where Christian wraps his arms tightly around her and speaks hushed soothing words in her ear when the cold wind blows around them. She fears her legs might collapse under her as her beloved Papà is lowered six feet into the soil, but Christian keeps her upright.

Alessandro holds a Bible in one hand and sprinkles the first lot of dirt over the grave in the other. With a deep sincerity, he prays aloud. 'Oh God, by whose mercy the faithful departed find rest, bless this grave and send your holy angel to watch over it. As we bury here the body of our brother, Virgilio, deliver his soul from every bond of sin, that he may rejoice in you with your saints forever. We ask this through Christ our Lord.'

While the others chant, 'Amen,' Mamma lets out a howl that pierces the air and Elena's heart. Elena reaches for Mamma and pulls her in close as their family and friends take turns covering Papà's grave with fistfuls of dirt and sprigs of rosemary.

Christian and Alessandro lead the group back to the Grand Canal. She walks arm in arm with Mamma in silence, and they support each other as they move further away from Papà, leaving him behind in the same plot as his son. Rotting, rotting.

When the procession leaves the cemetery, the heaviness of the funeral lifts from the people around Elena. Her cousins chat amicably with each other. The younger generation play a game of chase, and their mothers yell at them when they run right through the puddles in their good leather shoes. The worst is over for everyone. But for her and Mamma it's only the beginning of a lifetime of learning to live with the hollowness.

A few paces ahead of them, Alessandro points out landmarks to Christian. With her husband distracted, it's the perfect opportunity for Elena to tell Mamma everything.

Her heart races. 'Mamma, I need to tell you something.'

Mamma turns to her with eyes glazed. 'What is it, tesoro?' Her voice is shaky. She looks so fragile, it wouldn't take more than a gust of wind to blow her over.

Elena can't bring herself to make things worse for her. So all she says is, 'I'm sorry I didn't come when you asked me to.'

Mamma rubs Elena's gloved hand with her own. 'You're here now. That's what matters.'

She'll have to tell Mamma the truth tomorrow. There's no time to waste. But she might not get another chance alone with her. She'll write her a letter. Yes, that's what she'll do.

The family crowds onto the vaporetto to take them back to San Marcuola. When the vaporetto leaves the jetty, Zio Matteo, Papà's younger brother, seated with his arm around Mamma, begins to sing 'Grande Sei Tu': *'How Great Thou Art'*. By the end of the first verse, the entire family is singing with him. Their voices lift for the chorus, the melody sweeping Elena up in a hug. Surrounded by these people who have known and loved her all her life, here on the waters of home, it makes her wish she'd never left Venice in the first place.

The group disembarks at San Marcuola, walks through the Jewish Ghetto together and climbs the four flights of stairs of the ramshackle apartment block to Elena's childhood home.

Zio Bruno stands at the door, collecting everyone's coats. His wife, Zia Sonia, is already at the oven warming up food. The cousins stand around unsure what to do.

Christian claps his hands together in the centre of the tiny, overcrowded lounge room. 'Limoncello time!' he says with his trademark lopsided grin.

His question is met with applause and the mood instantly lifts.

Elena retreats to the same corner of the couch where she sat yesterday, making herself as small as she can. Every relative she has is squashed together in this room and not one of them seeks to engage with her. She wonders if they're leaving her alone because they respect her grief, or because of her long absence, or if it's just her size repelling them. Whatever it is, she's grateful for it.

Mamma's in the kitchen with her sisters and sisters-in-law, and Christian is once again surrounded by a crowd eager to get to know him better. He's the consummate host, making every guest feel welcome and important. 'Pietro, Elena tells me you're studying medicine in Bologna. So you want to be a doctor, hey? Let me tell you something, mate, get out while you still bloody can.' He laughs. 'Portia, don't think I'm leaving here today before you give us a song. I don't know anyone who sings opera.'

When he notices Elena alone on the couch, he comes to sit next to her and calls over Zio Matteo. 'Tell me, Matteo, what was Virgilio like growing up? Was he a troublemaker like his daughter?' He grins as he gives Elena a cuddle.

'Let me help you with that.' He jumps to his feet when the aunts bring out the trays with tramezzini.

'Sit, sit,' Zia Lina tells him, but he insists.

He's the only man in the room who lifts a finger and the women swoon.

'What a wonderful man. So humble and kind and a *surgeon*! You must be thrilled,' Zia Sonia says to Mamma within earshot of Elena.

'So handsome too,' Zia Romina adds, as her eyes roam over Elena's body, up and down, up and down.

Later, Christian's elbow-deep in dishes, charming her cousins Marta and Lara, when Mamma fills a plate to the brim with food and sets it on Elena's lap. 'Mangia.' She nods at the plate.

Elena's starving, but she can feel the eyes of all in the room on her. She twists her earring and looks down. 'I'll eat later at the hotel, Mamma. Everyone's watching me.'

Mamma places her fingers under Elena's chin and lifts her face so they're eye to eye. Her eyes are bloodshot, but they've lost the glassiness of before. 'Mangia, Elena,' she says firmly.

It's the first time since Elena arrived here yesterday that Mamma's given her a glimpse of the woman she still is beneath the grief. Without argument, Elena brings the fork to her lips. The chicken cutlet melts in her mouth. Greedily she eats the rest, avoiding eye contact with anyone until the plate is clean, popping the last fritole into her mouth whole.

'Brava.' Mamma pats her knee.

Christian comes out of the kitchen; the front of his shirt is wet from the sink. He rests his elbow on the mantelpiece while he speaks with Alessandro. They laugh together as if they've been friends forever.

Christian beckons Elena over, grinning. 'I'm finally uncovering the truth about you now, babe.'

'I'm telling him the story of how you came banging on my door in the middle of the night.' Alessandro laughs. 'How you tried to convince me that God spoke to you and told you that He did not want me to give up my life in service to Him. He instructed you, apparently, to tell me I was not supposed to become a priest at all.'

Elena smiles at the memory. 'I'd only lost my brother two years before. I wasn't ready to lose you too.'

'I had to become a priest. It was the only way to escape from you.' Alessandro flicks his hair out of his eyes. *'Alessandro, help me with my homework. Alessandro, I need money.'* He imitates her voice.

'Ha!' Christian snorts.

'Seriously though.' Alessandro smiles at her. 'You did not need to be so worried. You could never lose me, Elena.'

For a moment Elena's transported back to her childhood when Alessandro and Paolo took turns letting her sit on the handlebars of their bikes as they raced through the backstreets, all three of them without a worry in the world.

Christian's voice brings her back to the present. 'Looks like some of your relatives are going now, Ellie.'

When most of the mourners have left, Christian almost single-handedly finishes the cleaning up, gently guiding the women away from the kitchen and insisting they rest. She watches him trying his best to be everything she needs him to be, wishing so deeply she didn't hate him.

Gayle

Gayle and Mike have been waiting to be seated at the restaurant in Dorsoduro for close to ten minutes now, and Mike's sighs are getting more and more dramatic. A couple walks in behind them, letting the cold night air in as the door opens and, without hesitation, they head straight for a vacant table. Gayle and Mike look at each other with mouths agape.

'Did you see that?' Mike hisses. 'We were here first!'

'There are still four free tables, hon. Maybe we should go on over and sit at one? This might be the kind of place where you don't need to wait to be seated.'

The two young women and two young men who are run off their feet waiting on tables haven't so much as looked their way the whole time they've been standing near the front door.

'But the internet says you have to wait to be seated in countries like Europe,' Mike insists.

Gayle isn't so sure he's right. That's the second group of people who've walked in and sat down since they arrived. But she's saving challenging Mike for bigger things this evening, so she pats her perm, which is weather-beaten today after all the wind, and says nothing.

'What if we sat down and the table was reserved? That'd be a mighty embarrassing predicament, that,' Mike says when another couple of minutes pass and they're still waiting by the door.

Gayle wishes they'd stayed at the hotel and eaten dinner at Il Cuore, like they'd planned to. But that was before poor old Signore Bianchi had gone and had his heart attack yesterday. It isn't cheap to dine at Il Cuore by any means, so knowing that it would be Rocco and the young ones cooking again tonight, they ventured out of San Marco, taking a leisurely ten-minute stroll to this restaurant by a small canal in the district of Dorsoduro that Mike saw had good reviews on Tripadvisor. It's also a more budget-friendly restaurant, and now that they're here being ignored, she can see why.

At last an unsmiling young waiter approaches them. Shockingly, he starts speaking to them in Italian!

Mike holds up his hands. 'Whoa, son, I'm gonna have to stop you right there. Me and my wife, Gayle here, we're from Little Rock in Arkansas. That's in the United States of America,' he says proudly. 'Folk don't speak Italian in Little Rock, only English. Wait, no, no, I tell a lie. There was this one Italian family over on Anderson Road there some years back. Wait a minute, no, now that I think about it, they were Colombian.'

The young man, who's more of a boy than a man really, gestures to the empty tables. 'Sit anywhere,' he snaps before turning his back on them.

Mike scowls. 'Rude! Should we look for somewhere else with decent service?'

Gayle's lower back is aching; she's desperate to sit down. 'The food does look good here, hon,' she says. 'And it's good value too, remember?'

Mike grunts and unclips his fanny pack. 'All right then. But I've a mind to leave them a bad review.'

'How about we wait and see what the meal's like first?'

The meal is actually delicious, chilli mussels drowning in a rich tomato broth for Mike and jumbo prawns in a light, creamy garlic sauce for her. Between them is a bowl of crispy golden potatoes, roasted with lemon, and a small plate of steamed broccolini with salted butter. Of course it's not quite as delicious as Signora Bianchi's food, but then again, how could it be? Unfortunately, Gayle's too nervous to enjoy the food so she pushes her plate across the table towards Mike.

There's a small moment of alarm when his face turns bright red and he makes all kinds of gagging sounds. But he coughs up the offending piece of prawn shell into his napkin soon enough, and after a few gulps of water, he's okay.

He hails a waiter to complain that the low lighting nearly cost him his life, but unfortunately the waiter doesn't respond in a very sympathetic manner or offer any kind of refund.

When another equally harried waiter clears away their plates, and Gayle's sure that Mike's completely over the near-choking fiasco, she scrunches her paper napkin into a tight ball and sits up straighter. 'Hon, Venice is a beautiful city, and I'm ever so thankful you brought me here. But the only place I want to be next Christmas is at home with our family. The *whole* family.'

In years gone by, all the children, the grandchildren, even some of the neighbours, had gathered at their home on Christmas afternoon, each bringing a plate to go with the traditional roast honey ham she always prepared. Every year they would joke about how Justin would turn up late and, sure enough, he always did. It was tradition for Susan to bake the most decadently rich Christmas cake, dense with fruit. And Elizabeth, sweet Lizzie, would never let Gayle do the cleaning up, instead rounding up the grandchildren to help. After dessert, Noah would take a seat at the piano, and the family would gather around and sing carols while drinking non-alcoholic mulled 'wine' that Justin made with pomegranate juice, blackberries and spices.

These are the days Gayle holds dearest to her heart. They did right by the Lord, she and Mike. They were plentiful in creating these four beautiful children to honour Him, and God had rewarded them with a bounty of grandchildren, and now great-grandchildren.

Which is why it had cut her so deeply when Noah moved away to California. The rest of her children are no more than a quick drive away and she can get her fill of them whenever she chooses to.

Whether it's dropping in to see Justin at the office for a quick coffee or joining Susan for a walk around the lake on Tuesdays with baby Elsie in the pram, or doing the weekly grocery shop with Lizzie pushing her own shopping cart next to her and then having a club sandwich at Mae's Diner together afterwards, Gayle's children are always there.

But when Noah left, he didn't come home again. He didn't call, he didn't write. When Noah left, he really left.

'Hon,' she continues now, 'I've been meaning to talk to you about Noah.' Her throat tightens around the words.

Mike blows hard through his nose. 'There's nothing to talk about.'

When she opens her mouth to reply, an unexpected sob comes out.

'There, there.' Mike's tone instantly softens. He rests his hand over hers. He's never been able to see her cry without worrying. 'Don't you go crying now, it'll work itself out. Noah'll come around. Kids always do.'

'Noah's not a kid any more. He's pushing fifty and he's *not* coming around. I miss him so much.' She uses the napkin to wipe her nose, looking around to make sure nobody's watching her cry like a fool in public.

'I know you miss him. I do too. But it's written clear as day in the Bible that he's sinning.'

'We're all sinners in the eyes of the Lord.'

Mike guffaws. 'Well, there's sinning and there's *sinning*.'

'He's our son. We can't turn our backs on him.'

'But we didn't turn our backs on him,' he argues. '*He* turned away from *us*.'

She meets his eye. 'You know he only left because of your reaction to his wedding announcement.'

'I was only saying what's right. We promised to honour God above all else. God's word has to come first.'

The pull between being a good mother, like her religion demands of her, and being a submissive wife, like her religion also demands of her, is making Gayle's head hurt. Her hands shake as she lays down the challenge she's been rehearsing in her head all day. 'Well, I've been doing a lot of praying on that. And reading the scripture over and over. Why, I must have read the Gospels no less than three times from start to finish since Noah left. And hon, nowhere, *nowhere*, can I find Jesus saying anything about it being a sin.'

He frowns at her. 'But the Bible says—'

'None of what the Bible says about *that* is in Jesus' own words. And who's our Lord and Saviour? It's not Paul, and it's not Timothy, and even Pastor Bob preached that one time to take Leviticus with a pinch of salt, don't you remember?'

After a minute Mike says, 'You've got me confused now with all your Bible talk. How about we go visit Pastor Bob when we get back home and see what he thinks of all this? He's always had the best advice for us when we need it.'

Pastor Bob is pushing ninety years old now and living in an aged care facility. Mike has remained loyal to him over the years, but Gayle hasn't forgotten that the pastor's 'best advice' from decades ago is a big reason they're in this mess with Noah. 'Hon, we shouldn't need Pastor Bob to tell us right from wrong.' She dabs at her eyes. 'Doesn't it feel wrong that we wished all our children a Merry Christmas apart from one? And ain't it wrong not knowing our own son's whereabouts? For all we know, he could be in hospital, or worse.'

Mike shakes his head. 'We were having a nice dinner here, hon. Why'd you have to go and ruin it with this talk of hospitals and sinning? To me it's simple. Marriage is the union by which to honour God through procreation. And that marriage of Noah's sure as heck ain't a God-honouring one.'

'You don't need to agree with him, you just need to accept him.'

'He's asking us to accept too much.'

'He's our *child*, Mike. There shouldn't be limits to what we can accept when it comes to our children.'

He sighs a big sigh and rolls his eyes. 'What do you want from me? Go on and spit it out. What is it you actually want me to do?'

Gayle feels herself shrink in confidence, but she perseveres. 'I want you to call him and apologise. Say you're sorry for the way you reacted.'

His nostrils flare. 'Now, hang on just a minute. Dogs would have to mow the lawns and cats would have to hang out the washing before I apologise to that boy.'

Gayle gulps down her nerves and ploughs on. 'Hon, I've never asked you to do anything you didn't want to do now, have I? For every one of our fifty-five years of marriage, I've respected your authority, and I've done it gladly.' Her voice wobbles and she twists the napkin around her finger. 'But this is our *son*. I can't have another Christmas without my boy. We have to relent and accept Noah for who he is. We should've done it a long time ago.'

'Don't you see? That's what they want! They want good God-fearing folk to relent so the bad ones can carry on in all manner of sin.'

'Noah isn't bad. You know that. Please, let's call him and beg him to come home.'

'Beg him? I ain't doing any begging and that's for certain.'

'Fine, not begging, just asking.'

Mike's silent for a long time. He strokes his beard. Finally he shakes his head. 'I want to make you happy, hon, I really do. I hate seeing you this worked up. But I can't do it, simple as that. I can't go against my principles.'

Gayle's shoulders sag. The hope she had for father and son to find their way back to each other bursts like a popped balloon. But she'd already decided, before even talking to Mike, that she's not backing down. She's not giving up on Noah this time. If Mike won't reconcile with him, at least she can. If she can just open the door that leads to Noah even a fraction, Mike might be tempted to walk through it later and their family can become whole again. 'Will you let me call him, then? Can I do that?'

Mike stares at his hands, sucking in his bottom lip so it looks as if he's munching on his beard. 'I've got a proposal for you. How about we enjoy the rest of the Italy trip in peace first, without Noah and his problems bothering us, and then you can call him when we get back home to Little Rock?'

'How about I call him from our room tonight to ease the ache in my heart so I can actually enjoy Italy?' She reaches across the table to rest her palm on his bristly cheek. 'Please, hon, it would mean everything to me just to hear his voice and know he's okay.'

'What if he makes you talk to Chris? What will you do then?'

'Then I'll tell Chris how sorry I am for everything that happened and ask him to find it in his heart to forgive me.'

Mike points at her, his face redder than ever. 'I can tell you right now, you won't be apologising for a darned thing to the man who turned our son gay. You've got it all mixed up about who should be doing the apologising here.'

She's pushed him too far. *Silly, silly, silly.* She backtracks quickly. 'Okay, okay, no apologising to Chris, but please, hon, please let me call Noah.'

'Excuse me, signore, will you and la signora be ordering a dessert?' A young waitress in a black minidress leans her hand on the table.

'No, we won't, thank you all the same, sugar,' Gayle answers before Mike can be tempted by the cakes in the display cabinet. 'We need to be getting on back to our hotel. I've got an important phone call to make.'

'Okay,' Mike concedes when the waitress walks away. 'You can call him. But I want nothing to do with it. This is all on you, you hear?'

She jumps out of her seat and throws her arms around his neck. 'I'm so lucky to have you. Thank you, thank you!'

With renewed hope in her heart for a reconciliation with Noah, she's overcome with gratitude on the walk back to San Marco. The narrow streets are lit up with strings of colourful Christmas lights and hanging decorations of bells and angels. Every street they turn into is prettier than the last. Even the streetlights here have character, all shaped like lanterns.

This is the first night that they've been out walking this late, and Gayle's surprised by how quiet Venice is at only nine o'clock, considering how busy and crowded the piazzas are during the day. The shops are all shut, the cafes too. The lights are on in the upstairs apartments, but the shutters are closed. She loves Venice like this, when the only sound is of her and Mike's footsteps on the cobbled road.

But when the street opens onto another piazza, she sees that they aren't alone at all. A crowd is gathered at the far end of the square, looking up at flashing images projected onto the large brick wall of a church. The images increase in number. They're all photos of cars, all kinds of cars, hundreds, thousands of them.

They stand together, she and Mike, with the silent crowd, mesmerised as the number of cars grows, taking up more and more space until almost the entire church wall is covered. It becomes apparent that the cars are forming the shape of a ship. Every second, dozens more cars are superimposed. Once the ship is fully formed, it soon disappears and words in giant text emerge in its place, shining in bright white light on the wall. *UNA GRANDE NAVE = UN MILIONE DI MACCHINE. NO GRANDI NAVI!* Some seconds later, the wall is plunged into darkness. A few seconds after that, the cars flash up again, first ten, then hundreds and so it goes.

The flashes are bringing on a headache, so Gayle looks away. Some of the crowd disperses, while some stays to watch the whole thing again.

Two young women standing next to them speak in Italian to each other. Mike steps towards them. 'Evening. Do y'all know what this is about?'

One of the women helpfully replies in English, 'It's part of the *Venice Rising* exhibition.'

'Is there a meaning behind it?' Mike points at the cars on the wall.

'It is showing how one big cruise ship docking in the canal is equal to the pollution of one million cars,' the other woman says. '"No more big ships" is the message.'

'I see, thank you.' Mike leads Gayle away.

Arriving in Venice this week on the giant cruise ship was so exciting. Her heart leapt when the edges of the city first came into view from the top deck, as the greenery along the canal banks gave way to the ancient stone buildings packed so closely together, and then Mike pointed out the tall bell tower in the distance. As they approached San Marco, the vaporettos and speed boats grew in number around them and the white dome of the magnificent cathedral on the other side appeared on the water's edge. The closer the ship drew to the port, the more the city came alive, with Christmas decorations hanging across the streetlamps, pop-up market stalls lining the esplanade and people *everywhere*. Such a festive feeling! Her spirits soared when the ship's deep horn heralded their arrival.

At the time, she hadn't given much thought to the small group of flag-waving protestors in the speed boat who tried to intercept the ship. But now she knows it wasn't just a renegade threesome of disgruntled youth, like she'd assumed. The issue is big enough to warrant protest art that draws big crowds.

She doesn't speak until they're out of earshot of the women, then she says, 'It's because of us. The *Venice Rising* exhibition is a protest about people like us.' The shame creeps up her neck and into her face.

'How were we supposed to know about the pollution thing? Nobody told us. It's not our fault.' Mike's face is red.

She squeezes his hand. 'Maybe that's the point of the exhibition. Now we know.'

He scoffs. 'A light display in a backstreet alley won't do a damn thing. It should be on the internet.'

'Are we sure it isn't?'

'Well, I've never seen it and I'm on the internet all the time. Besides, I thought flying caused more pollution than boats. Isn't that why the airlines bully us to pay extra for carbon offset? How exactly do they expect us to travel anywhere without polluting?'

She can't come up with a response, so they walk in silence the rest of the way to the hotel.

Once they're back in their suite, she reminds Mike that he promised to let her call Noah.

'As long as you don't apologise for anything,' Mike says, 'And whatever you do, don't put me on the phone. I don't want to speak to that boy until he's ready to repent.'

'Definitely, absolutely.' She nods as she pulls her phone from her bag. 'Just saying hello is all. Let me look for his number . . . Here.'

'Put him on speaker.' Mike sits in the corner chair and unties the laces of his sneakers.

She frowns. 'You just said you didn't want to talk to him.'

'Doesn't mean I don't want to hear what he has to say for himself.'

Obeying, Gayle puts the phone on speaker. She holds her breath. An automated voice announces that the number doesn't exist.

Noah really has left.

Elena

When they arrive back at Il Cuore from Mamma's apartment, the lobby is empty and the lights are dimmed, which makes the fairy lights twinkling on the big Christmas tree sparkle even brighter. Papà will never see another Christmas tree. The restaurant is closed but Elena can hear laughter coming from the kitchen. The sound of it grates on her stinging heart.

Christian's unused to older-style lifts like the one here and refuses to take it. Every step up the carpeted stairway to the first floor is a mountain to climb as she holds on to the wooden banister. It's only nine-thirty, but it feels like it's past midnight.

In the suite, she unzips her stiletto boots. Her toes are screaming in pain. Slowly and carefully, she removes the layers of clothes. It's a relief to peel off the stockings that felt harsh and scratchy on her legs all day. As gently as she can, she wipes off the make-up, revealing her raw self. She doesn't look in the mirror.

When she emerges from the bathroom in only her knickers, she can feel Christian's eyes on her, making the hair on her arms stand on end. She pulls a fresh nightgown from the open suitcase, turning herself away from him.

He clears his throat. 'Want a coffee, babe? I know it's late, but I'm making myself one anyway.' He walks over to the small Nespresso machine by the minibar.

'Thanks, that'd be good.'

'I was thinking I might go out in a bit, get some air. I want to find those art installations that light up at night. Your cousins were saying it's best to go after ten when it's less crowded. You don't have to come, it's okay.'

'I think I will stay here, as long as you're sure you don't mind? I'm so tired.'

'Totally fine with me, babe, honestly.'

'Thank you again for today,' she says. 'You were amazing.'

'You don't have to thank me. Always here for you, you know that.' He lines up two small cups as the coffee machine hums into life. 'Just one thing, babe.' He keeps his eyes on the coffee coming out of the spout. 'I didn't want to have to say anything, especially today, but how about we be more careful with what we put in our mouths tomorrow, hey? You downed a shitload of food at your mum's.'

She looks at him and wonders what it would feel like to wrap her hands around his throat. To watch the life drain from his eyes.

'I know I did,' she replies. 'I hate myself for it.'

'Don't be too hard on yourself. I mean, it was understandable, given the circumstances. I get it. But I know how much you want to turn things around. Fresh start tomorrow, hey?'

She swallows the bile rising in her throat. 'Yep.'

He brings her the coffee with a smile. 'You've got this, babe.'

Twelve days. She has twelve days left in Venice to get herself out of this marriage.

And she's going to make sure she does get out while she's here, no matter what.

Because if she follows him back to Australia, there's no question that she's going to kill him.

Sophie

The last of the diners left over an hour ago and the kitchen is so clean, it's gleaming. Sophie throws her dirty apron in the wicker linen basket in the corner of the huge walk-in pantry.

Rocco seals the lid on a plastic takeaway container packed to the brim with leftover white bean soup and, with a permanent marker, he labels it before piling it on top of containers of eggplant parmigiana.

'What do you do with the leftovers?' she asks him.

'This we freeze, then on Sunday we take the frozen food to church. The nuns distribute it to families who need it. Every week we take maybe twenty-five, thirty containers.' He shrugs one shoulder. 'It's not much, but better than nothing, eh?'

'It's a lot better than nothing. I've seen so much waste in other restaurants, this is fantastic.' She watches him squat to load the containers into the freezer, thinking he just got a tiny bit hotter with his humanitarian goodwill on top of that sexy butt.

He slams the freezer door shut and stands up, reaching into the pocket of his tight pants to pull out a fat wad of cash. 'Take this, Sophie. It is not enough for all of your help today, but it is at least something.'

She laughs and waves it away. 'I don't want your money! Put that away.'

'Okay, then wait one second.' He walks out into the restaurant, returning with the jar of tips. He slides it on the bench towards her. 'You have been here working for over twelve hours. This is yours.'

'No, the tips are for us all to share.'

'Not today. Today it is yours. It is not just me who says so, the others insist as well. Apart from all your help cooking and serving and cleaning, if you were not here to translate, what would we have done with the Scottish guests tonight, eh? Not one word I understood! So fast the man talks, *och aye, och aye*. What is he even saying? Mammamia!' He flings his arms around.

'I did some work in Glasgow.' She laughs. 'I had the best time today. I feel like I should be the one paying you for letting me be a part of it.'

Even though they'd been under the pump with barely a minute to rest from morning until the final dish had been cleaned this evening, she'd loved every minute of working in the Bianchi kitchen. As well as the delightful Scottish couple, she'd had fun chatting with other tourists and some of the locals this evening. There hadn't been a single complaint about Signora Bianchi's absence.

It didn't hurt that the food was to die for. Sophie had been dazzled by Rocco in the kitchen, blown away by the skill with which he'd sliced dozens of eggplants so finely and salted them with a speed that had to be seen to be believed. Then he'd created the most perfect seasoning for the bean soup, with the genius touch of adding a splash of soy sauce to the pot – not something she'd have expected in an Italian kitchen. What she'd imagined might be a rather dull entrée had in fact been mouth-watering.

'Is this your mother's recipe?' she'd asked him when he fed her a mouthful of parmigiana sauce bursting with basil and oregano.

'No, this is something I throw together just now. Mamma would kill me for using dried herbs. But she is not here, so I cheat.' He'd grinned.

Once Rocco heard from Signora Bianchi, just before lunch, that his father had finally agreed to have the heart surgery, which has now been scheduled for two days' time, he was so buoyed by the news that he sang along (hilariously tunelessly) with the radio to English songs Sophie knew and Italian ones she didn't.

'I'm the only Venetian man in history who cannot sing,' he announced proudly, dancing around the kitchen to Taylor Swift. 'My papà could have been a professional singer if he wanted, and Mamma and Marina have the voices of angels. They all want to die of shame when they hear me sing.'

'This is correct. Please stop, my ears are bleeding,' Marina had quipped as she walked past.

While they worked, Rocco had regaled Sophie with stories of past hotel guests and restaurant mishaps, like the politician who'd brought his mistress out for dinner only to be met by his wife who, thinking he was away, had snuck a night out with her lover. Or the story of the day a distracted Signore Bianchi had mistaken the mayonnaise for custard and filled all the pastries with it, narrowly escaping death by rolling pin when Signora Bianchi had discovered his error. Rocco had her laughing until she was drying her eyes. But best of all, he hadn't probed into her personal life or her past, not even a little bit.

His cousin Salvatore had been with them all day too. He was a sweet and easygoing kid, quite shy. He hadn't spoken much, but his English was perfectly fluent just like the others.

Rocco had ribbed Salvatore mercilessly about a new girl appearing on his Instagram feed lately, and he'd taken the teasing with a smile.

Marina had kept to herself for most of the day; she'd been as quiet as Rocco had been extroverted, and she'd spent long periods of time glued to the phone and computer on the reception desk, looking terribly busy and important.

Salvatore's sister, Chiara, who was just as stunning as Marina, had been in and out between the kitchen and reception all day too, but she had a more relaxed nature than Marina. Which wasn't all that surprising. A person hurtling towards the ground with a parachute that refused to open would be more relaxed than Marina, whose movements had been fast and twitchy, and she'd barely cracked a smile, despite Sophie twisting herself into knots trying to get her to engage.

Sophie had even pulled out the big guns with anecdotes about celebrity chefs, like how Jamie Oliver's wife, Jules, had dropped in to visit him at work and how Jamie had run to Jules and lifted her up as if he hadn't seen her in months, making everyone swoon. And how Yotam Ottolenghi, after a day in the kitchen, had invited her back to his home, where he'd cooked the most amazing lamb meatballs that they had eaten wrapped in fresh pita bread, while sitting on outdoor ottomans by the pool with a few of his friends who had spontaneously stopped by.

Marina couldn't have cared less.

Why do you need her to like you?

Who cares?

Bec had replied when Sophie had messaged her in the afternoon to bitch about it.

Because I need EVERYONE to like me.

It's my toxic trait, you know that.

I thought your toxic trait was waking up on time but then staying in bed until you're running late.

So I have two toxic traits.

What are you, the toxic trait police?

What about how you always ask for advice and then never follow it?

Shut up

Sophie has thirteen days left in this hotel and she's going to crack that uptight Italian chick if it kills her.

Marina has already left the hotel tonight to go and see her parents at the hospital and Rocco's about to join her. He turns off the kitchen lights and together, he and Sophie leave the kitchen. She's desperate for a good lie-down.

Rocco leaves the concertina doors of the restaurant open and keeps the fairy lights in the trees switched on. 'Sometimes the guests come down at night to eat the leftover cakes and pastries we leave out on the table,' he explains.

Sophie thinks there's a very strong likelihood she'll be one such guest.

'Have a good night, Sophie. Thank you again. You are an angel – a very beautiful and clever Australian angel.' He picks up her hand when they're out in the lobby and plants a soft kiss on it, smiling at her sheepishly over his glasses, turning her insides to mush.

They head in opposite directions, he for the front door and she for the stairs leading up to her suite.

The second she's in her room, she reaches inside the sleeves of her dress to unclip her bra, breathing a sigh of relief. Two minutes later, she's in her *101 Dalmatians* pyjamas sprawled out on the bed, counting out the contents of the tips jar. She's surprised to find it adds up to over two hundred euro. So much for Bec thinking she was being taken advantage of.

Instead of working on her feature like she's supposed to, she instead browses the vintage-style dresses saved to her Pinterest board named *Shit I don't need but v much want*.

A few minutes later, there's a gentle knock at the door.

'Just a second!' She slips a robe over her pyjamas and opens the door to find a smiling Rocco. He's holding a silver tray with a pot of tea and two blueberry and lemon shortcake biscuits from the breakfast buffet.

'You're not legally contracted to bring me sweets every night, you know.' She laughs.

'To say thank you for all the help.' He beams at her.

'That's so kind of you. I've been eyeing off those biscuits all day.

Come in.' She scoops a pile of clothes off the armchair and gestures for him to sit.

'No, no, I am not staying. I only wanted to bring you the tea.'

'I thought you were going to the hospital.'

'I bumped into Mamma and Marina outside on the steps. Papà is asleep, so Mamma has come home to be in her own bed tonight. Yesterday she slept in a chair.'

'Poor thing, she must be so exhausted.'

'Yes.'

They fall into silence. Feeling awkward standing there, saying nothing, Sophie points at the painting of the Pope. 'Do you ever feel like his eyes are following you?'

He turns to look at it. 'All the time. Be careful, Sophie. Don't misbehave under the eyes of il Papa, eh?' He catches her eye and she feels herself redden.

What's the score with this guy? She's been watching him all day and has seen how gentle and kind he is with everyone he comes across. But he isn't vanilla like some of the other men she's known, who are lovely but have the personality of a brick. He's funny and enigmatic, and he's sexy as hell in his own sweet way, how he lopes around with his long legs, and his messy hair and those enormous honey-coloured eyes that are always smiling behind his glasses. Even the smell of his aftershave turns her on.

It also became more and more obvious to her during their conversations throughout the day that he's single, so there has to be a catch. There's *always* a catch. *What skeletons are you hiding, Rocco?*

'I should go and see if Mamma needs anything,' he says.

She watches him as he leaves, taking in his toned butt in the tight black pants for at least the tenth time today. Whatever Rocco's story is, he's definitely hot.

Back in her room, the shortbread is beyond delicious and the tea is brewed to perfection, making her crush even harder on him, a man who can make perfect tea!

Once she's finished, she slides on her ugg boots and walks down to the kitchen. There, she finds a sponge under the sink to give the tray a quick wipe down and then she washes and dries the crockery. As she puts everything away in the right drawers, she smiles at how at home she already feels in this kitchen.

When she heads back up the stairs, a man's coming down them. He's *gorgeous*. Hemsworth-level gorgeous. He smiles at her when they make eye contact.

'Hiya! How's it going?' She smiles back at him, wishing she was in something more glamorous than baggy sleepwear.

'Oh, hey, another Aussie!' He stops when they reach the same step. He's tall and built with wavy dark hair that falls in soft waves to his shoulders, which she instinctively wants to reach out and stroke. His eyes are a deep blue, his jaw so chiselled it could grate cheese.

'I'm heading out to see that *Venice Rising* exhibit,' he says. 'Have you seen it?'

'Not yet, no. I want to, though.'

'I'm looking for the ones that light up at night.'

'Enjoy! Let me know what they're like tomorrow. I'll be working in the restaurant.'

'For sure, I will, yeah. I'm Christian, by the way. And you?'

Excellent, I've found myself a religious nut on the staircase. Typical. 'Oh, sorry, I'm not really interested in religion, thanks.'

He laughs a big laugh. 'No, I mean my name's Christian.'

She slaps her head. 'Shit. Ugh, I'm such an idiot. I'm Sophie.'

'Don't worry about it.' He's still smiling. 'Thanks for the laugh, Sophie. I promise I'm not going to pull out a *Watchtower* mag from my back pocket.' This time he holds her eye for a fraction longer.

It's long enough for her to recognise something in him. Something that makes Sophie's gut tighten, not in a good way. For reasons she can't explain, that gorgeous smile of his doesn't feel so innocent any more. Her own smile disappears as his electric eyes on her feel more penetrative than friendly. Two words come crashing strong and hard into Sophie's head. *Aggressive mimicry*. This guy's looks are there to lure his prey. Of that she's one hundred per cent certain.

'Well, I'm off to bed. Have a good night,' she says quickly. She jogs up the stairs, resisting the urge to look over her shoulder, even though she's positive he's watching her.

'You too, hey?' he calls out.

She doesn't answer him.

As soon as she reaches the first floor, the lift bell dings and the doors open. She jumps, her breath catching, expecting him to walk out of the lift, thinking he's followed her up here.

She exhales when an elderly man, who's short and round and who, like her, is also dressed in pyjamas, steps out of the lift with a smile.

'Buonasera, signora!' He throws his arms in the air with flair.

If she didn't know better, she'd swear he was Signore Bianchi. He looks just like the photos she's seen of him, an older George Costanza.

'Buonasera,' she says before quickly walking to her suite.

She fumbles with the key card and closes the door behind her, checking twice that it's locked. The man on the staircase has made pins and needles race up and down her spine. She's never had such a visceral aversion to someone before, and she only hopes that the whole aggressive mimicry gig he's got going on hasn't been successful in luring someone to prey on.

But men like that always get what they want, don't they? Who is this man's victim, then? There has to be one.

Loretta

After being stuck in the ICU, Loretta imagined that once she was back in her spacious apartment, she'd throw herself on the white leather recliner and breathe a huge sigh of relief. Her apartment has always been her sanctuary. Most of the furniture, passed down the generations, was restored by Alberto years ago with a whitewash finish, giving the whole space a calm feel. And it's not just the restaurant that looks like an indoor forest; Loretta's been collecting plants all her life. Dozens upon dozens of them are dotted throughout the apartment, in every nook and cranny, in an assortment of large and small marble, terracotta and colourful mosaic pots. Being surrounded by green has always soothed her.

Loretta was born at Il Cuore and, God willing, she'll die here. Not in her wildest dreams would she consider living anywhere other than this apartment she adores. But right now there's nothing good about being home. She's trapped on the couch as Marina paces up and down the lounge room shouting, shouting.

'Can you come in here, please, and help me talk some sense into our deranged mother?' Marina yells at Rocco, who's in the kitchen, pouring himself a glass of water. 'Where did you go, anyway? One minute you were here and the next you were gone.'

Rocco leans against the kitchen doorway and has a long drink before replying. 'Relax, would you? I took some biscuits to Sophie. She worked all day without a break, with no pay. She barely had time to eat. Do you want our guest to starve?'

Marina arches an eyebrow. 'Okay, fine, feed your new girlfriend biscuits. But please tell Mamma that she's completely lost her mind if she thinks we're letting her back into the kitchen any time soon.'

'Letting?' Loretta shouts. 'What do you mean letting? You think you have any say in what I do? Ragazza stupida. You're talking about *my* kitchen and *my* hotel, and I'll do as I please until I join my parents in paradise.'

'The way you're behaving, that trip to paradise will be here sooner than you think!' Marina throws her hands in the air. 'Look at how much stress you're under. Please, please be reasonable. It's time you and Papà retired.'

'The only thing giving me stress is you fighting with me after everything your father has put me through these last two days. The restaurant is where I go for some peace.'

Marina turns to Rocco. 'Do something!' she yells.

Rocco kneels down in front of the couch and takes Loretta's hand in his. 'Mammina, please. We're worried. What if it ends up being *you* who has a heart attack next from all the stress? What would we do without you?' He speaks softly. 'Luca rang Marina today and said he was just as worried about you as he is about Papà. We've got it all worked out so you don't have to come back to work yet. I can go to the market in the morning and do the cooking. Sophie's here to help for the next two weeks. Salvatore says he can stay as late as we need him to every day as well. Why don't you rest until you get your strength back after the shock of yesterday, hmm?'

Loretta's having none of it. 'There's nothing wrong with my strength. Every day the people crowd our little restaurant for a taste of Signora Bianchi's cooking. Do you hear them asking for Rocco? No. Now, pass me the remote control. Let me watch *Il Commissario Montalbano* in peace. And then both of you, leave me alone. I've had enough of the pair of you in my face.'

Rocco shrugs and gives Loretta the remote.

Marina shoots him a withering look. 'That's it? You're not going to say any more? Honestly, you're as weak as bubbles of soap in Mamma's hands. I'm the only one who stands up to her.'

'I just did stand up to her! She won't listen,' Rocco protests.

Loretta shuts her eyes. 'Please, Marina, Rocco, enough,' she whispers. 'Enough.'

'Bene!' Marina snaps. 'Have it your way. But if you drop dead from exhaustion in that kitchen, don't come crying to me!'

Loretta doesn't reply. Instead, she pulls her hair out of the tight bun, taking out the pins that were pressing into her scalp. It falls in thick waves over her shoulders, and she enjoys the momentary sensation of letting go.

Only seconds later, a key's being jiggled into the lock of the front door and in walks Alberto, in his slippers with his jacket over his checked blue pyjamas, grinning from ear to ear like a lottery winner.

'Buonasera, famiglia mia!' he announces in the doorway, standing there with his arms in the air as if he's just scored a goal for Inter Milan.

Loretta's mouth drops open. Rocco and Marina race to the door and bombard Alberto with questions. He ignores them and walks over to the couch, flopping down next to Loretta.

'I had enough of the hospital,' he tells them. 'The food's terrible.'

'But, Papà, your surgery! It's in two days. You have to go back!' Marina's voice is shrill.

Alberto shakes his finger at her. 'No surgery. There's nothing wrong with me. All I need is a good sleep in my own bed.'

Loretta's temples throb. 'What the hell is the matter with you?' she yells, whacking him hard on the arm. 'It took me all morning to convince you to have the surgery. What changed?'

'Nothing changed.' He smirks. 'I only agreed so you'd stop nagging me.' He reaches across the table for his cigarettes and lighter, which Loretta intercepts.

'You're an even bigger idiot than I thought!' she shouts in his face. 'Stand up! I'm taking you straight back.'

Alberto laughs as he kicks off his slippers and rests his feet on the table. 'Relax, Loretta. Everything is good now, don't worry. Stop frowning so much. You're prettier when you smile.'

'Papà!' Marina begins, but Rocco interrupts her.

'Leave him alone. Let Papà relax, he's been through a lot.' Rocco gives Loretta a wink and a *simmer down* signal with his hand.

He's right, there's no point in arguing with Alberto now. If Alberto was determined enough to discharge himself from the hospital and walk all the way home in the freezing cold in his pyjamas, he's hardly going to turn around and go back there now.

Tomorrow morning, after he's had a good sleep, she'll talk sense into him. She forces herself to breathe slowly.

'By the way, I saw the new food writer out in the hallway,' Alberto says. 'She didn't say who she was, but I saw her going into suite four so I knew it was her.' He taps Loretta's leg. 'You should see her. *Oof!* That one samples the food more than she writes about it, let me tell you. She hardly fit through the door of her suite.' He chuckles.

'Papà!' Marina and Rocco yell in unison.

Loretta flicks his hand off her. 'Cretino.'

He takes the insult with a smile.

'If it wasn't for Sophie, what would we have done today?' Rocco's face is burning, his even temper suddenly gone. 'We should all be kissing her feet for what she did for our family – instead you're mocking her. And you're not one to talk, Papà. You're not exactly a butterfly yourself.'

Loretta looks closely at Rocco. This is more passion than he's shown about anything in a long time. Has he been charmed by this new Australian woman? There's no denying the spark in his eyes right now. Well, this is a surprise! He hasn't looked sideways at a woman since Gabriella.

And what about this stranger, Sophie, volunteering to work from morning till night for people she's only just met? Perhaps it was out of the goodness of her heart, but it could also be that she nominated herself for a day in the kitchen to be near Rocco.

Loretta can only hope that if anything is to happen, it will be a short and sweet holiday fling, because any more than that would be too complicated. And the last thing Rocco needs is complications, after everything he's been through.

She remembers something she meant to tell Rocco and forgot with all the drama. 'A proposito, Rocco, do you know that your old friend Alessandro di Rita is in town?'

'Yes, I heard a rumour he was back.'

Loretta detects the falter in his voice.

Rocco's eyes dart to Marina, who stands frozen in place. What is it about il padre that her children know and she doesn't? Has he been involved in some kind of scandal? Please, God, no, not Alessandro. His poor mother would be heartbroken.

She continues as if she hasn't noticed their reactions. 'Such a holy man, his parents must be so proud.'

Rocco and Marina exchange another meaningful look. Something's definitely going on here.

'Go to San Zaccaria and pay him your respects. I assume he'll be staying there in the rectory,' Loretta tells Rocco.

He nods. 'I will.'

'And ask for a benediction while you're there,' she adds. 'Padre Alessandro is loved by the Holy Father. A blessing from him is almost as good as being blessed by il Papa himself.'

'Si, Mamma.' Rocco walks towards his room. 'Buonanotte, everyone.'

Marina finally moves as well.

When they both close their doors, Loretta stands with a groan. 'Come on, Alberto. Let's go to bed.'

'I stood outside the door listening to all the shouting before I walked in, you know,' he says. 'I'm surprised the hotel's guests haven't called the police to our apartment. Marina's right, maybe my little faint was the sign we both need to work less.'

'Little faint? It may be time for *you* to retire, but there's nothing wrong with me.'

Loretta needs to work as much as she needs to breathe. If she lets the children run the kitchen for much longer, they'll quickly come to see how well they can cope without her. Rocco's an excellent cook; he's more than capable of taking over the restaurant. Once they realise they don't need her, what will become of her? If she isn't Signora Bianchi from the restaurant, who is she? She doesn't even have grandchildren to keep her busy.

Sighing, she walks into her bedroom and changes into her nightgown. She retrieves her mobile phone from her handbag to charge it overnight and freezes when she reads the text message flashing on the screen from an unknown number.

Come back to me.

Gayle

While Mike works on his blog in bed, Gayle opens up her Bible but finds that she's unable to focus. Noah changing his number without telling her is what she deserves, she knows that. But the knowing doesn't make it hurt any less.

It's quiet in the hotel now after the shouting that came from the Bianchi apartment, which is right next door to their suite. It was rather frustrating, Mike said, not being able to understand what the Bianchi women were arguing about.

For Gayle, a family argument is far less worrisome than the anguished screams of last night. The wrongdoing of having ignored those screams sits deep within her. Her eyes glaze over the words of the old leather-bound book, seeing nothing. If indeed she had read the words on the open page in front of her, she would have seen this: *Proverbs 31:8 Speak up for those who cannot speak for themselves.*

When Mike's finished his blog, she proofreads it for him, smiling at the good bits:

The mosaics at the basilica in Torcello are quite something! Mosaic art stretching all the way up the wall to the vaulted ceilings. And those ceilings aren't exactly low.

Let me tell you though, folks, these Italians are all about the Virgin Mary. It's Santa Maria this, Santa Maria that. The gift shop even sells Santa Maria pyjamas – imagine! Needless to say, we didn't buy any sacrilegious merchandise, but we did find some very nice

'I love Torcello' coasters (at quite a bargain price I might add), so we couldn't go past those.

And she frowns at the bad bits:

You'd think these Italian waiters have their eyes painted on. Thirteen minutes and forty-seven seconds they left us standing at the restaurant tonight. If an establishment in Arkansas tried on that kind of behaviour, they'd be shutting their doors within a week. Unfortunately, being rude to customers is accepted in Europe. I'd go so far as to say it's even expected. There's a fair degree of racism towards Americans that I can gather, and that's the truth.

The blog doesn't mention the *Venice Rising* protest art they saw on the church wall this evening.

Once the blog's posted, Mike complains, 'I know I had that big dinner, but I'm getting hungry again. There's nothing to eat here except for the dry biscuits from the minibar.'

Gayle closes the Bible. 'Remember when we checked in, young Rocco told us to help ourselves to the sweets they keep in the restaurant at the end of the day?'

'I do remember him saying that!' His voice lifts. 'A nice piece of cake would hit just the spot.'

'Let me go on down there and see what they've got.' She's already up and looking for her robe. 'I'll bring you back something good.'

'See if there's any of that almond cake left.'

'Sure, hon.' She's glad for the excuse to get out of the room; her shame's stifling her in there.

Out in the hallway, the door to another suite is wedged open with a Bible. It upsets Gayle to see the Lord's word being used as a doorstop.

Downstairs, the concertina doors leading from the foyer to the restaurant are open and the thousands of fairy lights in the potted trees create a bright glowing light. She spots a plate of cake slices and shortbread on the big trestle table and walks over to it, but stops dead in her tracks at a sudden movement from under the table. She bends down to see what's there and her breath catches.

Curled up small on the floor with a basket of pastries in her lap is a skeletally thin young woman, barefoot and in a flimsy nightgown. Gayle's seen her around; she's the wife of the wonderful Australian doctor who saved Signore Bianchi's life yesterday. Gayle thinks she must be around the same age as her oldest granddaughter, Ava, who's thirty. She even has her chestnut brown hair cropped short in a pixie cut like Ava's, but that's where the similarity ends. This young woman's head is too big for her tiny body. Her arms and legs are matchstick thin. It's as if she could break just by being hugged.

When the woman sees Gayle, she gasps. Her cheeks are bulging. She quickly chews and swallows, looking mortified. The poor little mite, gorging herself in secret like this, must have an eating disorder.

Gayle squats down, about to apologise for scaring her, but before she can say anything, she sees the marks. Oh, the marks! Too many to count. Both of the woman's eyes are blackened, her cheeks are bruised, there are red marks on her neck as well as scratches and bruises around her collarbones. Her shins are black and blue all over. And they're only the parts of her that are exposed. What else is hiding beneath that nightgown?

The woman remains silent, frozen, staring up at her. The terror in her expression brings tears to Gayle's eyes.

'Hey there, sugar. It's okay, don't be scared,' Gayle says gently, keeping a good distance away. She sits herself onto the cold floor, landing on her backside with a thud. She has no idea what to say, what to do. She just knows she can't leave that poor girl there alone. They sit facing each other in silence.

The woman eventually speaks. 'Christian, my husband, he's strict with my food. He's gone out for a while so . . .' She lets the sentence hang. Her voice is tinny, weak. Her accent is hard to decipher.

She looks Italian, with her dark eyes and dark hair, but she doesn't sound Italian.

'You poor child. Was it you I heard screaming last night?'

The woman nods.

Gayle gulps down a fresh wave of guilt.

The woman looks at the pastry that's crushed in her fists and crumbled over the floor. She tries to scoop the crumbs off the pavers without much success. 'I've made a mess.'

'Don't worry. They're nice people here.'

Gayle isn't the kind of person who likes to pry. Her whole life, she's stayed in her own lane. She's only ever made it her business to know the ins and outs of her own family. She follows the scriptures when it comes to that kind of thing, the way God tells her to do in Proverbs 21:23: *Whoever keeps his mouth and his tongue keeps himself out of trouble.* Gayle likes to keep herself out of trouble.

But this isn't a time where she's able to keep her mouth and her tongue. The Lord also asks his followers to be good Samaritans, and this beaten young woman, curled up on the floor, is in no less danger than the beaten man left on the side of the road over two thousand years ago in Jericho. Gayle's not about to pass by her again.

'My name's Gayle,' she says. 'Gayle Dawson. My husband, Mike, and I are here on vacation. What's your name, sugar?'

'Elena.'

'My, that's a pretty name. Elena, tell me what I can do to help you. Do you want me to report him to the police?'

Elena shakes her head fast. 'No! God, no. He'll kill me if he finds out I told anyone.'

What in the Lord's name are you doing with this monster? Why haven't you left him?

It's only when Elena answers that Gayle realises she said those things out loud.

'He wasn't always like this. He was lovely. He still can be.' Elena sighs. 'He's a powerful man, very well connected. He once showed me a document with the address of every women's shelter in Australia. I wouldn't have got far if I tried to leave with no money, no friends. I didn't have access to my passport.' Her hands glide along the marks on her neck.

'Tell me what I can do to help,' Gayle says again. 'I have money.'

Elena breathes in and out, raggedy nervous breaths. She's silent for a long time, staring down at her hands as she flicks her nails, before she finally speaks. 'There is something. It's a lot to ask though.'

'Tell me.' Gayle gives her an encouraging nod.

'I was planning to give my mother a letter. She lives here in Venice, and I need her help to escape. But I'm worried I won't get a chance to leave it in her apartment somewhere I know she'll find it without Christian noticing. He's always watching me. Could you take the letter to her? She lives in the Jewish Ghetto in the Cannaregio district. It's not that close, about half an hour by vaporetto.'

Gayle's pulse speeds. This isn't what she was expecting. What will Mike say? 'Yes, I can do that, of course. I'll go with Mike tomorrow. What else can I do for you?'

'The letter's all I need, thank you. I'll slip it under your door in the morning. Which suite are you in?'

'Three.'

'Thank you. I'm very grateful.'

'Please don't thank me. Let me give you my phone number just in—'

'I don't have a phone.' Elena crawls out from under the table. 'I have to get back to my room. If Christian doesn't find me there when he gets back, I'll be in trouble.'

'Where is he?'

'He's looking at the new art installations.'

So the man beat his wife black and blue, then walked around the city admiring art.

Gayle stands up too, using the table for support.

Elena gives her a small smile. 'Thank you so much for helping me.'

'It's the least I can do. God bless you, sugar. Everything will work out, don't you worry now.'

Elena takes a few steps towards the door and then stops. 'I used to be somebody. Five years ago I was impressive.'

'You still are, Elena.'

The young woman drops her head and leaves.

Gayle walks into the kitchen attached to the restaurant. She hunts around until she finds a dustpan and broom tucked away in a cupboard, which she uses to brush the crumbs off the ground as best she can.

Her body feels old and heavy as she lugs herself back up the stairs to the suite. Her head is filled with images of Elena, of her bony hands, and her big bulging eyes that were so solemn and so sad, and dear Lord, those strangle marks around her neck.

It's only when Gayle walks into their room and sees Mike's expectant face that she realises she forgot to bring him anything from the restaurant.

'Sorry, hon, I got talking and forgot about the cake.'

'I was wondering what took you so long. Who were you talking to?'

'It's a long story, I'll tell you all about it in the morning. I'll go back down and get your cake.'

'I'll go,' he says. 'You stay here, you look tired.'

As Mike heads out, she crawls under the covers and says an urgent silent prayer for the young woman whose life is in danger because of a man who bears the name of the Lord.

On the THIRD DAY *of* CHRISTMAS

Loretta

Loretta leans her head against her bedroom window while she nurses the coffee Rocco brewed for her. It's still dark out, the light from the streetlamps reflected in the shallow puddles along the path. It rained on and off through the night, and the gentle sound of it on the walls was a comfort to her through the slow hours when she couldn't sleep. Now, the streetscape below of Dom and Eva's pastry shop with all the cakes displayed in the window, the faded red apartment block next to it with Gino's cafe on the ground floor, and next to that Yolanda's hairdressing salon and Minh's souvenir shop with their shutters still drawn doesn't feel familiar. The view is different somehow, the colours deeper, the contrasts sharper. Flavia's in Venice and nothing is the same.

Alberto's bustling about cheerfully in the bathroom, having slept solidly while she didn't get a wink. She'd been too petrified that his heart would stop and she'd wake up to his cold, stiff body. Every time he'd stopped snoring, she'd sprung up to check he was still breathing. If only he'd stayed in hospital like he was supposed to. Now he's as fresh as a schoolboy, singing to himself with the confidence of Pavarotti while he shaves, which has her feeling more resentful than ever. All she can think about is walking out onto the rainy street to find Flavia.

She tells herself to stop obsessing, to think of something to be grateful for instead. So she thanks the Blessed Virgin that the puddles aren't deep enough this morning to require shoe coverings when stepping out.

The hotel was spared in last month's catastrophic acqua alta, thanks to the foresight of her ancestors who built it high off the ground. But whenever the city floods, it makes the hotel guests a little more demanding, edgier. It makes her job harder. So she's grateful that the rain has been light this time, saving her especially from the American guests, the obnoxious old man and his bumbling wife, who surely would've made her day long with their complaints. Loretta immediately feels guilty for thinking badly of the Dawsons. Any guests who keep Il Cuore afloat deserve her gratitude.

This reminds her of something else to be thankful for: the solvency of their little hotel. Ten years ago, with the surging popularity of Airbnb, the number of guests checking into the hotel reduced every month. Competing with Airbnb felt as if they were a children's lemonade stand fighting a giant like Coca-Cola. On top of that, the high tariffs on Venetian businesses and the growing number of 'eat and run' tourists using Venice as a day-trip destination made it just about impossible for boutique hotel owners to survive.

In a desperate bid to keep their heads above water, they sold off the top floor to foreign investors, who rented the rooms out to long-term tenants, but it didn't take long for much of the money that came in from the sale to dwindle. When the future of the hotel was at its most dire, a miracle occurred. Rocco, who was living in Milan, unexpectedly came home. It was true that Rocco's homecoming was overshadowed by the terrible circumstances of his return, but it was a miracle nonetheless. Because even though he came home a broken man, he did have a clear vision in his head for the future of Hotel Il Cuore. And that vision was of a hotel painted bright blue, a glistening jewel that paid homage to the canals, with a forest-themed restaurant inside that had Loretta as its star.

Rocco convinced her and Alberto to use every cent they had to build a restaurant with a glass dome ceiling and indoor trees, like a giant greenhouse. They bought back that small section of the top floor to make this possible. He encouraged Loretta to share her home cooking with the world.

It was risky. If the restaurant failed, they would have been left with nothing. But the restaurant became an almost overnight success, thanks to its launch at the exact time when the world's millions of Facebook users collectively decided it would be a grand idea to show their friends and family what they were having for dinner, and tagging restaurants in posts became a thing. Rocco was savvy enough to exploit Loretta's looks along with her swoon-worthy plates of authentic Venetian food.

In no time, word spread about the indoor forest restaurant in the bright blue hotel, run by the Sophia Loren lookalike, Signora Bianchi. Celebrity TV chefs soon came to film specials with Loretta, food magazines came knocking and Il Cuore's name grew.

Later, when Instagram influencers really came into their own, a whole new level of fame ensued. To this day, tourists come from around the world and the photos they post of the food and of the surrounds – and, of course, of her – keep the restaurant busy.

Loretta doesn't mind the attention as long as it benefits her family. Signora Bianchi is a character she's mastered perfectly by now. She's become a queen at small talk, at making every guest feel special. She has signature poses for photos, allowing herself only the faintest hint of a smile to keep up her alluring reputation, while avoiding looking like she's sucked on a lemon. She knows to keep her chin level with the ground and her nose pointing thirty degrees to the left for the most youthful angle of her face. Turning on the charisma comes naturally to her. And because she's charmed people the world over with her knowledge of Venetian cuisine, her family lives in comfort in a city where many natives struggle to survive. Now that's something to truly be grateful for.

Her phone vibrates on the bedside table. The sound makes her jump and the scalding coffee splashes onto the back of her hand. 'Merda!'

'Cos'é, Mamma?' Rocco calls out from her doorway.

'Nothing, don't worry.' She puts the cup down and reaches for a tissue, holding it tight against the red strip of skin.

Rocco walks into her room. 'What happened?'

'I spilt some coffee, that's all.'

'Show me.'

She reluctantly holds out her arm. 'See? I'm not dying.'

'Run it under cold water. That tissue will do nothing.' He looks out the window. 'I hope Sophie's dressed warmly enough for the Rialto. It's the windiest place in all of Venice.'

Marina comes into the bedroom with her hands up behind her head, twisting her long curls into a messy bun. 'Maybe she can get warm by cuddling against you.'

Rocco shoots her a look.

'We shared a womb, my friend.' Marina smirks. 'I know you.'

He lets out a small laugh. 'She's been good to us. It's not my fault if I can't help noticing she's beautiful as well.'

'Be careful, eh?' Marina raises an eyebrow.

'Your sister's right.' Loretta moves away from the window. 'We don't need drama with this food writer, Rocco.'

'Relax, Mamma. There won't be any drama.' He smiles.

'I'm not so sure about that,' Marina says. 'I know what you're like with your soft heart.'

'If anyone needs to be careful with their heart, it's not me.' Rocco's smile disappears and he meets Marina's eye.

Loretta whips her head around to Marina. 'What does he mean?' As far as she's aware, Marina's steadfastly single. What does Rocco know?

'Nothing, Mamma, ignore him.' Marina pushes Rocco lightly in the back. 'Go. You'll be late for your Australian girlfriend. Make sure you have a scarf, and take an extra umbrella in case she doesn't have one.'

'Wait, Rocco, I'm coming with you,' Alberto calls out. He appears in the doorway in his coat.

'The only place you're going is back to hospital!' Loretta yells at him.

Alberto launches into Shirley Bassey's 'Never, Never, Never', swinging his hips from side to side as he waddles towards her. Rocco's the only one who rewards him with a laugh.

All three of them have already tried talking sense to Alberto this morning to no avail. His stubbornness knows no bounds. Unless Loretta carries him to the hospital on her back, he's not going.

She points her finger at him. 'You may as well take off that coat, because the only way you're going to the market today is if you step over my dead body first. If you're not smart enough to know you should be in hospital, then you're certainly not smart enough to choose the produce for my restaurant. Rocco will go alone. And if you think I'm letting you set foot in the kitchen today, you're even thicker than you look.'

Alberto snorts and turns to Rocco. 'Let's go.'

Rocco shakes his head. 'Sorry, Papà, I like having my head attached to my neck, so I do what Mamma wants.'

'What will I do with myself all day?' Alberto whines.

'You can sit up here and think about how stupid you are.' Loretta gestures to him.

'At least keep me company, then. Let the children work,' he argues.

'If you want my company, go back to hospital. I'll come and sit with you all day. Otherwise I don't want to see your face.'

Alberto zips up his coat defiantly. 'You can't keep me locked up here like a prisoner.'

She quickly steps between him and the door. 'You're *not* going to the market.'

'Get out of the way, Loretta. I'm going to Eduardo's to complain to him about the dictator I married.'

Eduardo's cafe is only one lane away; it's the lesser of two evils. She steps out of Alberto's way. 'Walk slowly and don't eat anything that's bad for your heart. And don't you dare smoke, Alberto Alfredo Bianchi! Do you hear me?' she calls as he leaves.

He waves a dismissive hand in the air and enters the lift, the doors closing behind him.

'I'm going down now, Mamma.' Marina comes to the doorway.

'I'll meet you down there in a minute.'

'Are you really well enough to work?' Marina rests a hand on Loretta's lower back. 'I can set up for breakfast. Why don't you come down later, after Rocco returns from the market?'

Loretta throws her arms in the air. 'Child, we haven't even started the day and you're already getting on my nerves! This is the third time you've asked me if I'm well since I woke up. Do I need to remind you it was your father who had a heart attack, not me?'

'What's so terrible about me asking if you're fine?'

'If I'm not fine, you'll be the first to know. Until then, leave me alone.'

'Okay, okay! You can't expect me not to be concerned.'

'If only you were as concerned with finding yourself a husband as you are about being a pain in my arse.' Loretta takes the keys to the apartment off the hook by the door and slips them into her jeans pocket. 'Why don't you call Luca Falcone and invite him to join us for lunch? He's such a good man, a fine surgeon. This might be an opportunity for you.'

Marina rolls her eyes. 'Enough with Luca Falcone! How many thousands of times do we have to have the same conversation?'

'But he has that big penthouse in Martellago—'

'Mamma! I beg you, stop.'

'Bene!' Loretta's voice echoes through the apartment. 'Let those ovaries of yours shrivel up and die before you give me even a single grandchild. You and your brother are the curse of my life, neither of you with any prospects.'

Marina blinks, her face turning pink. Loretta instantly regrets her words but before she can apologise, Marina pushes past her and heads out the door.

Rocco comes out of his room, with so much aftershave on they'd be able to smell him in Athens. He's put product in his hair and has his best coat on.

'Go easy on Marina,' he says gently. 'Let her be. She doesn't need a matchmaker.'

Her eyes narrow. '*Why?* Who has she matched herself with that you're keeping from me?'

'Nobody.' He laughs, but it's clear from the way his cheek twitches that he's lying. 'Ciao, Mamma.' He kisses her cheek on his way out.

Loretta closes the front door behind him and walks back into her bedroom. She sits on the bed, letting her shoulders sag. She's already worn out from her interactions with her family today and she hasn't even served breakfast yet.

To the public, the Bianchis are the epitome of the close-knit happy family, all four of them living and working together in harmony. All the outside world sees are their smiling faces, their joviality with each other. But lately, all she does is argue with the others. The three of them exhaust her, more and more as time goes on, and she's craving to be left alone.

It's only now they're all out of the apartment that she dares look at the message on her phone that came earlier. Another message from *her*.

I'm waiting for you.

We can't, Flavia. We can't do this.

Oh, but how she wants to go to her! A few seconds pass with her hands gripped tight around the phone before she sends another message.

How did you get my number?

It wasn't hard. Come to me.

No

All I want is to touch you – just once.

Let me have that and then I'll leave you
alone, I promise.

Just once, Loretta.

Gesù Cristo. She reaches for the medal of the Madonna tucked inside her top. *This woman will be the end of me.*

She casts her mind back to when she was a young woman desperately in love. In the ten years Flavia and Loretta were together, not a single person knew. If they had been two unmarried Venetian men who spent every spare moment with each other, even vacationing together, the whole town would've been speculating about them. But they got away with it because they were living in the patriarchal Italy of the seventies, when women weren't credited with having sexual desires of their own and were only the child-bearing vessels for their husbands. The idea that two women would be lovers was a concept so unimaginable that Loretta and Flavia's relationship was never brought into question.

Loretta's parents pushed her to go to the local youth dances, to meet prospective suitors. They invited families with sons to dine at the hotel, but she was obsessed only with the girl from choir with the long blonde hair and the curvy hips who lived up the street. In Loretta's fantasies, it wasn't John Travolta or Massimo Troisi she dreamed about, like the other girls did. It was only Flavia, with her full lips and her almond-shaped hazel eyes, who filled Loretta's head.

Loretta knew for sure that it wasn't just a crush when Flavia started dating Aldo Gaetano from San Polo, and she thought she would die of jealousy. She hated Aldo. Sweet, loveable Aldo who would make a fine husband for Flavia. Loretta wished he was dead.

'My parents are nagging me to marry Aldo,' Flavia told her one day on their walk home from choir practice. 'They're worried if I take too long to accept him, he'll give up and then nobody else will want me.'

'Do you even love Aldo?' Loretta's heart hurt saying his name out loud.

Flavia hesitated. 'I don't. He doesn't make me laugh.'

'I make you laugh.' It was barely more than a whisper. An invitation: *please love me.*

Flavia lifted her hand, and with her thumb, she caressed Loretta's cheek.

They'd arrived at Flavia's front door.

'You do make me laugh. But you see, that's the problem. That's why I can't give my parents what they want.'

She turned away from Loretta and unlocked the door. Walking in, she left it open behind her and disappeared into the house. Loretta stood outside, knowing what she did next would change everything. Instead of walking home, she followed Flavia inside.

For the next ten years, Loretta gave her life to Flavia. They didn't live together, of course, accepting from the beginning that their love would have to be a secret. Sometimes Loretta fretted that they'd be caught and bring shame to their families, or that their parents would eventually force them to marry men. Most of all, she fretted that she was disappointing God by loving a woman. There was always guilt casting a shadow over her, always.

She confessed to Flavia once how worried she was for their souls. 'We're going to hell, aren't we? We'll never meet the Blessed Virgin in heaven because we disgust her.'

'You listen to me.' Flavia held her face in her hands. 'I'm prepared to live in eternal damnation in exchange for this.' She kissed Loretta's closed mouth. 'And this.' She separated her lips with her tongue. 'And this.' She unbuttoned Loretta's jeans and slid her hand inside her knickers, making her gasp. 'I'd give my soul for you,' she whispered.

After proclamations like this, it came as the greatest shock of Loretta's life when Flavia tearfully told her that she was leaving to join a convent after being called by God.

'What call?' Loretta cried. 'Since when did you have a calling?'

'Since before we even met. I never told you because I didn't want it to feel real. I tried and tried to ignore it, for years I pretended I couldn't hear Him. But now the Lord's voice is getting so loud in my heart that I can't hear anything else above it.'

'Your heart can't even hear me?'

'Even you, my darling, even you.'

Flavia left for a convent in Tuscany to begin her induction. She changed her name to Suora Teresa and disappeared from Loretta's life.

Years later, when Flavia's parents died one after the other and she returned to Venice briefly, Loretta was a married mother, and she made excuses to avoid the funerals. Her marriage vows were too important to her to risk seeing Flavia.

Over the years, she's tried her best to give Alberto and her children a good life, to be grateful for the family she was blessed with. But now Flavia's returned, and it's all coming undone.

She leaves Flavia's message on read, tips the rest of the coffee into the sink and gets dressed for the day. She puts on her sneakers and walks out into the hallway.

It takes all of her self-control not to keep on walking out of the hotel, all the way to San Zaccaria, to the woman she loves who asked her to come.

Sophie

Sophie stands by the Christmas tree in the empty lobby, waiting for Rocco. She pats her hot-pink handbag, feeling for the umbrella. Rocco warned her there wouldn't be much protection from the weather at the markets.

Marina glides down the stairs, graceful as a swan. Even with her hair pinned back, no make-up on and dressed in the plain Il Cuore uniform of black shirt and pants, she's nothing short of stunning. Meanwhile, Sophie's spent an hour curling her hair, doing her make-up, painting her nails, ironing her dress. She's ready to poke Marina's eye out with a fork over her effortless beauty.

When Marina sees her, she lifts her lips into a smile that definitely looks forced.

'Morning, Marina!' Sophie says cheerily, like Marina's her bestie and not an ice queen who terrifies her.

'Good morning, Sophie. Rocco is coming now. I hope you enjoy the Rialto.' With that she bustles off into the kitchen as if the future of the free world depends on her.

At least Sophie hasn't been forced into small talk. Marina's saved her from herself. She would have launched straight into some elaborate story that has absolutely no relevance to anything, the way she always does when she's intimidated.

A minute later, the lift clunks and bangs and out walks Rocco. He looks so Italian in his black woollen trench coat, tight black pants and dress shoes, cream knitted scarf wrapped high around his neck and black fedora – all to do the food shopping. The average Australian male would never dare try to pull off this look. For a fashion tragic like Sophie, Rocco's unabashed sense of style is *everything*. She works hard to look her best every day, deliberating over clothes and accessories, watching make-up tutorials and taking an age to copy them to get her eyeliner just right, so she's deliriously happy with Rocco's efforts.

He gives Sophie his over-the-top jazz-hands wave, smiling so big she can almost see his tonsils before he briefly disappears through a door next to the restaurant. He re-emerges a few seconds later with a pull-along plastic-lined cart.

'Buongiorno, Sophie!' He holds her by the shoulders, kissing both cheeks. He smells of expensive cologne.

Her heart flutters.

'Andiamo. Let's go!' He holds his arm out, bent at the elbow, an invitation.

Well, this is new. Sophie's never linked arms with a man in her life. Happily she slides her arm into the crook of his and lets him lead her out onto the cold cobbled street. She's a bit disappointed there's nobody there watching them make their glamorous exit from the hotel (shopping cart notwithstanding). They look so dolled up, the two of them together, that they deserve the street to be lined with paparazzi.

But San Marco is just about empty compared to when she arrived two days ago. The narrow lanes are devoid of tourists. Chairs are up on tables inside the cafes, and the wooden shutters are closed on the salt-stained red and grey apartment buildings that rise up out of the water. Pigeons roam the pavements, splashing around in the puddles. She didn't imagine a Venice this quiet and still, a Venice this serene.

Rocco's walking pace is faster than she'd like, as they turn corners, climb up and down stairs and walk across small bridges while daylight falls across the city. It's Sophie's first time outside of the hotel since her hurried arrival here, and she wishes she could take her time, stick her nose in the tourist shop windows that aren't yet open, or stop and snap some photos of the narrow canals, dark and luminous under the clouds, with soft waves lapping against the moored tugboats. But this isn't a leisurely stroll for Rocco; he's on the clock, so she stays quiet and walks quickly to keep up with his long strides. At least it's not raining.

He fills her in on the latest round of family arguments, how his father discharged himself from hospital. So it *was* Signore Bianchi she saw coming out of the lift last night! She's equally excited and nervous to learn that Signora Bianchi is coming into the kitchen to cook today after all. Bec will be pleased.

Remembering bumping into Signore Bianchi in the hallway reminds her of meeting Christian. She considers telling Rocco about him, but what could she say? *I met one of your guests last night and he gave me the ick.* She keeps her mouth shut.

They reach the Grand Canal and walk across the Rialto Bridge, magnificent in both its size and its gothic white arches, which stretch high above the water. On the other side of the bridge, the stillness of San Marco is left behind and it's a whole new world. Dozens of market stalls line the street. The stall owners, rugged up in coats and beanies, call out to each other, joking and laughing. People wander about, eyeing off the produce, many of them with pull-along carts similar to Rocco's. It's too early in the day for tourists, Rocco explains; these are the locals shopping for their families and their eateries.

An old, hunched-over woman at one of the fruit stalls carefully examines a green apple. She's covered in wrinkles, dressed head to toe in black, and her grey wiry hair pokes out from under her headscarf. Sophie asks if she can take her photo, using the sign language of holding up her camera, and the woman gives her a delighted smile, her entire face lighting up.

Rocco looks at the camera screen over Sophie's shoulder as she checks the composition. 'You have captured the atmosphere of the Rialto in less than a minute. Brava!'

She feels herself glow under his praise.

Rocco stops first at a fish stall, where a short old man in a plastic apron hugs him. They speak in hurried Italian while Sophie waits a little way behind. The smell of fish is overpowering, but the seafood laid out on the table in tubs packed with ice looks fresh and delicious. After a minute or two, the man packs several plastic bags full of sardines, wrapping them in thick layers of butcher's paper.

Rocco reaches for Sophie and gently pulls her closer, introducing her in Italian. Then he turns to her. 'Sophie, this is our good family friend Pasquale. He has sold the best seafood in Venice since I was a boy. The sardines were fished by his sons off the coast of the Adriatic Sea less than two hours ago.'

Pasquale gives her a warm, gap-toothed smile.

When it's time to pay, there's an outburst of shouting and much gesticulating between Pasquale and Rocco, until Pasquale finally holds up his arms in resignation. Rocco reaches into his pocket and pulls out a stash of cash.

'He tries to rob me,' Rocco tells her with a laugh as he hands the money over. 'It is the same every morning.'

'Ha! I'd love a photo of you both standing next to the fish, if I can?'

'Of course.'

The men, who were threatening World War Three seconds earlier, pose happily with their arms around each other's shoulders.

And so it goes as they visit the other stalls: the warm greetings (everyone knows Rocco by name); the showing off of produce, whether it be vegetables in wooden crates or herbs and spices in weaved baskets; the obligatory passionate bartering; the joyful shouts of 'Buon Natale!'

Sophie tries to capture as much of it as she can on camera, and she makes quick notes on her phone to jog her memory later. She already knows she won't be able to do justice to the Rialto and its people. Photos won't show just how juicy the cherry tomatoes she samples are or how vibrant Filomena who sells cannolis is, or how mouthwatering the freshly baked bread smells. Words can't adequately paint a picture of the very real sense of community here in the marketplace, the good-natured ribbing and the genuine camaraderie between sellers and buyers. There's a hospitality and a warmth to the Venetians that has her feeling all gooey inside.

They start the walk back to the hotel just under half an hour later, the rain still holding out. This time when they cross the Rialto Bridge, the shops are open, tourists in their bright yellow rain ponchos have begun to fill the streets and people stand under the awnings at the high tables outside the cafes, drinking their morning coffee.

Back at the hotel, Rocco holds the door open for her. 'Come, Sophie. Let's show Mamma what we bought. But be prepared, she will complain. Every day she insults my purchases, no matter how fresh the food is. Are you ready?'

'Ready.' Her heart rate speeds up as she follows Rocco into the kitchen.

Signora Bianchi's waiting for them. Sophie stops in her tracks when she sees her. The woman is a vision, tall and slender, with honey-coloured eyes, just like Rocco's and Marina's, and olive skin that looks like it belongs to someone half her age. She doesn't have a hint of make-up on, her grey hair is twisted in a low bun, and instead of wearing the uniform of black shirt and pants the others have on, she's dressed in straight leg blue jeans and a black long-sleeved turtleneck underneath a plain white apron – the iconic look she's famous for. She's hands-down the most beautiful woman Sophie's ever seen in the flesh. And when she walks over from the enormous marble bench in the centre of the kitchen to where Sophie stands in the doorway, it's as if she's floating. There's an elegance and a grace to her that's ethereal.

'Mamma, here is Sophie Black, the wonderful journalist from Australia. Sophie, this is my mother, Signora Loretta Bianchi, the most excellent cook in the world!' Rocco all but shouts.

'Benvenuta, Sophie.' Signora Bianchi holds both of Sophie's hands in hers. Her hands are warm and calloused. 'It is an honour for me to have you in my kitchen.' Her accent is a little thicker than her children's, but her English is perfect. She has a husky deep voice that reminds Sophie of an older Florence Pugh; it suits her.

'Thank you so much for letting me spend time with you, Signora Bianchi.'

'You must call me Loretta. Signora is much too formal for the good friends we are about to become.'

Good friends. Sophie's completely starstruck. 'Thank you. I hope you're feeling okay after the shock of your husband's cardiac arrest?'

'I feel fantastic, because you are here with us and this makes me very happy.' Loretta turns her attention to Rocco. 'Now, let me see what you have for me today.'

'Sardines so fresh you will be convinced you can still see them swimming.' Rocco gives a chef's kiss.

Loretta rolls her eyes. 'Sardines? Again? Have you forgotten there are other animals that live in the sea?'

'Wait until you see them.' Rocco presents her an unwrapped package of fish.

Loretta gives the sardines a perfunctory sniff. 'What else?'

'Peas!' he replies happily, undeterred by the filthy stare she gives him. 'For you to show Sophie how you make your famous risi e bisi.'

Loretta clicks her tongue. 'I tell you, Sophie, it is a miracle our restaurant is still open with this dull food my fool of a son brings me.'

Rocco grins. 'I told you. She complains every day, but when the patrons praise the food, she forgets to thank me for my good choices. Look! Look at her smiling. She knows it's true.'

'I am smiling because I was remembering a happy time in my life, before I had you.' Loretta laughs.

Rocco plants a fat kiss on his mother's cheek and she shoos him away with a tea towel.

Sophie can't remember the last time there was any of this kind of banter with her own mother.

'The first thing we do is clean the fish, Sophie,' Loretta says. 'The smell will be unpleasant. Take your time at breakfast and come back when we are finished with this part.'

'I'd love to help, if you'll let me.'

Loretta frowns at her. 'You want to clean sardines?'

'Yes, please. If you've a certain method you use, I'm keen to learn from you.'

Rocco puts his arm around Sophie's shoulders. 'What did I tell you, Mamma? Sophie is not like the other journalists. She is something special.' He gives Sophie a smile that makes her belly flip.

Loretta shrugs. 'If you insist, I am not going to refuse the help.'

Salvatore arrives then, hugs Rocco and greets Sophie like an old friend. 'Zia!' He rushes over to Loretta and gives her a bone-crushing hug.

They speak in fast Italian. Loretta touches his face tenderly. There is such warmth in this family, so much love. It's at once beautiful and heartbreaking for Sophie to be this close to it.

'Get something to eat quickly, all of you. We open the restaurant in ten minutes,' Loretta says. 'Sophie, hang your coat on the back of the door.'

Rocco helps Sophie out of her red trench coat and hangs it up for her. His eyes linger for a moment over her navy and white long-sleeved polka-dot dress, and a slow smile appears. It's her favourite dress, tight through the bodice, with a full skirt to just below the knees. It delights her to see the effect it has on him.

'Rocco, take the vacuum with you and give a quick clean around the buffet table,' Loretta says, drawing Rocco's attention away. 'There is a big mess there. Someone had a fun eating party yesterday after the cleaners left.'

'I guarantee it was the new Americans.' Rocco pulls a small vacuum out of a cupboard.

'Sophie,' Loretta adds, 'make sure you have enough to eat. Do not be shy.'

Sophie waves an arm over her body. 'Does this look like the figure of a person who's shy around food?' She laughs.

'You are perfect.' Loretta smiles at her.

'You are right, Mamma, she is.' Rocco looks right at her when he says this, and Sophie thinks she might just explode with lust.

Elena

Elena stands under the hot water. The scalding heat burns the wounds on her skin that are still broken. It's a good pain, a healing warmth to help wash away the trauma of what he did to her two nights ago on Christmas Day, on the eve of Papà's funeral. When it was time for bed that night, Christian remembered and became annoyed that she'd used an unacceptable tone with him when she didn't want to go out to see the art installations, so he *set things straight*.

The water pours on her now while she thinks.

Today's the start of it. The escape. She's twenty-eight years old, almost twenty-nine, and she's hitting the reset button. Her thirties won't be a repeat of the horror of her twenties. Some of the details of the escape are clear in her head, some not so clear. But whether she's completely prepared or not, she's going for it.

She looks at her wrists under the steam, at the red welts from his fingers that still circle them. Once these marks have faded, she'll never again be in pain because of him. She'll never go hungry, or feel her heart clench when he turns his key in the lock or when his face changes from a smile to something more sinister.

She mentally drafts the letter to Mamma. Then she steps out of the shower, leaving the water running, and wraps a towel around her body. She perches on the toilet with the hotel notepad and pen in her hands.

Please, God, keep him asleep while I do this.

With a shaking hand, she writes as quickly as she can.

Darling Mamma,

I've sent this woman to see you. Her name is Gayle Dawson, You can trust her.

I'm so sorry to burden you further when you're already going through so much, but, Mamma, I'm in trouble. Big trouble. My marriage isn't what it seems. Christian's not a good man. He hurts me and he starves me. I have to escape while I'm here and you have to escape with me or he'll come for you.

I know this is a shock, but we have no time to waste. This is what you need to do. Go to the bank and get as much cash as you can. If they let you take all your money in cash, take it all. Buy a new mobile phone and pay for it in cash. Pack your legal documents and your passport. Once you've done these things, stay home and wait for me.

When I get a chance, I'll come for you before the end of our trip and we'll leave together. I don't know which day I'll come or where we'll go. We have to go far away so he can't find us. Don't pack a case – we need to travel lightly. You need to know, Mamma, that we won't be returning to Venice for a long time, I'm sorry.

You mustn't speak a word of this to your sisters. We can't risk Christian finding out. When you see me with Christian, act as if nothing has changed or he'll be suspicious.

I'm so sorry, Mamma. I'll explain everything when we're alone.

Love,

E x

P.S. I wanted to be there for Papà. Christian wouldn't let me leave until he could come too. I'll never forgive myself for not coming when you asked me to.

Without reading over what she's written, she tears off the piece of paper and shoves it deep inside her make-up bag.

Then she starts a new note, this one in English.

Dear Gayle,

My mother's name is Anna-Maria Zanetti, and her address is Calle Ghetto Vecchio 10257. Take water bus #1 or #2 from San Marco to San Marcuola stop. My mother's apartment in the Jewish Ghetto is a short walk from there. She lives on the fourth floor in apt 404.

Could you please stay with her as she reads the letter? I don't want her to be alone when she does, she knows nothing of my situation.

Thank you, Gayle, I'm indebted to you.

Elena

P.S. The reason I'm in Venice is for my father's funeral, which was yesterday. The day Christian wouldn't let me come home to see my dying father was the day I decided I would run.

She hides the note with the other letter. When she stands up, Christian's behind her.

She gasps. 'Jesus! You scared me.'

His eyebrows draw together. 'Why's the shower still on?'

'Oh, it is too!' She feigns surprise. 'I was thinking about Papà. I didn't realise I hadn't turned it off.'

He leans across her and turns the tap off without taking his eyes off her. 'Why are you shaking?'

'I'm freezing.' She gives a little shiver for effect.

He's silent for a moment and then he pulls her in close. 'Come here.' He rubs his hands up and down her back. 'That better?'

She nods, her heart still pounding.

He kisses the top of her head. 'Babe, I want a quick shower myself before we head down.'

'I'll go get dressed.'

The letters in her make-up bag are a ticking bomb. The entire time he's in the bathroom, she can barely breathe. She paces the suite like a caged animal.

Christian emerges in his boxer shorts, showered, smelling of aftershave and with styling product in his hair. He's smiling; he didn't find the letters.

Minutes later, they walk down the stairs hand in hand.

'You're taking it easy on the food today, remember, babe?' he reminds her as they cross the lobby.

'Yep.' Her stomach growls as the smell of pancetta wafts from the restaurant.

They find a spare table and he pulls out a chair for her. 'I'll get you some water.'

He pours himself a coffee and brings their drinks to the table before he walks back to the buffet. She watches him load his plate with all the delicious things she's desperate to eat.

He joins her at the table, cracking open an egg with the back of a spoon, and he reads the news on his phone while he eats.

Elena needs to get the letters to Gayle before he finishes eating, but she has to wait for the right moment. She sips at the water as the slow minutes pass. Her hands start to twitch, so she hides them under the table.

Gayle walks in with her husband, Mike. They're in matching yellow polyester tracksuits bright enough to be seen from the moon. Mike ushers Gayle to a table where she's facing Elena.

Christian's meal is now half finished.

Elena stands, scraping her chair on the pavers. 'I need the bathroom. Can I please have the key card?'

He doesn't look up from his phone. 'Five minutes. I'm almost done.'

'I need to go now.' She doesn't have to fake the urgency in her voice.

'There's a toilet over there.' He indicates with his chin. 'Just use that one.'

'I don't want to use a public bathroom.' She grimaces. 'It's urgent, Christian. I feel sick.'

'This is because you overdid it with the food yesterday.' He keeps his voice low. 'I told you, didn't I?'

'You're right, I'm sorry. Key, please?'

He reaches into his pocket. 'I'll meet you up there.'

When Elena races past the table where the Dawsons are sitting, Mike announces, 'Dang it, hon, I forgot to take my morning tablet. Back in a minute.'

'I'll come with you, hon,' Gayle replies, way too loudly for it to be a natural conversation.

What the fuck are they doing? Why are they following her? This wasn't part of the plan.

She bolts up the stairs, taking them two at a time, feeling them behind her. Mike catches up to her on the landing of the first floor, Gayle lagging behind.

'Are you okay? Has he hurt you again?' Mike pants. His pink face is clammy. Sweat runs down onto his beard.

'What are you doing?' Elena hisses at him. 'He can't catch us talking!'

Gayle makes it to the top of the stairs. Her face is flushed too. 'Are you okay, sugar?'

'I'm fine. I told you I'd leave the letter under your door. I'll give it to you now, but we have to be quick.' Elena jogs down the hallway to her room with the Dawsons following her. Her hands are trembling so hard that she can't hold the key card steady for long enough to unlock the door.

'Here.' Mike takes the card from her and opens the door.

'Wait there.' Elena dashes to the bathroom and retrieves the letters. Mike holds out his hand, but she gives them to Gayle.

'Anything else we can do for you, sugar?' Gayle's still out of breath.

Elena's eyes dart up the hallway. 'No, just go. Go!'

She slams the door in their faces and goes into the bathroom. She flops down onto the toilet and leans back against the cistern, shutting her eyes.

Gayle has the note for Mamma. There's no turning back now.

Seconds later, she hears Christian come in.

She walks out of the bathroom, rubbing her stomach. 'Sorry I had to leave in such a hurry. I just made it back in time before I threw up.'

He sits on the bed, looking at her long and hard. She knows that look. Ice spreads through her chest.

'What were those fat Americans doing at our door?'

'Who?' she says innocently.

'The Americans, the old couple from across the hall. They were standing outside our door. What were they doing there?' He doesn't blink.

Fanculo. She musters a laugh. It comes out shrill. 'How should I know?' Can he hear how shaky her voice is?

He doesn't break his stare. 'He jumped when he saw me, the old dude. Literally jumped, like he'd been caught doing something bad. Mumbled some kind of apology about forgetting which room was his. The wife stood there like a stunned mullet.'

'That's weird.'

'It *is* weird. It's very weird.' He breathes in and out. 'There's nothing going on with him, is there, Ellie?'

'What? You can't be serious?'

'Well, with you running off like that in the middle of breakfast, and then him being up here *coincidentally* at the same time, something smells off.'

'Are you kidding me?' She fakes another laugh. 'He's like a hundred years old. He was wearing a sun visor at breakfast. A sun visor! In the middle of winter. Indoors! How could you possibly think there's anything going on?'

Christian's face softens. 'Don't know, just a weird feeling.'

The stress has made her dizzy. 'I feel faint all of a sudden. I need to lie down.'

She flops down onto her side of the bed and takes a few deep breaths.

'I wonder if you've caught a bug.' He touches her forehead with the back of his hand. 'No fever.'

The hardest thing she's ever accomplished is learning not to flinch when he touches her.

'Do you still feel like going out?' His tone is gentle now. 'We can stay in until you feel better.'

'I'll be okay to go out.'

The fact that he's using this trip to sightsee, when they came here to bury her papà, makes her incandescent with rage. But it was the only way to get him to agree to stay in Venice after the funeral. Now the rest of the trip is a tourist holiday for him, with visits to Mamma limited to the evenings.

He checks his watch. 'The Doge's Palace tour starts in an hour. We can cancel it if we need to.'

'I'll be fine, honestly.'

'All right. Well, how about you rest until it's time for the tour.' He looks out the window. 'It's not raining. I might go grab a quick coffee from up the street.' He reaches for his coat.

Once he's gone, she moves off the bed. From the window she watches him walk along the narrow lane with a spring in his step. As soon as he disappears from view, she flies down the stairs to reception.

'Can I please use your phone?' she asks the receptionist, who looks so much like Marina, they could be sisters.

'Of course, signora.' The smiley receptionist – Chiara, according to her name tag – lifts the phone up onto the desk for her.

Elena dials Mamma's home phone number. It rings and rings. She hangs up and tries the mobile number, even though Mamma never uses her mobile phone. A recorded message tells her the phone is switched off.

She thanks Chiara and quickly walks into the restaurant.

Gayle and Mike aren't there. Are they already on their way to Mamma's apartment? If Mamma isn't answering her phone, will she even be home when they get there?

Marina meets her at the breakfast buffet. She's holding a platter of melons. 'Signora, hello again. Did you forget something?'

It's strange to have Marina address her so formally in English, as if they're strangers. She has a sudden urge to tell Marina who she is. 'Actually, I didn't have any breakfast before, so I came back to grab a bite.'

'I noticed you did not eat.' Marina gives her a kind smile. 'How about this table here?'

'I don't need to sit, thank you. I'll be fast.'

'No problem. Help yourself to the buffet, signora. It warms my heart to know you will be eating this morning.'

Elena reaches for a hunk of bread and slaps pancetta and cheese on it. She gobbles mouthful after mouthful, hardly chewing what she swallows. The large lumps of food hurt her throat as they slide down. Next, she scoffs a Danish scroll. Her hunger overpowers the shame of gorging herself like this in public. Who knows when the next chance of a solid meal will be? When she's done with the scroll, she picks up a slice of melon.

'You are eating my food at last. Brava!' Signora Bianchi comes up from behind her and rubs her arm.

Her gentle touch almost makes Elena cry. She wants to ask all about poor Signore Bianchi, but instead she swallows the melon and hurries out of the restaurant.

Back in their room, she sits near the window, watching the street, wishing she could have used this opportunity to escape. But she needs a bigger head start to outrun him, and she's not prepared to ruin her one chance of doing this. She's thought up a possible way to get out of a day of exploring the sights with him so she can be alone for a few hours, but it's a risky idea. She's still undecided about whether to go through with it or not. She gnaws at a nail while she imagines all the ways in which her plan could go wrong.

Gayle

Gayle and Mike stand huddled together under a fold-up umbrella, waiting for the vaporetto to take them to Cannaregio. The air is blisteringly cold and the bottoms of their sweatpants and sneakers are fast getting soaked by the pounding rain that started up just as they left the hotel. Despite the weather, Gayle's on a high. She's helping a young woman gain her freedom and she's buoyant with the idea of it. She feels like she's in a movie, standing there in the rain with her love by her side, about to board a boat to deliver a secret letter to a stranger in a foreign land. And in a ghetto too! The whole thing makes her shiver with excitement.

Last night she was too shaken up by her encounter with Elena to tell Mike about it, but she told him everything as soon as he opened his eyes this morning. If she'd kept Elena's story to herself, then it would have meant lying to Mike about where she was going when she went off to deliver the letter. Gayle never lies, unless, of course, it's necessary to avoid hurting someone, like telling a friend her haircut suits her. She's hopeful those little white 'kindness fibs' will be glossed over on Judgement Day. Surely she wouldn't face purgatory (or worse) for telling Mike he has a good singing voice? Proper lies are different; proper lies are a sin. It says so, clear as day, in the Bible. And lying to one's headship – well, that's a whole extra layer of sin.

Just as standing under Mike's umbrella shields her from the rain now, living under the umbrella of his headship shields her through life's storms. Susan and Elizabeth have found wonderful God-fearing husbands to take over from Mike as their headships, and Justin now shelters his own family. Her head hurts when she thinks of Noah. How does a headship even work with him and Chris? Whose umbrella shelters who?

She shakes the thought from her head. Today is about Elena. She can go back to worrying about Noah and how she'll find him after her mission for Elena is complete.

Right at this moment, even though she's being shielded from life's storms under Mike's headship, his actual umbrella could be doing a better job. She's getting wetter by the second.

Thankfully the vaporetto pulls into the dock and they climb on board. Mike has their tickets and a map ready on his phone for when they reach their stop. He's so good at taking care of everything like that.

Inside, they spread out across a row, placing their backpacks between them. It's a trick Mike taught her, to take up as much space as possible so they don't end up getting squashed. She feels a little guilty about the people who are left standing, but not too guilty; they're young, after all.

On the boat, Mike researches the Jewish Ghetto. Gayle thinks of Elena's poor mother, living in a ghetto without a husband any more. She reaches across for Mike's arm, thankful for his reassuring presence.

He shuffles closer and tells her about the gates at the entrance to the ghetto that they used back in the day to lock the Jews inside the neighbourhood every night.

'It says here not many Jews live there any more,' he tells her. 'Priced out.'

'Priced out of a ghetto?'

'By the looks of it, yeah. It's got some well-reviewed restaurants there though, not so much of a slum these days. Should we stay for lunch afterwards? Lotta souvenir shops in these photos, and I know how much you love your souvenir shopping. Oh, look, it says here Shakespeare's play *The Merchant of Venice* is set there.' His eyes sparkle and she can see he's as excited as she is about this spontaneous adventure they're having.

He puts away his phone after a while and sings the chorus of Elvis's 'In the Ghetto'. It's loud enough for people to turn and look, which encourages Mike to sing a little louder still. She gives him an appreciative clap when he's done. Nobody else on the boat is polite enough to do the same.

By the time they arrive at the San Marcuola stop, it's no longer raining. They step off the vaporetto and have a drink from their water bottles before heading in the direction of Anna-Maria Zanetti's apartment. The Jewish Ghetto is less crowded than San Marco, but it's still bustling. The lanes are lined with rows of shops and cafes, and people wander about in rain jackets and plastic ponchos. Mike follows the map on his phone and they only get a little bit lost.

Anna-Maria's apartment is on a narrow alley, crammed with buildings on both sides that are six or seven storeys high, taller than any of the apartment blocks in San Marco. The buildings certainly look like they belong in a ghetto, with paint peeling off the wooden doors and window shutters hanging off their hinges. In San Marco there are colourful potted plants dotting the balconies; here there are lines of washing.

There's no buzzer on the wall of Anna-Maria's building, but the huge wooden front door is open, so they walk inside to an empty foyer with a damp concrete floor. Gayle wrinkles her nose at the smell.

'No lift,' Mike says.

'That can't be right. Elena's mother's on the fourth floor.' She looks around but Mike's right.

Her heart sinks, the stairs are steep.

'Would you rather wait down here, hon?' Mike offers. 'I can take the letter up.'

She considers it, but she owes it to Elena to give the letter to her mother herself. She's puffing by the end of the first flight of stairs and they stop for a sip of water after the second flight and again after the third. When they're finally outside Anna-Maria's door, they're both breathing hard, and she wonders if her face is as red and sweaty as Mike's.

There's no security door, just a brown wooden one. Mike knocks. Gayle's heart is speeding both from the exercise and from what she's about to do. This poor woman's life will never be the same after she reads the letter.

Mike knocks again, quite a lot louder this time. Loud enough to make Gayle wince. The door creaks open and a petite woman stands before them, dressed head to toe in black, including her headscarf and stockinged feet. Gayle's struck by how young Anna-Maria is, so awfully young to be left widowed. Her sense of adventure deserts her when she takes in the grief painted all over Anna-Maria's face, the puffy bags under her eyes.

Mike extends his hand. 'Hello, I'm Mike Dawson. This here's my wife, Gayle. We're very sorry for your loss.'

Anna-Maria doesn't accept his handshake, keeping her arms tightly crossed.

'We're praying for your husband's salvation, sugar,' Gayle adds.

'Your daughter Elena asked us to deliver a letter to you,' Mike says.

Anna-Maria narrows her eyes at him and doesn't respond.

Gayle produces the letter, but Anna-Maria doesn't take it. 'It's from Elena,' Gayle encourages her.

'Cosa non va in Elena?' Anna-Maria says sharply.

'Sorry, ma'am, we don't speak Italian,' Mike replies.

But Anna-Maria keeps talking, so he shouts, 'No Italian!' like the woman is deaf. 'Elena. Told. Us. To. Come.'

Gayle holds out the letter again. 'Take it, sugar. It's for you.'

Anna-Maria looks from one of them to the other and warily reaches out to take the letter. They watch on as she reads it, standing in the doorway.

Gayle's chest is tight.

Anna-Maria's face crumples, and just as Gayle is about to open her arms and gather the poor soul into a comforting hug, Anna-Maria does something unexpected. She shouts at them. The only words Gayle can make out among the barrage of sentences and flailing arms are 'Criminali! Banditi!'

'We ain't criminals,' Gayle reassures her. 'Elena sent us.'

Anna-Maria yells even louder. For such a small woman, her voice carries far. It echoes off the walls.

The door to a neighbouring apartment opens and an elderly man in flannelette pyjamas walks out. He speaks to Anna-Maria and she points at them and holds up the letter.

Again, Gayle catches a few words, 'Elena! . . . Banca! . . . Criminali!'

'No, you don't understand,' Mike appeals to the man. 'We're helping Elena.'

Mike's right, the man doesn't understand. He disappears into his apartment, then comes out again brandishing a broom. He lunges towards them, and they're left with no choice but to gallop down the stairs, holding on to the steel railings as they run down each flight. He chases them until they're all the way out of the building.

'Vaffanculo!' the old man growls and then slams the big entrance door shut in their faces.

Gayle and Mike stare at each other with open mouths, gasping for air. Gayle hasn't moved this fast in forty years.

'You okay there, hon?' Mike pants. 'He didn't get you with the broom, did he?'

'No.' She takes big gulps of air, which make her cough. 'He get you?'

'Nope, too fast for him.' He rests his hands on his thighs, and looks up at her, wheezing heavily. His face is redder than ever.

Despite the gravity of the situation, or perhaps because of it, Gayle starts laughing. And once she starts, she can't seem to stop.

Sophie

Sophie strategically makes herself useful in the kitchen throughout the breakfast service to avoid going out into the restaurant and coming face to face with Christian. Hopefully he's checking out today. It's only when Rocco announces that all the breakfast diners have left that she braves the restaurant to help with the clearing up.

Then it's onto cleaning the sardines. She cleans one fish to every five of the others, copying the way Loretta does it with short, fast strokes. Once the sardines are ready to cook, she helps shell peas for Loretta's risi e bisi.

Loretta's in full control in her enormous white kitchen; she's methodical and orderly and the others follow her lead. She barks orders at Rocco and Salvatore, but this just seems to be her way with them, rather than any actual aggression. She doesn't break a sweat when surrounded by steam or smoke and she's constantly in motion.

While they work, Loretta questions Sophie, prying with the skill of a senior detective. 'Sophie, are you married?'

'Nope, single as a Pringle!'

'But is there a nice man in Melbourne who has your heart?'

'No one at the moment.'

'And you have been married before?'

Sophie throws a quick glance Rocco's way. He's stirring an industrial-sized pot of rice, facing away from her, but from the tilt of his head, it's obvious he's listening.

'Nope, never married,' she replies. 'That's why I'm so happy, ha!'

Loretta doesn't laugh. 'What about a boyfriend?'

'I ended things with my last boyfriend around a year ago. More closet space for my impulse buys now, ha ha!'

'Hmm.' Loretta frowns. 'So you *lived* with this boyfriend?'

Shit. Rocco warned her how Catholic Loretta is. 'Yeah, yep, we lived together.'

'Why did you let this man live with you before he made you his wife?'

It feels like a sharp slap.

'Mamma!' Rocco yells. 'Sophie, I apologise for my mother.'

Sophie lifts her chin up. 'I'm quite relieved I didn't marry him, actually. I wasn't happy with him.'

'Ah.' Loretta nods. 'Then perhaps it is better this way.'

Sophie's proud of herself. She stood up to Loretta and made her back down.

Australia – One

Italy – Nil.

'How old are you, Sophie?' Loretta asks five seconds later.

'I just turned thirty.'

'Okay, bene. So you still have one or two years left. Do not take too long to find a good husband, eh, or your womb will get too dry for babies.'

Italy equalises.

'Why do you pressure Sophie to have children when you say the last time you were happy was before you had any?' Rocco calls out.

'Be quiet, nobody is speaking to you!' Loretta doesn't take her eyes off the garlic she's deftly peeling. 'Sophie, are you living at your parents' house since the man left you?'

'Um, *I* asked *him* to leave. And no, I'm still in my little flat in town. Mum lives about half an hour away.'

'And your father? He does not live with your mother?'

She gulps. 'My dad . . . he . . . ah . . . he passed away.'

Loretta puts down the knife. 'My condolences, Sophie. May God rest his soul.'

'Thank you.' The heaviness sits on her chest.

'Was it a long time ago?'

'Twenty years ago, yes.'

'Cancer?'

'No, it was . . . an unexpected thing. I'm sorry, Loretta, I don't like to speak of it much.'

Salvatore, who's at the sink operating the noisy dishwashing hose, looks up. 'Chi è morto?'

'In English!' Loretta snaps.

'Sophie's father passed away,' Rocco tells him.

'May God rest his soul,' Salvatore says sincerely.

'You do not have time for all this talking!' Loretta shouts at him. 'Look at how slow you are. The people will arrive for dinner and the breakfast dishes will still be dirty.'

'Relax, Zia.' Salvatore laughs and turns the hose back on.

Loretta picks up the knife again. 'Tell me, do you have brothers and sisters?'

Nothing can stop this woman!

Sophie takes a breath. 'Just the one brother, David. He's a year younger than me.' She figures she may as well answer the questions that are coming next and save Loretta the time. 'He's married to a woman called Courtney – she's really lovely. They don't have any children. They live about an hour out of Melbourne in a city called Geelong. They have the most enormous house, you should see it. They could lose each other for days in that place.' In her best effort to move the conversation away from her family dynamics, Sophie launches into a description of her brother's McMansion so detailed that if an architect was taking notes, the plans for the house could be drafted to council standards. If she talks for long enough, maybe Loretta will get so bored she stops with the intrusive questions.

'Are you close with your family?' Loretta locks eyes with her, not even a tiny bit distracted by all the waffle.

Sophie sighs. 'Not really, no.'

'That is very sad. I pray for Saint Joseph to bless your family.'

Why Saint Joseph in particular?

'Is this why you came to Venice alone at Christmas?' Loretta asks. 'Because you are on bad terms with your family?'

'No, that was just how the timing worked out.' Sophie's *really* desperate for a change of topic now. The smell of sardines on the charcoal grill fills the air. 'The sardines smell amazing, Loretta. Do you serve them cold?'

'No, of course we serve the sardines hot,' Loretta replies.

'So why are they being cooked now?'

'This is for us. We eat at noon what we serve for dinner. I taste and see if I need to change anything.'

It's nearly noon now and Sophie's stomach growls, forgetting it's already been fed a solid week's worth of food from the incredible breakfast buffet.

'You are staying until January ten, yes?' Loretta asks her.

'That's right.'

'Then you will be here for La Regata della Befana, the Venetian festival for the Epiphany. Rocco and Salvatore are racing a gondola in the regatta.' Loretta smiles proudly. 'You will join us for this celebration.'

'I'd love to, thank you.'

Rocco and Salvatore exchange a look that Sophie can't read.

'And, before that, on the first night of the new year,' Loretta continues, 'we have the Holy Feast for the Mother of our Lord at a church not far from here, San Zaccaria. The priest celebrating the Mass is a friend of our family who is returned from the Vatican. A very holy man. You will join us for this Mass.'

Sophie freezes. 'Thank you, but I'll pass on Mass. The gondola race sounds great though.'

The smile on Loretta's face vanishes. 'What do you mean, *I'll pass?* You do not want to attend Mass for the Mother of our Lord?'

'Per l'amor del cielo, Mamma!' Rocco throws his hands in the air. 'Leave her alone! Forgive my mother, Sophie, please. I'm very sorry.'

'You, keep your mouth shut and stir the rice!' Loretta shouts over her shoulder to Rocco, before turning back to her. 'Sophie, why do you hate Jesus?'

'What? I don't hate Jesus!'

'Bene, then you will attend this holy Mass with us on the first day of the year so the Blessed Virgin will look after you and no harm will come to you for the whole year.'

'A whole year of no harm? That's impressive for one church attendance,' Sophie deadpans.

Rocco and Salvatore reward her with a laugh but Loretta gives her a stern look.

Uh oh.

'Yes, a whole year of protection. Dress warmly that night when you come. Bring your gloves.' Loretta gives her a look that says, *don't fuck with me, young lady.* Then she pulls another knife from the block and starts to julienne carrots with a speed and precision that Sophie's never witnessed.

Sophie immediately stops slicing the pane di casa she's been assigned to and grabs her camera to get a record of this julienning magic. She can't let herself get sidetracked from the reason she's here, which is to capture these moments.

Rocco approaches her when Loretta disappears into the storeroom. 'Of course you don't have to come to Mass.'

'I don't mind, honestly.'

Sophie hasn't been inside a church since she moved out of home over ten years ago. But how bad could it be if the Mass is in Italian? She could zone out and nobody would know any different. It's important to keep Loretta on side. Plus, Loretta said the family's going, which means Rocco will be there, and that's a nice sweetener.

'Lunch!' Loretta announces, walking back in. 'Salvatore, tell Chiara and Marina. Rocco, go upstairs and bring your papà.' She loads a stack of plates onto her forearm, and Sophie follows her out into the restaurant, holding a tower of glasses in one hand and a jug of iced water in the other.

She helps Loretta bring out the rest of the food, just as Rocco comes in with his arm around Alberto, who he towers over.

'Ah, signorina, ciao, ciao!' Alberto's voice booms across the restaurant as he approaches Sophie with open arms. He pulls her into a hug and kisses both of her cheeks with force, scratching her with his stubble. He holds her by the arms and inspects her. 'You are a very beautiful woman.'

Sophie immediately loves him.

'Fat, yes, but very beautiful!' he announces happily.

She immediately loves him less.

Rocco yells at Alberto in a string of Italian words she imagines aren't congratulating him on his behaviour. His hands are going nineteen to the dozen.

Alberto shrugs, not looking the least bit bothered by Rocco's tirade.

When he's done yelling, Rocco pulls out a chair for Sophie to sit next to him at the table.

Sophie's cleaned dozens of sardines, sliced ten loaves of bread and shelled kilos of peas. It feels good to be off her feet.

'I don't know who I am more embarrassed by, my papà or my mamma. I am so sorry.' Rocco speaks in a low voice so only she can hear him.

'It's all good, don't worry,' she reassures him.

'Do you feel as if you have been in the boxing ring after your first morning with Mamma? I should have warned you this is what she is like.'

'It's fine, truly. She's an incredible cook. I'm in awe of her.'

'You also have a natural talent in the kitchen,' he says. 'You would not consider becoming a chef?'

'That's so sweet of you to say. No, I'm nothing special.'

'You are very wrong.' He smiles at her.

She leans her head a little closer to his. 'What's your story, Signore Bianchi? Why are you so nice to me? You're too good to be true.'

'And I want to know your story, Sophie Black.' He holds her stare. 'I want to know about the parts you have kept hidden from Mamma. And I want to beat up the man from Melbourne who did not make you happy.'

'Beat up?' She laughs. 'You've gone all cave-mannish now, have you? You didn't answer me though. What's your story?'

'I am worried that if you hear my story, maybe you will not smile at me any more in that sexy way.' The way he looks at her over the top of his glasses gives her a delicious longing low in her stomach.

'You've got me intrigued now,' she says softly.

'Mangia, Sophie, mangia!' Loretta puts an end to their conversation.

It doesn't stop the electricity buzzing between them.

Chiara and Salvatore join them at the table. 'Dov'é Marina?' Salvatore asks.

Loretta smacks his hand. 'In English.'

'She came upstairs to get her coat maybe half an hour ago,' Alberto replies. 'She has errands.'

Rocco frowns. 'What errands?'

Alberto shrugs.

Loretta pours herself a glass of water. Sophie's surprised there's no wine with lunch. Isn't day drinking what Italians are famous for?

Loretta turns to her. 'Tell us about the people at your work. Is there a man in your office who might make you a good husband?'

'God help you, Sophie.' Rocco laughs. 'Round two!'

And so the next Loretta interrogation begins. It's hard for Sophie to appreciate just how perfectly seasoned and charcoaled the sardines are and how fresh and crusty the bread is when she's besieged by question after question shot at her like tennis balls from a pitching machine. There's nowhere to duck.

Thankfully, a quarter of an hour later, Loretta boots Alberto, in no uncertain terms, back upstairs to rest and she heads into the kitchen again.

Sophie stands up too, but Chiara tugs on her hand. 'Zia always gets up before us. Stay and have a break from her questions.'

'Zia has been asking her a million questions all morning,' Salvatore tells her.

'Of course she has.' Marina appears from behind them. 'Please do not be too shy to tell my mother to stop intruding, Sophie. She has no boundaries, none.'

Marina takes Loretta's spot at the table. She looks flustered as she shrugs off Rocco's questions about where she's been.

'Be careful, Marina,' he says quietly.

Marina shifts in her seat. 'It is not what you think. I was watching the performance artist in the piazza.'

He blows out through his nostrils. 'You went out in weather like this to see the woman in the tank? Since when do you care so much about art?'

'Since our city is disappearing under the sea.'

They stare at each other like it's a competition to see who can go the longest without blinking.

Marina finally breaks the silence. 'Relax, okay?'

'I am not relaxed, not even one per cent,' Rocco replies. 'Zero per cent relaxed with the two of you.'

The two of who? Sophie's dying to know. Sadly, no more is said.

Rocco flattens two sardines with a fork on a thick slice of bread and passes it to Marina. 'Mangia.' He smiles and the tension between them evaporates like magic.

Sophie aches at the closeness of this family, at the easy way they argue and quickly make up, how they're so enmeshed in one another's lives.

Chiara distracts her from her envious thoughts by inviting her to visit them in Padua, where she shares a home with her parents,

Salvatore and one younger brother who's still in high school, along with her husband and two small children.

'It's lovely how you all live with your parents,' Sophie says.

'Living with our parents is not a choice,' Rocco replies, not unkindly. 'We cannot afford our own apartments.'

'At least you live in Venice.' Chiara points at him.

'Why don't you live here?' Sophie asks her.

'We used to when I was a girl,' Chiara replies. 'Now, like most Venetians, we cannot afford to.'

'We even have to pay entry tax so we can work here.' Salvatore tears a piece of bread. 'And the train fare is double for peak hours. Instead of encouraging Venetians to come and work, they punish us.'

It's the first time Sophie's seen Salvatore speak in a way that's not lighthearted.

'Is it hard to find a job in Padua? Is that why you travel here for work?' she asks him.

'No, there is plenty of work in Padua. But we come to work with our family.'

'Venice is our home,' Chiara adds. 'If we stop working here, then we have lost all connection to being Venetian.' She looks at her watch. 'And now it is time for us to leave our home again.'

They all clear up together, then Salvatore and Chiara leave. Marina starts her shift on reception and Rocco and Sophie head back into the kitchen. The next hour and a half is taken up helping Loretta bake cakes for tomorrow's breakfast and make mousse for the evening's dessert. Cake every day for breakfast is something Sophie can totally get on board with.

Just after two o'clock, Alberto appears in the kitchen. 'Loretta, andiamo a riposare.'

Loretta checks the clock on the wall. 'Sophie, now I go and have a lie-down, okay?' She wipes her hands on her apron before taking it off.

When Loretta leaves, Rocco rests his hand on Sophie's lower back. The unexpected touch sends tingles racing up between her shoulder blades. It's been a long time since she last felt this kind of attraction. She'd forgotten how thrilling it is.

'Can I bring you a coffee?' he asks.

'Ooh, yes, please. Do you have a lie-down now too?'

'No. Now I go to the gym and lift very heavy man weights. It is obvious, yes?' He holds up his skinny arm and pumps his non-existent biceps.

She laughs.

'And you?' he says. 'How will you pass the time now?'

'Well, I was planning to go out and explore the city, but now I'm considering a little siesta too. Your mum works us hard!'

'She does. It is a good idea to have a rest. If you like, tomorrow afternoon I can show you around Venice?'

'I'd love that.'

'Very good, then we have a date.' His words sound self-assured, but the nervous way he adjusts his glasses says otherwise.

A date! It's all she can do not to break into a celebratory dance.

'Do you want me to knock on your door when it is time to come back to the restaurant and we can walk down together?' he asks.

'That would be wonderful.'

'Okay, when you hear a knock at around five o'clock, you will know it's me, Rocco.' He taps his chest.

Her heart leaps. 'I'll know it's you.'

Loretta

After Alberto has a nap, with Loretta lying next to him awake, he goes to the window and comments that the rain has stopped, so they're able to go for their afternoon walk. She doesn't think Alberto should be heading out at all so soon after his heart attack, but he says he's going with or without her, so she joins him to at least keep her eye on him. They leave the hotel arm in arm, walking at a slower pace than usual.

Even outside, there's no escaping the smell of cigarettes on Alberto's breath.

Last night, Loretta threw out his cigarette cartons, along with his lighters and ashtrays, but he's obviously found a way. She suspects his supplier is that good-for-nothing Eduardo from the cafe around the corner, who Alberto visited this morning.

'Are you tired?' she asks as they stroll through the lanes, manoeuvring their way through the swarms of tourists and waving to the shop owners they know.

The smell of dough coming from a waterfront pizza cafe makes Loretta's mouth water. 'We can stop for a rest in here if you need to,' she offers, seeing some empty tables inside.

But Alberto says he feels good and wants to keep walking.

They make their way to Piazza San Marco, past the tourists lining up outside the Doge's Palace and more tourists posing in front of the Bridge of Sighs. The cool wind blows strands of Loretta's hair into her eyes and she regrets not wearing a headscarf. Her exhaustion as they walk makes her grateful for the easy dinner preparations this evening.

All they need to do is throw together the salad and grill the fish. Did Rocco choose today's menu deliberately to ensure an easier day for her or is she giving her son too much credit?

The extra pair of hands from Sophie also made an enormous difference. That girl is a godsend – fast, neat, a quick learner, competent – all the traits Loretta appreciates.

Sophie has a lovely nature; she's sunny and quick witted. She's not a pushover either, and Loretta likes that. With her peaches and cream skin, long blonde waves and light green eyes, she's very pretty too. And she dresses beautifully – her navy polka-dot dress today, bright red lipstick and fingernails, and pearl-drop earrings were as if she'd stepped out of a 1950s fashion shoot, not the dull copycat wardrobe of most women these days.

But Sophie's hiding big secrets, that much is clear, with the way her eyes darted all over the kitchen when Loretta asked about her life. Rocco's a sensitive soul, he's fragile and vulnerable. Loretta's worried for him. Despite how lovely Sophie appears to be and how helpful she is in the kitchen, Loretta wishes Sophie would board the next flight back to Melbourne where she belongs. There's trouble brewing for her son with that girl, she can feel it in her bones.

As if reading her thoughts, Alberto says, 'I like Sophie.'

'So does your son.'

'It's the other way around. Have you seen how she blushes around him? Our boy's a good catch.'

Immediately Loretta's thoughts turn to Gabriella, Rocco's ex-wife, who would certainly have laughed in Alberto's face at the suggestion of Rocco being a good catch.

'They like each other. It's mutual.'

'No, she's not his type. Too fat.'

Loretta rolls her eyes. 'He's bewitched by her, I know my son. Now to see if anything develops before she leaves.'

'Don't meddle, Loretta, I know what you're like.'

'Rocco's a grown man. Why would I meddle?'

Alberto sniffs and doesn't reply.

They stop in front of Hotel Danieli, where a large sculpture has been erected on the stone pavers. The sculpture is made entirely of painted aluminium. The detail is minute, a feat considering how large it is, almost half as wide as the hotel itself. Lying face down, with pained expressions, are sculpted gondoliers wearing wide-brimmed hats and striped jumpers, waiters in white tailcoats, artists with paintbrushes and Venetian masks in their hands, and chefs holding ladles. The metallic people are piled on each other, as squashed together as the sardines in their paper wrapping from the market this morning. On top of the bodies of the Venetian workers is a stampede of aluminium tourists, with exaggerated smiles and their arms raised holding phones. At the front of the sculpture is a metallic tour guide, waving a small yellow flag high in the air for the masses to follow her. The tourists' aluminium shoes dent the bodies and faces of the Venetians lying prone beneath them.

Alberto drops his arm, letting Loretta's drop too. They stand together in silence, staring at the sculpture. All around them, real-life tourists take selfies with it.

'Let's go home,' she says. 'I don't want you overexerting yourself.'

'Okay.' Alberto pulls a cigarette from his pocket and lights it.

She gives him an incredulous look, but he holds up his hand. 'Don't lecture me. What's the point of living if I can't enjoy life's simple pleasures?'

She's too fed up to argue so they walk back towards home in silence.

They pass Magdalena standing in the tank. The water reaches the tops of her thighs now. Each day the crowd around her gathers in size, morbidly looking on.

What's the point of Magdalena self-flagellating this way? It will achieve nothing. For years the people of Venice have been screaming into a void. The world is a slave to fossil fuels, and nothing will change that. Every day the cruise ships still come, dumping thousands of gallons of waste into the canals, literally shitting on Venice. Loretta remembers the blue canals from her youth, when it wasn't unusual to see swans gliding on the water. Even dolphins swam there. Nothing can survive in the toxic water now. The acqua alta, which used to be a once-every-few-years phenomenon when she was growing up, has struck six times since November.

She turns her back to Magdalena, who's shivering with the dirty water swirling around her stained white dress. No tokenistic exhibition, none of this feel-bad art will change the fact that the world doesn't care about the death of Venice. Nobody cares.

The disgusting smell of Alberto's cigarette hangs in the air between them. She thinks of Flavia waiting for her at San Zaccaria.

I'm sinking, right along with this cursed city.

Elena

It's five-thirty in the afternoon, the sun has disappeared behind the grey clouds and the chill in the air reaches Elena's bones. She pulls her knitted jacket tighter around herself and wills the red bars on the outdoor gas heater to be more effective. She wishes she could stand on a chair and stick her face closer to it.

'You're cold, babe,' Christian says. 'Let's go inside.'

'No, no, I'm fine.'

'Ellie, your teeth are chattering.' He laughs.

'I like being near the water.'

Most of the tables on the bar's balcony are empty. Aside from a couple of old men smoking and playing backgammon, it's just the two of them braving the cold on the canal bank.

She casts a quick look at the crowd in the bar. Inside, they could be anywhere, but out here it could only be Venice.

She cradles her steaming cup of tea and turns her attention back to the traffic jam of gondolas floating along the narrow canal, the gondoliers ducking as they pass under a low bridge.

'They're just about knocking into each other.' Christian sips his whiskey. 'Why's everyone so desperate for a gondola ride anyway? It's such a cliché.'

She keeps her eyes on the canal. 'The best way to see Venice is from the water.'

The gondoliers sing 'That's Amore' together, one of Papà's favourites. The tea warms her aching chest. It's been a painful day away from

Mamma, playing tourist in her own city. While they followed a tour through the Doge's Palace and the Gallerie dell'Accademia, as they climbed to the top of the clock tower and took selfies from the Rialto Bridge, all she could think about was Mamma and if she'd received the letter from Gayle. Had Mamma's life been upended while they were being serenaded by the orchestra outside Florian?

On a footbridge a few metres away, a woman with long black hair, wearing a pink chiffon evening gown and holding a white parasol, leans against the railing, while a man nearby takes photos of her on a camera set up on a tripod. Another man stands off to the side, holding her coat. The model poses so naturally, oozing confidence, seemingly oblivious to the cold wind whipping around her or the people who stop to gawk at her. The woman arches her back, tosses her hair over her shoulder, juts out her hips and stares down the barrel of the camera, revelling in her own beauty. It's hard for Elena to imagine ever feeling this good about herself.

Someone taps Elena on the shoulder and she flinches.

'Buonasera.' It's Padre Alessandro, smiling down at her.

Christian's out of his seat like a shot, extending his hand and grinning ear to ear. 'Alessandro! Good to see you, mate. Join us for a drink?'

'Yes, okay, why not?' Alessandro says. 'I am on my way to my parents' to eat but I can stop for a little drink.'

Christian drags a cane chair from a nearby table and Alessandro sits between them, facing the canal. He gives a shiver and turns to Elena. 'It's cold. You would not be more comfortable inside?'

'She won't be told,' Christian replies for her. 'Can't keep the Venetian girl away from the water. What can I get you to drink, mate?'

Alessandro requests a beer and Christian heads to the bar.

'Come inside before you freeze to death,' Alessandro says to her in Italian, as soon as Christian's out of earshot. 'You're trembling.'

'I like it out here,' she insists. 'Thank you for everything, yesterday. The service you gave for Papà was beautiful.'

Alessandro zips his charcoal puffer jacket all the way up and rubs his hands together. 'I loved your papà, you know that. It was an honour to celebrate his life.'

She gulps back the tears that spring.

He nods at her cup of tea. 'Tea? At a bar?'

'I haven't had a drink in years.'

'Why not?'

'No reason.'

Alessandro gives her a long look before he speaks again. 'You've changed. You used to be so full of opinions, so loud, always the life of the party. We could never shut you up. Now you're as timid as a mouse, hiding in the corner all of yesterday afternoon. What's wrong?'

She licks her dry lips. 'I'm grieving. It's hardly the time for me to be the life of the party.'

'No, it's more than that. What's happened to you, Elena? You can talk to me.'

She doesn't trust herself to speak. It's been a decade since she last spent any time with Alessandro, but growing up, he and Paolo were inseparable. She spent endless days tagging along with them as they played high stakes games of marbles in the narrow streets of Cannaregio and practised kicking goals at the neighbourhood football pitch, and she had a front-row seat to their hijinks and mishaps later on as teens and young men. Alessandro had begun speaking of joining the seminary only months after Paolo died. Two years later, he left for Rome and the priesthood. She's often wondered if the two things were connected.

She doesn't have a single friend left in Australia, nobody to notice she's not herself the way Alessandro has.

'You're so thin.' Alessandro's concerned eyes almost undo her. 'Are you getting any help?'

Christian's walking back towards them with Alessandro's drink in his hand.

'I'm okay.' She makes herself smile. 'Don't worry.'

Alessandro rests his hand on hers. 'I'm here if you need me. Don't forget that.'

Quickly, she slips her hand away from his. Priest or not, if Christian saw them holding hands, things would turn ugly.

Christian places Alessandro's beer on the table and waves away any offer of money.

Elena lets the conversation between them about the latest multi-million dollar signing of a Premier League player to Inter Milan wash over her. The model in the pink dress puts on the fur coat, handed to her by the assistant, and the posse crosses the footbridge before disappearing out of view on the other side of the canal.

Elena's eyes rest on the row of terracotta planter boxes hanging along the bar's balcony. The splashes of red and white of the potted pansies contrast with the dark water of the canal behind them. The petals dancing in the breeze hypnotise her. She drinks her tea and listens to the chorus of deep voices from the sea of gondoliers passing by, taking in the atmosphere on Papà's behalf.

She's pulled back to reality when Alessandro says he has to go.

'We should head back too, babe. It's almost dinner time at the hotel.' Christian stands up.

Alessandro pats Christian's back and kisses her cheek, holding her tight. 'You're not alone,' he says in her ear. 'I'm here for you.'

She watches him hurry away with his hands deep in the pockets of his jacket, weaving his way through the tourists, and she has to stop herself from running after him and telling him her secrets.

'Here.' Christian takes off his trench coat, which is warm from his body heat, and drapes it over her shoulders. It hangs to her ankles, dwarfing her. 'Let's get you home.'

He takes her hand and leads her past the crowded shops and the cafes that line the canal, through the streets that take them back to the hotel. Their suite is toasty warm.

'Babe, I'm wrecked. And you weren't well this morning, you must be wrecked too.' Christian walks to the bed. 'Let's give your mum's place a miss tonight.'

'What? No!' She shrugs off his coat and follows him. 'We have to go see her, Christian. It's why we're here.'

'We came here for your dad's funeral and so you could show me around Venice afterwards. We didn't come to sit in your mum's apartment. We'll see her tomorrow.' He kisses the top of her head.

It's final, there's no point arguing. 'Pass me your phone, please,' she says through gritted teeth. 'She'll be worried if we just don't turn up.'

'I'll do it.' He's already holding the phone to his ear. 'Anna-Maria! Come stai?' He's smiling his best smile. 'Ellie has a sore stomach . . . Yes, sick . . . We'll come tomorrow, okay? . . . She's sleeping . . . Okay, see you tomorrow . . . Ciao!' He hangs up. 'Off the hook.' He winks at her.

She wants to claw his eyes out.

'Come on, Ellie, don't look at me like that. You're as buggered as I am, admit it. Let's go down for dinner and have an early night, hey? We both need it.' He holds the door open for her.

Rocco greets them at the restaurant entrance. It's packed inside but Elena quickly finds the table where the Dawsons are sitting. The pair of them are easy to spot with their white hair and bright jackets. They couldn't be more obvious, gawping at her. These two don't know the meaning of discretion! While Christian's chatting to Rocco, she gives Gayle a questioning look. Gayle shakes her head with a pitiful expression. Mike gives her a thumbs down.

What the fuck does that mean? What went wrong?

What was she thinking, trusting hapless strangers with something so important? She should have given Mamma the letter herself. What an idiot she was complicating things this way.

Christian slides an arm around her waist, drawing her into his conversation with Rocco.

'What a shame you don't want dinner, signora. Can I make you a fresh juice instead for your nausea?' Rocco says. 'What would you like? We have everything: apple, orange, pine—'

'Anything's fine, thank you.' Her eyes are still on the Dawsons.

Rocco guides them to a corner table where Gayle and Mike are now hidden by a fern. Christian reaches his arm across the table to hold her hand. 'You're the most beautiful woman in the room tonight, Ellie.' He smiles at her and she smiles back, her heart racing with anything but affection.

Gayle

Although Elena's blocked from her line of vision by a potted tree, Gayle watches Christian. He's smiling at Elena as if they're any young couple in love on holiday in Venice. Then he throws his head back and laughs at something. How does Elena make conversation with this man? How can she even bear to look at him?

Gayle turns her attention back to Mike, grateful to be married to an honourable man who'd never dream of raising a hand to her. She leans across the table and, with her napkin, wipes a drip of marinara sauce that's caught in his beard.

Happily, Signora Bianchi is back in the restaurant today and the meal has been to die for. Signora Bianchi is subdued this evening though. She's been friendly enough and stopped by to enquire about their day, but she isn't as smiley or chatty as she was on their first night, leaving their table only a minute after she came.

'A husband's heart attack can do that to a woman,' Mike says.

Gayle wonders if it's more than that though, if perhaps the yelling they heard from the Bianchi apartment last night might also have something to do with Signora Bianchi's melancholy. Regardless, Gayle's thrilled that she's back and they can enjoy her amazing food again.

The lovely young Australian waitress, Sophie, comes out of the kitchen and catches Gayle's eye. Gayle gives her a wave and Sophie waves back, her round face lighting up with her smile. She looks as pretty as a picture in another fifties-style frock. Sophie approaches their table but then she freezes mid-step, her expression changing to one of terror.

Gayle quickly turns her head, following Sophie's gaze. And who should she find looking back at Sophie, with a wide grin, but Christian Taylor. What's going on? Has Christian hurt her too? She turns to Sophie again, but the girl has already disappeared, the door to the kitchen swinging shut behind her.

'Hon, there's something going on with Elena's husband and Sophie, the waitress,' Gayle tells Mike, describing to him what she's just seen.

He looks over his shoulder at Christian. 'You sure you're not imagining things?'

'I'm sure. You should've seen her face when she saw him. It was like she'd come face to face with Lucifer himself.'

Mike opens his mouth wide to fit half a sardine in. 'Don't you go taking on more people's problems now,' he says with his mouth full. 'We gave Elena the best part of our day today and for what? My thighs are still burning from those stairs. I say we put the whole thing behind us.' He tilts his head to get a better view of the kitchen. 'I wonder when they're bringing out the lemon mousse? Never had lemon mousse before. Never even knew lemon mousse was a thing. Wait till the kids read about that in the blog tonight. Suze and Lizzie will be looking up lemon mousse recipes on the internet, I'd guarantee it.'

Gayle feels another splitting headache coming on. Her doubts about following Mike's lead always and without question gnaw away at her heart.

Be happy to be here in this lovely restaurant, eating this lovely food. Don't resent him just because he doesn't care about strangers' lives. What's important is that he cares about you.

Mike burps. 'Ooh, pardon me. I blame that on the sauce – too rich, I say. You haven't finished your fish there. Want me to give you a hand with that?'

'Help yourself, hon.' As she slides her plate towards him, she can almost feel the cancer within her marriage grow.

On the
FOURTH
DAY *of*
CHRISTMAS

Loretta

'Mammina, you look pale. Let me take that from you.' Marina reaches for the tablecloths in Loretta's arms.

Loretta shoos her away. 'I swear on all the saints, Marina, if you don't stop nagging me, I'll find a train to throw myself under!' She loads the laundry into the industrial washer in the restaurant kitchen.

Marina swears under her breath and walks through to the office.

Through the doorway, Loretta watches Alberto lift the blackboard with a grunt. Writing the menu is the one job she's allowing him to do today before she banishes him back upstairs.

Her husband, who's always had the strength to hold Hotel Il Cuore on his shoulders, who's always been robust and indestructible, seems frail as he hunches over the blackboard, holding a long piece of white chalk. Her heart lurches.

Marina slides into the seat next to Alberto, her back to Loretta. 'Papà, can I talk to you about something?' she asks.

Loretta cranes her neck to listen.

'Of course, vita mia, anything,' Alberto replies.

'The hotel has an excellent name, business is solid. We can afford to employ good chefs. Mamma can pass on her recipes. Don't you agree it's time for you and Mamma to retire? Think about your heart and the rest it needs, Papà.'

Alberto puts the chalk down and rubs his eyes. 'It's not just my heart that needs rest. My bones are old, Marina. I'm tired and aching all over. In four years I'll be eighty. Do you think I enjoy setting an alarm before dawn every morning and trudging in the rain and the sleet across the canal to haggle with thieves? And then spend my days being yelled at by your mother in the kitchen for doing everything wrong? But you know as well as I do that the restaurant is the blood in your mother's veins. You're convincing the wrong person to retire. I'd be happy to never work again if I had Loretta to pass the time with me. But she's ten years younger than I am. If I retire now, she'll leave me to rot alone while she carries on working all day.'

'So, insist she retires too.'

'Insist? Insist nothing.' His tone hardens. 'You think she doesn't know I've had enough? You think I haven't told her every day for the last five years? What I say makes no difference to your mother. It never has and it never will.'

He picks up the sign and walks out to the front of the hotel with his head hanging forward and his shoulders slumped. The chalk residue stains his black pants.

Loretta watches as he puts the sign up on the landing. Immediately, passers-by stop to read the daily menu. He walks back in and heads for the lift, his face reflecting the sense of hopelessness of his words. Marina didn't argue with him, didn't convince him that he had it all wrong, that Loretta put his needs above hers. Of course she didn't argue, she can see for herself he's right.

On the other hand, Marina and Rocco have grown up witnessing Alberto's adoration for Loretta, which is obvious to everyone. Whenever he introduces himself as Signora Bianchi's husband, he almost grows in height.

Loretta has to get out of the hotel for some fresh air; she's being choked by her guilt in there. She hurries into the cloakroom and grabs her coat, sunglasses and headscarf.

In the lobby, Marina's mid-conversation with Chiara and Salvatore, who have just arrived. Loretta walks past them.

'Mamma! Where are you going? It's twenty minutes until breakfast,' Marina calls.

'Out!' she replies without turning. 'You keep telling me to rest. You do breakfast!'

Outside, she ignores the voice in her head that tells her to go to Flavia. There have been no text messages so far from her today. Loretta expected to be relieved, but all she feels is bereft.

Instead of heading towards San Zaccaria, she walks as quickly as her arthritic knees will let her to Piazza San Marco, where she stands behind the crowd to watch Magdalena shivering, hip deep in the water.

Magdalena stares out at the crowd, her eyes lingering on Loretta when she spots her, even at the back with her hair covered and her sunglasses on. It's been over twenty years since Loretta and Magdalena were in the same space, but every second of that encounter is burned in Loretta's mind forever, and it's become apparent that it's the same for Magdalena.

She watches Magdalena for a few minutes before the current inside her pulls her away from the piazza, not towards Flavia but towards home. The pull of home is always strongest, no matter what her heart wants.

Marina's standing over the stove in a cloud of steam, lifting eggs out of a pot of boiling water. Loretta takes the slotted spoon from Marina's hands and continues the task herself.

Marina tilts her head. 'I'm so worried about you, Mamma. You're not yourself.'

Loretta smiles at her intuitive daughter, feeling regretful about the way she snapped at her earlier. 'I'm okay, cara mia. Here, carry these out there for me.'

Before she walks into the restaurant, Loretta looks herself over in the office mirror, pins back flyaway hairs and activates Signora Bianchi mode, fixing a smile on her face.

Breakfast service passes in its usual busy blur, but nothing dulls her ache for Flavia, her guilt and worry over Alberto, and the unstoppable thought that with every minute, she's drowning more and more.

GAYLE

Gayle's grateful for the clear skies when she and Mike board the train to Verona. They climb the steep stairs to the top level.

'To unpath'd waters, undream'd shores,' Mike quotes Shakespeare, who's the reason for the impromptu trip. 'I wish I'd gone to college and studied Shakespeare.'

'It's a real shame you didn't, hon.' Mike's always looking up interesting facts on the internet. He'd have made a great college professor with all that knowledge. 'You sacrificed college to work at the tyre factory and provide for our family,' she reminds him. 'And we're all so thankful for you.'

'Not *all* of you,' he bristles.

She quickly changes the subject. 'Why don't you go on and take a photo of the scenery? Got your phone there?'

The view from the carriage is of sweeping fields of the Italian countryside as far as the eye can see, shimmering emerald green in the sunshine. Gayle leans against the window and again, like yesterday, she feels as if she could be in a movie, or at least a country music video.

When Mike found out today that Verona was where Juliet's thirteenth-century home from *Romeo and Juliet* was, he suggested they go there on the spur of the moment. He was inspired by their early morning tour of the Doge's Palace, a setting for *Othello,* the tour guide told them.

'*The Merchant of Venice, Othello, Romeo and Juliet.* This Italy trip is our Shakespearian odyssey, hon.' He holds the phone up to the window.

She loves it when Mike uses phrases like 'Shakespearian odyssey'. Knowing how much smarter he is than her is part of the reason Gayle's found it so troubling to be questioning his opinions lately.

Once they're in Verona, it's a ten-minute walk from the station through the town following Mike's phone map until they reach Juliet's cream brick house, still standing tall all these centuries later. They look up at the tiny, enclosed balcony where Juliet herself would have stood. There's no denying how quaint the balcony is, with arches carved into the stone, curved windows on either side and ivy creeping along the walls.

'Now, hon, I want you to picture Juliet there on the balcony. She's looking out over the garden. She doesn't know Romeo's down here, hiding behind this big old bush just here. And Romeo whispers to himself,' Mike reads from his phone, '"*O, that I were a glove upon that hand that I might touch that cheek!*" And then Juliet, not knowing Romeo's there, remember, calls out, "*O Romeo, Romeo! Wherefore art thou Romeo?*"'

Gayle has goosebumps all over as Mike reads out the rest of the scene.

Afterwards, they walk to the centre of town, which isn't as flush with tourists as San Marco but is just as pretty. They buy 'I love Verona' cushion covers from a street peddler for only three euro each. Then they enjoy a wonderful three-course lunch at a restaurant that was well reviewed online, but again, nothing matches Signora Bianchi's cooking. The chef sends them home with a mound of mozzarella (it's enormous!) freshly made on the premises after Mike gives the waiter some feedback that their glasses had dirty finger marks on them.

Gayle's hips ache after all the walking, so they stay on the lower carriage for the train ride back to San Marco.

On paper, and indeed as it will appear on Mike's blog tonight, it's been a perfect day so far. Another delicious breakfast at the hotel, touring Doge's Palace, the trip to pretty Verona. But through it all, Gayle has felt a weight in her chest and a heaviness in her limbs.

And her headache refuses to go away, no matter how many painkillers she takes. She rubs her temples.

'What's wrong, hon?' Mike says. 'Is your headache giving you trouble again?'

She nods.

'And we've been away from the bright pink walls of the hotel too.' He sighs.

Gayle's had a headache for six months. It's got nothing to do with pink walls and everything to do with God punishing her. It started the day that Noah walked out of their home. And she doesn't know how the headache will ever go away until she makes things right with her son.

She pulls out her phone to distract herself and scrolls Facebook. Even that reminds her of how Noah blocked her on there. Just then, a thought comes to her that's so brilliant, it's hard for her not to squeal.

With her heart racing and her hands twitching, one by one Gayle searches for Noah's friends. Noah may have blocked her, but his friends haven't. After much searching and clicking on profile photos to make sure she has the right people, she ends up finding six of his old school friends. She sends all of them the same message, asking if they're still in touch with Noah and begging them to help her find him.

She doesn't tell Mike.

Loretta

By mid-afternoon, Salvatore and Chiara have left for the day, Rocco and Sophie are upstairs getting ready to go out and explore some of the sights, Marina has taken over on reception and Alberto, who came down again to join them for lunch, is back upstairs for his afternoon nap. Loretta will meet him up there soon, but not just yet.

She walks around the kitchen checking everything first. The risotto's warming on the hob.

She smiles, remembering Sophie furiously taking notes this morning while Loretta explained that in risotto con tastasal, 'tastasal' literally means 'taste the salt'.

'My father used to make salami,' she told Sophie. 'He dried it right here in this kitchen, hanging it from the beams. To test if the salt in the salami was the correct quantity, my mother put a small amount of salami in the risotto. And that is how we have risotto con tastasal.'

The smell of the juniper berries in the risotto brings back strong memories of Loretta's mother. Mamma would have appreciated Sophie's wide-eyed wonder at their cooking methods. How simple things like adding a few drops of water to break down the tomato paste before stirring it into the pot had Sophie oohing and aahing with delight. Mamma had a soft spot for people who responded to food with joyful abandon, not treating it like the enemy as so many did. Sophie's devotion to good food runs deep, and Loretta loves her for it.

Earlier today Sophie had sighed with pleasure when Loretta gave her a spoonful of mascarpone mixed with coffee liqueur and icing sugar to taste before she added it to the cake.

'Mmm, my God! That is a dessert I would cheerfully die for!' Sophie exclaimed. 'If I had children, I'd sell them to the circus for a mouthful of this.'

Loretta absent-mindedly stirs the risotto with the wooden spoon that's resting in the pot.

As much as she's been charmed by Sophie, it continues to trouble her how completely besotted Rocco is.

Also troubling her is Padre Alessandro, who dropped by this morning, ostensibly to check in on Alberto after learning about his health scare. The whole time Alessandro was with Loretta though, he was agitated, looking from side to side as if he'd lost something. She invited him to come tomorrow for breakfast and to bring his parents. He paused to think about it before reluctantly agreeing, and only after she nagged him a little to accept, which was also strange. Invitations to eat at Il Cuore are always met with unbridled enthusiasm.

He then chatted to Rocco for a minute or two in a hushed voice and left. When she asked Rocco afterwards what they talked about, he dodged her question. There's definitely something fishy going on with that padre. Tomorrow when he comes for breakfast, she'll try to sniff out what it is.

Loretta also has the too-thin young guest, Signora Taylor, on her mind today. This morning her triangular elbows poked out so sharply from her skeletal arms it was as if her bones were about to burst through the skin. Yesterday, Signora Taylor ate nothing when she sat with her husband at breakfast, but then she came back to the restaurant by herself only minutes after they left and gorged herself, standing at the buffet, ramming the food down her throat, and Loretta had had to look away. Then there she was again this morning with nothing but a glass of water and only three cubes of watermelon on the plate in front of her, while her husband feasted on everything in sight. Why didn't she eat in front of him?

Loretta knows it's inappropriate to interfere in guests' private lives, but if that was her daughter, she'd want someone to intervene. So, this morning, she smashed a boiled egg with a fork, spread it over a chunk of fresh bread, put some pancetta and a few cubes of cheese next to it on a plate and walked it over to the table where the young couple sat.

'Signora, please, eat something. I cannot have any guest leave my restaurant hungry.'

'Ah, aren't you wonderful!' Il dottore clapped his hands together. 'Come on, Ellie, you can't let Signora Bianchi down. You have to eat something, babe.' His tone was cheerful, but he smiled at his wife in a way that looked more like he was baring his teeth.

The young woman stared back at him with eyes so dilated with fear that Loretta knew instantly and unequivocally that there was something dark at play. Perhaps the amazing doctor with the face of an angel who'd saved Alberto wasn't all he seemed to be after all.

As she walked away from their table, she had a tug on her memory that she wasn't able to place. Signora Taylor was familiar to her – she knew her from somewhere. But where?

Loretta puts the lid back on the risotto and wipes down the already clean white marble bench. Also in her thoughts are that infuriating old American couple, the Dawsons, who wear tacky matching tracksuits every day. The husband pulled Loretta aside this morning and asked her if it was possible to hang sheets off the pink walls because they give his wife a headache.

'Signore, the restaurant walls are sixteen feet high. How large are your bedsheets in America?' She had to stop herself from asking him if he'd considered that his wife might have a headache because whenever he opened his mouth to speak, it was as if he was trying to get the attention of someone in Positano. Instead she said, 'Perhaps, signore, if breakfast was complimentary for the rest of your stay, it might help la signora's head to feel a little better when she eats here surrounded by'—she waved her arm around—'... *the walls.*'

He huffed and sighed and scratched his beard as if he was actually giving her proposition some thought, when all along he couldn't hide his eyes that grew as big and round as dinner plates. Unsurprisingly, after more theatrical pondering, he finally agreed that yes, free breakfasts might indeed help.

Alberto won't be pleased when he finds out they've lost forty euro a day in income.

Loretta wipes down the sink and the front of the fridge, checks on the cakes and gives the risotto a final stir before she takes off her apron and hangs it on the back of the door. She looks around her sprawling, spotless kitchen one last time, making sure everything is where it should be.

To think that Dottore Luca, Marina, even Alberto, want her to retire. This room in all its shiny white glory is her sanctuary, her lifeline. If she didn't have her kitchen to help sort through her thoughts, she'd surely turn mad.

She passes Marina in the office on her way upstairs. There's something off about her daughter that Loretta can't quite put her finger on. How she wishes Marina had a partner to share her problems with.

Back in the apartment, Alberto's snoring. If there's one thing Loretta wants for Marina, it's that she doesn't end up like her. She hopes her daughter finds heart-thumping, passionate love. It's what everyone deserves.

It's what I deserve.

The thought grips her.

It's what I deserve.

It's what I deserve.

Without giving herself time to change her mind, she pulls her phone from her pocket and sends a text.

> I want to see you.
>
> When shall we meet?

She's done it. She's allowed the current inside her to drag her out to the stormy sea and it's as exhilarating as it is terrifying.

She climbs into bed next to Alberto, pulls her chain out from inside her turtleneck jumper and clutches the pendant of the Madonna.

What have I done?

Sophie

Rocco's leaning on the reception desk, chatting to Marina, when Sophie comes down the stairs.

He turns when she approaches and opens his arms wide to profess how lovely she looks. All she's done is throw on a coat and scarf. She loves a man who's this easy to delight.

'Marina!' he shouts. 'I'm taking this very beautiful guest on a tour. Can you believe Sophie has not seen any of the sights, not even one, since she arrived?'

'When has poor Sophie had time to go sightseeing? We have been working her like a slave from the minute she walked in. I am so sorry.' Marina gives a genuine smile and Sophie instantly forgives her all her standoffishness. *We're friends now!*

'No need to be sorry.' Sophie beams at her. 'I've loved every minute with you guys.'

Marina doesn't reply. She's staring at the computer again. Maybe 'friends' is a tad premature.

'Eh, Marina.' Rocco taps the desk. 'He came looking for you today.'

The blood drains from Marina's face. 'When?'

'Before. Where were you?'

Marina's eyes dart to Sophie and back to Rocco again. 'Nowhere. What did he say?'

'He asked about you, how you are, asked if you are happy,' Rocco says.

'And? What did you say?' Marina looks as if she wants to reach across the desk and shake the words out of him.

Whatever this is, it's clearly very juicy. Sophie's going to implode if one of them doesn't break this down for her right now, piece by piece, until she knows every last salacious detail about this mystery man of Marina's.

'I told him you were fine,' Rocco says. 'I only saw him for a minute. He pretended he came to check on Papà's health. He gave him a blessing.'

Gave him a blessing? WTF?

'Why are you saying he came looking for me, then? He obviously came to see Papà.' Marina's voice is quivering.

Rocco lets out a short sharp laugh. 'Andiamo, Sophie.'

No! She doesn't want to andiamo anywhere. She wants to stay right where she is until she finds out who they're talking about. But Rocco cocks his arm and leads her to the front door with her none the wiser.

Just before they walk out, he turns to look back at Marina. 'Mamma invited him to breakfast tomorrow with his parents, by the way,' he calls over his shoulder, escalating Sophie's curiosity.

She's busting to ask Rocco to dish, but she also wants him to think she's nonchalant, which is a whole lot more attractive than exposing how chalant as hell she actually is. So she acts as if the weird inuendo-filled conversation with Marina didn't just happen.

It's icy cold outside, but the sun's out and the sky is a brilliant blue. Venice is shining.

They walk at a slow pace, much more to her liking than the hotfooting they've been doing to the market the last two mornings. As she walks along the ancient Venetian streets on the arm of this gorgeous Italian, an afternoon of exploring the city ahead of her, she feels like the luckiest girl in the world.

'So where are you taking me, Signore Bianchi?'

'Where better to start my tour with a writer than to take her to a bookshop? But this is not a bookshop like you will find anywhere else in the world. Wait until you see. It is a long walk, eh? We walk and we talk.'

'Sounds perfect.'

'After that, I will show you some of my favourite places. You will see Rocco's Venezia.'

'Exciting!'

'Exciting for me too. This is like a vacation for me.'

'A vacation?' She laughs. 'That's a bit sad. Don't you ever take actual holidays?'

'Rarely. Where would I go?'

'You could come and visit me in Melbourne.' She keeps her eyes forward.

'You want me to come and visit you? Really?'

'I very much want you to.'

'In this case, how can I say no? I will come to visit you, Sophie. Because already I miss you when you are leaving.'

She turns to look at him and he holds her eye. He strokes the back of her hand with his thumb. Her skin comes alive under his touch.

They continue walking until, after a while, he stops. 'We are here. This is Libreria Acqua Alta.'

'Oh my!' She's never seen anything like it. There are books littered *everywhere* – in baskets, along the walls from floor to ceiling, piled high on tables and, most amazingly, in full-size gondolas! The shop is packed with tourists, it's messy and chaotic and there are cats strolling around among the shoppers and lounging on the books. Out the back of the store, a facade of leather-bound books is actually a set of stairs that overlooks a small canal.

'I am going to leave you to look in peace.' Rocco wanders off to a corner of the shop.

A cool wind whistles through the store. Sophie buttons up her coat and slowly makes her way around. All the titles are Italian. She hunts for the cookbook section and picks up a copy of an Antonio Carluccio hardcover, which she buys.

Only a few minutes after they leave the shop, she regrets choosing a book that heavy. As soon as she whines about it, Rocco takes it from her.

'Time for a gelato?' he asks.

'Ooh, yes please.'

'Great, come and meet Nunzio. He is an old friend of the family. When you taste his gelato, you will only want to eat gelato from his shop for the rest of your life.'

Old Nunzio limps out from behind the counter to embrace Rocco. He offers them samples on teeny wooden spoons. The dilemma of which flavour to choose among the rows of gelati in big steel tubs is very real and it takes Sophie an age to settle on mango, then immediately wish she'd chosen lemon instead. Nunzio waves away their offers of money.

Rocco finds them a bench to sit on in a small public garden tucked away at the end of a narrow lane. She'd never have guessed there'd be a leafy park here. The mango gelato puts to shame any she's ever had before, and she no longer regrets her choice – until Rocco offers her his cone for a lick and she tastes the Baci one.

Never in Melbourne would she think to go out and buy an ice cream and sit outside to eat it when it's ten degrees, but here it doesn't feel wrong to be doing so, rugged up in coats and scarves. It's a happy, wonderful strangeness. She licks her lips, savouring the last tastes of mango.

Next, Rocco takes her to a hole-in-the-wall shop, nestled between a beautician and a post office, that sells Murano glass jewellery. The shopkeeper, a woman with a glamorous updo and dripping in more jewels than you'd find at the Tower of London, greets them warmly. She stands behind a waist-high display cabinet, where sparkling beaded necklaces, earrings, brooches, rings and bracelets of every colour dazzle under fluorescent lights.

'Sophie, meet my friend Allegra,' Rocco says. 'Allegra was at school with Marina and me. She designs the most beautiful jewellery in all of San Marco.'

Sophie's drawn to a multicoloured beaded necklace, but Allegra insists she try on one that's made of only dark blue glass. 'This will make your green eyes look even prettier,' she says as she puts it around her neck.

'What do you think?' Sophie asks Rocco.

He pushes his glasses up his nose and looks at her for long enough to turn her beetroot red. When he speaks his voice is hoarse. 'I think you are perfection.'

Christ on a bike!

The necklace costs more than a day's wage, but Rocco called her perfection, so of course she buys it.

They stroll through the back streets of the city, arm in arm again, until they come to a tower in a hidden-away palazzo.

'Many tourists don't know about this place,' Rocco tells her.

'How would they? It's a maze to get here. Like the gelati shop and the jewellery shop and the bookshop. Everything you've shown me is hidden away.'

'I told you, this is *my* Venezia.' He points at the palazzo. 'See how the shape of the stairs is like a snail?'

He's right, the staircase snaking up the side of the tower looks just like a snail shell.

'It is called Scala Contarini del Bovolo,' he says. 'The spiral staircase of the snail. Shall we climb it? The view from the top is incredible.'

'I'll give it a go. Can't guarantee you I'll make it to the top, though.'

Rocco tells her to go first so she can set the pace. They stop intermittently and look out at the ever-increasing views of the city. When they reach the top, Sophie takes photos of the kaleidoscope of canals and red and cream buildings and church spires of San Marco.

Rocco asks for her phone. When she hands it to him, he drapes his arm around her, pulling her close, and takes selfies of the two of them with their heads together.

'So you don't forget me when you return to Australia, eh?'

'There's no chance I'll forget you.'

He gives her another one of his looks that makes her crazy with want.

Once they're back on solid ground, she stares up at the tower; it's as if it reaches the sky. Climbing it isn't something she would have attempted if he hadn't encouraged her. She promises herself that when she gets home she's going to go out for ice cream on winter days and try new things that push her outside her comfort zone.

Next they walk to Piazza San Marco and Sophie lays eyes on the majestic basilica for the first time. Even with all the scaffolding around it as repairs take place after last month's flooding, its sheer size and gothic beauty leave her awestruck.

The square itself is humming with activity. A small group of men dressed in tuxedos play classical music for the diners seated on red cane chairs outside the famous Caffè Florian. Other tourists browse the shops interspersed between the eateries that line the piazza. There are pop-up stalls in the middle of the square selling everything Venice themed from umbrellas to T-shirts to teddy bears. Flocks of pigeons hop around among the crowds of people, unintimidated in their search for snacks on the stone pavers.

Sophie pulls her water bottle out of her handbag, but Rocco stops her.

'It's against the law to drink in the piazza unless you are seated at a restaurant. The police will fine you.' He indicates two uniformed policemen standing nearby. 'They don't even let a baby drink from a bottle here.'

She realises he's serious, so she stifles her laugh and slips the bottle back into her bag.

'Come, I want to show you something.' He leads her a little further to the clock tower. 'Watch what will happen when it is five o'clock.'

A small crowd waits at the bottom of the tower. A minute later, at precisely five, the bells chime and sculptures of the three wise men pop out from the top of the tower, presided over by an angel as they twirl in time to the ringing bells.

'This happens every hour but only for the twelve days before the Epiphany,' Rocco explains.

It's magical. Everything about Venice is magical.

They walk a short way along the lagoon, where rows of empty gondolas rock in the water. The gondoliers, in their striped sweaters, stand in small groups on wooden decks, laughing together and smoking. The sun is lower in the sky now, sitting above the white domes of the cathedral on the other side of the water. Sophie takes out her camera to capture the hues of red and orange glowing in the clouds.

'Come and look at this sculpture for the *Venice Rising* exhibition,' Rocco says.

They approach a giant metal artwork of Venetians being stampeded by tourists. The sculpture makes Sophie want to cry. Rocco looks at it without expression. He's lost the smile he's had all afternoon.

'Is this true? Is this what it's like for you?' she asks.

He nods.

'I thought tourists were what kept Venice afloat.'

He lets out a small laugh; it's not a happy sound. 'Afloat? No. Three quarters of the tourists only visit San Marco for a few hours. They make us drown faster.'

'You're the person being trampled on, and I'm the person doing the trampling. This is awful.'

'No. You are not these people, you are better.'

'Not really.' She's ashamed by how ignorant she is about this city. She knows nothing about the whole Venice sinking situation beyond the fact that water levels are rising and the city's at risk.

'Let's go back, eh?' he says. 'Mamma will be waiting for us.'

'Thank you for making time to show me around when you're so busy.'

'Never too busy for you.'

His smile is so inherently kind. And he's now standing so close to her that he just needs to lean a tiny bit forward and their lips would touch. But he doesn't and the moment passes.

As they walk back through the piazza, there's a large crowd gathered at the opposite end to the basilica. They get closer and Sophie sees what the people are all looking at. Standing in a tank of muddy water is a woman in a white dress, with white hair that reaches her hips.

The gathered tourists stare at the woman with morbid fascination. Most have their phones out.

'I wonder how long she stands there for?' Sophie says.

'Seven hours every day. They give her water to drink but that is all. I hope her suffering is not for nothing.'

'It's not for nothing. Look at all the crowd.'

'Attention alone will not help us. We need action.' He turns away from the artist. 'You know, I was excited about *Venice Rising* before but now I feel depressed. This problem is too big for one woman standing in a tank to fix.' He sighs. 'Let's go.'

The orchestra gathered under the awning outside Florian continues to play, and the mournful sounds of violins follow them up the lane towards the hotel. Their bodies cast long shadows on the cobblestones in the fading afternoon light.

Rocco doesn't talk on the way back and neither does she.

Elena

It's freezing on the water at night. Even with the heavy layers of clothing Elena has on and Christian's arm around her, the cold rips right through to her bones as the vaporetto leaves San Marco for San Marcuola, where Mamma waits for them.

Christian's talking animatedly about the performance artist they saw earlier standing in the tank of water. He shows her the Twitter feed on his phone. 'This exhibition's going off. "Affogando"'s trending, look.'

His ability to dissociate from the fact it was her refusal to go look at the art a few nights ago that led to her begging for her life confounds her.

She pretends to listen to him tell her more about *Venice Rising*, while she plans her escape. It will have to be done without Mamma having received her letter, which makes it more difficult but not impossible. Hopefully God is on her side and Mamma will be home when she needs her to be.

She needs to send Christian off exploring without her so she can take the boat to Mamma's apartment. Together, they'll race to the train station nearby and catch whichever train is leaving Venice first. They'll find somewhere temporary to stay, change the colour of their hair, and begin a new life. She can't think about anything that comes after that. It's too much, too terrifying. *One step at a time.*

At least here in Italy, it will be harder for him to find her. He has no agency here, no multimillionaire father – director of a mining company – and all his Sydney contacts. But although it will be harder for Christian to find her in Italy, it won't be impossible. He'll be wild with fury. He won't simply let her go without a fight. He can afford private investigators to track her down. Her heart rate speeds up.

'Look at this, Ellie. This is the other installation I was telling you about, the Jesus one the Catholic Church is going nuts over. Check out the retweets. I'm telling you, this thing's getting traction.'

'Mmm, sounds like it.'

She has to make sure they leave no trail when they escape. She can't afford any mistakes. They'll have to stay absolutely hidden for a few months at least, until he returns to Australia having exhausted all options and having given up on ever finding her. He'll go home eventually; his career will lead him back to Sydney in the end. She's banking on him leaving Italy before she and Mamma run out of money.

If he doesn't give up, if he decides to stay in Italy, he'll find her eventually, this much is certain.

A shiver runs down her spine. She looks out over the black water, seeing nothing.

How did she get here? How did this become her life? She, Elena Zanetti, who was clever enough to win a prestigious scholarship from the University of Bologna for an exchange program with the University of Sydney. She, who had the independence and smarts to move alone to the other side of the world at eighteen and to graduate Law, in a foreign language, with distinction.

She was so desperate to hang on to her life of freedom in Australia, to stay far away from her grieving parents back in Venice, that when her student visa expired, she gratefully accepted the marriage proposal of the lovely doctor she'd been dating for less than a year.

Christian had been so easy to fall in love with. Hot, popular, ambitious – he was the whole package, even without his ostentatious wealth. He doted on her, besotted by her Italian accent and her olive skin. She loved being loved by someone like him.

Only six weeks after the wedding, while she was preparing for the bar exam, she found out she was pregnant.

Christian was overjoyed at the news. She wanted to die.

She was so ill with morning sickness, she could barely leave her bed, let alone study. There was no way she could take the exam in that condition. She had no choice but to wait for the next opportunity in a year.

In the early stages of her pregnancy, the only food that didn't make her sick was deep-fried. And while she couldn't drink water without gagging, she was somehow able to chug down litres of Diet Coke. It wasn't exactly an optimal diet, but she did what she had to do to get by.

As the weeks went on, she grew more and more resentful of the situation she was in.

'Did you have a good day?' Christian kissed her cheek one evening, walking in from yet another late night of hospital rounds.

'Best day ever,' Elena snapped.

'Why are you being snarky?' He flopped down onto the leather couch next to her in their apartment overlooking the harbour, which still didn't feel like home to her, and yawned. 'What happened?'

'Nothing happened. Nothing ever happens! I spend all day every day lying here feeling sick or hunched over the toilet vomiting because I'm carrying your child. That's my whole life now.'

He raised an eyebrow. 'My child? *Our* child, Ellie.'

'I didn't want this.' She waved at her still-flat abdomen. 'I'm only twenty-three, for fuck's sake. Do you think I studied as hard as I did to end up like this?'

'Hey, calm down, babe,' he said gently. 'This wasn't the plan, I know, but it'll all work out. It's okay.'

'It's not okay, nothing's okay! I'm losing my fucking mind!' Elena was annoyed at how shrill she sounded. 'My friends have forgotten about me. They all have careers now, and what do I have? Nothing! No job, no family. You're never home. And whenever you are home, you're buried under textbooks. I feel like a widow most of the time. Nobody calls me, nobody visits. I'm rotting away. This fucking baby's ruined my life.'

Christian gave her a look, and for a brief moment she had an unexpected knot of fear in her stomach and the wild notion that he might hit her. Then he pulled her in closer to him and kissed the top of her head.

'I'm so sorry things are shit for you, Ellie,' he murmured. 'It'll get better soon. You won't be sick for much longer, and then everything won't feel as bad as does it now. I wish I was around more. This post grad is killing me, babe, but it'll be worth it. Once I'm a consultant I'll make the best life for you and our family, I promise.' He stroked her dirty hair.

Elena convinced herself that she must have imagined the dangerous look in his eyes.

She was sixteen weeks along when she felt the baby kick for the first time, tiny butterfly tickles, so precious they brought tears to her eyes. In that moment, she had her first outpouring of love for her child. 'Hello, little one,' she whispered. 'I'm sorry I've been so sad. I'll try to be better.'

Two days later, she miscarried.

'Did you do it deliberately?' Christian asked her on the way home from the hospital, in a tone she'd never heard before that made the hair on her arms stand on end. 'You didn't want the baby, you made that pretty clear. Did you do it deliberately?' His lips formed a thin line.

Her eyes just about popped out of her head. '*What?*'

He didn't reply. He stared straight ahead for the rest of the drive, which they passed in silence. She didn't trust herself to speak.

They both remained silent as the lift ascended the eight floors to their apartment. As soon as they were inside, she pushed past him and pulled her phone out of her handbag to call Mamma, to cry to someone who would comfort her for what she'd just been through rather than accuse her of orchestrating it.

She screamed when Christian sent the phone flying out of her hand.

'I'm going to ask you again,' he said in a voice so low it was almost a whisper. 'Did you do it deliberately?'

She stared at him like she was seeing him for the first time. Who was this person? 'What are you doing?' she shouted, bending down to pick up the phone and showing him the shattered screen. 'Look what you did! What the fuck is wrong with you?'

He swung his arm back and punched her in the face with a force that sent her flying onto the hard floorboards. Then he squatted down next to her and grabbed a chunk of her hair, jerking her neck back in one swift motion.

His lips were on her ear. 'You're a disgusting pig.' He spoke slowly and softly. 'You've done nothing but stuff your face full of fried shit for weeks. You may as well have been feeding my baby rocket fuel with the amount of Coke you guzzled every day. You killed my child by rubbishing your body, you stupid bitch. And now you fucking owe me another one.' He rammed his knee into her stomach and she retched.

He left her like that, curled up on the floor in her own vomit, and took himself off for a walk. Elena was in a fog, aching from the miscarriage, from the beating, bewildered, terrified, too shocked to call anyone – her parents, his parents, the police. The shame of her husband beating her only hours after she'd endured a D&C kept her there, hugging her knees on the floor.

Now, as the esplanade lights of San Marcuola come into view, she judges herself for not having left him then and there. She could have left and caught the first flight home to Venice that very first day he hit her.

Instead, he came home an hour or so later, his face crumpling with regret. 'Ellie, I don't know what happened. I was beside myself, I wasn't thinking straight. I can't believe I hurt you. Jesus Christ! I'll never hurt you again as long as I live, I promise.'

He was so warm, so caring towards her in the weeks that followed, so completely back to his lovely self, that she forgave him without having to try too hard.

The next time he beat her was six months later when she spoke to him in a tone he didn't like. Again, she didn't tell anyone. Again, she didn't leave him. She knew then that she'd made the biggest mistake of her life in choosing him. It was the start of her crippling self-doubt. She was always told how smart she was, but how smart was she really? Look who she'd married.

When he cried and apologised and made promises all over again, she chose to believe him so that she didn't have to face the truth, that she was an idiot who'd been tricked by a monster.

When the next intake for the bar exam came around, it was impossible for her to apply. By then, they'd moved away from the city, closer to Christian's new placement at an outer suburban hospital. She wasn't allowed to leave the house without him. He took away her phone and made her close her bank account.

Elena never worked a day as a lawyer. From the day she married Christian, she never worked a day as anything. Her friends had long given up on her. She was all alone.

Now, she thinks, the most confusing part is that she still can't work out how she let it go so wrong. What she knows is that it didn't all happen at once – it was a gradual thing, a slow robbing of her life. Somewhere along the way she lost herself, and she believed him when he told her that she was worthless, stupid, completely dependent on him for survival.

Her job, Christian reminded her, was to get pregnant. But she wasn't able to conceive. He accused her of secretly being on the pill. She wasn't.

He threatened her that if she ever left, he'd kill her. 'Don't even think about running away,' he warned her. 'Believe me, I'll find you. And if you run back to Mummy and Daddy in Venice, I'll kill them too.'

She believed him. She never attempted to escape. Not once. Even when he began controlling her food intake in his mission to make her womb 'less toxic', and she lost more and more weight.

Christian remained his loving, charming self between the episodes of horror, which came on with increasing regularity as the years passed. The violence that began as a few times a year became a few times a month, then more.

The longer she didn't conceive, the more fixated he became with controlling her body through food. It was as if he genuinely couldn't see her fading away.

When the cancer came for Papà and he grew gravely ill, as much as she begged and cried, Christian absolutely would not allow her to go back to Venice on her own until his exams were over. Along with the tidal wave of regret came a blinding anger. The death of her beloved Papà finally lifted the fog.

'Here, babe.' Christian holds his hand out for her as the vaporetto comes to a slow stop and the passengers disembark at San Marcuola. 'Careful, the ground's wet,' he says, ever the gentleman, always looking out for her.

Sophie

In her suite, after another busy dinner in the restaurant, Sophie flops into bed and works on the *Foodie* feature. The biggest challenge is deciding what to leave out. She wishes she could bottle up every moment for the magazine's readers.

When she's written enough for today, she closes her laptop and sends Bec the selfies that Rocco took this afternoon.

He IS cute.

You look adorable together!

Now listen to me, you are allowed to shag this cute boy as long as you don't develop *feelings*.

> Very much hope to shag him.

> But so far lots of compliments and meaningful eye contact with zero action.

Why don't YOU start the action then?

> Hello?

> Have we met?

> I'd rather die. What if he rejects me?

> He had millions of opportunities to make a move and nada.

He's definitely not gay?

Gotta say that shirt's very tight and shiny.

> Accidentally brushed against his boner today.

Not so gay then!

Also, ew.

Sophie smiles to herself as she remembers the two strips of red that stained Rocco's cheeks when her hand accidentally brushed against him as he pulled her in for the selfie. He's clearly attracted to her. She's made it as obvious as she can that she's into him too.

What is it exactly that's stopping him from making a move?

Elena

When Mamma opens the door, it's written all over her face that she's seen the letter. She knows.

Mamma reaches for Christian first, kissing both his cheeks. When she hugs Elena, she grips her so tightly, her ribs hurt. It's almost impossible for Elena not to cry.

'I'm sorry I was rude to your friends,' Mamma whispers quickly in her ear before leading them inside.

What happened between Mamma and Gayle and Mike? Not knowing is killing her.

Mamma brings out a tray with leftover almond biscuits from the funeral. She's shaking all over. Elena can't imagine how many questions must be racing through her head right now.

Christian jumps to his feet and takes the tray. 'Anna-Maria, you spoil us! Look at these beautiful sweets.'

Mamma pours Elena a black tea. She never owned a kettle until Elena told her over the phone once that she enjoyed drinking tea. The next time she called home, Mamma told her she'd bought a kettle for the next time Elena was back in Venice. But she never came home after that, until now. Mamma held on to that kettle, waiting for her daughter to return for over five years. Did its presence in the kitchen make Mamma sad every time she saw it?

Elena doesn't know how she's ever going to get over the guilt of it all. She wishes Christian would go to the bathroom so she can at least tell Mamma how sorry she is, but he doesn't move off the couch.

It's difficult for Elena to make any kind of small talk when she's this anxious. Luckily Christian's a natural at carrying the conversation. So she sips her tea as Christian's voice fills the room. He engages Mamma on everything from the rising waters of Venice and the new art exhibition to Italy's refugee crisis, the restoration project of the Basilica San Marco and how corrupt the Italian government is. Christian defers regularly to Mamma for her opinion, and Mamma struggles to make herself understood with her broken English. Elena translates a bit for her and Christian listens respectfully and with patience.

Elena can see the confusion on Mamma's face. *This guy, Elena? Are you sure? But he's so lovely.*

Elena looks around the apartment while the two of them talk, and she tries to take it all in, knowing that very soon she'll never see any of it again. The threadbare brown couches are the same ones her parents have owned since she was a little girl. The family used to snuggle under thick blankets at night watching talent shows and comedies on television. They weren't a wealthy family, but they were a happy one. Then Paolo got cancer in the summer before his second year at university and everything changed.

There's a photo of Paolo on the mantelpiece, taken at his first Holy Communion, all dressed up in a white suit, smiling his big cheeky smile, his light brown curls greased slick with a wide side part. So full of mischief, those eyes. Even now, all these years later, it's hard for Elena to breathe when she sees his face. If he had stayed alive, she never would have run away from her grief to Australia, never would have been in that pub the night she met Christian.

Also on the mantelpiece are other family photos, dating back to her great-grandparents' weddings. Her ancestors look so young and solemn. Her own wedding photo in a brass frame, taken at Sydney's botanic gardens, turns her blood cold. Poor Mamma must have suffered not being able to share that day with all of her family and friends back home. She and Papà were fish out of water at the wedding.

Elena doesn't have enough fingers to tally the cruel things she's done to her mother. And now she's going to tear her away from this home, forcing her to leave everything behind just so they can be safe from the man who's currently standing behind Mamma, giving her a shoulder massage. He'd commented that she looked tense and he knew just the thing that would help – the magic Christian Taylor touch.

Mamma looks straight at her while Christian rubs her shoulders.

Elena tries to convey to Mamma with her eyes what's in her heart.

I'm so very sorry I did this to our lives.

Gayle

Gayle unplugs her phone from its charger on the dresser and logs in to her Facebook account. Four of Noah's friends have already seen her message, but not one has replied. It's hopeless.

She puts earbuds in and watches an old episode of her favourite show, *Say Yes to the Dress*. Those pretty Atlanta brides, so excited for their wedding day, always manage to make her smile, no matter how frayed her nerves are.

Part way through the show, a message from an unknown number pops up on the screen. Gayle's heart stops.

Jackson Parker says you're looking for
me. Here I am.

I miss you too, Mom x

Gayle hugs the phone to her chest.

Can I call you?

Sure.

She knows she should wake Mike. She knows he'd want her to talk with Noah on speakerphone. Instead, she leaps up and stubs her big toe on the leg of a chair, letting out a yelp. Mike doesn't stir. He's sleeping the sleep of the just.

Fumbling in the dark, she wraps the fluffy Il Cuore robe around her and slides her feet into woolly slippers. She leaves the suite, gently clicking the door closed behind her.

In the hallway, she leans against the wall and avoids the eyes of the Pope staring at her as she makes the call.

'Mom.'

'Boa,' she says through her tears, using the name her daughter Susan coined when he was born.

He chuckles and she eases her grip on the phone.

'I'm sorry, baby,' she cries. 'I'm so sorry for everything.'

'Feels good to hear that.'

She asks him where he's living – Montecito. Where he's working – for a Hollywood animation studio. And, with a dry throat, she asks about Chris.

'He's doing great. He's good to me, Mom. He makes me happy.'

She nods as the tears keep falling.

'Pop there?' he asks.

'He's asleep, sugar.'

'He know you've been trying to reach me?'

'Kinda.'

'Hmm. You gonna tell him we spoke?'

'Eventually. He needs some time, your pop. This is hard for him.'

Noah breathes down the line. 'It shouldn't be hard. It should *never* have been hard.'

'I know, sugar.' She wipes her eyes. 'Are you gonna come home soon? I miss you so much. So do your sisters and Justin. Lizzie was just telling me at Christmas how much she misses you. It's not the same without you, Noah. I feel like I'm breathing with one lung.'

'I miss everyone too.' He sighs. 'But I'm not coming home until Pop apologises. I can't see him until then.'

Her head hurts. 'What about the rest of us? What about me? *I* want to see you.'

Noah takes a long time to reply. 'It's not just him I'm mad at, Mom.'

Her stomach twists.

'Listen, I have to go. I'm at work. You've got my number now. You can give it to the others. When my husband can be properly welcomed into the family, by *all* of you, then you give me a call, okay? I'm not coming home just to sneak Chris around behind Pop's back.' He pauses and when he speaks again, his voice cracks. 'You shouldn't have let him make me dig that hole. You should've defended me. I was only a kid. I deserved better than how y'all treated me.'

The line goes dead before she can say, 'You're right.'

She casts her mind back to the day everything changed, the day she was changing the sheets in the boys' room and something moved inside Noah's duvet cover. He was sixteen then. Justin was twenty-two and living away at college.

That day she unzipped the duvet cover and a magazine fell out, landing at her feet. The magazine was full of photographs of men in the most ungodly scenarios she could ever have imagined. She didn't know how to handle such a situation, so she went to Mike.

Mike sure was angry. Noah, as scared as she'd ever seen him, confessed that he'd bought the magazine because he was tempted by the sealed section at the newsagents. He was curious, he said.

Gayle had grounded Noah, the naughtiest, most wilful of all her children, more times than she could count, but Mike said this time it was different. This time Noah wasn't just messing around like young boys were prone to do, this was sinning on a whole new level and it had to be stamped out of him quick smart.

For all the trouble Noah got himself into, Mike adored that boy, and Noah idolised his dad. It was the first time that things weren't right between them.

Why wasn't a boy his age curious about seeing naked women in magazines instead of naked men? they wondered aloud to each other. They weren't able to come up with an answer that didn't make them fret, so they resorted to what always helped, God.

God couldn't give them direct instructions Himself, so they turned to their local pastor, the next best thing. Pastor Bob told them that Noah needed time away to reflect on his sins and reconnect his spirit with the Lord's.

Mike sent Noah to a Christian military camp over the summer. Mike's friend Ron Wilson had a boy, Jeremy, who'd been in trouble with the law years earlier. Jeremy had been sent to the same camp. After six weeks, Jeremy had returned a reformed young man and was now happily married with two children and his own accounting firm.

Noah didn't want to go to that camp, not one little bit. But they made him go. Three weeks in, Noah was sent home in disgrace when he was caught kissing one of the boys.

Mike and Gayle once again turned to Pastor Bob, who said that Noah had to repent. The pastor said the Lord had spoken to him and told him that Noah's punishment should be to dig a hole out the back of the Dawsons' land. Noah was to use his digging time to cleanse his heart and mind from the sinful ideas he'd gotten from that ungodly magazine.

Mike made Noah set his alarm and go out to the backyard every morning to dig that hole before school, and then made him get back out there again every afternoon when school finished to keep digging until dinner time. Nobody in the house was allowed to speak to Noah while he was digging. He wasn't allowed to complain about it either.

Noah took Mike's big shovel out into the yard every day and he dug for a whole month. Some days it rained on him when he was digging, other days Gayle heard him crying in the shower after he came in at night. His hands were covered in blisters and scrapes.

Every evening when Noah came into the house, Mike asked him if he'd done a good amount of praying out there and every evening Noah said yes, sir, he had.

Pastor Bob found Bible passages for Noah to read to show him the error of his ways, and every night Mike made Noah read those passages and ask for the good Lord's forgiveness.

At the end of the month you could have fit a station wagon in that hole. Then the pastor said it was time for Noah to fill the hole back up again. Pastor Bob said that once the hole was full, Satan would be driven away from Noah, never to return.

There was no question about it, Noah changed after he dug that hole. He never got into any more trouble. Mike said the pastor was right: digging that hole had been just what their boy needed to find his way back to God.

Gayle's once rambunctious son who was always looking for the next bit of mischief was well and truly reformed. He became the most godly of all her children. Mike used to have to push Noah into reading God's word; now he locked himself away in his room and read the Bible for hours at a time.

Noah finished college and took a job as an animation artist at a local advertising company. He was such a handsome, talented young man, and there was no shortage of young ladies who made it a point to go up and talk to him after church every Sunday. Gayle's other children were all courting by his age, but Noah hadn't asked out any of the pretty girls who made eyes at him yet. So Mike and his friend Bud Forsyth took matters into their own hands and set Noah up on a dinner date with Bud's daughter, Kelsey.

Noah went along on the date without argument. In the days before he'd dug the hole, Gayle couldn't even get him to wear a shirt she chose for him without him giving her grief about it, and here he was letting his pop choose him a girl. She should have known that something wasn't right with her son, that the spirit had been sucked right out of him, but she was ashamed to admit that she liked the new quiet Noah better than the one who was always getting into trouble, so she stayed silent.

Kelsey was a sweet little thing, and she and Noah grew close. Eventually, they married. Gayle prayed and prayed for them to be blessed with children, but they never did have any. However, Noah had a good job and a lovely home and a wife who loved him, so she was grateful for how his life had turned out, even without the grandchildren.

And then, out of the blue, Noah came to visit without Kelsey. He'd left her, he said. He didn't love her. Noah and Kelsey had been married for over twenty years by then.

'You made a covenant before God to be with Kelsey for the rest of your life!' Mike hollered at him. 'Now you go on home, son, and apologise to that poor woman.'

'I can't live a lie any more,' Noah said.

As devastated as Mike and Gayle were to lose their sweet daughter-in-law, they couldn't exactly force Noah to stay married to Kelsey. The most peculiar thing was that when Noah's marriage fell apart, it was the happiest Gayle had ever seen him.

'The Lord works in mysterious ways,' Mike said. 'Maybe he was born to be a loner.'

Gayle wasn't convinced that being alone was why Noah was happy. She had a feeling there was more coming and, sure enough, a year later, more came. Noah came to visit and he sat his parents down. In a measured voice, he told them he was in love with a man named Chris and they were getting married.

'What the hell's the matter with you?' Mike shouted. 'You had a beautiful wife and a beautiful home, and you threw it all away so you could become this?'

Noah took a deep breath. 'I haven't *become* anything. It's who I've always been. It's who I am.'

'Who you are is sick. *Sick!*' Mike roared.

'Mike, please, stop!' Gayle didn't want him to say anything else he'd regret.

Mike went on as though she hadn't spoken. 'You know what the Bible says, you know you're a sodomiser. And now you wanna get married too? Marriage is between a man and a woman. The good Lord doesn't allow marriage between men. And I sure as hell won't allow it either!' The vein in his forehead pumped with blood.

Noah didn't speak for a long time.

Gayle held her breath.

Finally, he cleared his throat. 'I don't need you to allow it. You don't get to decide who I love.' Then he turned and walked out the front door.

She should've followed him, she should've said something, but she was too much of a coward to disobey Mike.

Noah didn't speak to them for a whole month, then he sent her a message, telling her he'd married Chris and moved to California.

She immediately called him, but he didn't pick up. She messaged him instead.

> I love you, Noah, and so does your pop.
>
> It was a shock for him is all. He didn't mean what he said.
>
> He'll come around, he just needs time.

Noah didn't reply. That was in June.

He never replied to a single one of her messages after that, and her voicemails went unanswered. She gave up after a while. Then he also disappeared from social media.

And all of it stemmed back to the magazine she'd found all those years ago in his bedroom. They should have let him be who he always was. Digging a hole didn't fix him, it broke him.

Noah's right, she should have defended him. She's done wrong by her son. Noah was born perfect just the way he was, but it took her losing him to realise that. And now she's worried it's too late to ever get him back again.

'Hon?' Mike's voice is husky from sleep. He stands in the open doorway in his pyjamas, rubbing his eyes. 'What are you doing out here? You had me worried when I woke up and couldn't find you.'

She's too upset to tell him what's happened. She doesn't only blame herself for losing Noah, she blames Mike. She blames him a lot.

'I'm sick of your snoring,' she hears herself snap. 'I came out here to get some peace and quiet.'

Mike looks as if he's been slapped. 'You shoulda said something.' His Adam's apple bobs up and down. 'I'll look up tips on the internet to help me stop. There are always good tips on the internet.'

She nods. 'Sorry. I'm just so tired is all.'

He holds his hand out for her. 'Come to bed.'

As she lies there in the dark, something becomes perfectly clear to her. The cancer in her marriage isn't the fact that she's doubting Mike's word. There isn't anything to doubt. She *knows* she's right. She *knows* he's wrong.

And a wife thinking she knows better than her husband is just about the worst thing that can happen in a godly marriage.

On the FIFTH DAY *of* CHRISTMAS

Sophie

On the way back to Il Cuore from the markets, Sophie and Rocco walk across the Rialto Bridge. It's an overcast morning and the canal is peaceful in the semi-darkness. The streetlights are still on, their yellow reflections shimmering on the water.

'Can I stop to get a picture of the canal? It's stunning in this light.' Sophie leans on the railing. 'I love how the waves lap right up against the buildings. You don't see that anywhere else in the world.'

'This is the magic of Venice,' Rocco says. 'The balance between water and stone.'

'I love that! I'm going to quote you in my feature.'

He laughs. 'Okay, but also write that water and stone is the magic *and* the disaster of Venice.' He leans on the railing next to her. 'The big ships that come through the canal make the waves too big. Every day the water washes away more of the clay. The buildings are eroding. They will crumble soon.'

Sophie shakes her head. 'I don't understand how the ships are still allowed to come through.'

'Come, let me show you something, but we have to walk back the other way.'

They turn back in the direction of the markets, Rocco dragging the cart full of food behind him. On the other side of the canal, he squats down and rubs the ground with his fingers. 'See this?' He looks up at her. 'This is concrete. When the ancient stones erode, instead of replacing them with new stones, the government fixes the cracks with concrete.' He stands up and kicks the concrete with the tip of his shoe. 'Centuries of beauty destroyed like this, piece by piece.'

The concrete is smeared messily into the surrounding stones. Sophie takes out her camera and photographs it.

He laughs through his nose. '*This* is what you want to photograph? Will your people at the magazine want a photo of concrete?'

'No, but *I* do. This is important.'

He takes her the long way back to the hotel, stopping at different places to point out more signs of destruction. 'See that step? When I was a child, my friend Armando lived in this building and we used to climb five stairs to the front door. Now the stairs are all under water, only this one step remains . . . That angel statue on the bank over there, it used to be two angels. You see how he is looking down? The other angel is looking up from under the water. A drowned angel.'

They arrive back at the hotel, where Loretta gives Rocco a mouthful about lagging behind with the food.

'I was showing Sophie the damaged stones on the ground. I want her to see what is happening to Venice.'

'Stones? This is why you let my fish rot in the heat? To stare at stones? Dio aiutami.' Loretta taps the back of his head. 'The only stones I am worried about are the ones in your head!'

Rocco spreads his arms out. 'What heat, Mamma? My toes are frozen and I'm wearing woollen socks. I could leave the fish outside for three days in this weather and it would still be fresh.'

'Go and unpack the food into the fridge and cut up the oranges on the bench. Save your staring at the ground for when you have time.' Loretta hands a basket of pastries to Sophie and softens her tone. 'Help me in the restaurant, please, Sophie? I cannot rely on my son.'

Sophie wants to say, 'Thanks, but no thanks, Loretta. I'm perfectly happy to keep hiding in here.' But she can't avoid the restaurant forever to avoid the one guest who makes her squirm. She takes the basket of pastries and follows Loretta out there, holding her breath.

The restaurant's packed. She does a quick scan of the room. No Christian. She exhales.

Loretta puts her to work and she's instantly busy, going between the restaurant and the kitchen, clearing tables, topping up the coffee pot and juice jugs, refilling fruit platters. She doesn't pay much attention to the diners with one notable exception.

The priest. Holy mackeroly, *the priest*!

Loretta calls Sophie over to a table and introduces her to Padre Alessandro and his parents, Signore and Signora di Rita. Loretta's practically frothing at the mouth as she tells Sophie twice in the space of a minute that the holy Alessandro has come home for a visit all the way from the Vatican itself. This holy Alessandro, Sophie thinks, is the unlikeliest of priests. If an antipriest was a thing, he'd be it.

The only priests she ever knew growing up were withered, rambling old men. But this guy, mother of God! His eyes are such a pale blue they're almost grey, and when he smiles, there's an altogether too-knowing look in them. He's dressed in a tight pinstripe black shirt and skinny jeans. The jeans are red. Red skinny jeans. *On a priest.* He's got a mop of blond wavy hair and a sexy three-day growth. He's tall and broad, with his sleeves pulled taut against his ripped arms. A thousand per cent there's a sixpack hiding under that shirt. This is the kind of priest she'd drag herself to early Mass for every Sunday morning.

'Welcome to Venezia, Sophie.' Alessandro gives her a lopsided smile.

Her tongue sits like lead in her mouth. 'Welcome you too, thanks,' she mumbles, immediately wishing for an earthquake to swallow her up before she says anything even more idiotic.

It's only when she walks away from the table a minute later, having thoroughly humiliated herself with her slack-jawed staring, that she remembers the weird conversation between Rocco and Marina yesterday about a mystery man who was coming to breakfast with his parents, and everything clicks into place.

Oh. Oh! *A Catholic priest, Marina. How very* Fleabag *of you.*

She's still smiling to herself at the salaciousness of it all when she walks straight into someone at the entrance to the restaurant. 'I'm so sorry!' She takes a step back.

'Hey, no worries.' Christian smiles. 'Nice to see you again.'

Her face feels numb. She forces herself to smile. 'Hi.'

Then she locks eyes with his partner, whose hand he's holding. The woman should be hospitalised for malnutrition. She's dressed in a grey jumper that's so big on her she could fit into it twice.

Aggressive mimicry. This woman is his prey. Sophie doesn't know much about a lot of things, but this she knows. She swallows. Her throat's so tight that it hurts. 'Ah, are you . . . are you after a table?'

'We are indeed.' Christian gives her another disarming smile.

Sophie never knew that it was possible to hate someone you don't know, but she wholeheartedly hates this man.

She leads them to a free table. The woman catches her eye again as she sits down. She needs help. Sophie doesn't need to be told to understand this. She leaves their table with her stomach in thick, bunched-up knots.

Marina comes into the kitchen. Sophie doesn't care about her illicit little romance with the hot priest any more, and she's already forgotten about Rocco's despair for his sinking city.

All she can think about is the woman in the restaurant with the sunken cheeks and thin brown hair cut shorter than a schoolboy's. She needs to find out more about this situation, because she's going to do whatever she can to help her.

Sophie knows a matter of life or death when she sees one.

Loretta

It's impossible for Loretta to focus on the restaurant. Her phone is a grenade in her jeans pocket as she waits for it to vibrate with a message from Flavia, who has yet to respond to the message Loretta sent her yesterday afternoon. What's taking her so long to reply? Has she left Venice? Or worse, is she still here but has changed her mind?

The waiting and the sleeplessness have made Loretta jittery. She hopes the guests don't notice. The only blessing is that she hasn't had to face Alberto yet today; he was still asleep when she came downstairs. She can't let herself think about him.

Just once, is her mantra today as she reaches for the pendant of the Madonna inside her top. *Just let me touch her once and I'll never ask for anything again.* She's devoted thirty-six years of her life to Alberto. Surely God can forgive her one moment of living for herself?

She almost drops the pot of coffee in her hands when her phone vibrates. Leaving the pot on the buffet table, she sprints to the restaurant's bathroom and pulls out the phone. She almost walks into Marina, who's standing in front of the full-length mirror.

'Where have you been?' Loretta snaps, sliding the phone back into her pocket. 'Breakfast is nearly over.'

Marina ignores her, turning from side to side, frowning at her own reflection.

'I can't rely on you or your brother to help me today,' Loretta continues. 'You nag me to rest, then you leave everything to me.'

She squints at Marina. 'Are you wearing make-up? Since when do you wear make-up to work?'

Marina doesn't take her eyes off the mirror, tucking the shirt tightly into her pants so that it pulls across her chest. 'This shirt is completely shapeless. It's so *ugly*. Why do we have such an ugly uniform?'

'Forget about the stupid shirt and get out there and help me!' Loretta huffs. 'The restaurant's full.'

'Ugh, relax. I'm coming.' Marina finally peels her eyes away from the mirror and opens the bathroom door.

Rocco walks past just at that moment. 'The di Ritas are here,' he says to Marina, looking less pleased than Loretta imagines he should, considering Alessandro is one of his oldest friends. 'Signora di Rita's asking for you, Mamma.'

'Again? I was just with her a few minutes ago.' Loretta sighs and follows Marina out into the restaurant. She'll need to check her phone when she has a minute of privacy.

Alessandro and his mother's blond heads are beacons shining from the best table in the house. She makes her way to them. Clara and her husband, Pedro, exclaim over the food. She's always liked the di Ritas. They're warm and gentle people. It's no wonder they produced a son holy enough to be called to Rome. Although Alessandro still has a strange air about him this morning; he's almost squirming in his seat and staring past Loretta at God knows what.

Clara tells her about a fundraiser for the church, and Loretta offers to donate a basket of her homemade shortbread. She hangs around the table for a few more minutes and talks with them about the weather (cold), Christmas (lovely having Alessandro home) and their insurance company (praise God, doing well), all the while wondering if the message on her phone is from Flavia and what it says.

Finally she excuses herself, too fraught to socialise any longer. On her way back to the bathroom, she notices that the cold meat platter is just about empty, and as much as she wants to check her phone, it's impossible for her to ignore it. So she stops and picks the platter up to take to the kitchen to replenish.

'Amazing spread once again.'

The voice belongs to the Australian doctor, Signore Taylor, who's appeared beside her.

'Prego, signore. I hope you enjoy.' She gives him a brief smile.

'Sure will.' He reaches for a pastry. 'I'm making up for my wife. She hasn't got much of an appetite. I don't know how she can resist all your delicious food.'

Loretta thinks about Signora Taylor gorging herself the other day.

He takes a step closer to her. 'I know Ellie can come across as a bit standoffish. She's really shy, that's all. She loves it here. I'd hate for you to get the wrong impression.'

Loretta turns to see Signora Taylor cradling a glass of water, looking the personification of misery. This isn't shyness, it's something much more sinister. 'Please let me know if there is anything I can do to make your wife's stay with us more comfortable, signore.'

'You're the best, Signora Bianchi.' He gives her a wink that makes her back muscles tense. 'How's your husband doing?' he asks, almost as if to remind her of the hero he is.

Before she can reply, Alessandro comes to stand next to them. 'Christian! Buongiorno, my friend.'

'Padre!' Christian grins.

Loretta frowns. 'You know my guest?' she says to Alessandro.

'Of course I know Christian.' Alessandro smiles. 'The reason I came home is for the funeral.'

She shakes her head and speaks to Alessandro in Italian. 'I don't understand. What's the connection between the funeral and this man?'

'Zia, have you forgotten that Signore Zanetti is Elena's father?' Alessandro points at Signora Taylor.

Loretta's breath catches in her throat. She whips her head around to look at the woman again.

'*That's* Elena Zanetti?' Her voice is shrill.

'You know my wife?' Christian frowns.

'I do know her!' Loretta holds her hand to her heart. Santa Maria, what's become of sweet little Elena? She was a teenager the last time Loretta saw her. Never in a million years would she have recognised this sad, skeletal woman as the vivacious girl she knew back then.

She walks over to where Elena's sitting and throws her arms open. 'Elena, cara! E bello vederti!'

Elena shrinks away from her and responds in English, with barely a hint of Italian left in her accent. 'I'm sorry, do we know each other?'

'Of course I know you,' Loretta replies in English. 'Don't you remember us? Rocco played football with Paolo. God rest his soul.' She crosses herself.

'I'm so sorry, Signora Bianchi, I . . . I don't.' It's clear she's lying.

Elena looks past her, and Loretta turns to see Christian standing behind her. He's looking at his wife with laser focus. His expression is dark.

'You know these people? Why didn't you let on, Ellie?' His voice has changed. It's low and still, and the way he says the word *Ellie* makes Loretta recoil.

'I swear I don't remember them.' Elena's words are shaky. Her eyes dart from Loretta to her husband. She wrings her bony hands together. The poor girl is beyond terrified of this man. What on earth is he doing to her?

Loretta thinks of Elena's mother, Anna-Maria, who's already lost her son and who now, only in her early fifties, has lost her husband too. It's obvious her daughter is in deep trouble. How can this much tragedy befall the same family?

'Excuse us, please, Signora Bianchi.' Christian's voice remains calm, but his jaw is clenched tight. 'I'd like to speak with my wife privately.'

'Of course.' Loretta gives Elena an apologetic look and walks out of the restaurant to the bathroom.

Taking a deep breath, she locks herself in a stall and checks her phone.

Flavia's message is there.

My love, I'm waiting for you at the
church. Hurry.

Elena

Christian's face is blood red, the veins bulging at his temples. He drags Elena up the stairs without a word, turning her fingers blue with his grip. She's almost airborne as he pushes her into the suite.

'What the fuck was that about?' he hisses as soon the door is closed. 'Why didn't you tell me you knew them?' His face is inches away from hers. His breath smells of eggs.

'I swear I don't know them, I don't!' She has a desperate urge to pee.

'Stop lying to me.' The tendons in his neck tighten.

Elena knows she only has seconds left to talk herself out of this. 'I'm not lying, I promise. Christian, please, you have to believe me! I was a child when Paolo played football.' Her words trip over each other. 'How am I supposed to remember some random teammate's family from twenty years ago? I don't remember them. I swear to you I don't.' She takes a step back from him. 'There's something else you should know though.'

'*What?* What else?' He narrows his eyes.

'That nausea I had . . . it keeps coming back. I feel really sick today. I'm wondering if I'm . . .' She lets the word hang unsaid, resting her hand on her stomach.

His eyes widen. 'Ellie, oh my God! Do you think you're pregnant?'

'Maybe.' She nods, her heart galloping.

'This is amazing!' He holds his hand up to his forehead. 'After all this time. Fuck!' His face melts into a smile. 'Let's go get a test.'

She shakes her head fast. 'I've already been to the toilet twice today. It won't be accurate. Let's do it tomorrow.'

She won't be pregnant tomorrow, but she'll make sure she's gone by then.

'A baby. I can't believe it!' He rests his hand over hers. 'I knew it would happen eventually, I *knew* it. I've got a really good feeling about this, Ellie.'

For a man intelligent enough to perform intricate brain surgery, it baffles her that he can even contemplate for a second that she might be pregnant. Not just because she's too malnourished to ever possibly conceive, but even if she was pregnant, how can he think any foetus could survive the kick after kick to her abdomen just days ago? And yet here he is, looking at her with a huge dorky grin on his face. The degree of his delusion is breathtaking.

A few minutes later, when he steps into the shower, she collapses on the bed with relief, ready to fake a serious bout of morning sickness. She'll say she's too sick to go out. There's no way Christian will want to be cooped up in the hotel all day. She'll encourage him to go sightseeing without her, somewhere far like Padua. And while he's out, she'll bolt. Even if Mamma's not ready, she'll take her along anyway.

Today is the day Elena escapes.

Gayle

'You ready to go, hon?' Mike says, once they're back in their suite after breakfast.

Gayle had been looking forward to the trip to the small island of Burano today, to walk along the pretty rows of coloured houses and watch a lace-making demonstration. But after seeing Elena in the restaurant at breakfast, cowering while Christian towered above her, interrogating her about goodness knows what, Gayle has to do more to help her. She needs to get through to Elena's mother somehow.

Anna-Maria's run-down apartment building, with the never-ending steep flights of stairs, and the aggressive neighbour with his broom are worth facing again if it means helping Elena escape. It took a bit of convincing for Mike to agree to come back to the Jewish Ghetto, but she's found her voice here in Venice and she's using it, even if it makes her quiver inside whenever she challenges him.

The trip back to Cannaregio has none of the sense of adventure that it did a couple of days ago. It's an icy wind that awaits them at the vaporetto stop, and when they pile onto the crowded boat, there are no seats. Twice on the journey, Mike holds on to Gayle to stop her falling when she's jostled by people disembarking. They finally get to sit down for the last two stops before San Marcuola.

To Gayle's surprise, when Mike knocks on Anna-Maria's door this time, she greets them both with bone-crushing hugs.

'Mi dispiace,' she says over and over. 'Sorry, sorry.' She rolls her Rs. Her face is racked with worry.

'Mike Dawson,' Mike pants. 'My wife, Gayle.'

Anna-Maria clutches Gayle's hands in hers. The lady's grip is fierce.

'Elena wants to escape.' Mike talks as loudly as he does to his deaf friend, Jim, back in Little Rock. 'She's coming for you.'

Anna-Maria nods. 'I ready, yes. Vieni dentro, vieni.' She motions for them to come inside.

They hesitantly follow her into the apartment. The small living area is crammed with furniture, all of it old, unmatching and worn. The walls are covered in a beige and gold paisley wallpaper that's peeling.

'Please, welcome.' Anna-Maria motions for them to sit on a worn sofa.

Mike removes his sun visor. No matter the situation, Mike never forgets his manners. It's one of his most endearing features.

Anna-Maria shows them a small white box on the formica coffee table. Inside is a new smart phone. 'Giacomo, he buy for me.'

'Giacomo?' Mike says.

'Si, yes. Giacomo, my friend.' She points in the direction of the apartment that belongs to the neighbour who chased them. 'You tell Elena, I have money.' She pats an unsealed package on the table and pulls a handful of money out to show them. Gayle's eyes almost pop out of her head. Each note is two hundred euro. There must be at least fifty, maybe more. By the looks of the apartment, this isn't a wealthy family. The amount in that package could very well be Anna-Maria's entire life savings. It's all so horribly sad.

Mike turns to Gayle and mutters, 'We didn't need to come back. She's got it all under control.'

Gayle can see the disappointment in his eyes. Mike likes to be a helper.

Anna-Maria holds her palm out in a stop sign. 'Aspettate. You wait, please.' She disappears further into the apartment.

Gayle looks at the photos on the mantelpiece. It seems Elena has a brother. She wonders where he is and if he knows what's unfolding with his mother and sister. She says a quick prayer for Elena's kindly looking father who passed away.

Anna-Maria returns with a dented blue cake tin in her hands. Much of the paint has peeled off. 'Please. For you.' She hands it to Gayle.

'Go on and open it, hon.' Mike's eyes are big.

Gayle takes off the lid to find a dozen or more delicate jam pastries crammed into the tin. She looks at Anna-Maria in awe. 'For us?'

'Yes.' Anna-Maria smiles shyly. 'For thank you.'

There's so much of Elena in Anna-Maria. Their large brown eyes and dark hair, the same olive skin.

'Why, that's very kind of you. Let me just sample one here.' Mike reaches across Gayle's lap for a pastry. 'Mmm, delicious.' His voice is muffled. The pastry crumbs fall onto his pants.

Anna-Maria sits on the armchair opposite them. 'You give one for Elena? She no eat.' She bites her lip.

Gayle's heart constricts. How on earth can she get pastries to Elena? But she knows what a mother needs to hear. 'Of course. I'll save some for Elena.'

'You and Elena, friends,' Anna-Maria states.

'Yes,' Gayle says. Elena may not think of them as friends, but she does.

'Christian, no good.' Anna-Maria's eyes brim with tears.

'Yes,' Gayle says again. A cold fear for Elena settles on her.

Mike finishes his pastry and licks his fingers clean. There's not much left to say, so they stand up to leave. Anna-Maria hugs them again and thanks them profusely.

'I've got a bad feeling about Elena's escape.' Gayle watches Cannaregio disappear behind them as their boat moves away from the esplanade. She's shivering but it's not because of the cold wind whipping around them. 'I do hope she stays safe.'

'Don't you worry, hon. Anna-Maria's got it in hand. Don't underestimate how far a parent will go for their child.'

She gapes at him, and he holds his hand up. 'Now, I know what you're gonna say, so you don't need to say it. But it's not as simple as all that.'

He's told her not to say it, so she doesn't, but she thinks it. How far would they go for *their* child? Not far enough, it seems.

The sights of Venice wash over her on the journey back to San Marco. Anna-Maria is risking it all for her daughter, and what has Gayle done for Noah? She has to fix this. God will never forgive her unless she fixes it. She looks over at Mike, who's recording the boat ride on his phone.

It's too late for her to go back to being the woman she was before she came to Venice. The new Gayle is finally going to be the mother Noah deserves, even if it means her marriage will never be the same. Her palms feel sweaty. If only being a good mother didn't make her a troublesome wife.

LORETTA

Loretta hurries along the streets, in the opposite direction to Piazza San Marco, where Magdalena's standing in the tank of water. She can't face the artist today.

Instead of staying with the family to eat lunch, she announced that she was meeting a foreign journalist at the waterfront for an interview. These requests from journalists come regularly, so nobody raised an eyebrow, not even Alberto, who had come down to join them. She was barely able to look at him, too afraid she'd change her mind if she did.

Ten minutes after leaving Il Cuore, she's standing at the bottom of the steps, outside the open front doors of San Zaccaria. She watches the people walking in and coming out but she remains outside, the enormity of what she's about to do hitting her with a sudden force.

She slips her gloves off, breathes warm air into her cupped hands and walks up the stairs into the church.

Tourists roam around inside. Some kneel in the pews, deep in prayer, a few light candles, others take photos of the altar and the fresco, despite the clearly marked signs forbidding it.

She spots Flavia off to the side of the pulpit, the sun rays streaming in from the stained-glass windows above shining directly on her. Even with her hair and body hidden away underneath the veil and dress, her beauty radiates from her. Loretta can't take her eyes off that heart-shaped face, that gorgeous smile, those enormous eyes. Flavia's deep in conversation with an elderly woman Loretta recognises as Signora Offreddo, her retired dentist's wife.

Loretta lights a candle. 'Nel nome del Padre, e del Figlio e dello Spirito Santo,' she whispers as she crosses herself, but then finds she's unable to pray. How can she speak to God when she's here in sin?

When Signora Offreddo leaves, Flavia catches Loretta's eye, sending her heart soaring to high heaven. Flavia gestures towards the sacristy and walks in there, leaving the door slightly ajar behind her. Loretta waits a minute, making sure nobody's watching, and then slowly, casually, follows her inside.

'Close the door.' Flavia's voice is hushed.

Loretta does. It's only then that she removes her sunglasses and headscarf, resting them on a vacant chair by the wall. 'Il padre?' she whispers.

'He's busy.' Flavia takes a step towards her and holds out her hands. 'It's safe. Come.'

Loretta stays exactly where she is, her heart thudding.

'Come, Loretta.'

Loretta closes the distance between them and slides her hands into Flavia's. They're soft and warm and, even though Flavia's acting like she's in control, her hands are trembling and her breath is ragged.

'Cara mia.' Flavia places her fingers under Loretta's chin and gently lifts it so they're eye to eye.

They've been the undoing of her, those hazel eyes.

'Have you missed me?' Flavia whispers.

'Do you even need to ask?' The tears, uncontrolled, unwanted, stream down Loretta's cheeks.

Flavia wipes them with her thumb. 'Are these tears of joy or sadness?'

'I don't know. Both.'

Flavia runs her fingers across the blister on Loretta's wrist where the coffee burned her the other day. 'You hurt yourself?'

'It's nothing.'

Flavia brings Loretta's hand to her mouth and kisses the burn mark. The feel of Flavia's lips against her skin makes Loretta shiver. She touches the veil that covers Flavia's hair and drapes heavily on her shoulders. Flavia's tan dress sits loose and long, and a chunky crucifix hangs from a thick silver chain over her chest.

'It's strange to see you dressed like this,' Loretta says.

'It's been part of me for so long that it's hard to remember a time when I wasn't hiding behind the habit.'

'I remember,' Loretta whispers. She slides her fingers underneath the veil, gently loosening it away from Flavia's face. It drops to the floor and Flavia's grey hair, still with wisps of blonde in it, falls in waves.

Flavia looks at Loretta from under her long lashes. 'Can I kiss you? Per favore?' A smile plays on her lips and the years melt away.

'A thousand times, yes.'

The second their mouths collide, Loretta's body comes alive for the first time in decades. Something inside her unravels as she finds Flavia's tongue with her own. Something primal and raw. She pushes Flavia against the wall of the sacristy, her knee between Flavia's legs, and she lets herself fall further and further into sin as their bodies smash together.

Nothing else matters to Loretta, nothing at all, apart from this moment, right here, right now.

Gayle

Back in San Marco, Gayle and Mike follow his phone map to a pizza cafe that's advertising a buy one, get one free lunch special.

Opposite the cafe in the piazza is a grand old white church with huge wooden doors. Gayle hasn't been inside an Italian church yet; the basilica's still closed after the November floods.

'Can we take a quick peek inside that church before lunch, hon?' she asks Mike.

He looks longingly at the cafe, at the enormous slices of salami pizza on display in the window. 'Sure.'

They walk in and she stares in pure wonderment. Every wall is decorated, and so is the ceiling. She doesn't know where to look first – statues, frescos, stained-glass windows, enormous pillars made of marble.

'You shall not set up a figured stone in your land and bow down to it.' Mike quotes the Bible under his breath, pointing to a statue of Jesus.

'Right you are, hon.'

Gayle doesn't admit to him that she can see why Catholics love art in their churches. It's impossible not to feel God's presence when the agonised face of the crucified Christ is right there.

Together, she and Mike circle around the church, following the torture of Jesus in the stations of the cross, painted in all its gory detail.

A priest in robes walks among the visitors, stopping to greet people. He's a dashingly handsome young man, tall and broad and blond like a movie star. Gayle blushes when he catches her eye and smiles at her.

'Forcing red-blooded young men to be celibate is unnatural,' Mike mutters, eyeing the priest. 'I'd bet my last dollar that priest has a woman tucked away somewhere. Stupid Catholic rules deciding his love life for him just ain't right.'

Mike's words remind Gayle of what Noah said the day he left and never came back.

You don't get to decide who I love.

Tomorrow she's going to challenge Mike. Tomorrow, just not today.

'I wonder what this leads to,' Mike says when they come to a door tucked off to the side of the altar. He turns the knob.

'I'm not sure we're allowed to go in there, hon.'

'If they don't want people in there, they'd lock it,' he replies, pushing the door open. It gives a slight creak. 'Sweet holy Moses!' Mike exclaims once the door is fully open.

It takes Gayle a few seconds to make sense of the scene before her.

The room is small and its walls are covered in religious art. But it's not the art Gayle's attention is drawn to. No, what Gayle can't tear her eyes away from are the two women locked in a clandestine embrace up against one of the walls.

The women, suddenly aware of their entry, jump apart from each other and stare back at her with the same amount of shock that Gayle's sure is plastered on her own face. One of the women is wearing a nun's habit, minus the veil that's crumpled on the floor by her feet. And the other woman, with a flushed face, wiping her lips with her hand, is none other than Signora Bianchi.

'What in the heck?' Mike's eyes are bulging and his mouth is agape.

Signora Bianchi lurches towards Mike, the panic clear in her eyes. 'Please,' she whispers. 'Please.' She clasps her hands in prayer. The colour has completely drained from her face. She looks as if she might faint.

Mike takes a big breath in, but Gayle squeezes his arm. 'We're ever so sorry,' she says to the women. 'We were just on our way out, you see. We were admiring the church and all the lovely paintings. Such beautiful art here in Italy. Puts us Americans to shame. Our churches are mighty plain, aren't they, Mike? None of these lovely mosaics and statues and what not.' Gayle can feel her face sweating. 'Anyway, we were off to get some lunch at that two-for-one pizza place across the piazza over there and we opened the wrong door by mistake. Whoopsie!'

Signora Bianchi and the nun are frozen. It's as if they aren't even breathing.

'It was my fault.' Gayle's panting now. 'I said to Mike, I'm sure this is the way out, hon. But it's clearly not. Oh dear. I'm terribly sorry. We're going right now, right this second. Pretend we were never here, okay? Bye, bye. Take care now. Goodbye.'

She tugs on Mike's arm, pulling him away. The women keep staring as she backs away.

Silently, Gayle leads Mike out of the church by the hand, as fast as her legs can carry her.

As soon as they're outside, Mike turns to her but doesn't say anything. It's the first time she's ever known him to be lost for words. When his words do come, she wishes they hadn't.

'We've gotta tell Signore Bianchi,' he says. 'He has to know about this.'

Elena

Elena rolls her neck to try and relieve the tension but it's no use. Her muscles are rock hard. Christian hasn't let her out of his sight all day. Faking morning sickness and encouraging him to take himself out for the day to Padua backfired on her spectacularly when he forced her to go with him.

He's been so desperate for so long for her to get pregnant that she banked on him wanting to wrap her up in cotton wool, insisting she rest, so she didn't risk the baby. She banked wrong.

'You can't just lie around doing nothing, babe. Up you get. It'll be the best thing for you.' He wouldn't hear any arguments.

She could kick herself for being so stupid. Why did she have to bring a pregnancy into it? Now he's going to make her take a test in the morning.

When their train back from Padua approaches Santa Lucia station, Christian announces that they won't be going to visit Mamma tonight. 'I haven't shown you the *Venice Rising* exhibits yet. I want you to see the lit-up ones. You can see your mum tomorrow – she won't mind.'

Elena looks at him dumbfounded. 'We can't not go to her again, Christian. Of course she'll mind!'

'She'll be right, don't stress.'

'Her apartment's only a few minutes away. Can't we go for a just a little while? We don't have to stay long. Please?'

'Tomorrow, babe. Come on.' He kisses the top of her head and stands, holding his hand out to her as the train screeches to a stop.

Instead of going to Mamma, they walk to the esplanade and board the next vaporetto back to San Marco.

On the boat, he talks to her about the art exhibition and she nods, staring at the passing buildings and the dark water lapping up against them. With her fingernails digging into her palms, she channels white light, visualising it streaming down to surround her. Doing this stops her from crying. Christian's voice becomes a faraway blur. Her breathing slows, her fists unclench.

As the vaporetto comes into San Marco, it passes the famous hands sculpture reaching up out of the water. They've gone past the sculpture several times on this trip but it's only now she's quietened her thoughts enough to really *see* it. The water sloshes around the enormous white forearms emerging from the canal. The hands' stone fingers splay over a storey high on the pink walls of the Ca' Sagredo Hotel.

The sculpture had been erected after she left for Sydney. She remembers how excited, how inspired she'd been, watching the Italian news on her phone, of the hands being ferried into San Marco, seeing the heavy machinery and the massive operation involved. The hands were the original climate action protest art for Venice, erected when helping slow down global warming was her biggest life goal. Back when she actually had goals.

The hands remind Elena that it's not just her who's drowning. She wants to be moved by this realisation. She wants the fragile state of the world to make the adrenaline pump through her with urgency like it once did. She wants to care again. Elena doesn't want this vast emptiness inside her any more.

She follows Christian off the vaporetto onto the lit-up esplanade of San Marco. He leads her along the lanes to Campo San Moisè, where he points to a metallic blue hologram, shining starkly bright against the black night. A large crowd has gathered around the art installation in the piazza.

'What do you think? Pretty cool, hey? This is the one the Church is trying to ban.'

The hologram of Jesus in blue robes hovers high above the ground. His arms are spread out, showing off the stigmata wounds in his hands and feet. Instead of blood, it's aqua water that pours from them. Beneath Jesus, a hologram version of Venice is brought to life in astonishing detail. The entire city is underwater. The sound of a waterfall comes from speakers positioned around the piazza, and a deep male voice echoes through the still air, repeating the same few words again and again.

'What does the recording say?' Christian speaks loudly to be heard above the boom of the speakers.

Elena stands on her tiptoes and puts her mouth to his ear. 'This is my Son, who has abandoned you.'

'Whoa!' Christian laughs. 'That explains why the Catholics are losing their shit.'

Elena doesn't take her eyes off the hologram. The city she was born and raised in is sinking. Art like this should make her weep. But she's no longer the fiery law student who used to wipe the floor with anyone who questioned global warming. Right now, she's no longer even a concerned Venetian. All she is is a woman whose empty stomach is twisted in knots because she has to stop the monster she married from finding out she's not pregnant in the morning.

She doesn't want to be this selfish person. She has to find a way to become herself once more; she has to care about the world again.

Sophie

'Did you have a good afternoon?' Rocco asks Sophie when they finally have a minute to talk after the evening diners have left.

'I did. I followed the *Venice Rising* trail around San Marco.'

The installations helped Sophie to stop obsessing about Christian and his terrified-looking partner she'd seen at breakfast this morning. She needs to find a way to communicate with the woman and help her somehow.

Rocco pulls her out of her thoughts. 'You know, yesterday I thought I don't want to see any more of this art. Today, I have changed my mind. I am worried I will regret it if I miss it.' He lays down a fresh tablecloth.

'Why don't you come with me to see the ones that light up at night?' she asks.

He pushes his glasses up his nose and gives her his heart-melting smile. 'Okay, andiamo!'

Marina walks through from the kitchen. 'Andiamo where, Rocco? Everywhere will be closed except for the bacari.' She gives him a pointed look.

'Eh, relax, Marina. Always so tense.' Rocco laughs. 'We are going to see the exhibition, that's all.'

'Come with us,' Sophie offers, hoping Marina will decline.

Marina does. She's having an early night, she says as she shoos them out of the restaurant. 'Go, have fun.'

Sophie and Rocco take the rickety lift up to their rooms. The TV blasts from the family's apartment when Rocco unlocks the door.

Loretta retired early tonight, pleading fatigue. She was awfully quiet in the kitchen today, and she was so pale too. Sophie hopes Loretta isn't getting sick. Alberto, however, came down to hang out in the kitchen this evening and he was full of the joys of spring, singing his lungs out as if he hadn't keeled over from a heart attack only days before.

In her suite Sophie reapplies her lipstick, sprays deodorant under her arms and perfume between her boobs (for luck), and slips on her warmest woollen coat in a bright royal blue. She adds a white beanie with a fluffy pompom on top before meeting Rocco out in the hallway again, where the ever-present eyes of the Pope watch them leave, arm in arm.

Outside in the cold, clear night, the shops and cafes are closed and the laneways, still prettily lit up with Christmas lights, are mostly quiet. The first installation that Sophie wants to see is only a few blocks away. Rocco knows the way.

When they come around a corner, Rocco says, 'Ah, look! Our guests, the doctor and Signora Taylor.'

Sophie's back stiffens as the couple, both dressed in trench coats, approaches them. Christian smiles at Sophie and gives Rocco a high five. While the men exchange pleasantries, Sophie locks eyes with the woman, whose tiny frame is buried under her coat. The woman looks away.

Sophie keeps watching her. The woman's make-up is flawless. Her dark pixie cut, huge brown eyes and high cheek bones remind Sophie of a young Audrey Hepburn, and that plaid green and black coat is definitely Burberry. Such beauty and terror wrapped up together.

Christian pulls the woman closer to him while he laughs with Rocco. The woman flinches at his touch, confirming to Sophie that she wasn't imagining things this morning. They stand in silence, her and the woman, until Rocco and Christian say their goodbyes a minute later.

'Good to see you again.' Christian gives Sophie another wide smile.

She makes herself smile back.

'He is a very nice man,' Rocco tells her when the couple walks away from them, back towards the hotel. 'Very smart too, a brain surgeon. He saved Papà's life on Christmas Day, you know.'

'What do you mean?'

She hears for the first time the details of Alberto's cardiac arrest and rescue. She hates that Christian is the hero of the story. *Really* hates that.

'But his wife is . . . ah, she is strange,' Rocco says.

'What makes you say that?'

'She is Venetian, Elena. We knew her very well many years ago. We did not recognise her this time because she has changed a lot since she left Venice. But she knows us, and she pretended she does not know us. This is strange, eh?'

'Yeah. I think there's something bad going on there, Rocco.'

'She is very thin, yes. Maybe she has an illness?'

'It's not that. I don't get a good feeling from her husband.'

He turns to her, his eyebrows drawn together. 'The doctor? Why?'

'Just a feeling I have.'

He nods but doesn't respond, instead pointing ahead of them. 'There it is.'

The enormous hologram in the piazza can be clearly seen from over a hundred feet away. Sophie lets the conversation drop for now as she and Rocco stand hypnotised by the illusion, along with dozens of other people.

Rocco puts his mouth close to Sophie's ear to translate the recording coming through the speakers. When he speaks, his warm breath sends tingles down the back of her neck.

They walk closer to the lit-up Messiah.

'I hope Mamma does not see this,' Rocco says.

'She'd be offended?'

'It would break her heart.'

'Because she's so religious?'

'Because she's Venetian.'

'Ah.' Sophie nods. 'My mum would be outraged by it.'

'Your mother is very religious?'

'Only since my dad died. Before that we only went to Mass at Christmas. We were more cultural Catholics than anything.'

'Ha! Cultural Catholics, I like this. Then she changed after your father died?'

'Yep, she started forcing us to go to Mass. She quoted the Bible to us all the time, telling us we had to repent for our sins. She's still the same now.'

He tilts his head towards her. 'You have problems with your mother, eh? I can tell.'

She takes a deep breath. 'We have our issues.'

'Do you want to talk to me about it?'

She looks up at his beautiful face, full of kindness. 'No.'

The water pours and pours from Jesus. The voice reminds Venetians that they've been abandoned, left to sink by everyone, even their God. No ark is being built to save them.

God let her family sink too.

She watches the hovering Jesus as memories of her dad fill her mind.

Martin Black was screamingly funny with his imitations and his anecdotes. He was warm and cuddly, and he showered little Sophie and David with affection. They grew up on his lap with his arms around them. He was generous, spoiling them rotten with gifts and treats.

Martin was also musically gifted. He sang and played piano and they all joined in, even her mother. All four of them sang in the car on the long trips when they went on holidays, harmonising together.

Martin was truly wonderful.

Except when he wasn't.

He wasn't so wonderful when he beat Penelope to a pulp, more and more regularly as the years went on. He wasn't wonderful when he tried to kill his entire family, twice.

The first time, they were in the car on the way to a party. It might have been someone's birthday. Tension had been brewing between Martin and Penelope all morning. Sophie was nine years old by then and had long given up keeping track of what the fights were about. Penelope had worn the wrong clothes, or used the wrong tone, or taken too long doing her hair, or not ironed a shirt well enough, or laughed at something on television that Martin didn't find funny. This was one of those mornings. David and Sophie did what they did whenever they knew trouble was coming: they stayed quiet and kept out of Martin's way.

The drive began peacefully enough even though it definitely wasn't the sort of drive where there would be any singing. David and Sophie were too wary to even talk to each other in the back seat.

'It's never going to get better,' Martin declared suddenly. 'You're never going to change, and you'll never make me happy. There's no point continuing with this life any more.'

Penelope stared out the window.

'Did you hear me?' Martin turned to her. 'I said there's no point continuing with this life any more.'

'I heard you,' Penelope snapped. 'Good. Now we can get a divorce.'

'That's not what I meant.' His voice was steady.

Martin looked at the children in the rear-view mirror. 'Sophie, David, you're better off dead than being raised by a mother who doesn't respect your father.'

Sophie's stomach clenched hard.

Martin pressed his foot on the accelerator. The car began to speed up.

'Daddy, what are you doing?' Sophie cried above the noise of the revving motor.

The car went faster and faster. Martin weaved in and out of the lanes on the freeway. 'It's over!' he shouted. 'It's over! I'm giving us peace from this miserable existence.'

'No, Daddy!' Sophie screamed.

'Daddy, I'm scared!' David cried.

Penelope turned herself towards Martin. His hands shook on the steering wheel. 'Darling, my darling!' Penelope cried. 'Forgive me. I love you! I love you with all my heart. I love you!'

Their car was flying past all the other cars. Sophie craned her neck to see the speed on the dash. The dial pointed to the maximum, two hundred kilometres per hour. Still, Martin drove like a maniac, changing lanes constantly. Sophie wet her pants, soaked them right through. David vomited all over the back of Martin's seat.

'Darling, we'll start over. I promise it will be better. I love you!' Penelope's voice became more and more shrill. 'I'll do everything you say. Whatever you want I'll do it. I'll never disrespect you again. Please, I love you!'

The car took a sudden swerve into the emergency lane. Martin slammed on the brakes and the car came to an abrupt and screeching stop. Penelope, David and Sophie all screamed as they hurtled forward. Martin dropped his head onto the steering wheel and sobbed like a baby. Penelope cradled him in her arms.

'I love you,' they told each other over and over again.

Penelope turned to Sophie and David after what felt like a very long time, looking at them as if she'd only just remembered they were there. 'Are you okay, you two?'

They nodded mutely.

'Oh, David, you vomited,' she groaned.

'I . . . I felt sick,' David stammered.

'It's all right,' Martin said gently. 'We'll go home and you can get changed.'

'I need to change too,' Sophie said, scared of their reaction. 'I'm all wet.'

Penelope shook her head. 'Daddy was upset but he'd never hurt us, would you, darling?'

'Of course not!' The indignation rang through Martin's voice. 'You kids overreact to everything.'

The children apologised.

Martin drove them home at a slower than normal speed, showing them what a careful driver he was. He and Penelope held hands the whole way and said kind things to each other.

At home, while David and Sophie changed their clothes, Martin cleaned the inside of the car and Penelope rang her mother to say they'd had car trouble and would be arriving late to the party. Sophie asked if she could have a shower, but Penelope said there wasn't time. She still smelled like pee, David still smelled like vomit.

They went to the party, they played with their cousins. Everything was normal again. For a while.

The second time Martin tried to kill them was just under a year later. Sophie was ten years old by then.

This time, it was premeditated. First, Martin had their home fitted with security blinds that were key-locked. Then he had deadbolts fitted to all the doors.

One night, after the dishes were washed and dried and put away, and David and Sophie had retreated to their bedrooms, Martin quietly set a pot of boiling oil on fire in the kitchen, then went to the lounge room and lit a cigarette.

It was David who first noticed the smoke. By then, the entire kitchen was in flames. They stood there, the two children, frozen, staring at the fire, uncomprehending.

'Get away from there!' Penelope screamed. 'Quick, run!'

They ran for the front door. It was locked. They ran to the back door. That was locked too. The keys to the doors were missing. Panicked, they dashed to the windows, from room to room, only to realise the steel blinds were also locked and those keys were missing too.

'Where's Dad?' Sophie was beginning to gag.

'Cover your mouths! Drop low!' Penelope shouted. She screamed Martin's name.

The children crawled along the floor after Penelope and found Martin sitting in the far corner of the lounge room, calmly smoking.

The fire behind them had spread to the dining room. Sophie could barely see through the smoke.

'Save us!' Penelope hugged Martin's legs. 'Save us! I'm begging you,' she spluttered and coughed. 'Please, I love you!'

'Please, Daddy!' Sophie cried.

David collapsed face down on the floor.

'David's dying!' Penelope screamed. 'I promise I'll change. I'll do whatever you want!'

Martin stubbed his cigarette out in the ashtray and threw a set of keys on the carpet next to Penelope's feet. Penelope lunged at them. Covering her mouth, she ran to the front door. She couldn't stop coughing and neither could Sophie. David was unconscious.

Penelope tried different keys until one finally unlocked the door. 'Help me!' she screamed at Sophie.

They dragged David along the floor. He was so incredibly heavy. Sophie's arms and legs were like jelly, her head swam. It was hard to keep her eyes open; they were raw from the stinging smoke. The fire was only a few metres away from them now and the heat coming off the flames made her face burn.

The sound of sirens blared in the distance. They managed to make it out into the front garden with David.

The neighbours, who had gathered on the footpath, raced to them. 'We thought you'd all died! Half the roof's gone.'

David was now alert and coughing up black spit on the ground.

A fire engine came flying up the road to the house and the firemen jumped out. Two firemen ran up the driveway and two more pulled hoses from the truck. 'Anyone left in the house?' one of them shouted.

'No,' Penelope said.

Sophie looked at her dumbfounded. 'Daddy's in there, Mummy!' she cried. 'My daddy's in there!' she shouted to the men, who ran into the house.

They quickly came out again, with Martin's arms draped over

their shoulders. His head was lolling about, his legs were slack and dragging. They had to resuscitate him.

The house was destroyed but the family survived.

Martin and Penelope made up. They were the happiest they'd ever been after that fire. It was as if something finally clicked between them, and the fights stopped. They moved into a new home and they used the insurance money to fill it with shiny new things.

Exactly three months from the day of the fire, Penelope killed him.

'Sophie? Sophie?' There's a look of concern on Rocco's face. 'You are far away, Sophie. What are you thinking about?'

She realises with a start that the hologram has been turned off and the crowd is clearing. 'I was just thinking about my dad,' she tells him.

'What was he like, your father?'

'Dad?' She sighs. 'Dad was wonderful.'

On the SIXTH DAY of CHRISTMAS

Gayle

Signora Bianchi has seen them. She juts out her chin, tugs on the sides of her white apron and walks over to the table where Gayle and Mike are having breakfast.

Mike refused to eat at Il Cuore last night. 'I'm not giving that cheating lesbian another dime. We won't be eating at this hotel again. Sorry, hon, but I can't condone that kind of sinning.'

Despite Mike's proclamations, breakfast at Il Cuore is now free, so this morning he made an exception about eating at the hotel after all, and here they are.

And now Signora Bianchi's standing at their table with a coffee pot in her hand, and Gayle's heart is beating as fast as if she's just run up all of Anna-Maria's four flights of stairs.

'Buongiorno, signore, buongiorno, signora.' Signora Bianchi's jaw is tense even as she smiles. 'Can I top up your coffee?'

Mike's cheeks are red and he stares at his plate. 'That won't be necessary, thank you.'

Gayle gives Signora Bianchi a smile. 'I'd love some more of your fine coffee, thank you. Mighty kind of you.'

Mike gives Gayle a look from under his bunched eyebrows and she knows she's annoyed him.

Signora Bianchi clears her throat. 'I want to apologise for what you saw in the church yesterday.'

Mike fiddles with his napkin. 'Yes, well, it wasn't exactly what we expec—'

'And I want to thank you for your discretion,' she continues over Mike. 'I am sure you understand the damage it would do to my family and our business if what you saw became known.'

Gayle nods obediently, but Mike looks up sharply at Signora Bianchi.

'It's your poor husband I feel for.' He scratches his beard. 'I think he should know the truth, but Gayle here convinced me yesterday that it's not the right time to tell him, so soon after his heart attack and all. That's the only reason he hasn't heard about it from me.'

Gayle had worked hard to stop Mike from announcing Signore Bianchi's wife's infidelity to him.

'But hon, she's got that big old painting of the Pope right out there in the hallway while she's sinning with *a nun* in *a church*. That's hypocrisy of the highest order, that is. She shouldn't be allowed to get away with that, it ain't right,' he'd argued. 'Someone has to let that poor fellow know he's been tricked.'

Signora Bianchi lowers her eyes. 'I am very grateful to you both for your kindness.' She pauses as if she's considering what to say next, but instead she gives Gayle a heartbreakingly sad smile and leaves their table. She's immediately stopped by two women at another table who request a selfie with her, and Gayle watches as Signora Bianchi poses and laughs with them.

Signore Bianchi walks into the restaurant then, and he makes his way around the tables, loudly and cheerfully chatting with various guests. 'Ciao a tutti! Ciao a tutti!' he calls out. When he passes by his wife, he stands on his toes to plant a fat kiss on her cheek. Signora Bianchi laughs and shoos him away, playing up to the crowd.

Mike glowers at them as he munches on a pastry, the flakes catching in his beard. 'I still think he should know the truth,' he mutters.

He should, she agrees, *but not from us*.

When Mike's helping himself to a second plate at the buffet table, Gayle's phone pings with a message from Lizzie.

Hey Mom, guess what? Noah
messaged me!

He said he's still waiting for Pop to
apologise.

I want us to all be a family again.
Please talk to Pop xx

Mike comes back with his plate heaving with food. 'You know, what we saw yesterday is still turning my stomach. We need to keep praying hard that our boy comes to his senses.'

He picks all the strawberries off his plate and puts them on Gayle's without a word. He knows how much she loves strawberries.

Gayle has never felt so tortured. How is she ever going to make things right?

Elena

Elena stands at the window, watching the street below. Having only booked the room last week, the suites with canal views were already taken. This annoyed Christian. But Elena loves the street view, watching Venice in motion.

An old woman across the road sets up a small metal table and two fold-out chairs outside her cafe. Elena doesn't know the woman but she knows the cafe, which has been there since she was a child. It's a feat for any business to survive here for over two decades. A solitary strand of flimsy red tinsel hangs across the cafe's front window. The woman's large breasts sit low over the striped apron tied around her waist and her swollen feet are spilling out of loafers. She already looks exhausted. It's eight a.m.

Elena feels the old woman's fatigue; she's been awake all night. She thought about making a run for it in the early hours of the morning, but without the boats and trains operating through the night, she wouldn't have got very far. She only has one shot at escaping, and she has to get it right.

'Let's go get that pregnancy test.' Christian comes out of the bathroom, his hair slicked back and his aftershave on. He claps his hands together. 'Chop, chop. If we're quick, we'll still make breakfast here.'

Elena turns away from the window. 'I was thinking we really should wait until we're back home.'

He tilts his head and looks down at her through narrowed eyes. 'Why?'

'It's just – I don't know – with Papà's funeral this week, if I'm pregnant, it's a lot to take on, mentally.' Her voice is squeaky. 'Can we wait a little longer before I take a test?'

'Sorry, babe, I can't wait. I have to know. Let's go.'

She's prepared for this answer.

Years ago, when things were first unravelling and she still had access to the internet, she looked up how to fake a positive result on a pregnancy test and kept it locked away in her head for the time it would come in handy. That time is now. If she can show him a positive test, he won't risk the baby by hurting her and she'll be safe until she escapes.

'Christian, I don't want to go out right now. My nausea's the worst it's been. Can I wait back here for you?'

He raises an eyebrow and smiles a slow smile. 'The nausea's a good sign. I really think this is happening, babe.' He pats his pocket, feeling for his wallet. 'I'll be back before you know it.' He kisses the top of her head before he leaves.

She watches from the window until she's sure he's left, then she runs to the bar fridge, pulls out a can of Coke and shoves it inside the bathroom cabinet. She wedges their bedroom door open and bolts from the room out into the hallway, slamming straight into the blonde Australian waitress from the restaurant. The knock makes Elena stagger backwards and the woman grabs onto her arm to stop her falling.

'I'm so sorry! Are you okay?'

'Sorry, I didn't see you.' Elena looks past her down the corridor. 'I need to talk to Signora Bianchi, or any of the Bianchis really.'

'They're all downstairs in the restaurant.' The woman lets go of her arm. 'Are you safe? Is he hurting you?'

Elena gives her an incredulous stare. 'What do you mean?'

'I just saw your husband leave. I came up to see if I can help you.'

'Who even are you?'

'My name's Sophie. I can tell you're in danger. Let me help.'

Elena makes a snap decision to trust her. 'Come in.' She beckons Sophie into her suite and goes to stand by the window so she can keep an eye on the street. 'Christian will be back soon.' Elena speaks quickly. 'My mother lives in Venice and I need to escape with her before our flight back to Australia. That's just over a week away. I need him distracted so I have a chance to get away. But he won't leave me alone for more than a few minutes at a time.'

'Shit. Do you want to hide in my room?'

'No. If he can't find me, he'll kick down every door here.' Elena's started shaking and now she can't stop. 'I need him to be occupied, for an hour or even longer. That's what I wanted to ask the Bianchis for help with.'

'I'll tell them. We'll work something out. You're here until the seventh, right?'

'Yes.' *How does this woman know everything?*

'Okay, good. Where's he gone to now?'

'Pharmacy. I told him I'm pregnant but I'm not.'

Sophie's eyes bulge. '*What?* Why did you do that?'

'I know, I know. It was a mistake. He's buying the pregnancy test right now.'

'What's going to happen when he finds out you're not?'

'I'm going to fake a positive result with Coke.' Elena doesn't take her eyes off the street.

'You mean Coke as in Coca-Cola?'

'Yes, you can use Coke instead of urine on the test. It's supposed to be foolproof. At least I hope it is.'

'Jesus.' Sophie bites her bottom lip.

Elena's heart is racing so fast she thinks she might faint. She blows into her hands, breathing slowly in and out. 'I need to sit down. Can you watch the street?'

'Yep.' Sophie moves to the window. 'I almost forgot. Here, I was bringing this up for you.' She produces a sandwich, wrapped in plastic, from her apron pocket. 'Eat this before he gets back. It's salami and cheese.'

'I'm too nervous to eat. Do you have a phone on you? I need to call my mother.'

'Of course.'

Elena takes the phone from Sophie and types in Mamma's number, praying she answers. She does. When she hears Mamma's voice, she breaks down. Mamma tells her that she has money and a phone as requested – she's ready.

'I'm sorry, Mamma. I'm sorry I'm taking you away from everything you love.'

'Vita mia, the only thing that matters to me is you.'

'He's coming,' Sophie whispers, her eyes wide.

Elena hangs up quickly and gives Sophie back the phone.

'I'll stick close by. Call out if you're in danger.' Sophie gives her a brief hug at the door. 'God, you're shaking like a leaf, you poor thing. We'll figure out a way you can escape, don't worry.'

Less than a minute after Sophie leaves, Christian walks in. He holds up a paper bag. 'Ready to take a leak?' He grins.

Elena closes the bathroom door behind her and sits on the toilet with her pants down for appearances, just in case he walks in. She reaches for the can hidden in the vanity. The sound of gas escaping when she opens the Coke feels spectacularly loud.

Merda. Why didn't I open it when he was out?

She freezes, expecting him to burst through the door to see her sitting there with the can in her hands. The door remains shut. She dips the test into the Coke and hides the can again.

Then she waits.

After a few seconds, he calls out, 'How's it going in there? You done?'

'Not yet.' There's a roaring in her ears.

'What's taking so long?'

'It's hard to go, I'm nervous.'

'Bloody hell, Ellie, just do it.'

'I'm trying!'

Her heart just about stops beating when she looks down at the test. It's positive.

The immediacy of her tears shocks her. She pulls up her knickers and walks out of the bathroom, holding up the test for him to see.

His jaw drops. 'We're having a baby!'

He swoops her up in his arms, and they laugh and cry. The relief has made her giddy.

When they walk out together for breakfast minutes later, both Rocco and Sophie are hanging around in the hallway outside their suite.

'Hey, Rocco!' Christian grins at him. 'You're the first to know, mate. Ellie's pregnant!'

Rocco gives him a high five. 'Congratulazioni! This is wonderful news!'

Sophie catches Elena's eye and smiles. Elena has no idea how Sophie knew what she knew, but this stranger might just be the one to save her life.

Sophie

The entire family is in the kitchen listening to Sophie. Elena and Christian are seated in the restaurant along with the last of the breakfast diners.

'We need to find a way to occupy him to give her time to get away,' Sophie finishes.

'We will tell the police. They will arrest him,' Loretta says.

'Arrest him for what?' Sophie replies. 'They can't do anything without proof. Elena needs to run. It's the only way.'

Loretta gnaws at a nail. 'Too dangerous.'

'It's more dangerous for her to stay.' Sophie turns to Rocco. 'What can we do to distract him?'

'I don't know,' he replies.

'What about inviting him to be in the protest?' Salvatore says.

'What protest?' Marina asks.

Rocco drums his fingers on the kitchen bench. He slowly shakes his head at his cousin.

'What protest, Rocco?' Sophie repeats.

Rocco sighs. 'You know about the festival for the Epiphany, yes?' he tells her. 'La Regata della Befana, where we race the gondolas to the Ponte di Rialto?'

Sophie nods.

He continues. 'This year, all of us in the race are planning a protest. We are going to block the canal with our gondolas to stop the cruise ships from entering, so—'

All hell breaks loose in the kitchen with everyone shouting at once. Piano accordion hands are flying around everywhere.

'You did not tell me about this!' Loretta shouts.

'Nobody was supposed to know.' Rocco throws Salvatore a filthy look.

'Sorry.' Salvatore doesn't sound sorry at all. 'If Christian joins our team in the regatta, she can escape then.'

Alberto, who's sitting at the bench stuffing himself with breakfast cake, begins to say something in Italian.

'In English,' Loretta interrupts him.

Alberto grunts. 'Too long to wait.'

'We have a meeting on Saturday to plan the protest. It will be for an hour or two at least,' Salvatore says. 'If he comes with us to the meeting, she can escape then, one day closer.'

'Too long, no good,' Alberto replies.

'Papà is right, even Saturday for your meeting is still five days away,' Marina says.

'She's survived this long, she can get through five more days,' Sophie argues. 'He's over the moon at the moment, so hopefully that means she'll be safe for a while. Getting him to the meeting on Saturday's a good idea.'

'No,' Loretta insists. 'We need to do something to save her now, today.'

'Like what?' Sophie asks her.

Loretta sighs and shrugs.

Sophie turns her attention back to Rocco. 'Please trust me on this. Ask him to be in the protest, take him to the meeting. Please.'

'Why would he even agree to be in the protest?' Rocco says. 'He is not Venetian. It makes no sense. He will say no.'

Loretta says something else and so does Marina, but Sophie isn't listening to them any more. She keeps her focus squarely on Rocco. 'I know how men like him think. Being asked will make him feel important. He won't say no. Please, Rocco, I know I'm right about this. He's sitting out there right now. Go and ask him.'

Rocco looks around the room at his family, then he nods at her and walks to the door that leads to the restaurant.

'Santa Maria, this is a big mistake,' Loretta says as Sophie follows him out.

Rocco walks towards Christian and Elena's table. He leans over to speak in Christian's ear and then leads him out to the lobby. The sight of Christian walking that cocky walk, with his perfect stubble and his trendy designer clothes, looking so pleased with himself, makes Sophie's insides burn with rage.

As soon as the men are out of sight, she goes straight to Elena. She keeps a casual smile on her face in case Christian comes back in and sees them talking. 'Apparently there's going to be a protest at the big regatta next week. They're going to block the entry to the canal with gondolas. Rocco's inviting Christian to be part of it. He's out there now asking him to attend a meeting this Saturday to plan the protest. You can escape while he's there.'

Elena clasps her hands. 'This is perfect, thank you so much.'

'Is there anything else you need?'

'No, I don't think so.'

'I'm so glad the pregnancy test worked.' Sophie smiles at her.

'God, me too.'

Sophie gives Elena's bony shoulder a gentle squeeze and leaves before Christian returns.

When she heads back into the kitchen, everyone looks at her expectantly.

'Elena said it's a perfect plan,' she says in a way that comes out a little too 'told you so'.

Marina and Loretta respond with death glares that are quite frankly terrifying. But she knows she's done the right thing by Elena and that's all that matters.

GAYLE

'Hon, do you know where my sun visor's at?' Mike asks.

'Have you looked in your backpack?'

'Yup. It's not there.'

Then Gayle remembers. 'You took it off yesterday in Anna-Maria's apartment. You must have left it there.'

Mike received the sun visor as a gift for taking part in a charity walk that raised funds for injured veterans. He always wears it with pride. The embossed words *They Fought For Us, We Walk For Them* are a reminder to all of Mike's patriotism.

'I sure did like that sun visor.' He flops onto the bed.

Gayle hopes he doesn't suggest going back to Cannaregio for it. What would she even say to Anna-Maria after Elena's strange behaviour this morning?

Mike seems to read her mind. 'Do you think Elena's sorted things out with her husband, then?'

'Maybe, for now.'

This morning at breakfast Elena was there, laughing and chatting away with her husband without a care in the world! They were holding hands across the table and couldn't have seemed more in love.

Signora Bianchi placed a plate of food in front of Elena, and Gayle watched her cheerfully eating. It was obvious that Elena was deliberately avoiding eye contact with Gayle, not even acknowledging her and Mike with a simple look. Gayle had no way of letting her know they'd been to see her mother again.

'Come on, hon,' Mike says. 'Let's get you out of here and take your mind off that girl.'

They pack their backpacks with water bottles and plastic rain ponchos.

'Got your headache tablets?' he asks.

'Packed them.'

Her head's pounding. She's glad for a quiet day staying in the local area today. She doesn't feel up to boat and train rides.

Outside, they walk to a part of San Marco they haven't seen yet. It looks just the same as the rest of the city. Every narrow street is lined with cafes, and shops selling masks and glass and clothes.

They happen across a store that specialises in letter openers. Mike's overjoyed. He has a collection of letter openers back home, gathered from their travels, all proudly displayed in a glass cabinet in the living room. He's been looking for a new one to add to his collection since they arrived in Venice.

Mike points to a letter opener he likes in the window and when the shopkeeper, a short man with a white moustache, walks out and tells them its price, Gayle inhales sharply.

'That's mighty expensive, hon,' she whispers to Mike.

'This is the cost of handblown Murano glass, signora,' the man says in a thick accent. 'It is a good price.'

She's embarrassed that he heard her.

'We bought *six* glass pendants the other day for half of this,' Mike says.

'Then I am sorry to tell you, signore, you bought replicas. Everything in my shop is made by Italian craftsmen with genuine Murano glass. The pendants you bought are from China.'

'But we bought 'em right here in Venice,' Mike argues.

'Yes.' The shopkeeper sighs heavily. 'How can we compete with replica prices, I ask you? Venice sinks, and Venetians, we sink too.' He launches into a story about his friend who made masks and was lucky to sell two a day because most tourists can't tell the difference between a mask that takes hours to paint by hand and one that's mass produced in minutes. The friend shut his business, unable to keep paying rent on his shop.

Gayle feels her cheeks redden with shame. Just yesterday, Mike bought eight masks for four euro each for his Tuesday canasta group.

Mike looks longingly at the letter opener. 'So you can't discount it at all, then?'

'No, signore. I run an honest business and this is an honest price, I promise you.'

'What should I do?' Mike turns to her.

The letter opener has a handle made of red and orange glass baubles with delicate gold etching. Gayle doesn't have Mike's passion for letter openers, but even she knows this one's a beauty. 'I think you should take it.'

Mike's a head taller when they walk out of that shop, so delighted is he with his new gift. Gayle's heart grows in size seeing his joy.

They walk into a coffee shop next. 'Have you heard?' the barista asks them. 'They have coloured the water of the Grand Canal!'

'Who has?' Mikes asks her.

'Protestors,' the young woman replies, her eyes sparkling. 'Amazing!'

So of course, as soon as they have their takeaway coffees in their hands, they walk to the canal where they jostle with what must be every tourist in Venice for a spot on the Rialto Bridge. Below them the water of the Grand Canal, as far as the eyes can see, is blood red.

The large man standing next to Gayle digs his elbow into the side of her breast and the lady behind is squashed up so close that the railing of the bridge presses into Gayle's stomach. She has a fleeting and horrifying thought that the bridge might collapse under the weight of all these people, sending them plunging into the canal. She expresses this fear in Mike's ear and he laughs.

'This bridge has been here since ancient times, hon. It's withstood wars, it can handle us. Don't you worry.' He pats her hand.

She feels a little reassured but it's still awful being this crammed in. It's hard to take a deep breath.

According to the people gossiping around them in English, the coloured water is a stunt to symbolise the death of Venice. A group called Viva Venezia have already claimed responsibility for it, apparently timing their protest with the *Venice Rising* exhibition for maximum exposure. The vision of the murky red water is reminiscent of a shark feeding frenzy.

'Won't this kind of thing do more damage to the environment?' Mike says to her.

A man standing next to them in a knitted beanie answers. 'Don't worry about some red food dye damaging the environment, signore. This will wash away by morning, but the oil and fuel and excrement from the ships will continue.'

'I wasn't talking to you.' Mike's face turns red.

'Forgive me for trying to educate you.' The man laughs a bitter laugh.

Gayle feels herself getting pushed harder against the railing as more and more people crowd onto the bridge. 'Hon, I don't feel good. Can we leave?' she asks Mike.

'Let's go.' Mike stops recording and puts away his phone. 'People are rude here anyway. Not making tourists feel very welcome when we're bringing in all the money,' he says pointedly to the man in the beanie, who shakes his head at him and mumbles something in Italian.

It's not easy to go against the flow of foot traffic but Mike's good at pushing through. Even if it does earn them a few shouts and some rather rude hand gestures, Gayle's grateful for his forcefulness.

Once they're finally back on land in San Marco, she can breathe properly.

A short walk later, the familiar hotel lobby is a welcome sight. Lovely Marina is behind the desk to greet them, and she's very sympathetic when Mike complains about the rude man on the bridge.

'Imagine if she knew what her mother was up to,' he stage-whispers as they head for the stairs.

Gayle looks over her shoulder, panicked that Marina heard him, but she doesn't seem to have.

As Mike sits on the edge of the bed, peeling off his sneakers and woollen socks, Gayle makes him a hot chocolate, rehearsing what she's about to say.

'Hon.' Her voice is wobbly as she hands him the steaming cup. 'I have something to tell you.'

'Let me guess, you're pregnant.' He winks and she laughs a little too loudly. 'What is it, hon?' He flicks the dirt from between his toes onto the carpet and has a big slurp of hot chocolate.

'I've been in contact with Noah.'

He holds the cup frozen in mid-air. 'You have? What'd he say?'

'Well.' She sits down on the bed next to him and clasps her hands in her lap. 'He'd really like to make up with everybody and see us again.'

'See? I told you he'd come around. I knew you were worrying for nothing. When's he coming to visit? I want to show him the new trailer.'

'We didn't get as far as organising a visit.'

'He's the only one who hasn't seen the trailer yet.'

'Yes.'

'Wait till I tell him the price I got it for. Reckon he'd be impressed with that. Noah likes a bargain.'

She takes a calming breath. 'Forgetting the trailer, just for now, what I need to tell you is that Noah wants to reconnect but he's still very upset.'

'*He's* upset? What about us? Look at what that boy's put us through. How many tears have you cried over him? Upset, he says! Hmph, I'll show him upset. Why, I—'

'Mike, please!' Her voice breaks. 'Let me finish.'

He grunts. 'Go on, then.'

'He wants an apology.'

'From who?'

'From us, from you.'

'Ha! He's dreaming!'

Gayle wills herself not to cry. 'We hurt him deeply with the things we said.' She hopes the *we* sounds less accusatory than *you*. 'We haven't supported his marriage and—'

'It's not even a real marriage,' Mike scoffs.

She swallows. 'It's a legal union in the eyes of the law.'

'Only because our country's been taken over by these left-wing fascists—'

'Would you *please* let me finish!' she snaps.

His jaw drops.

'I'm sorry, hon.' This was not how this conversation was supposed to go. She reaches for his hand. 'I'm sorry.'

He nods. 'Listen, I know you get overemotional when it comes to that boy, but we can't let him bully us.'

'He's not bullying us. He's only sharing how hurt he is. Please, hon, can't we just apologise? Then everything will be better.'

'But it won't be better. He'll still be married to a man.'

'It'll mean he's back in our lives. You've always said you'd do anything for us.'

'And I have!'

'I know you have, I know. And now I'm asking for you to do this for me too.'

He shakes his head. 'I won't bow down to threats from Noah. He's always welcome in our home, he knows that. But I won't be forced to apologise for my beliefs.'

She bites her cheek hard enough to taste blood.

'Let's stop talking about Noah, because it does nothing but bring us down.' Mike pushes himself up off the bed. 'In good time, he'll realise he was wrong and he'll come crawling back. You mark my words, that's what'll happen. Now, how about some of those lemon shortbread cookies we picked up at breakfast? That would go nicely with this hot chocolate here, I reckon.'

Gayle sits silently while Mike hunts around for the cookies.

You're weak and pathetic and a terrible mother and you deserve for Noah to never speak to you again.

Loretta

The pain in Loretta's fingers is almost too much to bear. She rubs cream into her swollen, misshapen joints. Alberto keeps buying this lavender cream for her from the Rialto. She's convinced it does nothing to help, but the jar sits on her bedside table so she uses it anyway.

Alberto watches her from his side of the bed, where they've come for an afternoon rest. 'Ezio makes very good dough. Let Rocco bring some back for you next time you want to make pizza. All this kneading is too much for you.'

'Listen to me, Alberto, don't ever talk to me about Ezio and his dough again. If I have to hear one more time how good Ezio's dough is, I swear on Santa Maria, I'll throw myself off the balcony.'

She knows he's right. Ezio Tricholli has a reputation throughout Venice for his delicious pizza bases, parbaked overnight and sold at the market every morning.

Loretta's been making pizza in the restaurant less and less over the last two years as osteoarthritis has ravaged her. But this morning she wanted to show Sophie how she makes it, to share with the readers of her magazine. Now she's paying the price. She takes a painkiller, then another.

The pain is worse than usual. Is God punishing her for what she did yesterday? *Thou shalt not commit adultery.* She deserves this pain and more. Regardless, she can't bring herself to regret it. Those stolen moments with Flavia will be treasured forever. If only the nosy old Americans hadn't ruined everything.

Loretta was convinced Signore Dawson would tell Alberto or, God forbid, post about it on social media. But it's been over twenty-four hours since he caught her, and it appears that so far he's kept quiet.

'At least let one of the boys do the kneading part for you.' Alberto pulls her from her thoughts. 'Your hands are so red.'

Alberto's right. Rocco and Salvatore are more than capable. It isn't exactly a fine art.

'People like it my way.'

'Why are you this stubborn?' he complains.

Loretta's nonna taught her how to knead. One of her earliest memories is of standing on a stool in the kitchen, her hands deep in the warm mixture of flour, yeast, oil and salted water, with Nonna right beside her.

'I've been making dough my whole life,' she replies. 'I'm not ready for that part of me to die yet.'

Alberto doesn't answer. His eyes are closed and he's breathing deeply. *Men!* Where are their thoughts when they lie down? Do they even have any?

She puts the lid back on the jar of cream and examines her hands, ugly and weathered. These hands have created food for decades, they've nursed and loved two babies. These hands have also loved in other ways, they've stroked and teased. They were once beautiful hands, with smooth skin and long lean fingers. Now her wedding rings don't fit over her inflamed knuckles, so she wears them on a chain instead, along with the pendant of the Madonna and the ruby ring from a long time ago. The ruby is a constant reminder of the life she once lived with Flavia, of the love that once sustained her.

She reads the message on her phone for what feels like the hundredth time today. Each time it's aroused her more and more.

I'm leaving the rectory tomorrow.

I told them I have a cousin to stay with,
but I'm booking into Hotel Mondo.

Come! We have three days before I
leave for the Vatican.

Once Flavia leaves, Loretta will go back to being the dutiful wife and mother and hotel owner everyone depends on. Before that, for a precious few days, she'll let herself experience the love she's fantasised about for decades.

Careful to move quietly, she leaves the bedroom and walks into the lounge, where the wall unit stands. The antique piece of furniture, fully restored by Alberto, belonged to her great-grandparents. At the back of the second drawer in the wall unit, she finds what she's looking for: an old cloth-bound album. She sits the album on her lap and takes her time with each page. The black and white photos are faded but the memories are there. Time has done nothing to dim them. She touches each photo, her fingers lingering over them.

How different would her life have been if Flavia hadn't left? She would never have become a mother, never become Signora Bianchi. She can't wish away those things. And despite his innate ability to drive her completely crazy simply by breathing, she loves her husband. She could never wish him away from her life either.

'What are you doing?' Alberto's voice makes her jump.

'I thought you were sleeping,' she says.

He moves closer and sees the album open to a photo of Flavia, in a fitted paisley shirt and flared jeans, her wavy hair falling to her waist, laughing at something out of view.

'Ah, Loretta.' His voice is soft. 'Why do you sit here and cry instead of resting your eyes?'

She wipes her tears away. 'I don't know.'

He gently takes the album from her. She doesn't resist. Without a word, he puts it back in the drawer. 'Shall we go for our walk? I've had enough sleep.' He holds his hand out.

She nods and lets him help her off the couch. 'Stay there,' he says. 'I'll get your things.'

He comes back into the room with her coat and gloves. He walks to her and takes both of her hands in his, lifting them up to his lips, and he plants warm kisses on her sore fingers.

She puts on her gloves, knowing she'll never deserve him. 'Let's go and look at the drowning woman,' she says.

Together, they stroll to the piazza. Alberto hums as they walk.

'Is it even worth me arguing with you today about going back to hospital for the surgery you need?' Loretta asks.

'Look at this. Is this a man who needs his heart operated on?' He lets go of her hand, jogs a few steps ahead of her, then jumps off to the side, clicking his heels together. It's a less than graceful movement and he lands clumsily, but the fact he even managed such a trick at his age impresses her.

'Idioto.' She laughs for the first time today.

She keeps her head down as they make their way to Piazza San Marco, avoiding eye contact with the shopkeepers and cafe owners she knows, ignoring the tourists who fill the streets. The only person she's interested in seeing is the woman in the tank. Magdalena makes her feel understood, like she can see into her soul.

The crowd around the artist is huge today, but when Loretta stands near the pillar on the stairs of the piazza, Magdalena finds her almost instantly and holds her hand up to the glass. The water reaches her chest and her once-white dress is now a filthy grey. Loretta holds her hand up for a few seconds. It's become their language.

Alberto snorts, bemused, and pulls out a cigarette.

The people around Magdalena are in a frenzy. The piazza is heaving. There are camera crews, and people jostle each other to get closer.

'Excuse me, do you know what is happening over there?' Loretta asks a woman standing on the step below her.

'George and Amal Clooney are here,' the woman replies. 'See them, over on the left there?' She points and then whips her head back around to Loretta, her eyes widening. 'Wait! Are you Signora Bianchi? *Oh my God!*'

'No, but I get mistaken for her often.' Loretta's not in the mood for selfies.

The woman turns back to gawk at the movie stars.

Loretta sees them. They're standing a short distance away from the tank, with their backs to Magdalena and microphones in their faces. George looks older than he does on the screen and is shorter than she imagined him to be. Amal is staggeringly beautiful. Even from a distance, and dressed casually in jeans and sweaters, the pair exudes star power.

She remembers the euphoria when George and Amal were married in Venice. The buzz in the air is no less now than it was then. Alberto stands on his toes to get a better look at them. Loretta should be excited too – Hollywood is here to bring attention to Venice's plight.

But she can't get excited, because there's an anguished look in Magdalena's eyes. Even though the chaos around her is the exact thing she set out to achieve, the days of standing for hours on end in the dirty, cold water are clearly taking their toll on her. And she's only halfway through her performance. *Affogando*.

Loretta wants to help her. But what can she do? Nothing. So she offers Magdalena support the only way she can, by holding her hand up in the air again. Magdalena does the same and the two women stand apart but together, pretending to touch. Their connection transcends the crowd and the distance between them, transporting Loretta back to when she first saw Magdalena in this very square, twenty years ago.

Already world-famous by then, Magdalena Jansen had left her home in Amsterdam and moved to the northern Italian town of Budrio. That year, she opened a new exhibition in San Marco. The exhibition's proximity to the basilica was causing all kinds of controversy, considering its theme – confession.

Magdalena had set up a confessional in a small tent in the middle of the piazza. The tent was bare inside apart from two whitewashed wooden chairs facing each other. Magdalena sat on one chair and visitors to the exhibition were invited to enter one at a time to sit on the other. The exhibit was titled 'The Keeper of Secrets', the concept being that Magdalena would listen to each person's confession without handing out any penance in the way Catholic priests did. The idea was that the act of confessing, in and of itself, was enough. Magdalena silently sat on her chair, with a promise to keep the sinful secrets of those who paid the twenty-five euro entry for five minutes alone with her.

Loretta was of course outraged at the blasphemy of it. But she was also fascinated. On a warm June afternoon, when the children were at school – this was before the hotel had a restaurant, when she had more free time – she went to the piazza and waited in line for almost an hour until it was her turn to confess.

She walked into the tent thinking that if she told the artist she still loved Flavia despite having been married to Alberto for fifteen years by then, if she got that off her chest, the guilt might abate, even just a little, enough to finally start feeling settled in the life she'd chosen.

The tent curtain closed behind Loretta, and she and Magdalena were alone. It was warm in there, too warm. A pedestal fan in the corner pushed the hot air around. Magdalena motioned for Loretta to sit, so she did, feeling herself blush. She gave Magdalena a questioning look. 'Do I start?' she asked in Italian.

Magdalena smiled without showing her teeth, tilting her head slightly. Her eyes were a deep dark brown and her skin was pale. Her waist-length straight hair had to be dyed white, as she was too young to have greyed naturally back then; she couldn't have been over twenty-five. She was thin and tall, and her posture was regal, legs crossed at the ankles, hands clasped in her lap. She had on a flowing white dress, her trademark look, which reached the floor. No jewellery. Neither her fingernails nor toenails were painted. A barefaced, barefoot angel, waiting to hear Loretta's secrets.

So Loretta told her about the woman she loved who ran away to the convent and left her heartbroken. She told her about the arranged marriage to a fun-loving, gentle man who loved her, and the gorgeous twins who filled her days with light. She told her how much she still ached for the nun and how guilty it made her feel.

She watched Magdalena's face as she spoke, expecting her to react, but her expression didn't change. Her serene smile stayed fixed. Loretta was both unnerved and encouraged by her silence, and she found herself telling Magdalena things she hadn't even admitted to herself before.

'It's only out of duty that I attend Mass. It tears me up inside every time I have Holy Communion. I'm not worthy of receiving the body of Christ. The eucharist is for those who go to confession, but of course I can't bring myself to go. Can you imagine me telling a priest any of this?'

Magdalena kept smiling.

Loretta continued. 'Whenever I enter a church these days there's a sick churning in my stomach. Church used to be my place of solace, but that's ruined now. Loving her has ruined everything.' Her eyes began to sting. 'And what's killing me is that no matter how much I love my children and my husband, part of me always dreams of escaping, of going to find her. Of course, I'd never do that. I'd never abandon my family, but I wish I was satisfied with the life I have instead of always pining for another.' Her voice broke.

A bell rang outside the tent. Loretta's time with Magdalena was up.

Magdalena's performance was billed as silent, but just before Loretta exited the tent, Magdalena cleared her throat. 'Be true to yourself, signora.' Her voice was soft and clear, her accent foreign.

Loretta turned. 'What do you mean? What are you suggesting?'

But Magdalena shut her mouth and smiled her serene smile again. A security guard held the door of the tent open for Loretta to step back out into the sun.

Now, all these years later, Magdalena watches Loretta standing in the same piazza, with her husband by her side. Magdalena's presence in Venice the very same week as Flavia's return can't be coincidental. Loretta's certain it was preordained. This is how it was always meant to be.

Yesterday, Loretta left Flavia in the church in a frantic rush, determined to be back at the hotel before Signore Dawson could get to Alberto. Who knows where her kisses with Flavia would have led to if they hadn't been interrupted. Would she, the devout Catholic that she is, actually have had sex with a nun in a sacristy of all places? Surely not. But, oh, how the idea of it makes her stomach tighten with pleasure.

George and Amal Clooney have left now. The crowd around Magdalena disperses a little. Alberto cocks his arm for Loretta and together they walk back to the hotel, Alberto singing Etta James' 'At Last' to himself and Loretta dreaming about Flavia.

Sophie

Sophie hoped Rocco might spend the afternoon with her again but he's nowhere to be seen. He was quiet and distant after the drama with Elena this morning, and now he's ghosted her. Is he really that annoyed that she pushed him to talk Christian into being part of the protest? Loretta barely spoke to her today after breakfast as well, and everyone was staring at their phones through a silent lunch. Do they all hate her now?

She messages Bec about it and laughs at her reply.

For the love of God, woman, stop overthinking it.

Go shopping!

Bec makes an excellent point, so Sophie drags herself off the bed, rugs up and steps out into the laneway. There's nothing like retail therapy to soothe her rattled nerves.

Outside, San Marco is bustling. The tourists are everywhere and the sound of the gondoliers singing can be heard from the street. Sophie enters a tiny shop around the corner that sells handbags and is immediately accosted by a bony old woman who forcefully drags her by the elbow towards the foggy full-length mirror. Without asking, the woman pulls bag after bag off the shelves and drapes them over Sophie's shoulder, one at a time, grunting her approval or shaking her head with a click of the tongue at each one. Sophie wants them all!

So many bold colours and all in the softest leather. After only a few minutes, she's the proud owner of three new handbags, of which she needs precisely none.

Next door to the bag shop is a fashion boutique with a twenty-something behind the counter wearing smudged black eyeliner and dark purple lipstick. She's as friendly and welcoming as a rottweiler. It takes Sophie no more than a second to figure out that none of the clothes come in her size, so she hotfoots it out of there. She walks past a few busy souvenir shops and then stops at another small boutique.

An immaculately dressed middle-aged man with gelled dark hair and a perfectly manicured goatee steps out from behind the counter. His peach cashmere jumper is half tucked into ripped jeans and his shiny white shoes are pointy enough to take out an eye. 'Happy Christmas, signora! Have you come to find a beautiful outfit to wear for your beloved?'

'My beloved? No.' She laughs. 'Do you have anything in my size?'

'Plenty! I have plenty.' He pats a green velvet chair. 'Come, sit, sit. Prego. Let me show you what I have.' He disappears through a door leading to another room and emerges minutes later, almost toppling backwards under the mountain of clothes in his arms. 'Stand up, signora. Take off your coat. If you come into the dressing room – this way, please – I will leave these pieces for you here. You must come out and show me what you try on.'

She holds up the first outfit on its hanger and looks it up and down, unconvinced. It's a white polyester jumpsuit with flowy sleeves, wide pants and a plaited gold belt. Very ABBA, circa Eurovision Song Contest. She would never have given it a second glance back home, but it feels rude not to at least try it on. When she does, she's amazed at how comfortable it is and how phenomenal she looks in it. She's avoided wearing white for a decade – too unflattering for her figure, she was told by her mother a million times over. But the colour's perfect on her. And she can pull off a jumpsuit! Who knew?

'I *love* this!' she calls out from the dressing room.

'Show me, show me!' her new shopping husband shouts.

She opens the door and gives him a twirl.

He lets out a low whistle. '*Wow, wow, wow!* Now this one, you must have! What size shoe, signora?'

'I'm a seven in Australia. What's that, a thirty-eight?'

'Let us try thirty-eight. I have just the shoe for this outfit. One second.' He disappears out the back and returns carrying a pair of patent gold ballet flats. 'Try on, please.'

Again, they're not her usual style, but the shoes fit perfectly and are so incredibly soft it's as if she's in slippers.

The shopkeeper blows a chef's kiss. 'Bellissima! You are a goddess, signora, in this outfit with your golden hair. You are only missing the jewellery.' He picks up a chunky red beaded-glass necklace from a jewellery rack on the counter and clasps it around her neck. 'Please, signora, look in the mirror. You are beautiful. I do not lie when I say this.'

The necklace and shoes finish off the outfit perfectly. The whole look makes her feel a million dollars.

Sophie's been wearing the same style of clothes since her university days: structured A-line dresses that fall below the knee, worn with light cardigans and Mary Janes in summer and belted trench coats and boots in winter. She's embraced the quirky vintage look by curling her hair and wearing bright red lipstick and heavy eye make-up. She's looked like this every day of her adult life. This outfit, though, has shown her she can be so much more than a plus-size throwback to the fifties.

She sends a photo of herself to Bec, who immediately replies with a string of fire emojis.

Look at you!

Never seen you in pants, I LOVE IT!

'Try on the other pieces, signora.' The man holds the dressing room door open and gestures for her to go back inside.

She points to a salmon pink wrap dress on the seat of a thousand dresses he's brought for her to try on. 'I like the look of this one. How much is it?'

'Please, signora, it is impolite for us to discuss money. All the pieces are designed here in Venice. It is money well spent.'

Holy shit. This dude's going to bankrupt me.

'What's your name?' she asks him.

'My name is Massimo.'

'Signore Massimo, let's do this!' She pulls the pink dress off its hanger.

Anything to support the Venetians.

Loretta

'Amal Clooney's personal assistant is on the phone. She wants to book out the entire restaurant for them tonight,' Marina announces.

'For who?' Loretta asks.

'For Amal and George, obviously.'

Loretta wipes her cocoa-covered hands on her apron. 'No bookings.'

'She said they're prepared to pay three times what we'd make if we opened to the public.'

These types of calls come whenever the rich and famous are in town. They know the walk-ins only rule, of course they do. It's part of the character that's made Loretta's little restaurant so popular. But these people think the rules don't apply to them. The very last thing she feels like doing is fawning over Hollywood types.

'No bookings,' Loretta repeats.

'The Clooneys are here for the exhibition, Mamma. They're doing a good deed, promoting our cause.'

'I know, I saw them in the piazza, posing like peacocks.'

'You saw them? Why didn't you say anything?'

'What was there to say?'

Marina rolls her eyes. 'Maybe just this once, we should let them have the restaurant, as a gesture of goodwill.'

Loretta sighs. 'Child, we have enough fish here to feed over fifty people. *Goodwill* means opening our doors to everyone. I won't waste good food so we can indulge an ageing actor and his do-gooder wife. Tell them no bookings.'

'You're impossible!' Marina throws her hands in the air. Her face is almost as red as her glasses' frames. 'Papà, please explain to her that this is one of the most powerful couples in the world. Having them eat here is a big deal. It would be *so* good for business. Tell her!'

'No bookings.' Alberto doesn't look up from where he's sitting polishing the silver candlesticks.

Loretta has a sudden surge of love for him. He always has her back, always. The guilt stabs her heart.

Marina swears under her breath and leaves.

Minutes later, Sophie walks into the kitchen, wearing a lime-green crossover top with a pink and black leopard-print skirt. The whole outfit hugs her body like a second skin. It's nothing like the conservative vintage dresses she's worn since she arrived in Venice, and she oozes a new confidence. She's ravishing, there's no other word for her. And she's showing so much cleavage, Rocco's eyes might just fall out of his head when he sees her.

Loretta hasn't forgotten how Rocco ignored her advice this morning about Elena and instead followed Sophie's orders. Sophie's influence on him alarms her. She can only hope her son will bounce back from the hurt that's sure to be coming his way once she leaves, and that he doesn't spiral again.

'Marina just told me you knocked back George and Amal Clooney.' Sophie's green eyes are sparkling. 'That's definitely making it into my feature.'

Loretta smiles at her. 'Very good.'

'Do you think they'll turn up for dinner anyway?' Sophie says.

Loretta shrugs. 'If they do, I am saving the smallest pieces of fish for them and the oldest-looking parsnips. Imagine trying to close a restaurant because you think you are too important to eat with other people. Cretini.'

Sophie hoots, and even after the emotionally gruelling day she's had, Loretta laughs too. She gave Sophie the cold shoulder today after she inserted herself so forcefully in Elena's business, but she can't stay mad at this girl. Sophie is just too loveable. It's no wonder Rocco's fallen for her so fast.

Sophie pulls out her camera and photographs Alberto polishing the candlesticks.

'Alberto, go upstairs and rest,' Loretta says. 'You have not had enough rest today.'

'Are you coming with me?' he asks her.

'I want to visit Anna-Maria Zanetti quickly, before dinner.'

He raises his eyebrows. 'Davvero?'

'Yes, really,' she replies in Italian, breaking her own rule of only speaking English in front of Sophie. 'Why shouldn't I visit her? Isn't she my friend whose husband died?'

'And when was the last time you visited this *friend*?'

'Mind your own business and stop polishing candlesticks that don't need polishing just so you can be here to annoy me.' She slams the tea towel on the bench, pulls her coat off the coat rack and walks out of the kitchen.

'Where are you going *now*?' Marina asks as she passes the reception desk.

'Why do I need to report my movements to everyone in this place?' Loretta snaps at her. 'I'll be back for dinner, that's all you need to know.'

She wishes she could go to Flavia. It's killing her knowing Flavia has been so close by all day without having seen her. But she can't be disappearing from the hotel all the time, and she absolutely has to see Anna-Maria Zanetti and help in any way she can, before Anna-Maria loses another child to tragedy. She walks quickly along the lanes, stopping to talk to no one until she arrives at the canal, where she catches the boat to Cannaregio and watches San Marco disappear from view.

It's been more than a decade since Loretta last saw Anna-Maria, at Paolo's funeral. Loretta and Anna-Maria were once the closest of friends, but after Paolo died, Loretta quietly disappeared from

Anna-Maria's life. She justified it to herself by thinking that her continued presence in Anna-Maria's life, flaunting her son of the same age who was still very much alive, would only serve as a painful reminder to Anna-Maria of what she had lost. But the truth of it was that Loretta couldn't bear to be around the other woman's boundless grief. Over the years, the guilt gnawed away at her in a subtle-enough way that she was able to bury it, but Elena's return to Venice has changed that.

Loretta hasn't had reason to go to the Jewish Quarter since her friendship with Anna-Maria ended. When she reaches Campo di Ghetto Nuovo, she's shocked by how authentically Venetian it still is, how little it's changed all these years. There are still tourists, of course, and it's brimming with souvenir shops, but most of the people in the square are obviously locals. There are children everywhere, kicking footballs and riding scooters. It fills her heart to find a part of Venice where Italians still live.

The old men still sit under the canopies and have an ombra, just like they used to when she was young. This reminds her to tell Sophie, who loves to know the meaning behind everything, that 'ombra' means shade, but it's also the Venetian word for a small glass of wine in the afternoon because the fishermen in the old days used to gather under the shade of the clock tower when their work for the day was done, and a man would be waiting with his wine cart to serve them a drink. This thought distracts her until she arrives at Anna-Maria's apartment building, where she says a quick prayer to the Blessed Virgin before she begins the long climb up the concrete stairs to the fourth floor.

Loretta rarely cries – it's never been who she is – but this week she's shed more tears than she has in years. When Anna-Maria opens her front door and Loretta sees how the grief has ravaged her friend, her tears start up again.

Anna-Maria's eyes widen. 'Loretta Bianchi? It's really you?'

'Mi dispiace, mi dispiace,' Loretta sobs as Anna-Maria gathers her in her arms.

Anna-Maria welcomes Loretta into her home with a grace and kindness she doesn't deserve. 'What are you doing here?' Anna-Maria says once they're sitting in the lounge room that's barely changed in all these years.

'I want to help you and Elena with the escape.'

Anna-Maria's eyes bulge. 'How do you know?'

'She asked us to help her.'

'She came to you to ask for help?'

'They're staying with us.'

Anna-Maria's jaw drops. 'She didn't say. There's so much I don't know.' She begins to weep.

Loretta cries with her while they talk about Anna-Maria's dead son and her dead husband, and about her daughter who has married an evil man, about the friendship they've lost and the years they've missed.

Loretta tells Anna-Maria of the plan for Elena's escape, which will take place while Christian's at the meeting for the protest of La Befana, and of the fake pregnancy.

Anna-Maria covers her face with her hands. 'He'll never stop looking for her if he believes she's carrying his child!'

Loretta reaches for Anna-Maria's hand. 'I'm scared for you. I told the others we should call the police.'

'I told her that on the phone too, but she insists on doing it her way. They're coming for dinner tonight. I'll try and convince her again if I get a chance, but he doesn't give us a second alone.' Anna-Maria picks at imaginary fluff on her black pants. 'I don't want to leave Venice.'

'I don't understand why you have to go too?'

'She says it will be dangerous for me to stay.'

'But there are many of us who could hide you from him until he leaves,' Loretta insists.

Anna-Maria tilts her head. 'Would you let your daughter go alone?'

Loretta sighs. 'No.'

Before she leaves, Loretta helps Anna-Maria the only way she can, by pulling an envelope out of her handbag.

Anna-Maria looks inside the envelope and gasps. 'Loretta, what is this? Sei pazza.'

'It's nothing.'

Anna-Maria tries to give her back the envelope, but Loretta holds down her hand. 'I remember what it was like not to have much money. These days, I have it to spare. Let me help you. It's my way to try and make it up to you for the terrible friend I've been.'

'You don't need to make it up to me. I love you, I always have.' Anna-Maria tearfully holds the five thousand euro to her chest. 'Grazie.'

Loretta looks at her watch. 'I have to go. They'll have a stroke if I'm not back before dinner.'

'Tell me, how is dear Alberto?' Anna-Maria holds open the door for her.

'That's a story for another day.' Loretta reaches for Anna-Maria and hugs her fiercely. 'Anything you need, I'm here for you, I promise.'

'You're a good woman, Loretta.'

'Hardly.' She quickly leaves before she cries again.

Elena

As the vaporetto approaches the stop at San Marcuola, Elena sees Signora Bianchi on the platform. It's unmistakably her – tall, thin, perfect posture with her silver hair in its high bun, in jeans and a long cream coat, looking as elegant as always.

Elena remembers well how hurt Mamma was by Signora Bianchi after Paolo died. The two women haven't seen each other in years, and now here Signora Bianchi is at the Jewish Quarter. It's too coincidental for her to be here for any other reason when it was today that she found out the truth about Elena.

If Christian sees Signora Bianchi this close to Mamma's house, he'll be instantly suspicious.

'Babe.' She taps his leg. 'Let's not tell my mother about the baby yet.'

'Why not?'

'She's already grieving Papà. I don't want to give her anything else to worry about. I'd rather wait and tell her after the twelve-week scan.'

He nods. 'Fair enough.'

She touches his cheek, stroking his stubble with her fingers. 'I've got an idea. Let's not get off the boat at this stop. Let's explore somewhere new instead. I feel so happy tonight, I want to soak up more of Venice with you instead of having dinner in her apartment.'

'Are you sure?' He raises an eyebrow. 'I thought you really wanted to see her.'

The boat comes to a halt. She needs him to keep his eyes on her and not Signora Bianchi on the platform.

'I'm absolutely sure. I just want to be alone with you.' She pulls him in for a kiss.

He kisses her back with passion, his tongue darting all over her mouth.

She keeps him there, not caring who can see them, until she feels the boat pull away from the stop.

'Wow.' He exhales, chuckling. 'That was unexpected. You've gone and made me all horny now.'

The boat picks up speed, leaving Signora Bianchi far behind and out of view.

Elena thinks of Mamma, who would have prepared dinner for them and now faces another lonely night. It's worth it.

It takes every ounce of self-control for her not to wipe his saliva off her lips.

On the SEVENTH DAY *of* CHRISTMAS

Sophie

Sophie smiles as she sends Bec a photo taken in the restaurant last night of George Clooney with his arm around her.

HOLY SHIT!

They came! Did Signora Bianchi close
the restaurant for them after all?

> Nope! They came anyway. Sat at
> a table in the corner.

> When I saw them I legit nearly
> wet my pants.

Ha! What's he like?

> Old. She's a goddess though!

> Both super lovely people.

You get to have all the fun! Meanwhile
I had to WFH today neck deep in
toddler vomit.

That bloody day care centre is a cesspit
of disease.

Hey, did you see the red water in the
Grand Canal? Looked freakish on TV!

> By the time I got there after the shopping spree, it had washed away.

Totally worth it for that jumpsuit.

When the conversation with Bec ends, Sophie stays in bed with the phone in her hand and pulls a piece of loose skin from her lip until it bleeds. With a tissue pressed against the cut, she clicks on her mother's name and presses 'call'.

The phone rings.

Don't pick up. Don't pick up. Don't pick up.

'Hullo, darling!'

Fuck. 'Hey, Mum. How are things over there?'

'Well, it hasn't been too hot today so that's a start. It was thirty-eight yesterday, had the aircon on non-stop. Have you been following the news about the fires?'

'I have. It's awful.'

'I thought you might have wanted to check in with me and make sure I was okay. I can see the smoke in the sky, you know, that's how close the fires are.'

'Sorry.' In true form, it's only taken a few seconds for her mother to make Sophie feel like a terrible person, even though Penelope lives in central Melbourne, nowhere near where the bushfires have been.

'Never mind, dear,' Penelope says. 'It's good of you to finally call me. I haven't had the chance to wish you a Merry Christmas yet, Fee. It's been terribly hard to pin you down. I was just telling Lois next door, it'd be easier to arrange a private audience with the Pope than it is to speak to my own daughter on the telephone.'

'Sorry, I've been busy working.'

'Not to worry, darling, we're chatting now, aren't we? Is it nice there in Venice? Not too smelly with all that sewage?'

'What sewage?'

'You know what they say.'

'I don't, actually. Anyway, yes, Venice is beautiful. You should visit one day.'

'Oh, gosh, no, not for me. Italians are so . . . how do I put it? Well, *Italian*.' Penelope laughs.

Sophie's been on the phone to Penelope for just under a minute. Surely that's enough to count? 'Mum, I need to go, I have to help with breakfast service.'

'Oh, okay, darling, but just quickly before you go, are you being careful with what you eat over there? It's all carbs, carbs, carbs in Italy, isn't it? It's like a big carb truck coming straight at you!'

'Mum, for Christ's sake, I don't need you policing what I eat! I'm not a five-year-old.'

'Don't take the name of the Lord in vain.' Penelope's voice hardens.

Sophie stays silent.

'Come on, Fee, let's not be cross with each other. I'm only trying to help you, sweetheart. Did you have a chance to read the information I emailed you last week about the gastric sleeve surgery?'

'Yes, I got the email.'

'Oh, well, I didn't know whether you had or not, because you never replied. Anyway, it's supposed to be very good.'

'I'm not interested in surgery.'

The seconds tick by before Penelope replies. 'You're not prepared to even consider it? That's rather disappointing, to be honest.'

Sophie gulps down the hurt. 'I know you wish I was thin like you. I know I'm a disappointment. I'm sorry I got the fat genes. Sorry I turned out like Dad.'

'Don't you *ever* say that again. You're *nothing* like him.' Penelope spits out her words like cannons.

'Whatever,' Sophie says under her breath.

'I don't know why you have to take such a nasty tone.' Penelope sniffs. 'When I saw your number, I thought to myself, how lovely, I can have a good chat with my daughter. Now look what you've done. You can be very cruel, you know.'

'*I'm* being cruel?' Sophie lets out a laugh.

'And I don't know what you find so amusing either. You've ruined my day, Sophie Louise. I hope you feel better now.'

'Mum, let me make something very clear. I *never* feel better when I speak to you.'

Sophie ends the call and sobs into her hands.

Gayle

Mike's fast asleep when Gayle's phone pings with a message from Lizzie.

Mom, Noah video called me last
night. So good to see his face!

Did you know he's grown a beard?
Looks great!

How did you go talking to Pop
about him?

    Gayle's heart constricts.

                            Not as well as I hoped, sugar. Your pop
                         is set in his ways. He won't back down.

Keep trying, Mom.

    Mike opens his eyes. 'Everything okay, hon?'
    Gayle puts down the phone and pats his shoulder. 'Everything's fine. Go back to sleep.'
    He rubs his eyes and checks the digital clock on the bedside table. 'I've slept enough. I'll have a quick shower and fix us a coffee before breakfast.'
    Bolstered by Lizzie's message, she says, 'Hon, about Noah.'
    He groans. 'Again with Noah? I just opened my eyes.'

'I know you're sick of talking about it, and to be completely honest with you, so am I. But it's kept me up all night and I just have to get this out or I never will.' Her voice is shaky and her palms are sweaty. 'Noah and Lizzie video chatted yesterday. Do you know he's grown a beard? Lizzie told me just now and it's made me wonder, is his beard brown or grey or a bit of both? And I don't want to be *wondering* what my son looks like, I want to *know*. This has gone on for long enough, and I want Noah back in my life, even if that means I have to do it without you. I won't lose my son forever over this feud, I just won't. So when we get back home, I'm going to LA to see Noah, with or without you.' She's trembling all over by the time she finishes saying that.

'Huh? What do you mean? For how long?'

'As long as it takes to make things right. I'm not prepared to wait any longer for you to accept him for who he is.'

Mike's fully awake now, his eyes wide. 'You sound like you hate me.'

Her instinct is to immediately back down and apologise. 'I could never hate you. I love you dearly and I always will. But I love my son too,' she says firmly. 'It's time we admit how badly we've treated him. And I'm not just talking about the argument you had about his marriage, I'm talking about *all* of it. We never should've made him dig that hole.' She keeps her arms crossed and adds, rather unnecessarily, but it's the phrase that she can't get out of her head so she says it anyway: 'Love is love.'

'*Love is love?*' Mike spits. 'Heck, I feel like you've switched sides to join the radical left. Who's brainwashed you? Have you been listening to a podcast or something? It's that Oprah Winfrey, isn't it? Or Jon Stewart. Is it Jon Stewart?'

Gayle's cheeks burn. 'Can't I have a mind of my own?'

'But you're talking rubbish! *Love is love*. Are you going to march in Mardi Gras next?'

Gayle doesn't answer. She throws back the covers and puts on her gown and slippers.

'Where are you going?' Mike sits up, alarmed.

'I'm going to stand out in the hallway again. Don't follow me out there.'

'But I, but . . .' Mike trails off, looking lost.

Gayle resists the urge to comfort him and walks out, closing the door behind her.

Out in the hallway, she exhales and leans back against the wall. Her nerves have made her knees wobble, but she's proud of herself for finally standing up for Noah the way he deserves.

A door up the hallway opens and out walks the young Australian girl, Sophie. She doesn't see Gayle as she checks that her door is locked. Sophie is as pretty as ever with her bouncy blonde ponytail, wearing a beautiful red woollen trench coat with black tights and knee-high boots. She looks up to see Gayle and, despite the bright red lipstick and pink blush she has on, Sophie looks drawn.

'Oh, hi, Mrs Dawson.' She pins a watery smile on her face. 'Are you okay there?'

Gayle smiles back at her. 'I'm fine, thank you, sugar. Just giving Mr Dawson some time to think about his behaviour.' She can see that Sophie's eyes are wet. 'Are *you* okay? You look like you've been doing some crying there.'

'Oh, no, is it that obvious?' Sophie wipes her face. 'I'd better get my act together before I head off to the market, then.'

'Do you need a hug?'

To her surprise, Sophie nods and crosses the hallway into her waiting arms. The young woman, who's always so smiley and chirpy in the restaurant, has a good cry on her shoulder.

'There, there,' Gayle soothes. 'Is there anything I can do to help?'

Sophie pulls away. 'You already have, Mrs Dawson. Thank you. I needed that.' She sniffs and hunts for a tissue in her coat pocket.

Gayle pulls one out of her dressing gown and Sophie gratefully takes it.

'I wish I had a mum like you.' Sophie pats her face with the tissue. 'You're so kind.'

Gayle sighs. 'No, I'm not really. My youngest, Noah, wouldn't agree with you anyway.'

'Well, *I* think you're lovely.' Sophie gestures to Gayle's closed apartment door. 'I hope Mr Dawson apologises for whatever it is he's done.'

'Oh, he won't.' Gayle chuckles. 'But that's okay. It's nothing some of Signora Bianchi's breakfast cake can't fix.'

'How good is cake for breakfast, though?' Sophie smiles.

'It's the best thing ever,' Gayle agrees.

Sophie heads down the stairs and Gayle steels herself before going back into the apartment. She finds Mike sitting up in bed with his arms crossed. 'I don't like this new version of you. Not one little bit,' he says with a humph. His face is red and blotchy and his eyebrows are knitted together. 'I hate this hotel and I hate what it's done to you. I think that wicked Signora Bianchi's been a bad influence. You've changed, and I want you to change back.'

'Or you could try changing with me,' she says calmly.

Loretta

There's something wrong with Sophie. Her make-up may be perfectly applied, but it can't hide how bloodshot those pretty green eyes are. Sophie, who's always so quick to laugh, hasn't smiled once since coming back from the markets with Rocco. Elena Zanetti's sitting out in the restaurant with her husband, and Sophie, who was obsessed with her yesterday, hasn't so much as looked at her. And, just a minute ago, Sophie realised she'd left her camera up in her room. Instead of fetching it, she shrugged and said she'd get it later. That girl's camera is an extension of her hand. Things aren't right.

While Sophie's out in the restaurant, Loretta finds Rocco stacking the freezer. 'What's the matter with your friend?'

'What do you mean?'

'Don't play the idiot, you know what I mean. What's wrong with Sophie?'

He turns his attention back to the fridge. 'She said she didn't want to talk about it, so I didn't push her.'

'Cretino.' Honestly, *men*!

Sophie comes back into the kitchen and Loretta watches her as she empties scraps into the bin. Sophie's face is raw with sadness.

'Is it time to slice the meat, Zia?' Salvatore asks.

'Leave the meat for another day,' Loretta answers. 'Today we make gnocchi.'

'Gnocchi?' Alberto looks up from reading the paper. 'We just spent a fortune on veal!'

'Nobody asked your son to waste money on meat I don't want.' Loretta snaps. 'Today we make gnocchi.'

'But I've written veal on the menu,' Alberto argues. 'People will be expecting your cutlets at dinner.'

'Well, stop sitting there like your arse is glued to the chair. Go outside and change the menu!' She waves her arm at him. 'And don't even think about sneaking a cigarette out there.'

Alberto mutters under his breath as he walks out.

Sophie's a girl after Loretta's heart, one who takes comfort from preparing food. And there's no greater balm for a troubled soul than kneading warm potato dough. Loretta needs this therapy almost as much, if not more, than Sophie does today. Something has to get her through the day without her succumbing to her nerves. Tonight she will meet Flavia at the hotel.

So the veal can wait.

Loretta instructs Rocco to go back to the market for potatoes, sage and eggs. He opens his mouth to protest but she gives him a look that keeps him quiet.

'Take Sophie with you,' she says. 'Another walk in the fresh air will do her good.'

While Rocco and Sophie are at the market, Loretta and Salvatore get a head start on the cakes. Her nephew is good company; he keeps quiet and leaves her alone with her thoughts.

When Sophie and Rocco return with the produce, Alberto follows them in from the office, and Loretta announces that she wants the restaurant tables set up in a new way. 'I'm sick of the way the restaurant looks. It's been the same, year after year. I want the tables and chairs lined up in two neat rows.'

'Have you lost your mind?' Alberto says. 'Why would we make the restaurant look like an army barrack with rows of tables?'

'Why are you even still here?' she barks. 'There's nothing for you to do with your weak heart. Can't you go and find one of your friends to annoy up the street instead of staying here like a thorn in my side?'

Alberto snorts a laugh and stays exactly where he is. It's almost as if he can sense what she's planning and is determined to make her feel as guilty as possible by showing her his face all day.

'Papà's right, Mamma. The restaurant won't look good that way,' Rocco adds.

Loretta acts as if she hasn't heard them. 'Sophie, come, put on your apron. First, we boil the potatoes in their skins, and then I will show you my nonna's way to make the dough. The secret is a sprinkle of nutmeg in the flour.'

'Mamma, it will take all morning to rearrange the tables. We don't have time,' Rocco complains.

'You will have more time if you stop talking and start moving. And find the white tablecloths, I am bored with these pink ones.'

'The white tablecloths will be creased.'

'So? Iron them.' She turns her back to him. 'Salvatore, fill two of the big stockpots with salted water and put them on the stove. Then go and help Rocco.'

Rocco and Salvatore finally finish griping and leave the kitchen, followed by Alberto. Loretta works beside Sophie, filling the silence by telling her stories about the history behind some of the more popular Venetian dishes. Every dish has its own tale and Loretta knows them all. Sophie listens while they pick the sage and chop the garlic.

'Did you know, Sophie, that it took many centuries from when rice was first introduced to Venice for Venetians to actually cook it as whole grains instead of grinding it with pestle and mortar?'

'Really? I assumed risi e bisi was an ancient dish.'

'It is old enough, yes. It was the main food of the peasants from long ago. But I am talking about even before then, when the trading ships first came from the East. Venetians thought that rice could only be used if it was ground as a thickener in soups and stews. It was hundreds of years before they realised it could be cooked as a whole grain.'

'Wow! Hang on, I want to make a note of that so I don't forget it.'

While the potatoes are boiling, they sift and season the flour. When the potatoes are done, Loretta teaches Sophie how she makes the dough. She speaks to her in her gentlest tone, calm and reassuring, guiding her along. It doesn't take long for the kneading to take effect.

With egg yolk running between her fingers and her hands deep in flour, Sophie begins to cry. 'I'm sorry,' she whispers. 'I'm not myself today.'

Loretta nods and says nothing.

'I had an argument with my mother on the phone this morning. She criticised my weight. I'm a disappointment to her.'

Loretta wipes the sticky dough off her hands. She walks around to Sophie's side of the bench.

'Look at how *beautiful* you are.' She holds Sophie by the shoulders. 'You are so accomplished, so talented, so kind and intelligent. How can your mother be disappointed?'

'She literally said those words.'

'You know something, not a day goes by that I do not criticise my children. Do not mistake your mother's sharp words for what is in her heart. Trust me, I know.'

'Maybe.' Sophie sniffs.

Loretta hands her a tissue. 'Relationships between mothers and daughters are never uncomplicated.'

'I see how much love there is in your family, though, how close you all are. I'm happy for you, but it makes me so sad for myself.'

'Marina wishes for an easier mother too, believe me. Would it help you to talk to me about it?'

Sophie shakes her head. 'I wouldn't know where to start.'

'Okay, but if you change your mind, I am here.' Loretta sprinkles a handful of white flour onto the bench and spreads it around with the palm of her hand. 'Now we roll the dough into rows and cut the gnocchi, and then we make the sauce.'

Sophie wipes away her tears. 'What sauce are we making?'

'Burnt butter.'

'My favourite.'

'And mine. Rocco hates it when I make this sauce because the butter sticks to the bottom of the pots, but it is not you and I who have to do the scrubbing, so what do we care?'

It's the first laugh to come from Sophie all day. 'Do you mind if I quickly run upstairs and get my camera?'

Sophie leaves the kitchen with a spring in her step and Loretta allows herself a smile.

Rocco comes in. 'Mamma, come and see the restaurant. We've changed it the way you want. It's not so bad the new way.'

She walks into the restaurant and gives it a perfunctory glance. 'You were right, it looked better before. Change it back.'

She avoids eye contact with Alberto as she speaks. The less she sees of him today, the better.

Elena

Christian's a changed man. He's been nothing but kind and loving to Elena since the pregnancy test yesterday morning. Last night he ordered enough dinner for both of them to eat, and this morning, when Signora Bianchi brought Elena breakfast again, he didn't act annoyed. In fact, he hasn't controlled her food intake at all.

'Just promise me you'll lay off the caffeine and fried food?' was all he said last night.

It's an odd feeling, being allowed to eat. The lack of hunger pangs makes her feel as if she's in another woman's skin. She's being careful and only eating small amounts; she doesn't want her food privileges revoked if she shows too little self-control.

After breakfast, Christian asked her what she'd like to do today and when she said she wanted to spend it with Mamma, he readily agreed. She just about fell off her chair with shock.

Now they're walking through the winding streets with Mamma towards her apartment after taking a tour of the Ghetto, rugged up in their coats. The clouds are heavy and the forecast is for rain, but so far they've managed to stay dry. Mamma walks beside Elena in silence, staring ahead. Elena's dying to know what's going on in Mamma's mind.

They've exchanged a few stolen glances today where Mamma's grief and heartache have been unmasked, but she's put on a magnificent show for Christian, laughing at his jokes, impressing him with her knowledge of the Levantine architecture of the ancient synagogue they visited, finding the best coffee for him to sample from her friend Umberta's bakery on the esplanade.

It's late afternoon now. The cafes are emptying out and the shops closing up for the day as everyone prepares to welcome in a new year. When they arrive at the cold, run-down apartment building, Mamma looks at the steep stairs with a sigh.

'It's a lot for you to climb these stairs every day, Anna-Maria.' Christian performs an inspection of the ground level of the building, knocking on the stone walls. 'I wonder if we could install a lift?'

'And who'd pay for that?' Elena laughs.

He looks at her earnestly. 'Us. I want your mum to be able to come and go as she likes. She's okay for now, but these stairs will get harder for her to manage the older she gets. We can look into it. Hey, Anna-Maria!' he calls up the staircase to where Mamma's already nearing the second flight. 'Would you like a lift in this apartment building?'

'Lift?' Mamma leans on the banister. 'What is "lift"?'

'Un ascensore,' Elena translates.

'Yes, I like,' Mamma calls down. 'Is not possible. Building very old.'

'Anything's possible at the right price, Anna-Maria. Give me the name of the building manager. I'll see what I can do.' Christian smiles.

Elena shakes her head. 'You're probably looking at a million dollars minimum, you know.' She shivers. 'God, it's cold. It's a wind tunnel down here. Let's go up.'

'I get access to my trust fund when I'm thirty-five next year, remember? A million's a drop in the ocean once that money's ours.'

'I forgot about that,' she says truthfully.

'You forgot?' He snorts. 'Isn't that the reason you married me?'

She laughs and he takes her hand.

'Ellie, I want to do this for your mum.'

'It's a nice thought. But dealing with Italian bureaucracy and tradespeople – you have no idea how hard it will be.'

'I'm a tenacious man when I want something, babe. I always get what I want. And I want to look after your mum. She's important to you, so she's important to me too.'

Today has reminded her of what Christian was like when she first fell for him – generous, warm, charming, funny. But as chivalrous as he's being about installing the lift, it's something he won't have to worry about. Mamma will be long gone by then and so will she.

Gayle

Gayle and Mike aren't going to the New Year's Eve fireworks. Mike's been in a mood all day, and even though the fireworks were a highlight on their itinerary, he's just announced that he doesn't feel like it any more.

'Why would I want to go out and celebrate a new year when it's the year my wife will leave me for LA?' he mutters.

'Hon, I'm hardly leaving you! I'm going to visit Noah is all. Please, won't you come with me? You know I want you there. All you have to do is tell him you're sorry.'

'I'm not compromising my values.' He huffs and walks into the bathroom, closing the door behind him with more force than necessary.

It's forecast to rain tonight. The esplanade is sure to be overcrowded with thousands of tourists and Gayle has a splitting headache. So she isn't upset to be missing the fireworks, but what is upsetting her is the friction she's brought into their marriage.

If she had stayed in her lane and not gone against Mike's wishes as the head of the house, they wouldn't have had this terrible simmering tension between them all day. Mike would be excitedly making sure his fanny pack had all the supplies it needed for their midnight outing to the esplanade. Instead, as they've explored more of Venice today, their walks have been mostly silent and any conversation stilted and awkward.

Mike's her best friend in the whole world. Even though he's been right by her side today, she's missed him – their easy camaraderie, their closeness. But she's determined to make things right with Noah and nothing will stop her now, not even this uneasiness in her marriage.

Mike emerges from the bathroom and scowls at her before climbing into bed.

'You want me to bring you your iPad, hon, so you can post your final blog of the year?' she offers.

'May as well. The kids would be mighty disappointed if I didn't.' He gives her a sideways glance. 'Should I write that you're going to LA without me?'

'I haven't even told Noah I'm coming to visit yet. Besides, the blog's for you to share the daily adventures with the children. Why don't you go ahead and tell them about the museum we visited or the art gallery? You might even like to mention those amazing crepes we had this afternoon.'

He softens a little. 'I did enjoy the crepes.'

'There you go.' She hands over the iPad and slides under the covers next to him.

'Thank you,' he mumbles. No matter how put out Mike may be, he never forgets his manners.

As he starts to type, Gayle stares at the picture frame in their room. It contains the prayer of St Francis of Assisi. Mike was annoyed by the idolatry of it and was going to complain when they first arrived. 'It's bad enough we've got that painting out in the hall of the Pope to contend with, and now they're pushing their paganism on us good Christian folk paying for a private suite?'

She'd convinced him to let it go; she didn't want to get off on the wrong foot with the Bianchis. Now, she reads the words of the prayer for the first time.

Lord, make me an instrument of your peace. Where there is hatred, let me sow love.

It's as if the Lord is speaking to her directly through the words of a Catholic saint.

'Blog's done. Do you want to read what I've written or not?' Mike says gruffly.

'Of course I do. I love reading your blogs.'

He passes her the iPad.

She smiles at his description of the art at the Peggy Guggenheim collection they visited.

I'm sorry, but painting six squares in different shades of brown isn't what I'd rate as art. I could've painted that in first grade. I asked for a refund and the wiry young man on the front desk, who looked like Stalin, rudely refused.

She reads the rest of the blog, suggesting an edit or two, enough for him to see that she takes her role as a proofreader seriously, but not so many changes as to cause offence. She's caused enough offence already for one day.

When she's finished, he makes the blog go live and then turns the iPad off.

'Want to watch something on TV?' she asks.

He shakes his head, still scowling. 'I want to go to sleep and put this rotten day behind me.'

Her heart squeezes to see him so unhappy. 'You know I love you as much as I ever have, don't you, hon? But I need to make amends with Noah for my spirit to be at peace.'

'Why couldn't he have just been like the others?' he complains.

'It's not the way God made him,' she says gently.

He blows through his nose. 'God doesn't make mistakes.'

'*Exactly.*' She meets his eye.

'I don't want to talk about this any more.' He reaches for the light switch and plunges the room into darkness. 'Happy New Year then,' he grumbles.

'Happy New Year, hon,' she says with a heavy heart.

She lies awake thinking about how she can't let them enter a new year – a new decade – this way. It's not right. God wants her to sow love. No matter how much they disagree about Noah, she needs to be an instrument of peace in their marriage.

'Hon,' she whispers. 'Would you like to make love?'

He sharply inhales. 'You tryin' to make me less mad at you?'

'Yes,' she admits with a chuckle.

'It ain't that simple.'

'I know. But I love you and I want us to feel close again.'

He doesn't answer.

She rolls onto her side, facing him. 'What do you say?'

He sighs. 'It's been so long since we did it. I haven't packed the pills. Didn't think I'd be needing them.'

She smiles in the dark. 'I packed them.'

He switches the light back on and turns to face her, squinting. 'Did you really?'

She cradles his face in her hands and nods. 'You were bringing me to this romantic city. I thought we might want some romance ourselves while we were here.' She wiggles her eyebrows, and he smiles for the first time all day. 'Wait right there.' She climbs out of bed and hunts around in the small vinyl medicine bag inside her suitcase, finding what she's after.

Mike takes the pill from her hand and gulps it down with a big mouthful of water from the glass on his bedside table, dribbling some onto his pyjama shirt. 'Come here, then,' he says gruffly, taking her into his arms. He kisses her fully on the mouth.

Even after all these years together, Gayle's heart still beats faster when his lips touch hers. Maybe this is the cure for the cancer growing in the marriage – less talking, more loving.

He pulls away suddenly. 'This doesn't mean I'm not upset with you for siding with Noah.'

'I know,' she says breathlessly as she undoes the buttons of his pyjamas as fast as her fingers let her.

His breath quickens and he slides his hands under her nightdress. 'As long as you know I'm still mad.'

'Gotcha.'

He kisses her again and she kisses him back, the tickle of his beard on her skin filling her with desire. They neck like teenagers while they wait for the magic pill to take effect and make Mike young again.

LORETTA

Loretta lies in the dark and waits. Soon Alberto's snoring. He never wakes once he's asleep. Both of the children are out. Rocco has taken Sophie to the cinema at the Lido, and Marina is out with friends. The coast is clear.

Quietly, she dresses in the dark and slips out of the apartment, taking her coat, headscarf and gloves from the hatstand by the front door before she leaves.

The hotel is silent, the hum of the bar heater along the walls of the hallway the only noise. She avoids the eyes of il Papa.

Downstairs, she applies lipstick, gives her hair a quick going over with spray and dabs perfume on her wrists. She looks at herself in the mirror; her skin's glowing. The adrenaline rush has made her look younger.

You deserve this, she tells herself. *You deserve to have passion.*

Her insides are dancing.

The streets of San Marco are abandoned – everyone's at the lagoon for New Year's. Flavia's hotel is far enough away for Loretta not to be friends with the owners but close enough to be within walking distance. The clouds are full of promise for rain, not an ideal night for fireworks. She hurries, walking fast to beat the predicted downpour.

This evening's dinner service felt interminable. She was so jittery that she was almost twitching in front of the guests. Alberto was in such a joyful mood, walking between the tables wishing every diner 'buon anno!'

Loretta might be the face of the hotel, but Alberto is its heartbeat. Even this week, when he's officially been off work, his presence at mealtimes continues to make Il Cuore what it is.

It felt like it took an age for the clean-up to be over and their evening shows to be watched, for their showers to be taken and for Alberto to finally, finally fall asleep.

Loretta can't remember the last time she walked these streets alone at night. Without the flavour and colour of the day, San Marco's beauty in the dark is more of an echo than a shout. She loves this district, this city, she loves it deep in her bones.

People are shocked when they hear she's never lived anywhere else except at Il Cuore from the day she was born, but she wouldn't have it any other way. How lucky she is to have lived a life with the water as much a part of her as the blood running through her veins. She knows every building, every piazza, like she knows her own body. Venice is in her skin.

She turns a corner and walks past Chiesa di Santo Stefano, the huge stone church where the twins were baptised, and she's hit with a memory so powerful it knocks the wind out of her: Alberto standing on the pavement where she now walks, juggling a twin in each arm and beaming at her.

'Loretta!' he'd called out to her as their family and friends flowed out onto the church steps after the service. He planted a fat kiss on Rocco and Marina's chubby cheeks.

The twins were three months old, in matching satin bonnets and billowing white gowns. Both of them were delighted to be bounced around on their papà's hips on that sunny spring day.

'Look what you gave me! Which man could ever ask for more?' He laughed with unbridled joy.

Loretta looks away from the church and hurries on towards the hotel where Flavia waits.

As she crosses over a footbridge, a neon sign from Ristorante Sale e Pepe catches her eye. It was a newly opened restaurant when Alberto brought her here, the talk of the town with three Michelin stars and a celebrity chef who hailed from Naples. It was hard to get into, but Alberto had booked well in advance.

She remembers him sitting opposite her at one of its terrace tables, celebrating their twenty-fifth wedding anniversary. He had greased back his thinning hair and placed a rose in the buttonhole of his suit jacket. She'd laughed and asked if he was hoping to meet someone new with all the effort he was putting in.

He laughed back. 'When you're married to the most beautiful woman in Italy, perhaps in the world, and you look like a slapped arse ninety-nine per cent of the time, then for one per cent of the time you should make an effort.'

Holding her hand across the candlelit table that night, he looked earnestly into her eyes. 'When we met, you asked me if I was prepared to marry a broken woman and I said yes. I told you I would help you mend. I promised to make you happy. Have I made you happy, Loretta? Have I helped you mend?'

What had she answered? She can't remember the exact words she used. She knows that when she answered she was thinking of Flavia and her heart ached.

Loretta's walking slows down. This city she loves is a reflection of the life she's made with Alberto. He's everywhere, he's part of the fabric of Venice – the gardens where they've taken the children, the schools they've been parents at, the markets where they do business, the cafes where they eat and the churches where they pray. He's been by her side, as solid as a rock, through financial hardship; he was her strength when she buried her adored parents; he was the one they all leaned on to pick up the pieces when their children's hearts were broken through failed relationships. It's always been Alberto. He's been happy to let her shine and take the spotlight, never jealous or threatened. He's accepted her and never judged her, even when she told him on their first blind date that she was a gay woman in need of a husband.

Alberto was a simple man looking for a wife to love, and he never asked anything of her except for her to make a home with him. The last few days she's convinced herself that her marriage is a sham. It's not. It's the most honest marriage of anyone she knows.

She's been focused on how much she deserves to be loved by Flavia, but what about Alberto? What does he deserve? Her heart is torn in two.

She reaches the street where Flavia's hotel is and stops outside for a moment before she enters the hotel lobby. It's a much larger hotel than Il Cuore. The lights are bright, there's elevator Christmas music playing and a man and woman are behind the front desk.

She sends Flavia a text: *I'm here.* Then she sits and waits with her heart galloping.

She hears the lift bell ring a minute or two later and out walks Flavia with an excited look on her beautiful face. She's dressed in lay person's clothing. Her wavy grey-blonde hair falls over her shoulders, and her slender body is hugged by a cream cable knit sweater and dusky pink jeans. She looks like a woman in her forties, not her sixties, and Loretta's filled with a deep visceral longing.

Flavia smiles at her and all Loretta wants to do is take her to bed.

When Flavia reaches her, they keep their distance, aware of the hotel staff watching them. Loretta's hiding under an oversized coat and a headscarf, but she could still be easily recognisable.

'Che bella,' Flavia says softly, homing in on Loretta's mouth. 'Come upstairs?' Her eyes are hazy and her intentions are clear.

The air is thick between the two of them.

Loretta gulps. 'I can't do this, I'm sorry.'

'What do you mean?'

'I came to tell you that I can't cheat on my husband.' The words feel caught in her throat.

'But I thought you wanted this? The other day at the church . . . your text messages.'

Loretta looks away from her, unable to maintain eye contact and stay strong. 'I want you, I do. But I can't.'

'One night, Loretta.' Flavia's voice wobbles. 'Give me one night. That's all. I can leave tomorrow, first thing.'

Loretta shakes her head. 'I can't, amore.'

Flavia blinks away tears. 'I understand.'

'You don't hate me?'

'How could I ever hate you?' Flavia whispers. 'Will you at least come for a walk with me if you won't come upstairs?'

'Yes.'

'Let me get my coat.'

Flavia returns in a grey knitted beanie and woollen coat, and Loretta's stomach flips upon seeing her again. It's all she can do not to reach out for her.

Together the women leave the hotel, walking a respectable distance apart. The rain has held off and they find a bench further up the street, overlooking a small canal. A streetlamp above them illuminates the water. They sit close together.

'Can I hold your hand at least?' Flavia asks.

Loretta shakes her head and keeps her hands inside her coat pockets.

Flavia sighs. 'Are you going to explain this change of heart to me?'

Loretta stares at the water lapping against the apartment block on the opposite side of the canal. 'Can we just leave it at I love you, but I'm married?'

'We can.'

They sit in silence for a while.

'Do you still sing?' The steam that Flavia breathes glows in the dark night.

'No. Not since we broke up really. I left the choir when you left.'

'That makes me sad to hear. Your voice is so beautiful.'

Loretta's cheeks warm at the compliment. 'Alberto loves to sing. He's filled our home with music. It's enough.'

'You don't sing together?'

'No. Never.' She swallows. 'Do you still sing?'

Flavia lets out a giggle. 'I'm a nun, cara. Of course I sing. We sing every day.'

'I always loved your voice.' Loretta still doesn't trust herself to look at her and not kiss her. So she reaches for her medallion inside her top.

'Is that the pendant of the Madonna your nonna gave you? You still have that?' Flavia asks.

'Of course I do.' Loretta pulls it out to show her.

'Oh, Loretta, you still carry my ring. And this is your wedding ring?' Flavia holds the chain in her hand, her breath hot near Loretta's neck.

Loretta nods. 'My fingers are swollen. I can't wear rings any more.'

Flavia examines the medallion. 'I remember this pendant so clearly. It hasn't changed and neither have you. Whenever you were nervous, you'd reach for it and you still do.'

'The Madonna brings me comfort.'

Flavia lets go of the pendant and, turning to face the water again, lets out a long sigh. 'Can I ask you something? Do you ever wonder if it's even true?'

'If what's true?' Loretta says.

'The Madonna. The annunciation, the virgin birth, all of it.'

'What are you talking about? Of course it's true.'

'Is it, though?' Flavia stretches her legs out long, and Loretta's drawn to their shapeliness. The desire inside her intensifies.

'Do you know what happened to girls in Jesus' time who became pregnant out of wedlock?' Flavia asks, drawing Loretta back to the conversation about the Madonna. 'They were stoned to death. I mean, what would you do if you were Mary's mother, and it became obvious your daughter was pregnant and the man she was betrothed to swore the baby wasn't his?'

Loretta winces at Flavia's casual use of 'Mary', like she's any regular person, not the Blessed Virgin. She clutches the pendant and stays silent.

'Isn't it possible,' Flavia says, 'living in an era where the obsession among Jews was the impending arrival of a Messiah, that a devout Jewish mother, familiar with scripture and trying to protect her daughter from certain death, would call this pregnancy a miracle, a gift from God, and convince her daughter that this is what it was?'

Loretta looks hard into Flavia's eyes. She's not joking. Loretta can't quite believe what she's hearing. 'Where's this coming from? I don't understand what's happening.'

'I'm sorry.' Flavia bites her lip. 'I know this is hard for you to hear. I remember well how deep your devotion to Mary was. But I need to share my doubts with someone, and I can't speak to any of the sisters at the convent, obviously.'

'I didn't know you had any doubts.'

'I'm crippled by them.'

'But, cara, what you're saying about the Blessed Virgin doesn't even make sense. The Angel Gabriel came to Saint Joseph in a dream and told him it was God's baby. It wasn't just the Madonna who said so.'

Flavia clears her throat. 'Isn't it possible that Joseph, who by all accounts was a good and decent man, took pity on Mary and agreed to this story and to say he was the father to save her life?'

'So everyone's lying? The Blessed Virgin, Saint Anne, Saint Joseph?' Loretta scoffs. 'Who was the father, then? If you're saying the virgin birth was a lie and that it wasn't Saint Joseph's baby either, then who was the father?'

'I don't know. Back then, girls were married by the time they were fourteen at the latest, which would have made Mary twelve or thirteen when she fell pregnant. Maybe it was her own father, or another relative, a soldier. It could've been anyone.' Flavia sounds as if she's talking about characters on a television show, not the blessed event of the immaculate conception. 'Whoever the father was, though, Mary wasn't at an age where she would have *wanted* to have sex.'

Flavia stops talking as a young couple walk past, rugged up in coats and hand in hand, talking to each other in German.

Loretta waits for them to be out of earshot before she speaks. 'Are you suggesting that the Mother of God was *raped*?' Her mouth is quite suddenly dry. She finds it hard to believe she started out this evening thinking she'd be in Flavia's bed and instead they're out here on a cold bench in the dark arguing about theology.

'I think it's a plausible explanation,' Flavia replies. 'More plausible, at least, than the story the church has come up with.'

Loretta shakes her head in disbelief. 'How can you say these things? How can you even think them? Of course the Madonna was a virgin, that's what makes her holy! You're a *nun* and you don't believe such a miracle is possible?'

Flavia takes a while to answer. Her eyes search Loretta's. 'What if there's no miracle? What if instead of a miracle, our entire religion was founded on a lie? What if I left our life together, our beautiful perfect life'—her voice breaks—'for something that's not even real?'

Loretta's heart softens. 'Oh, Flavia. You didn't waste your life. You've been in service to God. There's no higher calling.'

'I just don't know.' Flavia begins to cry. 'A couple of months ago it dawned on me that I was living a lie. That none of it was real.'

'None of it?' Loretta asks her gently.

Flavia nods. 'Once I questioned one thing, I started to question everything. The more I read, the less I believed.'

'You're reading rubbish! You were chosen by God. You told me yourself how powerful and persistent that calling was until you could no longer ignore it. Don't you remember?'

'The more I think about it, the more I think that was me being fanciful.'

'You think you *imagined* a calling that made you leave everything behind and join the convent?'

Flavia nods again.

'Do you believe Jesus even existed?' Loretta's so shocked, the words are hard to get out.

'I believe he lived in the time the Bible says he did and that he died by crucifixion in his early thirties.' Flavia sounds so cold, so analytical, when discussing the Lord. 'It's not disputed that he had a big following once he began to preach publicly, and that the momentum swelled after he died. Those are the facts.'

'Facts? What about *faith*? What about the resurrection?'

Flavia doesn't blink. 'No.'

'What happened to you?' Loretta says softly.

'I think what happened to me,' Flavia says through her tears, 'is that I was so deeply indoctrinated, I devoted my whole life to a fictional story.'

Loretta stares out at the water. The silence between them lingers. After a while she says, 'What will you do? Will you leave the convent?'

'The convent is the only life I know. The Vatican is my home. I don't have the fortitude to start all over again on my own. The only way I would leave is if I had someone to start a new life with.' She pauses. 'If I had you.'

She looks at Loretta hopefully and Loretta understands then that Flavia's homecoming has absolutely nothing to do with their love. Flavia's home because she's running away. Flavia's home because she's lost. And she's looking for someone to save her.

Sophie

'Pronta?' Rocco cocks his elbow.

'Si, sono pronta. I'm ready.'

'Brava, Sophie! Your Italian impresses me.'

'Grazie mille, signore. I love that movie. Such a beautiful theatre too.' She links her arm through his.

When Rocco invited her to the movies and then to see the New Year's fireworks, he was so awkward and nervous about it that she was sure this was him asking her out on a real date. And the fact he chose a rom-com like *Sleepless in Seattle* just about confirmed to her that he had an ulterior motive.

So she dressed to the nines, curling her hair to perfection and painting her fingernails fire-engine red. Beneath her coat, she wore the sexiest of the dresses she'd bought yesterday from Massimo, a clingy plum wrap, cut extra low to show off her look-at-me cleavage.

The location of the date itself couldn't have been any more romantic – a ferry ride in the dark, flanked by the thousands of twinkling lights of the canal, out onto the Adriatic Sea to a stunning old theatre on the Lido, home of the Venice Film Festival.

But throughout the movie, Rocco kept his hands to himself. Sophie was on tenterhooks for the whole film, willing him to touch her leg, drape his arm around her, *anything*. It felt like she was back in high school, wondering if the boy she liked would ever notice her. Whenever he leaned over to whisper something in her ear, his coffee-scented breath made her stomach tighten with want. But nothing happened.

Now, as they wait for the last ferry of the night to take them back to San Marco, she's beginning to wonder whether she's imagined his whole attraction to her. Maybe she's misinterpreted his natural friendliness as something more. Perhaps this is his way with all women. Is this just what Italian men are like?

Earlier, Bec insisted she message her with every last detail once she was back from the fireworks. It's beginning to look like there's going to be nothing to report. At this rate, Rocco will give her a hearty backslap when the clock strikes twelve and be done with it.

It's eleven-thirty when the boat pulls into their stop at San Marco. She expected it to be busy around the harbour but everything's shut. 'So quiet for New Year's Eve,' she remarks.

'Everyone is on the other side, at the lagoon,' Rocco replies. 'Let's go.'

On their walk to join the throng, a light rain starts. Rocco opens his black golf umbrella and she huddles under it. Her mind wanders. She's still carrying the hurt from the phone call with her mother this morning, but being around the bustling Bianchi family all day, and a particularly wonderful session of cooking gnocchi with Loretta, has helped comfort her. Sophie's at her happiest in that kitchen.

A thought comes to her with a sudden force.

I don't want to leave Venice.

The rain gets heavier.

'This is not good for the fireworks,' Rocco says. 'The people stand so close to each other on the esplanade, like sardines. Five years ago it rained on this night, and it was a disaster. There was a stampede at the end, when all the people tried to get out of the rain quickly at the same time. Some people were hurt very badly.'

'You're not exactly selling the fireworks to me.' She laughs.

'You know, we can see them from your window. Your side of the hotel faces the lagoon. What do you think if we forget about the esplanade and go instead to the hotel?'

She doesn't need to think. Just the two of them in her room at midnight compared to getting jostled around in a crowd of thousands in the rain? 'Sounds perfect.'

'You are sure? For me, there is always next year, but this is your one chance to be here.'

It hits her again. *I don't want to leave Venice.* 'I can always come back next year.'

'Yes! Come back every year!' He stops to check his watch. 'We only have fifteen minutes. I want to show you the basilica quickly. We must walk fast to still make it back to the hotel in time.'

'I already saw the basilica the other day, remember? Let's just head to the hotel.'

'Ah, but you must see it at night in the rain. There is nothing more beautiful, I promise you.'

So they walk on to Piazza San Marco. The piazza is completely abandoned, aside from three women in their twenties taking selfies under the rows of fairy lights that hang from the eaves along the edge of the square.

Rocco points to the basilica. 'Guarda! Look! She is beautiful, eh?'

Sophie struggles to find words. Her arms are covered in goosebumps. The contrast of the black sky behind the illuminated basilica makes the building appear even bigger and whiter than it did during the day. It shines magnificently over the wet square, casting its reflection in the puddles. The basilica's opulent domes and arches and spires, all sparkling in the rain, give it a more magical appearance than a Disneyland castle.

She turns to face him. 'This is absolutely the most beautiful thing I've ever seen in my life.'

He tucks a strand of her hair behind her ear before stroking her cheek with his thumb. There's no mistaking how he's staring at her now. She hasn't imagined it this time.

'I am also looking at the most beautiful thing I have ever seen in my life.' His voice is assured and his gaze is intense. He's lost all of his dorkiness. 'I am so happy you came to Venice, Sophie. Being around you has made me feel more alive than I have in a very long time.'

'I feel the same way.' She shivers.

'You are cold?'

'No, just happy.'

'Come.' He pulls her in closer to him.

Around them, the rain pours harder. The women who were taking photos leave the piazza and walk towards the lagoon. Sophie and Rocco are all alone.

'I was beginning to wonder if you didn't actually like me after all, Signore Bianchi,' she laughs nervously.

'Like you? I fell *in love* with you from the first evening when you came to help in the kitchen.' His eyes linger on her mouth. 'Do you know how many times I have wanted to kiss you?'

'Why didn't you?'

'I had the romantic idea of the first kiss to be when the fireworks are above us, at midnight. And now midnight is only minutes away, but I cannot wait for the fireworks.' He looks at her in a way that makes her breath catch. 'I cannot wait for even one more minute.' He smiles. 'Happy New Year, Sophie.'

'Buon anno, Rocco.'

And it's there, standing in the middle of the empty piazza, holding on to each other under his big umbrella, with the night rain falling all around and the basilica shining its golden light on them, that Rocco kisses her.

Elena

The rain comes down hard on the crowd gathered by the lagoon. Christian's umbrella is knocking against the others, and Elena keeps getting bumped by the people around them.

'You all right, babe?' Christian pulls her nearer to him. 'One minute to go.'

'I'm okay.'

Elena says one last silent prayer for the decade. *Help me run, Lord.* Then she joins Christian and the thousands of people around them chanting the countdown to midnight in English. The blast of an air horn makes her jump, and everyone cheers.

'Happy New Year, Ellie!' Christian yells over the noise, leaning down to kiss her lips. 'Happy New Year, baby!' He rubs her stomach over her coat.

The fireworks start and Elena looks up, mesmerised. Rainbows of colour explode above the buildings on the other side of the lagoon, lighting up the black sky and then cascading down, disappearing into the night before they reach the dark water.

Ten minutes later, just like that, it's over.

The rain intensifies and the crowd moves as one towards the piazza, crushing in around them. Elena struggles to keep herself from being lifted off the ground. More and more bodies join in the push from behind, separating her from Christian.

'Ellie!' He holds his hand out, but she pretends not to see it.

This is it. This is the opportunity she's been waiting for. She doesn't have her passport or any money, but she can work that out later. All she has to do is lose him in this crowd. Her heart fills with hope.

But only a moment later, her ankle twists, giving way. She loses her footing and falls on the ground.

People step around her, some even step on top of her, their shoes crushing her fingers and digging into her back. The stream of people is never ending and the pain in her ankle is searing. There's no room to stand. Nobody stops to help her up.

And then Christian's by her side, his eyes wide with worry. 'Ellie, Jesus! What happened?'

'I twisted my ankle,' she cries.

He scoops her up and carries her in his arms. With the umbrella left behind, the rain pours on them as Christian pushes people out of the way. 'Move! Make room!' He weaves his way through the sea of people, bit by bit, taking advantage of his height and bulk and commanding voice. Finally, they reach the piazza, and the crowd disperses into the square. Christian lowers her down.

She lets out a yelp when her foot hits the ground. 'I can't put weight on it. I can't walk. Oh my God, I can't walk!'

'It's all right, don't panic.' He picks her up again. 'I've got you, babe.'

Her ankle's on fire. She can already feel the swelling pressing against her boot. How can she run away if she can't even walk? She sobs into Christian's chest, huge, racking sobs.

He kisses the top of her head. 'It's okay, Ellie. I'm here. Shh, it's okay.' His voice is gentle and calm.

As he carries her through the crowded lanes leading back to the hotel, with his hair and clothes dripping, he plants soft kisses on her wet cheek. It makes Elena wonder, for what feels like the millionth time, how it all went so wrong with them.

He carries her all the way up the hotel stairs, and it's only when they reach their suite that he finally puts her down. He brings her an icepack from the kitchen downstairs and wraps it around her ankle with a pair of her tights. He stacks pillows under her leg, elevating her foot and her pain begins to ease. When her ankle is numb, he removes the icepack and performs a brief assessment, assuring her that it isn't broken, just sprained.

Elena thinks about how she sent a prayer to heaven to help her run and minutes later she couldn't walk. Is God trying to tell her something? Should she be trying to make her marriage work instead of running away? Christian's been so good to her these last two days. Maybe things between them are finally changing for the better.

He catches her eye and smiles. 'You're so sexy wet.' Softly, he kisses her mouth and then her neck. 'We should get you out of these clothes,' he murmurs as he helps her strip off, taking extra care with her injured foot. Then he lies on top of her and makes slow love to her, and she lets him.

Afterwards, he rolls onto his back. 'Ellie, I hope the baby's okay after your fall.' He strokes her stomach and she remembers with a jolt the only reason he's been good to her and why she absolutely has to run away.

'I'm sure she's fine.' She smiles at him.

'You said "she". You think it's a girl?'

'I do.'

'I do too.' He grins. 'I want her to be just like you.'

Even if she can't walk and has to crawl across Venice on her hands and knees, Elena's leaving on Saturday.

On the
EIGHTH
DAY *of*
CHRISTMAS

Sophie

Sophie never did see the fireworks. She and Rocco barely made it back to her suite before they were tearing each other's clothes off. She wakes up now to the gorgeous sight of a naked Venetian in her bed.

'Rocco,' she whispers.

He opens his eyes and rolls onto his side to face her. Somehow it feels more intimate to see him without his glasses on than it does to see him undressed. She traces the stubble forming along his jawline. She's only known him to be clean shaven until now, in the early hours of the morning before he's found his razor. She likes him better this way.

'What is the time?' His honey-brown eyes are soft and dozy.

She checks her phone. 'Five-thirty.'

He gives her a sleepy smile and kisses her bare shoulder. 'I should go to my room before the others wake up.'

'Don't leave yet.' She runs her fingers over his chest hair. The masculinity of it is intoxicating, a bold display of testosterone that she's unused to. 'How am I going to keep my hands off you today?' She sighs.

'Don't worry.' He grins. 'My number one priority is for you to keep your hands *on* me. We will work fast today, eh, so we can finish quickly after lunch and then we will come back to this bed and we will make love.'

'Mmm, okay. Work fast. Got it.'

'Then we will work fast again in the evening so we finish quickly again, and then we will come back to this bed and will make love some more.'

'Hate to ruin this most excellent plan of yours, signore, but we have the Mass with your family tonight after dinner.'

'Fanculo.'

'Sadly, no, there'll be none of that going on in church.'

He snorts a laugh and slides his warm hand between her legs.

She holds her breath.

'So, we wait a little longer. And then after Mass,' he murmurs, 'we will come back to this bed and will make love all over each other. And this is what we will do every day and every night.'

She gasps as his touch intensifies. 'What happened to you showing me around Venice?'

'You have seen enough of Venice.' His eyes rest on hers while his fingers explore. Any hint of Rocco's goofiness has disappeared in her bed. There's nothing awkward about what he's doing to her now. 'You are so beautiful in the morning, Sophie.'

'Only in the morning?' She smiles, becoming breathless.

'You are beautiful at every hour of the day and night. Bella, bella, bella,' he breathes into her ear.

He doesn't tell her she's beautiful in the way every man before him has. He doesn't say that she has a beautiful *face,* or that curvy girls turn him on, or that there's more of her for him to enjoy, or that she's *still* pretty. He hasn't said a word about her weight. He's accepted her exactly as she is without congratulating himself out loud for doing so.

For the first time in her life, Sophie feels seen by a man she's with. 'Ti amo,' she tells him.

'I love you,' he replies.

It took her almost a year to say 'I love you' in her last relationship, and even then, she wasn't sure she meant it. She and Rocco have said it to each other at least a dozen times through the night, and there's not even a tiny part of her that doubts it's true.

But it's not just Rocco who's stolen her heart, it's this city, this hotel. This life.

She's due to leave in a week.

'Rocco, I don't want to leave Venice.'
'Then stay.' He climbs on top of her.
'Stay?'
'Si. Stay and let me love you.'
Sophie shuts her eyes and lets herself be loved.

Elena

Elena's palms are slick with sweat. The zipper of Christian's document wallet slides out of her grip.

Calm down. Breathe.

Sitting on the floor next to Christian's suitcase, she takes two slow breaths. He's singing along to his Spotify that's playing in the bathroom while he showers.

Elena unzips the wallet and finds what she's looking for. Their passports are tucked together behind the printed airline tickets. Her ankle immediately throbs when she stands. Hobbling to the wardrobe, she slips the passports into the inside pocket of her coat, along with three hundred euro. They haven't used any of the cash in the wallet Christian carries on him since they arrived in Venice, so she's confident he won't come looking for the extra stash they kept here. If he does end up needing it, she can pretend they were robbed. Faking a robbery is the only reason she's hiding his passport along with hers. She'll leave it for him on the morning of her escape. The last thing she wants is to make it difficult for him to leave the country.

'Hey.' Christian's voice is right behind her.

Her heart just about stops beating.

The shower's still going. Shawn Mendes' 'Act Like You Love Me' blares from the bathroom.

She turns to find him standing there naked, wet.

'Come in the shower with me.' The water drips down from his hair onto his face. He kisses her mouth. 'I need to fuck you again.' He takes her trembling hand and puts it around his penis. 'Look at you all shaky.' He grins.

She does what the song tells her to as she leans back against the wall with him pressed up against her, soaking her clothes with his steaming body.

His eyes are closed but she can't take hers off the brown leather document wallet that's lying wide open on the floor next to the suitcase, with the passports and money very obviously missing. *Idiot.* Why didn't she put it away *before* she stood up? If he sees it, she's a dead woman.

'Get back in the shower,' she says between kisses. 'Go. I'll follow you. I want the water *hot* in there.' She gives him a playful smile.

'Okay.' He obediently jogs back to the shower.

The second he's gone, she slides the document wallet under the bed.

'Ellie,' he calls out. 'Come on!'

'Coming.' She throws her clothes into a pile on the floor and limps into the bathroom, sore, stressed, but prepared to do whatever it takes to keep him distracted.

Gayle

Mike walks into the room, puffing. 'Those stairs are so darned steep. No staff at reception. Guess where I found them all? In the restaurant! Sitting at the table eating, happy as you please, like they don't have any guests to look after.'

'Those people have to eat too some time, hon.'

He sits next to her. 'Signore Bianchi was there, poor old fella. Sitting there looking proud as punch with himself while his wife goes around kissing nuns willy-nilly behind his back. He asked me why we haven't been going to the restaurant for dinner.'

'What did you say?'

'I said your headaches have been giving you extra trouble, so I've been picking up takeaways instead.'

Thank goodness.

'You know what *she* said when I said that?' He raises his eyebrows, waiting for Gayle to say 'what'.

'What?'

'She said she was going to go on and fix us a hot meal right now. Said they were testing out for lunch what they're serving for dinner, and she had leftovers. Said if we eat a big meal now, then she can send us up a sandwich for tonight instead of us needing to spend money on takeaways. She's bringing up a plate for each of us. *And* it's on the house!' He rubs his hands together. 'Smelled pretty good too. Some kind of casserole, I think.'

'That's very generous of Signora Bianchi.'

'She knows she owes us for keeping her dirty secret, that's what that is. It's a good saving, though.'

Things have been a little easier with Mike today. Making love last night did what she hoped it would and thawed out the ice between them. They haven't spoken about Noah at all today, but the tension is there, lurking in the background more subtly than before, but always there.

And her headache is as bad as ever. Will it ever go away?

There's a knock at the door and Mike lets Signora Bianchi in. She's carrying a silver tray with two covered plates, as well as an ice compress.

'Buon anno, signora.' She smiles a small tight-lipped smile as she sets the tray down on the side table. 'This means "happy new year". Your husband tells me you are not well.' Signora Bianchi's holding her head high, but the strain is showing in her eyes.

'It's my headache is all,' Gayle says.

Signora Bianchi gives her a long look. 'You have had a headache every day since you arrived, signora. This is no good.'

'It's like I said,' Mike says. 'The pink walls in the restaurant, they set her right off.'

'It is not the walls,' Signora Bianchi says brusquely. She doesn't look at Mike. 'There is a Mass tonight,' she tells Gayle. 'A very special Mass, for the Feast of the Mother of our Lord. We are all going. Come. If you pray for your headaches to be healed at this Mass, the Blessed Virgin will intercede for you. The Lord listens to His mother.'

Mike steps forward. 'I don't know about—'

'Where's the Mass?' Gayle asks.

Signora Bianchi swallows. 'It is at San Zaccaria.'

'San Zaccaria?' Mike says. 'You've a nerve inviting us back there—'

'I made a mistake, signore,' Signora Bianchi interrupts, making a stop sign with her hand. 'I made a mistake and I am very, *very* sorry that you saw this. Even though I ask myself why you were even in the sacristy, which is off limits to tourists.' She adjusts her bun and turns her attention back to Gayle. 'Come to the holy Mass. If you set your intentions on this special day, it will work, believe me. This Mass brings miracles every year. Last year, a couple who were infertile became pregnant after the Mass. Another year, a man's cancer was completely cured.'

Mike crosses his arms. 'Now, listen here, San Zaccaria is a Catholic Church. Gayle and I, we're not Catholic. It wouldn't be right for us to be there.'

Signora Bianchi turns to him. 'Signore, it is *never* wrong to visit the house of God. You had no problem to go there as a tourist. The reason for a church is prayer, not tourism. Your wife has been unwell since you arrived. Mass is at nine. You are welcome to sit with us, but come early because it is a very popular Mass.' She looks at Gayle again and it's as if she can see right into her heart. 'Come and share your worries with the Madonna, signora. She will not abandon you.'

'Hold up, is Madonna gonna be there? If that demonic woman's going, then we certainly won't be.' Mike puffs out his chest.

'I don't think she means *that* Madonna, hon.' Gayle tries not to laugh at the look Signora Bianchi is giving Mike. 'I think I'd like to go. Would that be okay with you?' she asks him.

Signora Bianchi speaks before Mike can answer. 'Of course. Il signore knows it is not his place to come between his wife and God.'

Mike opens his mouth, but nothing comes out.

'I will send some sandwiches up to your room at six so you can eat away from the pink walls.' She flashes Mike a look, then smiles at Gayle. 'Have your lunch, signora. The food will fortify you. And here is the cold compress signore came into the restaurant *when it was closed* to ask for. I am putting it in the freezer for you. Eat first. You too, signore.' She takes the steel lids off the plates and a mouth-watering aroma fills the room. 'Prego.'

Mike is instantly mollified. 'Well, well, what've we got here, then?'

'This is my rabbit stew. The mushrooms were foraged from the Treviso forest only yesterday. It is very fresh.' Signora Bianchi nods proudly.

The stew is accompanied by creamy-looking mashed potatoes and chunky bread, dripping in juices.

How difficult it must be for Signora Bianchi to be around them after the debacle at the church. But instead of avoiding them, she's brought this delicious food. She could have sent someone else up with it, but she came herself.

'It's very kind of you to bring lunch for us, Signora Bianchi. I appreciate it,' Gayle says.

'Loretta.' Signora Bianchi taps her own chest. 'You call me Loretta.'

'Thank you, Loretta. I love your name. It's so exotic. Me, I'm just plain old Gayle.'

'Gayle is a fine name.' Loretta gives Gayle's shoulder a pat. 'Buon appetito. I hope I see you at Mass. We will sit at the front. Come and find us.' She lets herself out, clicking the door closed.

Mike puts a hunk of bread in his mouth. 'We're not really gonna go to that quack church, are we? It's pagan worship, hon.' He shoves a forkful of rabbit in too. 'Idolatry is what it is,' he says with his mouth full.

Catholics have always confounded Gayle with their strange fixation on the mother of Christ. But what if Loretta's right? She must passionately believe that the Mass will truly help Gayle, or why else would she draw their attention to that ill-fated church? What if they go along to this Mass and her headaches are healed? Or an even greater family miracle occurs?

'I want to go, hon,' she insists.

Mike rolls his eyes and shrugs. 'Well, you seem to be doing whatever it is you like these days whether I agree or not, so I guess we're going, then.'

Elena

Elena, Christian and Mamma arrive at San Zaccaria fifteen minutes before Mass is due to start. The Feast of the Mother of our Lord is always a big deal, but with their own representative from the Vatican celebrating the Mass tonight, the church is bursting at the seams. Everyone wants to see Padre Alessandro; he's a rockstar here.

Christian continues to be the best version of himself, not complaining about attending a second Italian service in a week.

Mamma walks ahead of them and Christian helps Elena up the aisle. She leans onto his arm, keeping the weight off her swollen ankle that he's strapped up for her. Not for love nor money could they find crutches to hire in San Marco today, not even at the hospital.

Mamma is stopped by well-wishers every few steps she takes. Papà was loved in the community. They ran their little grocery store for over thirty years before selling it when Papà became ill. He's sorely missed, but by nobody more than Elena. Being back in the church, where his funeral was held just last week, makes her chest feel like it's being crushed.

Mamma waves to Signore and Signora Bianchi, who are seated in the front pew. Signore Bianchi beckons them over. Merda, now Christian will see how well their families know each other despite her earlier denials to him.

Marina, sitting on the end in the aisle seat, gives Christian a brief smile before catching Elena's eye with a look of solidarity.

Marina is particularly stunning tonight. Her lips are painted blood red and her dark curls, usually wild and loose, are smooth and straight, held up in a lush high ponytail. Her face looks different when she's not hiding behind those huge red frames; she seems softer somehow. She's dressed in a satin white shirt that shows off her olive complexion, tucked into tight leather leggings that hug her slim long legs.

When Elena sees who's sitting next to the Bianchis, her stomach sinks. *What are the Dawsons doing here? They're not even Italian!*

Mamma makes her way along the row, hugging the Bianchis one by one. Elena wills her to ignore the Dawsons when she comes upon them. Of course Mamma doesn't. She clasps Gayle by the arms and warmly kisses both her cheeks, and then does the same with Mike. Elena watches Christian's face as he clocks it.

Mike pats the seat next to him, which is still free, and Mamma sits down.

'Mamma.' Elena reaches for her hand, trying to pull her back up. 'Wouldn't you be more comfortable in a side pew where there's more space?' She gives her a strained look. *We can't sit next to these people.*

Mamma waves her off. Elena has no choice but to sit next to her.

'Your mum knows the Americans. How?' Christian hisses in her ear.

'No idea.' She gives him a vacant stare. 'He's asking how you know the Americans,' she whispers to Mamma.

Mamma's face falls. 'I'm sorry, I didn't think.'

'It's okay. Don't worry.' Turning to Christian, she switches back to English. 'She doesn't know them. She was being polite.'

Christian chuckles. 'Italians! Everyone's a long-lost friend, even people you've never met.'

'I know, right?' Elena laughs with him, overwhelmed with relief.

'And she knows the Bianchis from when your brother played soccer with Rocco?' he asks.

'Must be.'

He nods, satisfied.

The organist begins to play as more people take their seats. The crowd may be huge, but so is the church. There's room for everyone.

Mamma, Signora Bianchi and Marina kneel in prayer. Elena joins them. She clasps her hands tightly, looking up at the painting of the Madonna behind the altar.

Quietly she prays. 'Madre di Dio, aiutami a correre.'
Mother of God, help me run.
Blessed Virgin, she continues, *lead me to safety. Guide me.*
Christian taps her shoulder. 'Rocco's here.'

Elena pushes herself off her knees and smiles at Rocco and Sophie, who walk towards them. Rocco smiles back but Sophie, looking agitated, barely acknowledges her. They take the seats next to Christian. Marina moves to the spot next to Sophie, making way for a nun who's just turned up and is now seated next to Signora Bianchi.

A hush descends over the church and the congregation rises. Elena winces when she stands, her ankle throbbing inside her boot. The organist starts a new song, and the choir, a group of twenty or so, mostly women, all dressed in black, begins to sing. The procession enters from the back of the church.

Elena watches Alessandro follow the altar boys up the aisle. The instant he reaches the pulpit and turns to face the congregation, it hits her like a thunderbolt. The light shining from behind him is like a halo of the Holy Spirit surrounding him. He's an angel. An angel right before her eyes. Of course! How could she not have thought of this before?

When Alessandro speaks, his deep voice washes over her. She's too mesmerised to listen, intoxicated by his beautiful flawless face, by the light surrounding him. She mouths a heartfelt thank you to the Madonna, who has granted her prayer within seconds of it being said. Here is her guide, her light bearer. Here is the man who'll lead her to safety. Her beloved old friend, back just in time to save her. She closes her eyes.

Later, as Alessandro gives his homily, Mamma grips her hand hard. It's as if every word he speaks is about them. He tells the story of Mary, Mother of Christ, who saved her child from certain death at the hands of an evil maniac. He speaks of how mother and child escaped their home and found refuge someplace new, how God led them to safety.

Alessandro sits as the choir sings 'Alleluia'. Elena finds herself singing along with them. Actually singing! When was the last time she sang? Certainly not since she was married.

Christian turns to her, the delight clear on his face. She smiles back at him and rests a hand on her stomach, giving it a little pat. His smile widens.

Elena lets her voice ring through the church in praise of the Lord, who she now knows with conviction will deliver her safely from the man standing next to her. She's been granted a miracle in the form of Alessandro. For where in Italy, or in the whole world for that matter, is there a safer place to find refuge than within the walls of the Vatican?

And that's precisely where she's headed.

Loretta

Loretta can't think straight, let alone pray. With Flavia on one side and Alberto on the other, this Mass is its own unique form of torture.

Last night, she and Flavia watched the fireworks in silence. The heralding of a new year signalled the end of their reunion. It was decided that Flavia would return to the Vatican in the morning and that they would not see each other again.

Loretta returned to the hotel in the early hours of the morning to find both her children still out and Alberto fast asleep. She stayed up and watched the sun rise over the buildings from her bedroom window.

She was so distraught at having said goodbye to Flavia that today she led her family to believe she was unwell. It was the only way to explain her brokenness. She came to Mass tonight to appeal to the Madonna to heal her fractured heart and to help her be a better wife to Alberto.

And then, only seconds before Mass began, Flavia appeared and asked Marina to make room for her. Now it's as if time has stood still. The Mass is never-ending. *What's Flavia doing here? Why didn't she go back to Rome?*

Alberto, completely oblivious, offers Flavia a mint when there's a break in the service for the collection plate to be passed around. Flavia looks at him as if he's mad and declines.

Loretta doesn't trust herself to look at Flavia or to speak to her.

When Alberto is distracted by his watch lighting up with updated football scores, Flavia leans her head close to Loretta's and whispers, 'I wanted to sing with you before I left. For old time's sake.'

Just at that moment, the organist starts playing 'This Day God Gives Me'. Flavia rests the back of her hand ever so gently against the back of Loretta's hand that hangs by her side. To anyone looking, there's nothing to see, but Loretta's skin is on fire.

Flavia begins to sing and, despite the anguish she's in, Loretta joins her. Together they raise their voices in harmony. For three and a half magical minutes, Loretta's transported back to when she was a young woman, singing once again with her love by her side. Alberto sings too, in his booming operatic voice, but it's only Flavia that Loretta can hear.

And then the hymn is over and, without saying goodbye, Flavia slips out of the pew and out of the church. Out of Loretta's life. It's all Loretta can do not to double over and wail.

Alberto smiles at her appreciatively. 'Your singing was magnificent, cara. Brava!'

Through the next part of the Mass, Loretta tries to talk to the Madonna. She desperately needs the comfort of the Blessed Virgin. But for the first time in her life, she can't feel Santa Maria's presence in her heart. When she looks at the painting of the Madonna cradling the baby Christ, all she hears in her head are Flavia's doubts about the truth of the Bible stories.

As much as she wants to forget what Flavia said, to put it down to the ramblings of a disillusioned nun, her arguments are impossible to ignore. The doubt Flavia has cast over the origins of Christianity has shaken Loretta's foundations. What she considered for her entire life to be an absolute and unwavering faith has been thrown into chaos by a few sentences whispered near a canal in the dark of night. Could what Flavia said be true? Is the miracle of the virgin birth not a miracle at all? Is it a horror story instead?

Santa Maria, forgive me.

She focuses her attention on Padre Alessandro, hoping his words of wisdom will give her the assurance she craves. But instead, when she follows il padre's intense gaze, she realises with a crushing certainty what's behind Alessandro's odd behaviour this last week.

The discovery makes her blood turn cold.

Gayle

Gayle has come to realise that Mass can be rather tedious when you don't speak the language. As beguiling as the (*very* handsome) young priest up at the altar is, the service has been interminable.

Mike has sat with his arms crossed over his belly and a set scowl on his face for the entirety of the Mass so far. The creases in his forehead have been extra deep since the last hymn with the truly extraordinary harmonising of Loretta and the nun. Their voices lifted above everyone else's, sounding so exquisite they sent shivers down Gayle's spine.

Gayle can understand Mike's solidarity with Signore Bianchi, but the way the two women sang was as if they were crying out together. There was so much emotion, so much *pain* in their voices, that Gayle can't help but feel just as much pity for Loretta as she does for poor old Signore Bianchi.

Now the nun has left, and the anguish is as plain as day on Loretta's face. Despite that, Loretta looks ravishingly beautiful tonight in a simple black shift dress, with small pearl studs in her ears and her silver hair pinned back. It's the first time Gayle's seen Loretta out of jeans and with make-up on. Albeit barely there, the mascara and blush only add to her beauty.

Gayle feels certain that Loretta didn't expect the nun to come and sit with her this evening. Surely Loretta wouldn't have insisted she and Mike be there if she knew the nun was coming too?

Her attention is drawn away from Loretta when they're ordered to stand up again by the priest. Mike groans and shakes his head. Neither of them was expecting all this sitting and standing and kneeling; the service has been a veritable aerobics class.

Gayle hasn't said her prayers to Mary yet, which was the whole reason Loretta invited them. She owes it to Loretta to at least try. So she looks at the painting of Mary behind the altar and prays to it. It feels silly and wrong, but she does it anyway. She prays for healing, for her headaches and for the cancer in her marriage. She prays for peace between Noah and Mike and for her own relationship with Noah. She prays for Loretta and all the problems she's having. But most of all she prays for Elena.

Nobody needs prayers more than that young woman, who tonight caught Gayle's eye when she arrived at the church, flanked by Anna-Maria and Christian, and conveyed with one brief look how much trouble she's still in. Gayle's never seen more frightened eyes.

Once she's finished praying for Elena, Gayle's satisfied that her prayers are done. Did she ask for too many things? Is there a limit to the number of requests a person should make when praying to a painting?

All she can do now is wait and see if it was a hoax or not.

Sophie

The smoky smell of incense hangs thick in the air as the choir sings in Italian. There are people everywhere. Too many people, all around her. A flutter sweeps across Sophie's chest and she wipes her clammy hands on her coat. She should never have agreed to come.

'Okay?' Rocco smiles at her.

'I'm okay.'

'Now is Holy Communion and closing hymn, then finished.'

She'll believe that when she sees it. This Mass has been going since the dawn of time.

Rocco reaches for her hand. His touch calms her a little.

Marina briefly looks down at their intertwined hands and says nothing, turning her attention back to Padre Alessandro, transfixed by him.

Elena's also focused on the priest. She has a beatific smile on her face. It's creepy, the way she's staring at him. Christian's scrolling on his phone, completely oblivious to his wife's fixation on the other man.

Both Mrs Dawson (whose presence here with her grumpy husband remains a mystery to Sophie) and Elena's mother also watch the priest with expressions of wonder and awe. He has every woman captivated.

But Padre Alessandro only has eyes for Marina. He holds his arms up in the classic preacher pose as he prays, his voice husky and deep. Does nobody else see that this man's clearly mouthing words he doesn't mean while not taking his eyes off Marina? Not for one second. Seriously, is he even blinking?

Sophie looks between Marina and the priest as he rattles off more prayers. Marina's red lips are slightly parted. *Jesus.*

Eternally cheerful Rocco watches Padre Alessandro through narrowed eyes. He rolls his tongue around his cheek. It's as if he wants to climb the few steps to the altar and belt his old friend a good one.

Behind the priest, an oil painting of Mary stares straight through Sophie with glazed blue eyes. It's unnerving.

The congregation chants another prayer and more incense is released into the church, overpowering her. People start to form lines for Holy Communion. Sophie's just beginning to think she might get through this Mass after all, when the next hymn starts. 'Ave Maria'.

A memory hits her with full force. Her mother, all those years ago, standing next to her at St Francis Cathedral on a sweltering Christmas Eve in Melbourne. Penelope had sung the Latin words to 'Ave Maria' in her serene voice, when she knew that once they were home she was going to end Sophie's father's life while young Sophie and David slept soundly in their beds. There wasn't the slightest waver in Penelope's singing voice that night, even as the man she was about to kill happily sang the hymn in baritone right next to her.

The choir builds up momentum. 'Ave, ave dominus.'

All around Sophie are people. People queuing up for Holy Communion, people walking back to their seats, more people blocking the altar and the aisles. People, people everywhere.

'I have to get out.' She slides her hand out of Rocco's.

'Nearly finished,' he whispers. 'Five more minutes maximum.'

'No. I have to get out *now*.' She doesn't give him a chance to reply. She climbs right over Marina, stumbling into the aisle.

Marina grabs onto her to stop her from falling. 'Sophie! What's the matter?'

She shakes her off and walks into the queue. 'Excuse me, excuse me!'

Nobody moves; the aisle is blocked as far as she can see. She squeezes between people, pushing them, forcing her way through.

The choir sings. 'Ventris tuae, Jesus.'

'Sophie!' Rocco's behind her.

She's sweating. It's hard to breathe. She elbows more people out of the way. They mutter at her. She doesn't care, she keeps pushing through until she reaches the back of the church.

A soprano soloist takes over; her notes are shrill. 'Ave Maria.'

Sophie flings the door open and runs down the stairs.

'Wait!' Rocco calls.

She doesn't stop running until she's at the opposite end of the piazza, where she bends over and dry retches.

Rocco catches up to her. 'What happened? Dio mio, you're sick!'

She turns to face him, with saliva and tears and snot sliding down her face. 'I'm sorry. I had to get out.'

'It's okay. Come.' He wraps her up in his arms and holds her tight. When her breathing finally slows down, he says, 'Andiamo. I will bring you tea to your room and you will feel better.'

'No, stay here with your family.' She hunts for a tissue in her pocket. Not finding one, she wipes her face with her coat sleeve. 'I'll find my way back to the hotel.'

'Sophie, come on, you are in Venice. No tourist can find their way back to anywhere.' He smiles. 'I am taking you home.'

'But the special Mass, your family.'

'Pfft, what special Mass?' He cocks his arm for her and she accepts it.

Slowly they make their way back to the hotel, Rocco whistling softly as he guides her through the lit-up alleyways and piazzas. When was the last time she knew someone to whistle while they walked, she wonders. It must be years. The happy melody soothes her.

Before too long, she spots the blue Il Cuore shimmering under spotlights. When she unlocks the door to her suite, she has the same sense of relief that she gets whenever she steps into her apartment in Melbourne. After only a week, Il Cuore has become home.

She heads straight for bed and Rocco follows her. They lie facing each other on top of the fluffy pink covers. She's still in her coat and boots. The panic has passed, and all she feels now is overwhelming fatigue.

'Do you want me to bring you a piece of cake?' Rocco's voice is gentle.

'No, thanks. I'm not hungry.'

They lie in silence.

'Hey, can I ask you something?' she says after a while.

'Of course, anything.'

'Marina and Padre Alessandro. They're together, right?'

He chuckles. 'You noticed, eh?'

'Not to put too fine a point on it, but I'm pretty sure every last person in that church noticed. So they're a couple?'

He sighs. 'They used to be when Marina lived in Rome. It was my fault, you know, that they were together in the first place.'

'What do you mean?'

'Marina was engaged to a man here, Nico. He was a teacher like her.'

'Wait, Marina's a teacher?'

'She was. Not any more. So, anyway, two months before the wedding to Nico, she found naked photos of her best friend, Helena, on his phone. They were all working in the same school. Helena was going to be her bridesmaid.'

'Oh my God. That's awful.'

'Yes. Of course the engagement ended after this. Marina wanted to escape so she took a teaching position in Rome. But she had no friends there and I was worried about her being lonely. Her apartment was close to the Vatican. Alessandro was my old friend and he was an assistant to a bishop there.'

'Oh, no.'

'Oh, yes.' He smiles a sheepish smile. 'So I think to myself, who is better than a priest to look after my sister?'

Sophie laughs and the sound of it shocks her. It's years since she's been as distressed as she was in church, and now, just being around

Rocco has calmed her enough that she can laugh. 'I'm sorry,' she says, still giggling, 'but any idiot could've seen what would happen there.'

'Are you calling me an idiot?' He tilts his head, a smile on his face.

She links her fingers through his. 'Indeed I am. You really think Alessandro comes across as someone who's going to be strict about celibacy? He's the poster boy for priests down to fuck.'

He snorts a laugh. 'Be quiet, let me finish the story.'

'Okay, go.'

'So, as you were smart enough to predict, they became lovers.'

'Shocked to my very core! Did you know though? At the time?'

'Yes, she told me. I was not happy about it, but there was not much I could do. Nobody else knew for the two years they were together.'

'They didn't get caught?'

'No. Alessandro did not have a parish, you understand. So it was only people who work at the Vatican who knew him in Rome. And let's just say, he was not the only one doing what he was doing. So they turned a blind eye. At least this is what I think happened.'

'Then what?'

'Well, then, Marina was nearly thirty. She wanted to get married, start a family, the normal things.'

'Let me guess, he wanted to keep being a priest and having her on the side?'

'Exactly this.'

Alessandro immediately goes from hot to not in Sophie's head.

'So she came home from Rome, more heartbroken than when she left.' He sighs. 'She wanted a break from the classroom. So she started working here with us and that is how things stayed.'

'Did she find another partner?'

'No, nobody. She left Alessandro because she wanted children, and then she would not look at another man. Mamma is always trying to matchmake, but Marina has no interest.'

'This is such a sad story.'

'I know,' he agrees. 'She never stopped loving him. And now, this week, it is the first time they have seen each other in five years.'

'Poor Marina.'

'Mmm.'

They fall into silence again.

Rocco still hasn't pried about her past, but she feels so close to him right now that she wants to share it with him. She takes a deep breath. 'That hymn the choir sang tonight, "Ave Maria". It brought back memories for me.'

He twirls a lock of her hair around his finger. 'Bad memories?'

'Yeah. Twenty years ago, my family went to Christmas Eve Mass, and the choir sang that hymn. When we went home that night, my mum killed my dad.'

Rocco's jaw drops. 'She ki—? *Why?*'

'He was violent. It was only a matter of time before he killed her, and possibly David and me. So'—she takes another big breath—'she killed him first.'

'*Santa Maria.* I thought you said your father was wonderful?'

'He was, and he wasn't.'

He shakes his head. 'I cannot believe this. Did you see her kill him?'

'No. David and I were asleep. She dropped sleeping pills into his wine, then she smothered him with a pillow while he slept. When we woke up, she told us he wasn't feeling well, that he was resting in bed. We opened our presents, the three of us had breakfast, and then she went to check on him. We heard her screaming and there he was, dead. She called the ambulance, they came and took him away and that was that.'

'What do you mean "and that was that"? Your mother did not go to jail?'

'No, she got away with it.'

'How is this possible?'

'The cause of death was inconclusive. Mum told the paramedics that after Mass Dad complained of chest pain. I suppose the coroner saw a fat middle-aged man with a history of heart disease, who'd mixed sleeping pills with alcohol, and it didn't seem that unlikely that Dad died in his sleep.'

'Gesù Cristo. So how did you know your mother killed him? She told you?'

'Not for years and years. She only told me last month when I was at her place for dinner. She was very drunk. She didn't remember it afterwards.' Sophie fiddles with Rocco's tie. 'She still thinks I don't know.' She laughs nervously, worried she's overshared. 'It's all very tragic, isn't it?'

'It *is* a tragedy. You were only a child.' He rests his hand on her cheek.

'It wasn't much of a childhood before then anyway, if I'm honest.'

'It makes me sad to know your life has been this hard. You have suffered.'

'I'm okay now. Well, if you don't count panic attacks at church.' She gives him a small smile.

'After what you have been through, to me you are amazing.' He pulls her in close to him and she snuggles up to his chest.

'So, now you know my story. What's your story? Let's hear it.'

'My story? You really want to know?'

'I do.'

'Okay, I will tell you.' His chest rises and falls. 'You say your mother was drunk when she confessed. Is your mother an alcoholic?'

Sophie swallows. 'She is.'

'I should have told you this before now.' He stops. 'I am also an alcoholic.'

Her breath catches. 'Oh.'

'Yes. *Oh*. Exactly. I am sorry I have not told you until now.'

'Why didn't you?' Her voice is strangled.

'I was scared you would not want to be with me if you knew.'

She doesn't answer.

'Sophie, I have been sober for eight years, I promise you this is the truth. I am committed one hundred per cent to staying sober.'

'I see.'

'Do you want to hear the story of my addiction? It is a long story.'

'I want to hear it,' she says, even though she feels heavy inside. So unutterably heavy.

'When I was twenty, I met a girl,' he begins. 'Gabriella. She came here to the hotel on holiday. After, I followed her to Milan. Her father owned a hotel, much bigger than this one, and I left here to work at that hotel. Anyway, we got married after a while.'

Sophie's eyes almost pop out of her head. 'Wait, what? You're married?' She thinks she might be sick.

He shakes his head violently. 'Divorced. Divorced, for a long time. Don't worry.'

She's worried. She's extremely worried. 'Go on.'

'It was not a happy marriage. We rushed into it. I felt stuck, I did not know what to do. She was a nice girl, but we had nothing in common. Everyone told us it was a mistake to get married, but we did not listen. We were young, we thought we knew everything better than anyone.' He flings his arms about. 'After we were married, I was not in love with her any more and she was not in love with me, but nobody gets divorced here. It is considered a big failure and I did not want to fail. I know this is not an excuse to drink, but that is what I did. And soon, it was a lot of drinking and then it was a big problem.'

'Is that why you got divorced?'

'Eventually, yes. But she stayed with me at first. I went to rehab for the first time when I was twenty-three.'

She raises her eyebrows. 'The *first* time?'

'There were four times,' he admits.

'Christ alive.'

'I know. Every time I went I was okay for six months, sometimes up to one year, then I drank again. Finally, my parents sold the top floor of the hotel to pay for me to stay at a clinic that was very well known for being the best one in Europe. It was in Switzerland. Three and a half thousand euro a night. I stayed two months.'

'Holy crap, that's a lot of money.'

'Yes. My parents risked everything for me. So, I went to this clinic, and it was finally there I realised I had to leave my wife. I understood that I was drinking to cover up the problems I had with Gabriella.' He blows out through his nose. 'I came back from Switzerland and we were divorced. I was twenty-seven and I have been sober since then.'

'How did Gabriella take it?'

'There was crying, of course. It was messy. But I think also she was relieved. After that I returned to Venice, broke, with no career, a failed marriage. It was a very low point for me. Because of me, my parents lost half the hotel. I had to do something to make it up to them. So I came up with the idea of the restaurant. And I helped build it and market it, and it gave me purpose, you know? It still gives me purpose. I like my life now, I like being sober. So that is my story, Sophie. I am so sorry I did not tell you. And I am sorry that this is who I am.' He looks into her eyes, the angst written all over his face. 'Say something, please.'

Her mouth is dry when she finally speaks. 'How could you tell me you loved me before telling me about all of this? How could you let me fall for you without warning me?'

'I was a coward. I am so sorry. What can I do to make it better?'

He's so sincere, so worried, she can already feel herself wanting to reassure him. She doesn't, though. She turns her head away from him and shuts her eyes.

So that's the catch. She knew there had to be one. Of course she wasn't just going to meet someone wonderful and have him love her without there being a catch.

That's not how things go for her.

Loretta

Loretta wipes the make-up from her face and examines herself under the harsh fluorescent light of the ensuite. The dark circles under her eyes, the deep lines around her mouth and the greyish tone of her skin reveal themselves. 'I look so *old*,' she grumbles.

Alberto, who's perched on the edge of the bed, replies, 'You're the most beautiful woman in Italy. No, the world.'

'Put out that cigarette!' She applies night cream to her cheeks. 'Who smokes at this hour? And with your heart the way it is.'

He takes one last, long drag and stubs the cigarette into an ashtray without complaint. 'Your singing in Mass was amazing.' He removes his shoes. 'You should join the choir.'

'Join the choir? In all my spare time?'

He shrugs. 'At least let us hear you sing, then. You don't need to be in a choir for that. You have the voice of an angel, and you never sing.'

Loretta doesn't answer. She unpins her hair and it falls to her waist. She joins him on the bed and brushes it out slowly.

Flavia's gone and Loretta knows in her heart of hearts she'll never see her again. Her grief is palpable, compounded by the shame and guilt of going behind Alberto's back.

Alberto looks at his watch and groans. 'It's almost midnight already. Merda.'

'Don't curse on the Holy Mother's feast day.'

He rolls his eyes. 'What were you talking to Pia Falcone about after Mass anyway?'

'Nothing. I was wishing her a happy Christmas.'

He snorts. 'The two of you looked like you were planning a rebellion with your heads bent together like that. What were you saying to her? Tell me.'

'I invited Pia for breakfast. They're coming the day after tomorrow.'

'*They*. Who else is coming?'

She swallows. 'Her son.'

'Ah, Loretta. Again, with Luca Falcone? Poor Marina. Why do you waste your time like this? Can't you see this matchmaking obsession of yours is useless?'

'Luca saved your life last week. Can we not thank the man?'

'What are you talking about? He didn't save my life at all. I was ready to run a marathon by the time he examined me.'

Alberto pulls back the covers and they climb beside each other into the four-poster bed. He switches off the light. 'We both know Luca's medical expertise isn't the reason he's invited to dine at our restaurant. Weren't you sitting right next to me in church tonight? Didn't you see the way your holy priest from the Vatican was looking at our daughter?'

She sighs a long sigh. 'Of course I saw. Everyone saw.'

'Did you know?' he asks. 'Did she tell you?'

'No. Did *you* know?'

'No.'

This doesn't surprise her. Alberto's only thoughts are about the rising cost of produce at the market or if Inter Milan are playing well. What does surprise her is that she herself never suspected it. She knew, of course, that there must have been a heartbreak to explain Marina's sudden return to Venice five years ago when she seemed so happy in Rome. The sadness was written in Marina's eyes. But it didn't once cross Loretta's mind that it was Alessandro who was responsible for it. She'd tried and tried over the years to get her daughter to open up to her. It was no use, Marina was a closed book.

She also tried to find a suitable man for Marina, someone to make her smile again, but Marina was resolutely disinterested in any of the men Loretta presented her with. She was a ghost, that girl, going through the motions of life as if she was already dead.

Tonight, with Marina looking so jaw-droppingly beautiful with her hair blow-dried straight, her glamorous make-up, wearing pants so tight they looked painted on, and walking all the way to San Zaccaria, in the freezing cold, with her bare feet in sky-high strappy heels, Loretta suspected that Marina was in love again. But even then, she didn't for a minute entertain the idea that it was the priest her daughter was off to seduce.

It was only when she saw Alessandro, the only priest she'd ever known who was holy enough to be chosen to do God's work in the Vatican, stare at Marina for most of the Mass, with that clear and intense longing in his eyes, that she knew.

And now it stuns her that she didn't figure it out earlier.

Of course, only a complicated love affair could affect someone the way Marina was affected on her return from Rome. Her daughter was too good-hearted to ever compete with another woman for the love of a man, especially after she'd been burned herself, so *of course* it was the priest. The reason Marina was so tortured was because her competition for the person she loved was God Himself.

La figlia è uguale la madre. Like mother, like daughter.

'What are we going to do about Marina?' she asks Alberto.

'What can we do?' he replies. 'We can do nothing.'

'She's throwing her life away for a man she can't have. Are we going to stand by and not say anything?'

'Like I said, what can we do?'

'Can you for once in your life not be so, so . . .' She can't find the words. 'Why are you like this?'

'Like what?'

'Like a dead fish. You should be crazy with worry!'

'Tranquilla, Loretta, tranquilla. There's only room for one crazy person in this bed.' He rolls onto his side, facing away from her. 'He'll go back to Rome soon, don't worry.'

'And then what? It'll be a fresh wound in her heart all over again.' She sighs. 'I want to fix it.'

'You can't. There are some things even the great Loretta Bianchi can't fix.'

'And what about Rocco and Sophie? Another thing to worry about.'

He chuckles. 'You're starting on Rocco now? He's the happiest he's ever been.'

'Why do you think Sophie ran out of church like that? She has problems, that girl, big problems.'

'We've known the woman for five minutes – we know nothing about her. And she'll be gone soon enough too. You worry too much.' Alberto yawns. 'Let me get some sleep.'

'Okay, sleep then, if that's what's so important to you. I may worry too much, but you don't worry enough. These are our *children*.'

'Who are both adults!'

'They're still our children. If we don't worry about them, who will?'

He changes position again, lying on his back now. 'Do you know what I worry about? I worry about my wife, who works like a slave and who pretends to be happy in public but who is never happy in private.' His voice wobbles. 'My wife who only days after my heart attack was so eager to get back to work just to escape from me, and who finds extra things to do every minute, so she doesn't have to spend time with me. That's what I worry about.'

'There's no need to be so melodramatic.' The words are caught in her throat. 'I've been busy, Alberto, I have a hotel to run.' The guilt twists like a corkscrew in her chest.

'So I've gone from being a dead fish to melodramatic, depending on what suits you. Let me sleep, Loretta. I've never felt as old and tired as I have this last week.'

His words make her heart splinter. In the dark, she reaches for his hand under the covers. 'Alberto, I beg you, please have the heart surgery. I know you're scared, but we both know you need it. I'm terrified you're going to die.'

'Sometimes I think you'd be relieved if I died.'

She gives his limp hand a squeeze. There's so much she wants to apologise for, she doesn't even know where to begin. But when she opens her mouth, all that comes out is, 'Per favore, Alberto.'

He wheezes in and out, in and out. 'Okay,' he says finally. 'I'll have the surgery.'

She doesn't let go of his hand until he falls asleep.

On the NINTH DAY of CHRISTMAS

Loretta

Loretta slips from their bed and quietly dresses in the dim light of the moon. How is she ever going to sleep again? The guilt keeps her eyes from closing.

Alberto stirs. 'Che fai?'

'I can't sleep. I'm going for a walk.'

He squints at his phone by the bed. 'It's four-thirty in the morning. What's wrong with you?'

'I need some air.'

'I'll come with you.' He flicks the covers off.

'I want to be alone. Go back to sleep.' She makes for the door, not giving him a chance to argue.

'Ti amo.' He's already half asleep again.

'Ti amo, Alberto.'

She tries to pray as she walks along the empty lanes but her prayers are hollow. It rained hard for most of the night and the water on the ground sloshes around her boots. Venice is bleak in the flooded darkness. Piazza San Marco is abandoned but for the pigeons. She walks past Florian, with its wet red wicker chairs stacked on the tables; past the basilica, battered by the acqua alta of November but still standing; past the giant illuminated Christmas tree, the clock tower and archways of the Doge's Palace, and onto the esplanade.

She reaches the installation in front of Hotel Danieli. The metal sculpture is in pieces, smashed by the stampeding crowd who were escaping the rain after the fireworks on New Year's Eve. The aluminium Venetian workers – the gondoliers, chefs and shopkeepers – who were being crushed by the metal tourists now lie scattered and broken from the feet of real tourists. What strikes her is that the tourists destroyed the metal versions of themselves as well; the tourists destroyed everything.

Yesterday, the mayor stood in front of the broken structure and spoke of the need to limit the daily visitor intake for Venice and to impose a tourist tax. 'These eat-and-run visitors are killing us!' he shouted at the gathered journalists.

Whatever has caused it, whether it's Magdalena standing in the tank of water, the visit from the Clooneys (who were actually quite pleasant in the end) or the impassioned speech from the mayor, this art exhibition is getting the world talking. The internet can't get enough of it.

A small stray dog trots past her. He cocks his leg at the sculpture and pisses on the face of a chef before trotting away.

Loretta looks down at the water swirling around her ankles. A day, at least, of acqua alta lies ahead for San Marco before the water drains. Soon the council workers will be out laying wooden footbridges all over the city. If only all the talking and tweeting would lead to action to stop this from happening over and over.

The rain begins to fall again. In her sleep-deprived state, she forgot to pack an umbrella, so she heads back towards home. Piazza San Marco is still in predawn darkness when she passes through it. Magdalena's tank is filled with dirty water the height of Loretta's chest. Magdalena hasn't yet arrived for the day.

Loretta walks to the tank and places her palm on the glass. The rain comes down harder now. She isn't dressed for it, in a woollen trench instead of a raincoat. She keeps her hand up against the tank and leans her forehead on it. The sign at her feet says '*affogando*'.

'Me too,' she says, a sob escaping her. 'Me too.'

The sound of a camera shutter makes her jump. A few metres

away, a man, standing under the awning of the gelato shop, takes a second photo of her.

'What are you doing?' she shouts. 'Stop it!'

'I don't speak Italian, love,' he says, so she repeats it in English.

'Sorry, couldn't resist. It's a great shot.' He has an Irish accent.

'I did not consent to you taking this photo.'

'I don't need your consent. You're in a public place.'

She joins him under the awning. 'Why are you here? It is not even five in the morning.'

'Waiting for the artist. Nobody's taken a photo of her climbing into the tank.'

'Why do you want to photograph that? It will ruin the illusion.'

He lights a cigarette. 'On the contrary – makes it more potent. Her willingness to return, to suffer again.'

She takes a step closer to him. 'Delete my photo. Please, I am asking you nicely.'

His eyes rest on hers. 'You're that famous cook, Signora Bianchi.'

She doesn't answer.

'I'm Dan.' He turns his face to blow the smoke away from her. 'It's too good a shot to delete.' He shows her the photo on his camera screen. 'It's magic, look at it. Just you, in the rain, in the dark. Beautiful.'

She's shocked by how broken she looks in it.

'Are you worried about your city sinking?' he asks.

'What a stupid question to ask a Venetian.'

'All I'm saying is this shot will help more than the whole exhibition, trust me. You can give people facts about the rising water, you can stick a professional artist in a tank, it's not going to achieve anything. This here'—he taps the camera screen—'a Venetian icon who everyone loves standing by herself in the flood, this is the emotional connection people need to get on board with change. I have to publish this.'

'You do not *have* to at all, but you are going to do what you want anyway.' She turns her back to him and walks to the hotel as the rain pours on her.

She doesn't notice how cold she is until she reaches their apartment and has trouble unlocking the door – her hand is shaking so much. The unflinching eyes of il Papa are glued on her. Alberto's snoring can be heard through the door; it's loud enough to wake people in Barcelona.

She has to tell him about Flavia. He deserves to know.

Elena

Christian's waiting by the toaster when Elena spots Sophie chatting with another guest. Sophie behaved weirdly at church last night, running out of there during the final hymn like she was in an action movie. But this morning she seems to be back to her put-together, bubbly self.

Elena has one thing on her to-do list today and it's securing Alessandro's help to escape.

The second Sophie looks at her, Elena beckons her over. The waitress comes immediately. 'Are you in danger? Do you need anything?' Sophie asks with a casual smile.

Elena speaks fast. 'I need Padre Alessandro to take my mother and me to the Vatican and hide us there. Can someone get a message to him to meet me at my mother's apartment on Saturday while Christian's out?'

'Of course. Anything else?'

Christian appears behind Sophie.

Elena touches her stomach. 'As long as they're healthy, we'll be happy either way.'

Sophie's eyes widen. 'Have you picked out names yet?'

God love this woman.

'We've settled on Rose for a girl,' Christian answers for her. 'That was my grandmother's name. The jury's still out if it's a boy.'

'Rose – how gorgeous!' Sophie claps her hands together.

Before she leaves their table, Sophie gives Elena a wink. Sophie won't let her down. She'll get the message to Alessandro. And Elena knows without any doubt that Alessandro won't let her down either.

She watches Sophie sharing a laugh with Signore Bianchi. Her blonde curls are in a high ponytail, her make-up is flawless and she's wearing a stunning pastel-pink sweater and pinstriped wide-leg pants under her Il Cuore apron. She's beyond beautiful, and Elena feels more than a little intimidated by Sophie's sense of style. She has it all going on – the padded pink headband, the jingly silver bangles, the gemstone rings stacked three and four deep. Nobody can miss Sophie. She's a rainbow of colour and glamour.

Elena thinks of her bare lobes and self-consciously tugs at the grey knit dress she has on. Christian chooses her clothes. They're always high-end, classic pieces but her entire wardrobe is so dull and muted, she may as well be invisible.

She adds *dress differently* to the mental list of things she'll change when she has her freedom back.

Everything's going to change. Everything.

Gayle

Gayle finds herself standing in front of yet another *Venice Rising* art installation.

Each exhibit at this art festival is more depressing than the last, and across the city, the main streets and piazzas are now covered in wooden planks to walk on because of the incessant rain. She hates the plastic shoe coverings with their elastic that digs into her calves, and she's worried that she or Mike will slip in the wet and break a hip. She missed Christmas at home to be here, and all this miserable place has done is give her things to worry about.

Whether it's because of Elena and Signora Bianchi and their complicated secrets, or whether it's because of the dystopian exhibition, or the fact that they can now see the city literally sinking before their very eyes, San Marco feels nothing but sinister. Her prayers at the church did nothing at all to help the unrelenting headaches, either.

All she wants to do is leave and never come back.

She holds on to Mike's arm. 'Hon, I want to go home.'

'Okay.'

'I don't mean back to the hotel.' Her voice wobbles and she knows she's about to cry. 'I want go *home*, home. Back to Little Rock.'

He scratches his beard. 'We're going home on Tuesday.'

'I can't wait until Tuesday. I'm just so unhappy here.'

'Let's go back to the hotel and talk about it.' He takes her hand and leads her on the planks and footbridges to Il Cuore. They ignore Chiara at the front desk and walk straight up to their room.

'What about the big festival coming up?' Mike says. 'With the regatta race and all. You don't want to miss that, do you?'

'I don't care if I miss it. I hate it here. We only came to Venice in the first place to eat dinner at this hotel, but we're not even doing that any more.'

'Look, if it means that much to you, we can have dinner at the restaurant again.' He sits next to her. 'I don't want to encourage that woman and her philandering ways, not one little bit. But I'll do it for you.'

'I still want to go home.'

He blows through his nostrils. 'Is it so you can go to Noah faster? Because we won't get out of this cheaply. The airline will make us pay a small fortune to change our flights, and that's a fact.'

'I promise that's not it. Please, hon. Please take me home.'

He sighs. 'I don't know what's gotten into you lately.' He rings Andrea, their travel agent back in Arkansas, who says she'll look into their options and call them back.

They sit and wait, with the TV on. Gayle's stomach is clenched while on Fox News, Tucker Carlson froths at the mouth about communism again.

Andrea rings twenty minutes later to say there are no vacant seats on flights back to Arkansas before Tuesday unless they take an extra connecting flight and pay twice the amount.

They don't have the budget for that.

'Well, we tried,' Mike says.

Gayle's trapped in Venice, just like the woman trapped in the tank of water. She isn't usually one for superstition, but her sense of foreboding is deep; something bad is headed to Hotel Il Cuore.

Sophie

As soon as Sophie has a minute to herself after the breakfast rush, she messages Bec with her worries about Rocco's revelations last night.

Sober for how long?

                                                                Eight years

No relapses?

                                                                No relapses

Do you trust him?

                                                                Completely

I think it'll be okay, babe.

Don't overthink it. Just enjoy the hot
sex with your Italian stud!

    Sophie desperately wants to believe Bec's right, and she very much wants to keep enjoying the hot sex with her Italian stud, so she decides that the best way to deal with Rocco's confession about his struggles with alcohol is not to deal with it at all. Instead of thinking about how the first man she's fallen for in ages comes with enough baggage to fill a Boeing 747, she chooses to immerse herself in life at the hotel, with its comforting daily routine and predictability that helps her ignore the red flags waving madly in her head.

There's so much to love here, so much to distract her from the fact there's an ex-wife of Rocco's whose life he quite possibly ruined with his addiction and that she herself might well be next in line for the life ruining.

Rocco bursts into the empty restaurant with as much enthusiasm as a litter of golden retriever puppies at mealtime. 'I was looking for you. I missed you!'

She laughs. 'I've been gone for ninety seconds.'

'The longest ninety seconds of my whole life! Mamma is sending me back to the Rialto for a few more things. She does not care that we have gone to the market today in the rain already. Do you want to come?' He pushes his glasses up his nose and beams at her.

It's easy to let herself believe a man this adorable could never hurt her.

Outside, they navigate the flooded laneways arm in arm, under Rocco's big umbrella. There's an extra spring in Rocco's step, and she's more than a little smug knowing she's responsible for it. As they walk, she tells him about her conversation with Elena about Alessandro.

'The Vatican?' he all but shouts. 'Does she think anyone can just go and stay at the Vatican like it is a hotel?'

'Hey, I'm just the messenger.'

'I suppose we can ask him and see what he says, eh?' he replies before he teaches her some more Italian, which is what he does every morning on the way to the market.

'Questo costa troppo,' she repeats after him. *This costs too much.*

'The words are not enough. Use your hands, like this.'

'Questo costa troppo,' she says again, with her thumb and fingertips pressed together.

He laughs. 'You say it like you are complimenting them. We are fighting for a better price, Sophie. Questo è troppo costoso!' he shouts.

She tries once again with more passion this time.

'Very good!' He's finally satisfied.

Minutes later she gets to practise the phrase, hand gestures and all, on Pasquale, the fish vendor, who's so impressed by her that he throws in half a kilo of extra anchovies for free.

Sophie knows all the Bianchis' regular vendors at the Rialto by name now. None of their spirits are dampened by the flood and they greet her for the second time that morning as warmly as they do Rocco. She haggles over the price of eggs with Sebastiano, whose well-behaved hens sit in raised cages by his feet. Elisabetta, with her array of nuts, calls out when she sees Sophie coming and offers her a small handful of pistachios in exchange for Sophie taking a photo of her toothy smile. Elisabetta loves having her photo taken by la signorina bionda. Carmelina, who sells all kinds of cheese, vies for Sophie's attention, pressing a small round of salty goat's curd into her hand to taste.

When they're back at the hotel, Sophie dries herself off and then immerses herself in Loretta's kitchen. She helps Loretta wrap anchovies around bocconcini balls to be served with crusty bread for primi. For secondi, she peels artichokes for roasting and chops peppers for stuffing in chicken breasts.

Loretta is so organised and fast today that, for the first time since Sophie arrived in San Marco, they have time to make the dolci before lunch instead of after. They bake three tarts for the evening with lemons as big as rockmelons.

'These lemons need to be tested for anabolic steroids,' Sophie quips.

'These are our cousin Emilia's lemons from the Amalfi coast,' Salvatore tells her proudly. 'They came with a big box when they visited before Christmas.'

Each lemon produces enough juice to take a bath in.

When the tarts are in the oven, Sophie helps Loretta bake the daily marantega cake. She claps her hands when Loretta announces they're also making bussolai, the crumbly doughnut-shaped cookie that's become her favourite, for tomorrow's breakfast.

Loretta is as patient and kind as ever with her, but she's not talking much. She doesn't speak to anyone, really, except to give instructions. The men seem oblivious to Loretta's quietness and continue to banter with each other like normal.

'Is everything okay, Loretta?' Sophie asks.

Loretta gives her a quick smile. 'Yes, of course.'

'You just seem a little quiet, that's all.'

Loretta indicates with her chin to Rocco, who's gesticulating wildly at Chiara. 'My son is loud enough for three people this morning. What is he so excited about?'

Sophie blushes.

Rocco comes up behind her when Loretta sends her to the pantry for baking powder. 'If you do not come with me to your bed the minute lunch is finished and let me make love to you, I will die, I am telling you,' he whispers into her ear, making her insides flutter.

'We wouldn't want you to die, now, would we?' She turns to face him and lets her hand drop over the front of his pants.

He rewards her touch with a shudder. 'Now, you make it so I cannot wait until after lunch.' He closes the door to the pantry behind him.

'We can't,' she whispers. 'Your mum's waiting for the baking powder.'

'Let her wait,' he murmurs. 'This will not take long, believe me.'

The silent sex is thrillingly fast, with Sophie's sweaty palms up against the door and his family only feet away.

Loretta

The family gathers in the restaurant for lunch.

Sophie clears her throat and announces that she has a request from Elena. 'She wants to get a message to Padre Alessandro to meet her at her mother's apartment on Saturday and to take them to the Vatican and hide them there.' She gives Marina an apologetic smile.

'It is not possible,' Marina answers before anyone else can. 'Alessandro is not planning a return to Rome yet.'

Loretta snaps her head towards Marina. 'How do *you* know what il padre's plans are?'

Marina gulps. 'I . . . ah . . . His mother told me when they were here the other day.'

'If it means getting Elena to safety, of course he would agree to return earlier,' Chiara says.

Marina gives her cousin a filthy stare. 'How do we even know he *can* hide her there? He is an assistant to a bishop. He is not the Pope. What power does he have to hide people in the Vatican?'

Chiara frowns. 'He can try!'

'Fine. I will go to San Zaccaria and ask him.' Marina sighs.

'*I* will go.' Rocco gives her a look.

'No, *I* will go,' she shoots back.

So Rocco knows about Alessandro and Marina. By the look on her face, Sophie clearly knows too. Is there anyone who *doesn't* know, or was Loretta the only fool?

'What if Alessandro says no?' Salvatore says. 'Do we know anyone else who can hide her?'

In that moment, it all becomes apparent to Loretta. God sent Flavia back to Venice not to torture her, but to save Elena. It was all part of His plan. Flavia may have lost her faith, but the Lord is still doing His work through her. Any doubts Loretta has been harbouring about her faith these last couple of days vanish, just like that.

Her heart is racing with hope. She can turn her sin, her shame, into something good.

'I know a nun living at the Vatican who can hide Elena and Anna-Maria in the monastery,' she says. 'All Alessandro will have to do is accompany them there.'

'That's perfect!' Sophie's face lights up.

'Which nun at the Vatican do you know?' Alberto squints at her.

'I will tell you about it on our walk,' she replies, pretending not to notice his expression. 'I will call her now.' She leaves the table and locks herself in the bathroom to make the call.

'Amore! You've changed your mind?' Flavia answers breathlessly.

Loretta's stomach squeezes at the sound of her voice. 'No, sorry. I need something from you.' She tells Flavia about Elena.

'Of course we can take care of them, for as long as they need.'

'Grazie, I'm so grateful to you.'

When the details are sorted, she hangs up and takes a cleansing breath before she walks back into the kitchen.

Alberto's watching her. As soon as they lock eyes, she knows that he knows. While the others carry on the conversation around him, his eyes bore straight through her, the pain and anger clear in his stare.

She thinks she might be sick.

'Are you ready for our walk?' He stands.

'I'm ready.' With trembling hands, she slips her feet into knee-high rubber boots and puts on her raincoat and headscarf.

'Shall we go to the park?' he says when they're outside. 'I don't want to see any more stupid art exhibits.'

'We can go anywhere you want to go.'

Together they wade through the flooded Piazza San Marco in silence. It's unbearably quiet without him singing or humming.

The crowds are smaller than other days this week. People are scared of the water. Thankfully there's a break in the rain and they find a bench to sit on in Giardini Reali. The pansies are in bloom, splashing purple and orange throughout the park. The bell tower stands proud behind the trees. The garden is free of tourists. Their only company is the pigeons playing happily in the deep puddles.

It amazes Loretta how few tourists know this beautiful park is here, when it borders the most famous square in all of Venice. People's lack of curiosity about their surroundings is extraordinary.

Alberto lights a cigarette, and she edges a little further away from him on the bench, too nervous to tell him off.

'The gardeners are lazy. Look at the weeds,' he says.

She doesn't answer. They sit in silence. On any other day it would have been a companionable silence. Alberto finishes his cigarette and stubs it out on the pavement with his boot before bending down to pick it up and putting it in his coat pocket.

Finally, he speaks. 'It's her, isn't it? The Vatican nun.'

'Yes.'

'I was a fool to trust you when you told me it was over. I should never have married you.'

His words feel like a kick in the throat. 'It *was* over! You weren't a fool. I swear to you, the first I heard from her since the day I met you was last week.'

'Last week? Why last week, suddenly?'

'She came looking for me. I don't know why, after all these years, but that's what happened.'

His eyebrows shoot up. 'What do you mean she came looking for you? She was *here*? You saw her?'

She nods. 'I was going to tell you.'

'When?'

'Today.'

He snorts. 'That's convenient. You were going to tell me after I figured it out.'

'That's not why. I promise you I was going to tell you today.'

'Is that where you went sneaking off to this morning? To see her?' His tone is harsh. Alberto's tone is never harsh.

'No. She's back in Rome. She's not coming back. I went for a walk by myself this morning. I felt guilty, I needed some air.'

'Guilty about what? What did you do?' His jaw drops. 'Wait a minute! The nun at Mass. Was that her?'

Loretta hangs her head.

'You were singing with her while I stood right next to you.'

She can't speak.

He lights another cigarette, flicking the lighter with more force than needed.

She finds her voice. 'Please don't smoke. Think of your heart. When are we going to go to Luca and tell him you're prepared to have the surgery?'

He looks at her with disgust. 'It's not the cigarette that's bad for my heart, it's my wife.' He takes a deep drag. 'Tell me everything. And don't lie. I deserve the truth.'

So she tells him. He listens and he smokes, and the pigeons dance in the water. The secrets pour from her, one after the other, until there's nothing he doesn't know.

They've had more arguments than she can count over the years, but never has he looked at her with this kind of contempt.

'Did you fuck her when she was here this week?' The venom drips from his voice.

She feels so fragile, so vulnerable, that it's as if her skin has peeled away and left her organs exposed. 'No. We only kissed that one time.'

He laughs to himself. It's a bitter hollow sound. '*Only*. You *only* broke our marriage vows once? Brava.'

'I'm sorry. I know how badly I've hurt you.'

'You know nothing,' he spits. 'Nothing.' His wheeze is louder than usual. Every breath he takes is more laboured than the last.

'I didn't tell you,' he says, 'how painful that heart attack was. It was like being stabbed between the ribs.'

'Oh, Alberto.'

'I thought nothing could hurt me more than that.' He stops. 'I was wrong.'

She bites on her cheek. 'Mi dispiace, caro. I don't deserve you to forgive me.'

'No. You don't.' He puffs on the cigarette. 'I loved you from the moment our parents introduced us. I wanted to heal that broken heart of yours. I thought I could make you happy, that *we* could be happy, together. How stupid I was.'

'You're not stupid,' she whispers.

He exhales. 'So, what happens now?'

'Well.' She sighs. 'What I want to happen is for you to have the operation and for me to spend the rest of my life trying to make it up to you. But what I want doesn't matter. What happens now is up to you.'

'I never want you to speak to her or see her again.'

'I won't.'

'How can I believe you, Loretta?' His voice cracks, making her gut twist with guilt.

'I promise.'

He lets out a shaky sigh and stands up. 'Let's go home, I'm tired.' He cocks his elbow for her.

Her knees creak painfully as she stands.

They link arms and walk slowly through the water along the lanes back to the hotel, ignoring the planks that have been laid down over the worst of the flood. Neither of them speaks.

Once they're back inside the lobby of Il Cuore, she says, 'I'm calling the hospital to book in your heart surgery.'

'Do what you want.' His voice is flat, his expression dull.

Ten minutes after she calls the hospital, an administrator rings her back with a date for Alberto to have the defibrillator inserted.

'Surgery's booked for you in eight days,' she tells him after hanging up.

He doesn't respond apart from a long sigh. She's broken him. She's broken Alberto.

She couldn't hate herself more.

Elena

For reasons beyond Elena's comprehension, the Dawsons have come and sat themselves at the table right next to her and Christian for dinner, and they haven't taken their eyes off her. Every time she sneaks a peek at them, they're gawping at her.

Eventually, Christian notices it too. 'What are you looking at, mate?' he says to Mike.

Mike's already ruddy cheeks turn even redder.

Christian puts his napkin down and stands up so that he towers over Mike. 'Listen, Santa, I don't know what your story is, but you need to stop staring at my wife.' His voice is low. 'Stay away from her. Do you understand me?'

Mike crosses his arms and gives Christian a defiant scowl. 'What are you talking about? I don't even know Elena.'

Mike's voice is as loud as Christian's is quiet, and people at nearby tables turn to stare.

Christian lowers his face to Mike's. 'Then how *the fuck* do you know her name?' he says softly.

'I heard people saying it! What's your problem, anyhow? Why don't you sit yourself back down and let me eat my dinner in peace.'

Gayle's mouth is agape.

Christian's jaw clenches.

'Christian, please.' Elena grabs his arm, but he flicks her off in one quick swipe. He turns on his heels and glares at her.

She knows that look.

Christian's voice has lowered to barely above a whisper. His breath is hot in her eye. 'There's something going on with this guy. I know it.'

'Elena! Christian!' Rocco appears from nowhere and gives Christian a friendly pat on the back. 'Is something the matter, my friend?'

Elena could throw herself at his feet with gratitude.

Christian's posture softens under Rocco's touch. 'All good, mate. All good.'

'Ah, bene.' Rocco turns to Mike. 'Signore, good news! Dinner tonight is on the house for you and for la signora.' He drops his voice to talk to Christian. 'Can I talk to you for a moment, my friend, about the, ah . . . the private business?'

'Sure, mate. Back in a tick, Ellie.' Just like that, Christian's mood lifts. He walks out into the lobby with Rocco, their arms around each other. The best of friends.

As soon as they're gone Elena turns to Gayle and Mike. She's trying not to cry.

'He's a menace, that husband of yours.' Mike's hands are trembling.

'I know. I'm so sorry. I haven't even had a chance to thank you both for all you've done for me.'

'We're the ones who should be sorry for putting you in danger,' Gayle says, casting a look at Mike. 'Are you still planning to leave him?'

'Yes, I'm escaping on Saturday. The Bianchis are helping me.'

'Is there anything else we can do for you, sugar?' Gayle's eyebrows are knitted together.

'No, but thank you.'

When Christian returns, the Dawsons have left and Elena's minding her own business, eating her stuffed artichoke.

'The protest's going to be *epic*.' He swallows a mouthful of rosé. 'I can't believe I get to be part of something this big! It'll be one for the history books. The meeting on Saturday's at eleven.'

It's like his run-in with Mike didn't even happen.

'That's exciting.' She smiles sweetly at him. 'Saturday's only two days away.'

Only two more days.

Gayle

Gayle and Mike are so shaken by the encounter with Christian that they leave their meals unfinished. When they return to their suite, they don't turn on the TV or take out their screens, or call any of the children like they have on other nights. Instead, they hug steaming mugs of hot chocolate while Mike convinces himself that saying Elena's name to Christian wasn't his fault.

The incident has left Gayle more certain than ever that something sinister is about to go down at Hotel Il Cuore. She has a sick feeling about Saturday.

Outside the rain continues to pelt down.

Gayle's phone pings with a message from Noah. Seeing his name on the screen makes her heart leap.

Lizzie said you're planning to come to LA.

Were you ever going to tell me about this or were you just planning to turn up unannounced?

She's taken aback by his tone.

> Hi sugar.
>
> I was going to check dates with you once we got home from Italy.

Pop coming with you?

'Who's messaging you?' Mike asks.
'It's Noah.'
'Has he woken up to himself yet?'

>Pop's not quite ready to come visit yet.
>I'm sure he'll come around soon.

If you don't care enough about me
to stand up to him, don't bother
coming at all.

'Show me what he's saying,' Mike says.
She hands over her phone, not because she wants Mike to read what Noah said but because she's given up.

Sophie

When the last guest has left and the restaurant and kitchen are spotless, Rocco takes Sophie by the hand. 'I have a surprise for you. Get your coat.'

He's waiting in the lobby for her when she comes back downstairs. He's particularly debonair tonight in his grey tweed coat and bowler hat.

She points to the picnic basket in his arms. 'What's all this about, Signore Bianchi?'

'You have been in Venice over a week and not taken a gondola ride. It is time we fix this problem, no?'

'It's nine-thirty. Do they do them this late?'

'For tourists, no. For me, yes.' He grins.

'But it's still raining out.'

'Even better. Venice is the most beautiful in the rain. You remember the basilica?'

She smiles. 'Kinda hard to forget.'

'Andiamo, bella.'

For the first time since she arrived, Rocco leads Sophie to the red door at the rear of the hotel that backs onto the canal, instead of the street. Shielding her from the rain with his umbrella, he holds her hand as she steps down to where a lone gondola awaits them. The gondolier, a youngish man dressed in black pants, a red striped top and the iconic straw boater, helps Sophie onto the gondola, where a bigger umbrella is positioned over the seats.

Rocco introduces him as his old friend Sergio.

'Is there anyone in Venice who isn't an old friend of yours?' She laughs.

As they float away from the bank, Rocco pulls her in close to him. It's cold on the black water, even huddled together under a heavy woollen blanket. Standing behind them, and seemingly not bothered by the rain, Sergio wordlessly steers the gondola around the corner.

'Guarda.' Rocco points up. 'Your window, Sophie.'

She looks up at the red shutters and remembers him opening them for her that first night, letting the sights and sounds of San Marco into her room. The bright blue stone of the hotel, its cream balconies and colourful planter boxes along the arched windows appear even more beautiful from the water than they do from the street. Then the gondola narrowly passes under a footbridge, and the hotel disappears into the dark behind them.

Sergio weaves them through the maze of canals that they have completely to themselves. The only sound is that of the soft waves. Venice is sleeping.

Rocco opens the picnic basket and produces small glass containers of roasted chestnuts and thinly sliced pears and pecorino. If someone had asked Sophie what the ultimate food for a night-time picnic on a gondola would be, she couldn't have dreamed up a better combination than chestnuts, fruit and cheese.

Rocco pours her a glass of rosé from a leftover bottle from dinner and serves himself sparkling water.

Stop thinking about his addiction. Live in the moment!

He catches the look in her eye. 'I promise you, cara, my sobriety is the number one priority in my life. Please believe me.'

He's so darned earnest, she can't not believe him. She nuzzles into his shoulder.

'Rest now, bella,' he says softly. 'Because I am going to do some very bad things to you when we get home. You will need your energy.'

'Your sex voice is so husky.' She smiles at him.

'What sex voice?'

'You know, the voice you get when you're thinking about sex.'

He snorts. 'Bella, if I have a voice for when I am thinking about sex, then that is the only voice I have every second I am with you.'

She's already imagining Bec's reaction when she tells her that line. Only an Italian could get away with it.

Half an hour later, they're back at the lagoon where all the other gondolas rock in the water, covered by blue tarps. Sergio helps them step out onto the pier as the rain comes down harder. Rocco grabs her arm and starts walking along the abandoned lit-up piazza like he's late for the bus.

'Slow down!' She laughs. 'I can't keep up.'

'I am walking fast to get you out of the rain.'

'Liar, you're just trying to get me to bed faster.'

'This is true. Andiamo!' With that he takes her hand and starts jogging in earnest, dragging her behind him. It's hard to run when she's laughing this much.

Her laughter abruptly stops when they approach Il Cuore.

Standing under a spotlight on the front steps of the hotel, a suitcase beside her, is the unmistakable figure of Penelope Black in a long yellow raincoat.

Ice runs through Sophie's veins.

Penelope's hair is sopping wet and her mascara's running down her cheeks in black streaks. She's madly typing on her phone with thumbs poking out of fingerless gloves, swaying as she texts.

'Mum?'

'Fee!' Penelope cries. 'Surprise! It's *meee*! Gosh, this place was hard to find. I got myself thoroughly lost with all the narrow lanes and bridges. It's not for the faint of heart, Venice, is it? Honestly, I thought I'd never make it here. The rain! And they confiscated my umbrella at check-in, would you believe? Anyhow, I finally found this place and it was locked! I tried calling you, but it went to your voicemail like it always does. You really do need to record a new message, darling. You sound awfully nasal. Anyway, I thought I'd try messaging you instead and then you showed up. Isn't that amazing?'

Sophie's dizzy, trying to keep up. 'What are you doing here?'

'Darling, I simply couldn't bear the way things ended in our last call. It left the most bitter taste in my mouth.' Penelope's voice echoes down the street. 'I had to make things right. And you said I should come to Venice, didn't you? You said that on the phone. So, *tada*! Here I am!' She waves an arm in the air and almost loses her balance. It's only Rocco quickly steadying Penelope that prevents her from falling face first down the stairs.

Penelope eyes Rocco up and down. 'Well, well. And who do we have here?'

Rocco gives her his big smile. 'I am Rocco Bianchi, son of Loretta Bianchi. It is an honour to meet Sophie's mother.'

'Goodness me,' Penelope squeals. 'Aren't you just delicious?'

Sophie struggles to speak. 'Are you staying here?'

Penelope tilts her head. 'Well, I mean, I haven't had time to book anything yet. I assumed I could stay with you, dear.'

Is she serious?

'Some mother–daughter bonding time. Wouldn't that be lovely?' Penelope slurs.

Oh God, she's serious. Sophie stares at her, unable to reply.

'You are in luck, signora.' Rocco fills the silence. 'We have a room that became vacant this afternoon. You are welcome to stay.'

'How marvellous. What a delight you are.' Penelope flirtatiously touches his chest.

Rocco unlocks the glass door and takes hold of Penelope's luggage. Sophie follows her mother's unsteady steps inside.

'What a splendid Christmas tree!' Penelope shouts.

'Cara, it will be okay,' Rocco whispers to her. 'At least we have a room, so you don't share.'

'Nothing's okay,' she whispers back.

Penelope staggers towards her and Sophie recoils at her stale breath. 'Come on, sweetie. How about a hug for your old lady?' Penelope's arms drag on Sophie's neck. 'It's always been you and me against the world, hasn't it, darling?'

Sophie disentangles herself from her mother's arms. 'It's never been like that.'

It's over, it's all over. She has to leave this city, this hotel, this man, all of whom she adores, as fast as she possibly can. Penelope has reminded her that she only has room for one alcoholic in her life, and that position's already been filled.

Sophie leaves Rocco with her mother and bolts up the stairs to her room.

'It's always been you and me against the world' rings in her ears as she locks the door.

When Sophie's father was alive, the only place Penelope could escape from him was the toilet, the one room in their house that had a lock. So whenever Martin turned violent, if she was quick enough, Penelope would run and lock herself in there until it was safe to come out.

But Martin Black had stamina. He could go on for hour after hour, ranting and swearing and smoking and pacing and punching the walls before he ran out of steam.

The house only had one toilet. When David or Sophie needed to go while Penelope was locked up in there, they had to do it in the back garden. There were times they needed to do more than pee. When that happened, they knocked on the toilet door and told Penelope about it in urgent voices. She never answered. When she locked herself in there, she was gone from them.

So the children walked to the neighbours' houses and begged to use their toilets. They knocked on a different door each time, so as not to arouse suspicion.

The neighbours must have known, surely. Martin's shouting must have easily been heard all the way up the street, and Penelope's screams were ear splitting. But no one ever said a word. They let Sophie and David use their toilets, and then the children went home and hoped they wouldn't need to go again until Penelope let herself out.

Sometimes lunch, then dinner passed by and still she stayed locked away. Neither Sophie nor David knew how to cook. They were still young enough to have missing front teeth. They weren't allowed to use the oven or the stove, in any case. So they dragged stools to the pantry and fossicked for food. Sophie did the best she could to bring together something that resembled a meal – a tin of peas or Spam, some sliced bread, a tomato.

Martin sometimes watched them while he smoked. Other times it was as if they weren't there as he paced lap after lap of the carpeted hallway, yelling and cursing and making all kinds of threats.

'Let's have a packet of chips for lunch,' David sometimes suggested.

But Sophie felt responsible for his wellbeing. 'No, eat your sandwich.'

'I don't like tuna.'

'Shh, just eat it. You can have a cream biscuit after.'

Of course it was a terrible situation for Penelope. She'd married young, in love and swept up in a daring romance with a much older man, who was all the more alluring to her because her parents disapproved of him. Nobody could have predicted what he'd become. It wasn't her fault.

After Martin died, Penelope turned to the church for comfort, and she turned to alcohol. She became unreliable, forgetful, often neglectful. She was more of a liability than a mother. Sophie did everything she could to keep her safe and functioning. Even then, Sophie didn't resent her, she pitied her.

But from the day Sophie left home, once she finally had space, that's when the resentment began. Over the years, that resentment blossomed and grew so large that its branches covered her entire relationship with her mother, throwing it into shade and locking out any possible light.

She went to counselling. It didn't work. She tried forgiveness – she really, honestly tried. That didn't work either. It's almost impossible to forgive someone who isn't sorry they hurt you, and Penelope was doing too much praying and drinking to be sorry about anything.

So Sophie made more room for the resentment to bury its roots so deep inside her that it became rather impossible to dig it out.

When Penelope locked that toilet door, she abandoned her children. And to Sophie, that was unforgivable.

On the
TENTH
DAY *of*
CHRISTMAS

Elena

Elena stares at the blood on her underwear in disbelief. Her period has been sporadic for years. Now, just a day before her escape, here it is – obtrusive, unwanted, terrifying.

When she was hurriedly packing in Sydney, adding tampons to her suitcase was the last thing on her mind. Thankfully, she finds a single pad with the complimentary hotel toiletries.

Her abdomen spasms, making her wince. Now there's cramping to contend with as well as her injured ankle.

Why does it have to be this hard?

She blames the food for the bleeding. It's the first time in years she hasn't been starving. Her body finally had the nutrition it needed to function normally – so it did. She could kick herself for eating enough to create this complication. Hunger is safer than this.

'What's going on in there, Ellie?' Christian calls out, never giving her a single fucking minute to herself.

'Coming!' She washes her hands and walks out.

They head downstairs to find Signore Bianchi at the entrance to the restaurant. He tips his hat to them. 'Buongiorno, signore! Buongiorno, signora!' He guides them to an empty table and when she sits, he gives her back a quick pat. His fatherly touch makes her ache for Papà.

With Rocco and Christian caught up in conversation by the buffet, Elena seizes the opportunity to manically wave Signora Bianchi over to her table.

Elena speaks to her quickly and, for the first time, in Italian. 'I have my period but no tampons or pads. He'll kill me if he finds out.'

'Ah, cara mia.' Signora Bianchi shakes her head. 'I'll take supplies up to your room now. Where do you want me to leave them?'

'In my make-up bag in the bathroom vanity. I'm so sorry for all the trouble I've caused.'

Signora Bianchi cups Elena's face in her hand. 'You have nothing to be sorry for. You're a brave girl. A friend of mine, Suora Teresa, will be waiting for you and Anna-Maria at the Vatican tomorrow. You'll be safe at the monastery there, don't worry.'

'Mille grazie, Zia. And Alessandro? Is he escorting us?'

Before Signora Bianchi can reply, Christian's back and Elena's none the wiser.

Loretta

The bright ceiling light in the Taylors' bathroom is hard on Loretta's eyes. After yet another sleepless night, she'd give anything to crawl back into bed for an hour or two. Instead, the hotel has been inundated with phone calls and emails from people asking her to comment on the photo of her that the Irish journalist published. She's ignoring those requests. There's enough drama in her life already.

Loretta moves quickly, finding Elena's make-up bag and hiding two boxes of tampons underneath the collection of foundations and powders and brushes. The suite looks like any other young couple's – clothes falling out of suitcases, souvenirs on the table, bed unmade. There's nothing sinister-looking about their room, which makes it even more disturbing.

Quickly, she leaves, locking the door behind her, only to find more drama waiting for her back in the kitchen. The whole family's huddled together around the bench, and she's faced with a multitude of accusing stares.

Santa Maria, has Alberto told them about Flavia and me?

'Why are you all looking at me like that?' Loretta croaks.

'Mamma!' Marina storms up to her. 'What's Luca Falcone doing out there?' Her tone is dangerous.

Loretta exhales. It's only about Luca. With everything else going on, she forgot all about inviting him for breakfast. She avoids Marina's eye. 'So what if he's here?' She puts her apron back on and turns to Rocco. 'Where's Sophie? Did she come to the market with you?'

'She's in her room. She's not feeling well.'

She wants to question him about that, but Marina isn't through with her yet.

'I've told you a million times to stop interfering in my life! Why don't you *ever* listen?' Marina sounds like she might cry.

'Why do you assume it has anything to do with you?' Loretta replies calmly. 'I did it to say thank you for the way he looked after your father.'

Marina points at Alberto. 'And were you in on this little plan too?'

'Your mother tells me nothing,' he answers, giving Loretta a stare that turns her insides cold.

Marina slams her hand down on the bench right in front of Loretta. 'Stay out of my business!'

'I have to get back to the front desk.' Chiara rubs Marina's arm on her way out, lowering her eyes when she passes by Loretta.

The men quickly mumble reasons for being needed in the restaurant and follow Chiara out, leaving Loretta and Marina alone in the kitchen.

Loretta hoists herself up onto a stool. 'Cara, I'm saving you from yourself. At least Luca's a man you can have a future with.'

'What do you mean by that?' Marina lifts her chin, giving her a defiant stare.

'I know about Alessandro.'

Marina takes a sharp breath in. 'Did Rocco tell you?'

'He didn't need to.'

'Please don't make me talk about it.'

Loretta wishes she could take Marina into her arms. *My darling girl*, she wants to say. *Do you know how special you are? Do you know that you deserve a partner to cherish you above all else? Do you know that you're too good to be the secret lover of a priest?*

Marina would think she's lost her mind if she spoke to her this way. Instead she says, 'Okay, tesoro. But tell me, did you speak to him about Elena? She asked me about him this morning.'

Marina nods. 'He's going to travel with her.' She purses her lips. 'It's dangerous for him. That lunatic husband of Elena's could track them down. What if he hurts him?' Her eyes are full of worry.

Gesù Cristo, her daughter really does love this man.

'The Blessed Virgin will keep him safe,' Loretta says. 'It'll be okay.'

'He wasn't supposed to go back there. He was going to resign. He's only returning because of *her*.' There's resentment in Marina's voice.

'Resign? He's leaving the priesthood?' Loretta can't hide her shock.

Marina nods but her expression is closed. It's clear she won't be divulging anything else.

Loretta rests her hand over Marina's. 'I'm sorry about inviting Luca.'

'You had no right.' Marina's voice cracks. 'His mother told him the invitation came from me. You humiliated us both.'

'I was only trying to help.'

'Stop helping. I'm begging you.'

'Okay, I promise. But I'm here if you want to talk. You don't have to be alone with your worries. I understand more than you can imagine about your situation.'

'You understand nothing, Mamma.' Marina pulls her hand away. 'I have to get back to work.' She leaves the kitchen just as Rocco walks back in.

'How long have you known about your sister and the priest?' Loretta stares him down.

He looks at the ground. 'Since Rome.'

She sighs. 'Nobody tells me anything.'

'It's not exactly the kind of thing you rush to tell your parents.' Rocco pours himself a juice. She's been distracted by one thing after another this morning and only now notices that Rocco isn't himself. He hasn't smiled once, and his shoulders are drooping.

She pats the stool next to her. 'Sit.'

He obeys.

'What's wrong?'

'Nothing.'

'Tell me.' She ruffles his hair.

'Sophie's avoiding me.'

'Why? What did you do?'

'Straight away you assume it's my fault.'

'Am I wrong?'

He adjusts his glasses. 'I told her about my past.'

She feels a surge of protective love for him. 'You're in love with her, aren't you?'

He nods.

'What happens when she leaves next week? Don't tell me you're thinking of following her to Australia.'

'I could never leave you and Papà, you know that. She wants to move here.'

'Does she? That's wonderful! I was so worried you'd be heartbroken after she left. Sophie's wonderful, I'm happy for you.'

'Don't pop the champagne yet.' He lets out a sad laugh. 'She locked herself in her room and is refusing to talk to me. I think I remind her too much of her mother.'

'Why? Her mother's an alcoholic?'

'Yes. Sophie didn't react well when she arrived last night.'

Loretta frowns. 'What did you just say?'

'Her mother arrived last night. I checked her into the free room. She's up there now. Sophie hasn't spoken to me since.'

'Sophie's mother is here, and you were planning to tell me when exactly?' Loretta taps him on the back of the head. 'Honestly, you get more stupid by the day! Look after the restaurant.' She slides off the chair and walks towards the door.

'Where are you going?' he calls after her.

She turns to him. 'I'm not going to let you lose her because of her issues with her mother.'

She marches up the stairs, ready to put out another fire.

Sophie

There's a gentle knock on Sophie's door. She freezes. Rocco's already been up here knocking twice. She can't let herself see him or she'll weaken.

She's leaving Venice today. Rocco has the potential to ruin her life, which means that even though it kills her to leave, she knows she has to. The knocking continues.

'Sophie? It is me, Loretta. Can I bring you something to eat?'

Sophie stays still and doesn't answer.

'Cara? Please. Open the door.'

When Loretta Bianchi tells you to open the door, you do it. Although she hates anyone seeing her without make-up, Sophie obediently unlocks the door and stands there, barefoot in her spotty pyjamas and white hotel robe, facing Loretta.

'Ah, bella, don't cry.' Loretta closes the gap between them and opens her arms.

For someone so lean, Loretta hugs fiercely. She points to the suitcase that lies open on the unmade bed, surrounded by a mountain of clothes. 'You are leaving?'

'I've booked a flight home this afternoon. I can't get involved with Rocco, knowing he's got an addiction. And it's awful because . . .' A sob escapes her. 'Because I love him. I've fallen in love with him. Already. And I love being here, with all of you. The happiest I've ever been is in the kitchen cooking with your family.'

'Please stay. All of us want you to stay.'

'I can't. One unreliable person in my life is enough.'

'Rocco is not like your mother, Sophie,' Loretta says gently. 'He is recovered. He is very, very reliable.'

'How can I guarantee he won't relapse?' Sophie heaves. 'I can't take the risk.'

'You are right, we cannot predict the future.' Loretta walks over to the window and perches herself on the ledge. 'But Rocco is doing everything he can to stay sober.'

'He said that. How do I know it's true?'

'Because I am telling you it is true. He never puts himself in a situation where he is tempted to drink. He never misses the AA meetings, even though he has to travel far to attend. He even went to a meeting this week. He knows how much he hurt our family, and he is truly remorseful.' She pauses. 'And I know, of course, that it is a risk to love him. But *that is love*, Sophie. Loving anyone is a risk. I cannot tell you what to do. If you want to leave, of course I cannot make you stay. But I promise you that Rocco is a good and dependable person. I am not just saying this because he is my son. He is the kindest man you will ever meet.'

Far out! It's not Rocco she needed to worry about weakening her resolve, it's Loretta effing Bianchi!

Sophie wipes her tears. 'You're wasted in this hotel, Loretta. You should have been a barrister.'

Loretta smiles. 'He loves you. I have never seen him this way with anyone before. Not even his wife.'

Sophie's heart squeezes. 'Really?'

'Yes, really.'

Sophie picks at the skin around a fingernail. 'I'm so hurt that he offered her a room here. It's really hard for me to open up to anyone about my past, but I told him everything. Then he invited her to stay.'

'Ah, this is something you have to understand about Italians. We lose our heads when it comes to hospitality. He would have offered Putin a bed. He is heartbroken this morning. You should see him.'

Loretta gestures towards the door. 'He was basting the pastries as solemnly as a mortician preparing a body for an open casket. He misses you. And he is very worried he has lost you.'

Sophie chews her lip. 'I've already booked my ticket home.'

'You still have time to cancel it.'

Sophie doesn't answer.

Loretta walks to the door. 'You cannot think clearly on an empty stomach. Let me bring you up some food. Then you can think about what you want to do. And I can arrange for your mother to go to another hotel today. But you know, perhaps being here, away from home, it is a chance to have a talk with her.'

'I'm not sure she's ready to hear what I have to say.'

'Try,' Loretta insists.

And because Loretta is essentially a deity who must be obeyed at all times, Sophie nods. 'Okay, I'll give it a go.' She throws a look towards the door. 'I just need her to sleep off yesterday first, then I'll go and talk to her.'

'So you are not leaving?'

'No. You're right, *again*. I have to give Rocco a chance.'

'I can tell Rocco to come up and see you? Please say yes. I cannot look at his face so sad for another minute.'

'You can send him up here only if he brings a slice of your marantega cake.'

'I will give him a plate of all the pastries for you, not just the cake.'

Sophie smiles back at the woman who already knows the way to her heart better than almost anyone.

Gayle

The article is the first news item Gayle sees on her phone. The photo of Loretta all alone in the flood in Piazza San Marco is underneath the headline *Life Imitates Art in Venice*. She clicks on the link and reads the article.

Venetian local Loretta Bianchi, known the world over as Signora Bianchi from the forest-like restaurant Hotel Il Cuore, cut a solitary figure early on Thursday morning. Signora Bianchi was photographed standing ankle deep in the flooded Piazza San Marco next to Magdalena Jansen's *Venice Rising* exhibit, *affogando*, highlighting the very real climate crisis facing Venetians.

Swedish environmental activist Greta Thunberg retweeted the photograph with the caption #SaveVenice. Thunberg's tweet has since been retweeted over 50k times and #SaveVenice is trending worldwide.

Former United States First Lady Michelle Obama also shared the photograph on her Instagram account and captioned it: 'I'm devastated by this image of Signora Bianchi, who our family had the pleasure of meeting in 2015 when she cooked for us in San Marco. Please save beautiful Venice before it's too late. #affogando.'

The mayor of Venice, Luigi Brugnaro, spoke to CNN this morning about the recent spate of floods in Venice. Says Brugnaro, 'Signora Bianchi represents all Venetians. We are all broken-hearted, we are all drowning. We cannot continue to live like this. We have the technology to stop the floods with the Mose Project. How many more catastrophes do Venetians have to endure before the Mose Project is finally operational?'

Construction on the Mose Project, a complex system of barriers that can be raised during periods of high water levels, remains unfinished, having been besieged by over three decades of delays due to red tape and corruption.

Venice Rising curator Franca Menori argues that the answer to saving Venice doesn't lie with the Mose Project. 'Yes, of course it will be useful once it is finished, if we ever see that day. But even then, it's designed to be used a maximum of fifteen times a year. Venice has flooded seven times in the last eight weeks. The Mose Project isn't the solution. What we need is a collective effort across the world to lower emissions. We need to stop the cruise ships from entering our port, and we need to place a limit on the number of tourists who visit Venice every year. The Venetian way of life is on the brink of destruction. We must act now.'

Neither the Italian Prime Minister nor the Minister of Environment could be reached for comment.

The *Venice Rising* exhibition culminates on 5 January, on the eve of the traditional Venetian festival La Regata della Befana.

This year, as the gondolas race across the Grand Canal, the same thing will be on everyone's minds: can Venice be saved before it's too late?

Gayle puts down her phone and moves to the window. The rain continues to bucket down, and the street remains flooded. In the crowded lane, people's umbrellas knock against each other and everyone is in rubber boots. Fancy having the technology to prevent all of this and not using it.

Mike has a hitlist of sights to see today, but Gayle has no interest in seeing anything.

Things still aren't back to normal between them, and she's beginning to wonder if they ever will be again. She created disharmony in her marriage and for what? It wasn't enough for Noah anyway.

She turns away from the window, from the city that's sinking, just like she is.

Sophie

Sophie unlocks the door to Penelope's suite. She takes the tray of food from Rocco's hands. 'I'll be okay from here,' she whispers.

'Good luck.' He kisses her cheek.

She enters the darkened room. The smell of whiskey hangs thick in the air. The shutters are drawn, but she can make out her mother's shape in the bed. 'Mum?'

There's no reply.

She puts the tray down on the dressing table. 'Mum?'

Penelope sighs.

Sophie switches on the bedside lamp. Penelope turns her head away from the light, squinting.

'Are you okay?' Sophie perches herself on the edge of the bed, next to her mother.

'I shouldn't have come.' Penelope's voice is scratchy.

'I brought you some lunch. White bean soup.'

Penelope makes a face.

There's so much that Sophie wants to say, she doesn't know where to begin. They sit in silence.

'Are you sleeping with that Italian man I met last night?' Penelope says eventually.

'So no small talk, then? Just diving straight into my sex life?'

'Be careful, Fee. Italian men have a certain *reputation*. I don't want you getting hurt.'

'Nobody's ever hurt me more than you have.'

Penelope scoffs. 'How on earth have I hurt you?'

'How *haven't* you is the question. For a start, you've been shaming me about my size since I was a teenager.'

'I only mention it because I want what's best for you. I wish you'd consider the gastric sleeve. It might solve all your problems.'

'For fuck's sake, Mum! This is exactly what I'm talking about.'

Penelope turns her head and looks Sophie in the eye for the first time. 'Fee, I adore you. You must know that. I'm only trying to help.'

Sophie's avoided prolonged eye contact with her mother for as long as she can remember. Now she takes a good long look at her, and what she sees shocks her. She doesn't see the unstable alcoholic who immediately comes to mind when she thinks of Penelope, she doesn't see a cold-blooded murderer, or even a critical mother. All she sees is a deeply sad shell of a woman.

'All I want is your happiness, Fee,' Penelope says, and Sophie believes her.

'If you want me to be happy, please don't mention my size again.'

'I'll try, darling.' Penelope sits up. 'My head hurts.' She has a sip from the glass of water on the bedside table. 'Your Italian fellow, what's his name again?'

'Rocco.'

'That's right. I made a fool of myself in front of him.'

'Rocco understands. He's had addiction issues too,' Sophie says quietly.

Penelope's jaw clenches. She looks away.

'He's been sober for eight years,' Sophie continues. 'He was telling me about a rehab clinic he stayed at in Geneva. It's excellent, apparently. Lovely views of the lake, big private rooms. The staff all speak English there.'

Penelope remains stony-faced.

Sophie takes a deep breath and summons the courage to say what she's been too nervous to say for over a decade. 'Mum, you need help to stop drinking.'

Penelope's knuckles turn white around the glass of water. 'I don't have the money to check myself into a posh clinic in Switzerland.'

'It doesn't have to be Switzerland. And I'll pay for it, wherever you want to go,' Sophie says quickly. 'I have savings.'

'I can't let you do that. Your savings are for you.'

'Of course you can. There's nothing I want more than to help you get well.'

'Not even the sexy Italian?' Penelope gives a small smile, showing a glimpse of her old self.

Sophie smiles back. 'Well, maybe, except for the sexy Italian. Will you go to rehab? Please, Mum?'

'Let me think about it.'

Whenever Sophie's imagined how her mother would react if she confronted her about her alcohol abuse, she never pictured a response this calm and reasonable. It makes her wish she'd had the guts to do it years ago. 'Thank you for thinking about it.' She takes Penelope's hand in hers. 'I'm glad you came. It's good to see you.'

Penelope squeezes her hand. 'I'm sorry I embarrassed you in front of Rocco.'

'S'okay.'

'I do love you, Fee. You have to know that.'

'I do.'

She isn't saying it back. Not yet.

Elena

Christian has baby fever. While they shop for souvenirs in Piazza San Marco, he excitedly plans how they'll turn the study into a nursery, debates with himself whether they should find out the sex or keep it a surprise, and suggests his old university friends as potential godparents.

He stops at a market stall and holds up a tiny canary-yellow 'I Love Venice' romper, the joy written all over his face.

The flood waters have filled the whole square and the rain shows no sign of abating. The wind whips around Elena's head, blasting her ears. 'Shall we go? Mamma's waiting for us.'

'Sure. Let's drop this stuff back at the hotel first.'

The lanes leading to Il Cuore are quiet. Some of the shops and cafes are closed, their shutters drawn and sandbags stacked on top of each other to keep the water away. But other workers are embracing the conditions, standing at their shop entrances in gumboots, cheerfully calling out their cheap prices for umbrellas and plastic ponchos and shoe coverings.

Elena's jeans are wet, so once they're back at the hotel, she sits on the edge of the bed and peels them off.

Christian watches her undress with a glint in his eye and she pretends not to notice.

As she's pulling on fresh jeans, he stops her. He raises an eyebrow and drops his voice. 'I mean, we're not in that much of a rush to get to your mum's, are we?' He licks the hollow of her neck.

She shudders and he mistakes it for excitement, which encourages him to pull her closer and kiss her behind the ear. She has to stop him before he discovers the tampon, but Christian doesn't take kindly to having his advances rejected. She has to play this right or everything will come undone.

'Babe,' she whispers. 'I'm really sore down there.'

He pulls away abruptly. 'What do you mean? You shouldn't have pain this early on. Have you had any spotting?'

'No, no, nothing like that,' she quickly reassures him. 'It's just . . .' She tries to look coy. 'We've been doing it *a lot* this week.' She giggles. 'You've kind of worn me out.'

He brushes her lips with his. 'It's because you're so fucking hot, Ellie,' he murmurs. 'I can't help it.' He's not taking no for an answer.

Fanculo.

There's a firm tap on the door.

Christian grunts and goes to open it. Elena quickly pulls on a fresh pair of jeans. Signora Bianchi is standing there. She seems agitated.

'Mi scusi, Dottore. My Alberto, he won't give up the cigarettes and I am so worried. Please would you speak with him. He will listen to a doctor.'

'Of course. We were just on our way out but I'm happy to help. Where is he?'

'He is on the front steps. Smoking. Always smoking.' She throws her hands in the air.

Christian turns to Elena with a wink. 'Looks like you get a pass.' Then he smiles at Signora Bianchi. 'I'll go see what I can do.'

When he's gone, Elena rushes to Signora Bianchi, her saviour twice today, and hugs her as tightly as she can.

Gayle

Gayle's proofreading Mike's latest blog post when her phone pings with a message from her daughter Susan.

Mom, did you and Pop get a message from Chris?

We all got the same message on Messenger.

We're worried!

Feeling as if the air has been sucked out of her, Gayle opens her Messenger app. Sure enough, there's a message request from a Chris Mullins.

Hello, I'm Noah's partner. Sorry to disturb you but it's about Noah.

I came home from work to a note from Noah saying that he 'can't live like this anymore'. His car's still here but he's taken a suitcase. He's not answering his phone or replying to any messages.

Noah's never done anything like this before and I'm very worried. I know he's recently been back in touch with his

family, so I thought I'd see if any of you
have heard from him. If not, I'm sorry to
alarm you in this way.

Please contact me if you hear anything.

> Gayle covers her mouth with her hand and lets out a whimper.
> 'What is it?' Mike asks.
> She shows him the message. 'We have to do something!'
> 'What can we do from here?'
> She bites her lip. 'I don't know. Let's see what else the others know.'
> She messages the group chat with Susan, Lizzie and Justin.
> 'What are you telling them?' Mike looks over her shoulder.
> She repositions herself so he can get a better view of her screen.

I saw Chris's message.

Have any of you heard anything else?

> Justin replies.

Hi Mom.

I've had a few messages with Chris.
Noah's been missing since yesterday.

Chris went to the police station but
because Noah left a note and packed a
case, there's nothing the police can do.

We've tried calling and messaging
Noah, but there's no response.

> Gayle's breath catches. *Gone for a day.* Nobody has heard from Noah or known where he is for a whole day. *Oh Lord,* she prays, *please help my boy be found.*
> 'It's us,' she cries to Mike. 'It's because of us.'

'Now, now, hon. Don't get yourself all worked up. That boy's always been impulsive, hasn't he? For all we know, he might have had an argument with this Chris fellow. Maybe Noah's come to his senses and walked out. He might be making his way back to Arkansas right now.'

Gayle turns to look at him. 'If anything happens to our son'—she points a shaky finger at him—'I will never forgive you, Michael James Dawson!'

His mouth hangs open, but he doesn't reply.

She throws on her robe and slippers and, without turning to look at him, marches out of the room with her phone in her hand. She stomps down all the stairs and walks into the empty restaurant. The ceiling lights are off but the room glows with the thousands of fairy lights draped around the trees.

She heads to the buffet and cuts herself a big slice of cake, before sitting at one of the vacant tables where she cries into her hands.

She tries calling Noah but there's no answer. Her heart skips a beat at the sound of his voice on the voicemail recording. She hangs up and sends Chris a message.

> Hello Chris,
>
> It's nice to make your acquaintance. I only wish it was under better circumstances.
>
> I'm sorry but I haven't heard from Noah. Please let me know if you hear anything.
>
> Bless you, Gayle Dawson.

Then she sends Noah a message.

> Sugar, you deserve so much better than the way we treated you.

> I'll do everything I can to fix it.
> I promise to help your dad
> change his ways.
>
> All of us are so worried about you.
>
> Please let us know you're okay.
> I love you.

And then Gayle prays harder than she's ever prayed before.

Loretta

Loretta sighs wearily as she climbs into bed. The phone hasn't stopped ringing all day with journalists wanting a comment about her photo at Magdalena's tank.

'How nice that the whole world now knows how miserable you are with your life,' Alberto grumbled bitterly this afternoon.

He hasn't smiled once today. At dinner he stayed upstairs instead of mingling with the guests. He must be worried about his upcoming surgery, but he hasn't shared his concerns with her. The lifelong bond between them has been broken and she doesn't know how to fix it.

She reaches into the drawer of her bedside table for the rosary, but the aqua glass beads don't allay her worries at all. After a while she flicks off the covers and leaves the warmth of the bed. She puts on a robe and slippers.

Alberto rolls over and looks at her. 'Where are you going now? Another escapade we can enjoy photos of in the news tomorrow?'

She clicks her tongue. 'Does it look like I'm going on an excursion dressed like this? I can't sleep. I'm just getting some cake and something to drink.'

He huffs and rolls over again.

'I'll be back soon,' she says to his back.

La signora Americana is sitting in the restaurant, alone at a table with an untouched slice of cake, when Loretta wanders in. Loretta curses inwardly but smiles at Gayle. Of all the people, why does it have to be her, the woman who knows her darkest secret, who's here when Loretta's at her most vulnerable? At least Gayle's insufferable husband isn't here.

'We had the same idea.' Loretta nods at the slice of marantega cake in front of her guest. Walking to the buffet table, she cuts herself a generous slice of cake, and from the bar, she pours two shot glasses of sherry.

'Thank you, but I don't drink.' Gayle pats her tight white curls when Loretta sets the sherry in front of her. Her eyes are bloodshot and she clutches a ball of saturated tissues. She hasn't taken off her make-up; the blue eyeshadow is as bright as ever and her eyelashes are clumped together with blue mascara.

Loretta slides the drink closer to Gayle. 'For tonight, you make an exception. It looks like you need it as much as I do.' She clinks her glass against Gayle's. 'Salute.'

'You twisted my arm.' Gayle copies Loretta, throwing back the shot. She licks her lips afterwards and looks appreciatively at the empty glass.

'You see?' Loretta smiles. She chews the first bite of cake. It came out a little dry today.

'Still raining out there,' Gayle says. 'Never seen a place get so wet.'

'The acqua alta is a curse.' She watches Gayle use her fork to play with the cake. 'You do not like the cake?'

'I love it! Everything you cook is just wonderful.'

'You do not seem like you are enjoying it.'

'I gotta headache is all,' Gayle says.

'Still?'

'Still. I've had this headache coming on six months now. Can't seem to shake it, no matter what I do.'

'So your headache did not start here, in my hotel?'

'No, ma'am.'

Loretta shakes her head. 'Then why does your husband insist it is the pink walls of this room that caused the problem?'

Gayle sighs. 'That's Mike, he's always looking for something to blame. The truth is, I know the reason I keep getting these headaches. And deep down, so does Mike.'

'And now you must tell me what the reason is.'

'It's because of my son.' Gayle's eyes tear up at the mention of her child. 'We're not exactly on speaking terms at the moment.'

'A mother cannot be happy if there is trouble with her son.'

'I think my headaches are the Lord's punishment. The thing is, Noah, my boy, he's gay.'

Loretta's skin prickles all over. 'You think God is punishing you because your son is gay?'

'No, no! God's punishing me for being a bad mother. You see, Noah got married and Mike, well, he's opposed to gay marriage.'

Loretta has to work hard not to roll her eyes. Of course Mike's opposed to gay marriage. What's he not opposed to?

Gayle continues. 'They had a big argument and we haven't seen Noah since. I didn't do a thing to stop it – I didn't defend my son. The Lord's punishing me for not loving him enough. Now Noah's missing. Nobody knows where he is since yesterday. He's not answering his phone. His husband, Chris, sent me this message today.'

Loretta reads the message on Gayle's phone. 'I have received messages like this many years ago about my own son,' she says, handing the phone back. 'This is a terrible thing for a mother. But you know, to me, it sounds like your son is safe. These are the actions of a man who wants time alone to think, that is all. It has only been a day. Maybe he had an argument with this Chris?'

'That's what Mike thinks too. I hope you're both right.'

Loretta's annoyed at sharing even a single thought with that moronic man.

'I think it's because he's upset with us that he's gone missing.' Gayle wrings her chubby red hands together. 'I'm telling you, the Lord's punishing me for not loving him enough.'

'The reason you suffer is because you love your son too much, not because you do not love him enough. Why would your head hurt for six months if you do not love him? Why would you be sitting here at this hour instead of sleeping?'

'I didn't love him the way I should have when he was growing up.' Gayle's nose drips. She wipes it with the used bunch of tissues. 'He gave me so much trouble, that boy. I resented him and that's the truth. I loved the other children more.'

'What do you mean?'

'It's a long story, Loretta. I'm sure you're too busy for my nonsense.'

'Do I look busy? I am sitting here doing nothing but eating cake.' Loretta's pleased for the distraction. 'Tell me this long story. I am interested.'

'Settle in, sugar, and I'll tell you.' Gayle lets out a shaky sigh. 'It started with my awful pregnancy – nausea like I'd never known, sciatic pain, haemorrhoids you needed a wheelbarrow for. I'd been blessed with easy pregnancies before, so it was a shock. Meanwhile, I had three little ones under five to look after. So I think I resented poor Noah before he even took his first breath.'

'You had three children less than five years old when you were pregnant?' Loretta's jaw drops.

'I sure did. Mike doesn't believe in birth control.'

Of course he doesn't, Loretta thinks.

'We let ourselves accept as many children as the Lord knew we could handle,' Gayle says.

Loretta shakes her head. 'Your poor body. So the pregnancy was difficult, and then?'

'And then Noah came into the world a whole fourteen weeks before he was due. There was a terrible storm that day. I remember it was a Wednesday. There's an old poem that has a line in it: "Wednesday's child is full of woe". Do you know it?'

'No.'

'Well, let me tell you, that child was full of woe. Even the sky was crying the day Noah was born.' She pauses. 'He was in the neo-natal unit for twelve weeks.'

'This sounds like a very difficult time.'

'It was. I had to have an emergency hysterectomy.'

'So the Lord decided that the number of children you could handle was four,' Loretta says acerbically but Gayle simply nods.

'Noah was an itty-bitty little thing when we brought him home, smaller than a doll. But boy did he have a set of lungs on him! That child screamed all the day long for the first year of his life. Sometimes I wonder if he knew, even back then, the struggles that lay ahead for him. He was a miserable baby, and I was a miserable mom.'

'Of course you were miserable. You had four young children to care for, you were recovering from surgery, your baby was born too soon. This is hard for anyone.'

'I thought it would get better but it didn't. The misery followed me into Noah's childhood. My other three were well behaved, but Noah? Oh, Loretta, he was the most wilful of boys. Trouble always seemed to find him.'

Loretta laughs. 'He sounds like Marina as a child.'

Gayle looks surprised. 'Really? And did you treat her differently to Rocco?'

'Of course! I used to take off my shoe to smack her with it so often that on many days I spent more time with my shoe in my hand than on my foot.'

'But did you love her less?'

Loretta shakes her head. 'I adored her.'

'That's where I went wrong.' Gayle tears up again. 'I favoured the other children, the ones who didn't give me trouble. I convinced myself that Noah's wilfulness was God's way of punishing me for not loving him enough. Now I know better. His wilfulness wasn't my punishment, him turning his back on me is.'

Loretta stands up, wincing as her knees creak. She brings the tissue box from the buffet table over to Gayle and sits back down again. 'Perhaps you appreciated your other children more because they were easier, like any mother would. This does not mean you loved your son less. Everything you have told me makes me think you love your son as much as any mother loves her child.'

Gayle blows her nose. 'You really think so?'

'God is not punishing you, Gayle. You are punishing yourself.'

Gayle looks off into the distance. 'You might be right about that. How'd you get to be so wise?'

Loretta chuckles. 'I am wise only when it concerns the lives of other people. When it comes to my own children, I am stupid. My daughter has been in love with a man for seven years and I never knew until now.'

'The priest?'

Loretta's eyes bulge. 'Even *you* knew?'

'Marina's a lovely young woman. I hope the good Lord brings her happiness.' They sit in silence for a minute, then Gayle says, 'I saw the photo of you in the piazza. Broke my heart to see you like that. You're going through a lot, aren't you?'

Loretta considers another sherry but remains seated. 'It has been perhaps the most difficult ten days of my life.'

'You wanna talk about it, sugar?'

There's such an honesty and openness to Gayle that Loretta finds herself sharing her story. 'And what has surprised me the most,' she finishes, 'is that I am much more devastated about hurting Alberto than losing Flavia.'

'You've built a life with Alberto. It makes sense. Give him some time, things will get better. It's easy to see how much he loves you.'

'You know who I feel like? The artist Magdalena in the tank. The water is up to here.' Loretta puts her hand up to her own neck.

'We saw her today. It was pouring rain on her, and she was standing there, shivering and shaking, with the crowd heaving around her. I had to look away.'

'I hate this exhibition,' Loretta says bitterly. 'I will be happy when it is finished.'

'I'd be lying if I said I enjoyed it, but I have to admit it's taught Mike and me a whole lot. We're changing how we do things now.'

Loretta frowns. 'How?'

'Well, for one, we're checking that everything we buy is made in Venice. And when we get home, we're gonna tell everyone not to come here on the cruise ship like we did. We know how bad that is now.'

'Hmm, perhaps the exhibition will be useful after all.'

Gayle takes a small bite of the cake. 'This really is delicious.'

'This cake is torta dea marantega, the cake of the witch.'

Gayle raises her eyebrows. 'Why the witch?'

'Tradition. The witch is the symbol of the Epiphany. In the old days on the trading ships, dried fruit and raisins were precious because they were rare. So this fruit cake was baked only at Christmas time as a special celebration.'

Gayle gives a faint smile. 'What a fine tradition.'

'It is a very simple recipe,' Loretta says. 'I can write it for you.'

'Thank you, but Mike, well, he doesn't like fruit cake.'

Loretta waves her arm at Gayle. 'What about what *you* like?'

'Oh, come on now, I wouldn't bake a cake just for me. Seems a waste if Mike isn't enjoying it too.'

'I hope he appreciates how lucky he is to have such a good wife.'

'I'm the lucky one. I've been giving him such a hard time lately, about Noah and everything. And even though he's upset with me, he still puts my needs before his every minute of the day. I left our suite in a huff tonight – we're always arguing about Noah these days. But the truth of it is I owe my Mike everything. He rescued me when he married me.'

'What is marriage for if not for rescuing each other?'

'He *literally* rescued me though. I was never a Christian before I met him, but he turned my face to the Lord,' Gayle says. 'We were only kids when we got married, straight outta high school. Mike was saving to go to college to become a doctor or a lawyer, something important, you know? He's so smart, he could've been anything he wanted to be.'

Loretta holds back a laugh.

'But no sooner were we married than out popped little Susan. So instead of college, he took a job at a tyre company, and he was a diligent worker for over fifty years. All our lives, Mike put himself last. He was the best daddy to our kids, always goofing 'round with them, and he's treated me like a queen. I owe that man everything. I just wish we could all be a family again. I know he loves Noah, he really does. But I'm worried it's too late and that something awful's happened to Noah.'

'We will pray for the safety of your son. I am sure he is well and you are worrying for nothing.'

Hearing Gayle talk so lovingly about her husband sends a pang of guilt through Loretta. It's not just Mike who has been a diligent worker; Alberto's worked hard from morning till night from the day they were married, showing as much devotion to the hotel as she has. He's also been the most wonderful father to their children and has never treated her as anything less than a queen. But while Gayle openly praises her husband, Loretta has always been quick to snipe at Alberto. She has to make it up to him – he deserves better. So much better.

Loretta eats the last mouthful of her cake. 'It is getting very late. I have to try and sleep so I can work tomorrow.'

'Bedtime for me too. That drop of sherry's done the trick. I can feel my eyelids growing heavy.' Gayle pushes her chair back.

Loretta stacks their dirty plates and glasses on the buffet table, too tired to take them to the kitchen.

As they walk up the stairs together, she slips her arm through Gayle's. 'I am sure you will hear from Noah tomorrow.'

'I hope so. I really appreciate you listening to me tonight. I've been a fan of yours for so long. Now I can call you my friend.'

'And you have seen me at my worst and shown me true kindness. You have been a true friend to me. And Elena's mother tells me how kind you have been to her too. You are a wonderful woman, Gayle.'

'Oh, sweet Elena. I'm so worried for her tomorrow.'

'Me too.' Loretta squeezes her hand. 'But we will pray, yes?'

'There's always prayer. Sleep well, sugar.'

'Sweet dreams.'

They each go to their own doors.

Alberto stirs when Loretta walks into the bedroom. 'You were gone for a long time,' he mumbles. 'Did you find another nun to kiss?'

'No nun, just cake.' She crawls into bed and kisses the top of his head. 'Alberto, you know how much you mean to me, don't you? You know how grateful I am for all you've done for our family?'

His eyes pop wide open. 'Are you dying?'

'What? No!'

A look of panic crosses his face. 'Is there something you're not telling me? Have you got cancer?'

'And why would I suddenly discover I have cancer at eleven o'clock at night?'

'I don't know. Why are you acting like you're dying?'

'Forget it,' she snaps. 'Go to sleep.'

Alberto grumbles to himself and shuts his eyes.

When he's snoring again, she whispers into the dark, 'Ti amo, Alberto.'

As soon as she lies down, she realises she hasn't emptied her bladder yet. Annoyed, she flicks the covers off and pads to the ensuite. She comes back to bed, again waking Alberto.

This time he gets up. He takes a step in the direction of the toilet and stops, clutching his shoulder. A weird sound comes from him and then he collapses onto the floor. Loretta flies out of bed and races to him. He's lying face down, unmoving.

'Alberto! Alberto!' She drops to her knees and turns Alberto onto his back. His body is limp and heavy to move. *Dio mio, not his heart again!*

'Alberto! Wake up!' She grabs him by the shoulders and shakes him.

He still doesn't respond. His head lolls. His eyes are rolled backwards.

'Rocco! Marina!'

She runs to the bedside table, lunging for her phone, and calls for an ambulance. The operator drawls, asking her to slow down, making her repeat the address twice. He's in no hurry whatsoever.

'Stop wasting time!' she yells at him.

Alberto is still unconscious. *Is he even alive?*

She runs in her bare feet, her nightgown flapping around her legs, out of their apartment and across the hallway, moving faster than she has in years. Her whole body's shaking as she bangs on the Taylors' door with both fists.

'Dottore!' she screams. 'Elena! Aiutami! Help!'

The door opens and Christian appears, with Elena behind him. She explains quickly, dragging Christian, who's dressed only in briefs, by the hand to her apartment. She and Elena watch Christian administer CPR to Alberto, just like he did last week. He doesn't stop until the ambulance arrives and the paramedics take over.

The whole time the paramedics are working on Alberto's limp body, shocking him with electric current, Loretta prays to the Blessed Virgin. She makes every bargain she can think of. It's when she promises the Madonna that if Alberto is spared she'll retire from the restaurant and spend the rest of her days caring for him that Alberto opens his eyes and gasps for air.

On the ELEVENTH DAY *of* CHRISTMAS

Loretta

'Signora?'

Loretta startles at the tap on her knee. She squints at the young nurse in front of her.

'Signora, you can see him now.'

'What time is it?' Loretta rubs her eyes.

'Five in the morning.' The nurse has a kind face, his voice gentle.

She pushes herself up off the couch in the visitor's lounge. Two hours ago, Luca came to find her with the news that Alberto had survived the operation of a cardiac defibrillator being inserted into his chest.

'I've tested it, it's working well. If he stops smoking, he has a lot of life left in him yet.' Luca smiled.

Now, Loretta follows the nurse towards Alberto's room in the ICU. 'Is he awake?' she asks him.

'Si, signora. He asked for you as soon as he opened his eyes.' He leads her up the sterile white hallway. 'Just so you know, there are some wires and tubes attached to him. But he's doing very well, so try not to worry when you see him. Here we are.' He nudges the door open and indicates for her to enter.

The top half of Alberto's bed is tilted to a forty-five-degree angle, facing the doorway, and she makes eye contact with him as soon as she steps into the room. The nurse was right to warn her. Alberto looks so fragile, so old, it's hard for her not to gasp.

'Loretta,' he whispers. 'You're here.'

'Of course I'm here, caro.' She rushes to his bedside. 'Where else would I be?'

The hospital gown is loose, exposing the left side of his chest, which is shaved and covered with a large patch of white gauze under his collarbone.

'Does it hurt?' She strokes the top of his head, where his hair is long gone.

'A little.' He pulls the prongs from his nose. 'This annoys me.'

The matronly looking nurse stationed by his bedside clicks her tongue as she readjusts the prongs. 'You need this, signore. I already told you, it's the oxygen. Stop pulling it out. And I told you to keep that left arm still for another couple of hours, remember?'

'Can you hear that?' Alberto's voice is hoarse as he addresses the nurse. 'They're paging you. You better go see what they want. Quick, go.'

The nurse snorts a laugh. 'How are you feeling?'

'I feel ready for a cigarette.' He grins at her.

The nurse rolls her eyes at Loretta. 'Is he always this much trouble?'

Loretta looks at Alberto with great affection, hardly believing her luck that God has given them a chance to start over again together. 'Always.'

Sophie

Sophie's eyes snap open at the sound of wild banging on her door. She flies out of bed and slips into her robe while Rocco, still half asleep, stumbles towards the door in his briefs.

It's Marina who's there when he opens it.

'Cos'é, Marina?'

'Papà! He had another heart attack!'

Fuck.

Rocco's face falls. He speaks in hurried Italian.

'He is alive,' Marina reassures him. 'He had surgery.'

Rocco reaches for Marina and they cling to each other.

'Let's go,' Marina says to him.

'You go,' he replies. 'I have to stay here.'

'You should both go.' Sophie steps forward. 'I can go to the market and get breakfast ready. I know how it all works.'

Rocco grips her arm. 'You are sure, Sophie? It is a lot for you.'

'I'll be absolutely fine,' she insists. 'Your cousins will be here to help soon. Go to your dad.'

'You are amazing.' Rocco kisses her cheek.

She smiles at him. 'Go.'

He throws on his clothes and he and Marina are out the door seconds later.

Sophie gets herself dressed and is on her way to the market soon after the others leave. The rain has stopped and the flood waters have receded a little, but she still has to use the boardwalks to roll the cart along.

Rocco calls her when she's almost at the Rialto with the news that Alberto's awake and recovering well. 'Can you believe we did not hear anything last night? Mamma was angry with me. She said she was calling for me,' he says. 'I think maybe the ambulance came when we were in the shower.'

Sophie's belly tightens at the memory of Rocco on his knees in front of her under the water last night. 'Please tell me you didn't tell Loretta that.'

'I told her. What else could I say?'

'Oh, God. What did she say?'

'She said some things I cannot repeat.' He lets out a chuckle.

'Well, I guess that means I'll never be able to make eye contact with your mother again.'

'She loves you, and I love you, and all of Venice loves you!' he declares before hanging up.

At the Rialto, market vendors converge on her like seagulls on chips, demanding to know where Rocco is, and then pushing her for every last detail about Alberto. She tells them what little she knows and in no time, she finds her shopping cart full to the brim with fresh food. Not a single seller agrees to take money from her.

On the walk back to the hotel, two nuns approach from the other direction on the Rialto bridge, their habits flying behind them in the wind.

'Dio vi benedica,' they say in unison when they pass her.

The cafe store owners have set up tables and chairs in the flooded lanes. They greet her by name and make her stop to explain why Rocco isn't with her. Everyone's concerned about Alberto.

Her neighbours of the last six years in Melbourne don't even know her name. *This is my community*, she thinks. *These are my people*. It's the first time in her life that she's felt such a deep sense of belonging.

She thinks of how close she came to leaving Venice yesterday and it scares her. Her knee-jerk reaction of booking the first flight home when her mother arrived actually had very little to do with Rocco and everything to do with her own unpredictable upbringing, she realises.

'I'll be careful with your heart,' Rocco promised her yesterday. 'I won't hurt you. You can trust me.'

She wholeheartedly does.

Back at the hotel, she begins putting together breakfast in the restaurant. She's soon joined by Chiara and Salvatore. They're busy but not overrun, thanks to Loretta's supreme organisational skills, which mean everything is ready to serve except for a few last-minute jobs, like boiling the eggs.

Sophie remembers the veal cutlets that were stashed in the freezer the other day and pulls them out to defrost. At the Rialto, she was given a whole rainbow of root vegetables by Bianca, the always-smiling greengrocer, which she'll roast in olive oil and balsamic vinegar to go with the veal. She has scallops from dear old Pasquale, which she'll grill for primi and serve with a tomato salad and the crusty baguettes that Ezio, her baker friend, gave her. She has enough eggs from Sebastiano's charming hens to make a custard dessert. It might not be traditional Venetian fare, but it will all be delicious and fresh.

She writes the menu on the chalk board, asking Chiara to proofread the Italian for her. Underneath, she writes, *Menu prepared by Sophie Black from Foodie Magazine*, making it sound like a guest cook is a treat, not a last-minute stand-in after a family emergency.

The breakfast crowd starts arriving. Elena and Christian walk in together and she remembers that this morning is when Elena is running away.

Christian looks around the restaurant. 'Is Rocco here?'

'He's at the hospital with Alberto,' Sophie replies. It's hard for her to even look at him.

'Ah, right.' He lowers his voice. 'We have a pretty important meeting later this morning. Do you know if it's still on?'

A look of terror crosses Elena's face.

'It's definitely on,' Sophie says. 'I'm not sure if Rocco will be back in time for it, but Salvatore's going. You know Salvatore, don't you?'

Upon hearing his name, Salvatore joins her at the restaurant entrance. 'Ciao, signore. If you meet me at ten-thirty in the lobby, we will go to the meeting together. I know the way.'

Elena and Sophie exchange the briefest of glances. It's enough for her to get the message across to Elena that they all have her back.

'Will you be okay if I am gone for two hours, Sophie? Maybe longer?' Salvatore asks her in the kitchen.

'It's all under control, don't worry,' she says with confidence, knowing she has a tool in her arsenal that will make all the difference to her meal preparations today. She's enlisting the help of the best home cook she's ever known, even better than Loretta: Penelope.

Sophie's love of cooking came from her mother. When things were peaceful in their home, Sophie spent Sundays watching her mother lovingly prepare roast lamb with all the trimmings, and waiting to be allowed to lick the beaters when Penelope baked the world's best chocolate cake. Penelope was a passionate cook right up until the day she killed Martin.

After that, she lost all interest in the kitchen. She swapped homemade pies for shop-bought ones, roast potatoes for frozen chips. By then, ten-year-old Sophie had learned enough from her mother to be a competent cook herself and she soon took over preparing the family meals.

In her teens, Sophie dreamed of becoming a chef and running her own restaurant one day. But she was academically strong, with a particular gift for writing, so she was encouraged – pressured – by her careers advisor and teachers to go to university instead. She ended up becoming a journalist who wrote about food instead of a chef who created it.

Although it is under the terrible circumstance of Alberto's heart attack, today is the day that Sophie's longest held dream comes true. She's running her own restaurant.

But half an hour later, Penelope hasn't come downstairs yet, even though she agreed to help when Sophie knocked on her door after the market this morning. The breakfast diners have almost cleared out and Sophie's just beginning to fret when Penelope breezes into the restaurant, looking a million dollars in a hot-pink floaty kaftan, her white hair held back under a yellow bandana.

'Hello, darling,' Penelope sing-songs. 'What fun, us girls reunited in the kitchen again!'

Sophie's relieved to see that her mother's as sober as a judge.

After the breakfast dishes are cleared away, Sophie sets up the kitchen just how she wants it. She puts Chiara to work chopping vegetables, Salvatore expertly slices the scallops in half and Sophie and Penelope prepare the cutlets.

Mother and daughter work seamlessly together, Sophie patting the cutlets with seasoned flour and dipping them in egg, then passing them to Penelope to coat in breadcrumbs and parmesan. She manages to quieten her brain down enough to let herself enjoy this rare moment of harmony with her mother.

Just before ten-thirty, Salvatore excuses himself to meet Christian in the lobby. Sophie hugs him fiercely.

Penelope's face darkens when Sophie tells her about Elena and Christian. 'I wish I'd had the courage to leave,' Penelope whispers.

It's the first time her mother has ever acknowledged her abusive marriage.

'I'm sorry I wasn't brave enough, Fee,' she continues. 'I'm so terribly sorry.'

Sophie tries to answer but the words are caught in her throat. She keeps her eyes down, staring at the dishes she's washing.

'It's the reason I drink, you know,' Penelope says. 'It helps me forget.'

Sophie meets Penelope's eye. 'Please go to rehab, Mum. Please get some help.'

'I told you I'll think about it, darling.'

GAYLE

Mike and Gayle are too stressed about Noah to do much adventuring today, so they sit in their room with the TV on.

Mike's initial bravado over Noah's disappearance has evaporated now that another day has gone by and he's not been heard from. Not ten minutes have passed all morning that Mike hasn't asked her if there are any new updates from 'Noah's fellow'.

Although he hasn't explicitly said so, she can feel Mike's resentment towards Chris weakening. It's clear in the messages Chris has sent Gayle today how much he loves their son, and she's beginning to think that even Mike can see that too. 'Can't be easy on him,' Mike conceded after a particularly panicked message from Chris.

She checks her phone now for what feels like the millionth time.

'Nothing?' Mike asks.

'Nothing, hon.'

She stares at the TV screen, not paying attention to the game show that's on. 'Do you think Elena's gone yet?'

She didn't catch Elena at breakfast today which means she'll never see her again.

Mike shrugs. 'Who knows? I tell you what, for what was supposed to be a relaxing two weeks on vacation in Italy, there's been a helluva lot of drama.'

'You can say that again.'

He turns to her. 'Are you still as desperate to leave?'

She thinks about it. 'Not so much any more. I just want to hear that Noah's okay. If we know he's safe, then I think I'd actually be happy if we stayed for the Epiphany regatta.'

Even with the acqua alta, when they went out for a takeaway coffee this morning, the streets of San Marco were buzzing as new hanging decorations were spread around the town for La Regata della Befana. The new decorations are all of witches on broomsticks. There's even a witch atop the giant Christmas tree in Piazza San Marco.

Mike read that on Epiphany Eve, la Befana, the witch, delivers presents to all the children in Venice, like Santa Claus. Gayle isn't sure exactly how a witch became the central figure for a Christian feast day, but then again, there's so little that actually does make sense to her these days.

'The Epiphany is still two days away,' Mike says. 'Surely we'll hear from Noah before then.'

Gayle nods. 'Surely.' She can't bear to think of the alternative.

Elena

Christian's gone. It's time.

Without a backwards glance, Elena hobbles out of the suite and takes the lift to the lobby. She bursts into the kitchen where she finds Sophie at the bench. She wraps her arms around her new friend. 'I'll never be able to repay you for what you've done for me. Thank you, thank you. Thank the Bianchis for me, will you? I wish I could have said goodbye in person. And Gayle and Mike too.'

'Go, go.' Sophie pushes her out the door. 'This is it now, you're free!'

'Pray for me.'

'You don't need prayers, you'll be fine.'

Elena walks out of Hotel Il Cuore with nothing but a small handbag and the clothes she has on.

Outside, the clouds hang low and heavy. The buildings on either side of the alleyways crowd her. She didn't think about shoe coverings before she left, and she doesn't want to backtrack, so she has no choice but to walk along the footbridges leading the way to the canal. With her injured ankle, the wooden planks feel as tenuous as balance beams.

She doesn't let herself look over her shoulder; it's easier to keep her balance if she looks ahead. Any second now, she expects him to catch up to her. All the while, the sky and the city close in on her.

She finally makes it to the vaporetto stop, where she disappears into the small crowd waiting for the boat to San Marcuola.

In her handbag are a handful of tampons, her passport, pen and paper she took from the hotel suite and another hundred euro she stole from Christian, just in case.

The boat arrives mercifully quickly and she climbs on board. There's a tap on her shoulder and she gasps, but it's just the conductor wanting to check her ticket. It's only when the boat pulls out into the canal, without Christian on board, that she exhales.

She checks her watch. It's eleven am. Christian's meeting has started. She's worried for Salvatore when Christian realises she's gone. Salvatore's little more than a boy; she hates that he's been dragged into this mess. She hates that the rest of the family have been too, and the Dawsons, and Sophie. Which one of them will bear the brunt of Christian's rage? Thinking about it makes her breathe faster.

Now the nun at the Vatican is involved too, and possibly Alessandro. So many people are risking themselves for her. She can't fuck this up.

The boat trip takes forever. She wants to scream at the people to hurry as they board and disembark in slow motion at every stop, and she has to restrain herself from pushing people out of the way when the boat finally docks at San Marcuola.

Thankfully, Cannaregio isn't flooded. She runs on solid ground now, ignoring the pain shooting from her ankle all the way up her shin. She doesn't stop running until she reaches Mamma's apartment building.

Mamma and Alessandro are waiting for her on the ground floor. She throws herself into Mamma's arms and they embrace the way they haven't been able to under Christian's watchful eye.

Alessandro's carrying a bundle of clothes. 'Marina gave me these for you. It's better if you change into them in case he describes your clothing to the police.'

Elena takes a brown woollen trench coat from him.

'Put this one on first.' He holds up a thick sweater. 'It'll bulk up your frame.'

She's sweating from her dash across the Ghetto, but she layers up in the sweater, coat and beanie that Alessandro gives her.

'They gave me clothes too,' Mamma says. She's rugged up in a long coat and woollen hat, which is pulled low over her forehead, hiding her hair.

Alessandro also gives Elena a handbag and gloves. They've thought of everything.

'I paid some boys to smash the CCTV cameras in the neighbourhood,' he tells Elena as she empties the contents of her handbag into the new one. 'There'll be no footage of you arriving or of us leaving. Keep your heads down, just in case. I'll walk ahead and stand away from you at the station. We'll board different carriages and meet when we leave the station in Rome. There'll be a driver waiting for us there. Are you ready?'

Elena nods. 'Pronta.'

He looks at his phone. 'The next train leaves in twelve minutes. We don't have much time. I'll go first, okay?'

'Alessandro!' Elena calls to his back as he walks out. 'Grazie.'

He gives her a quick smile and leaves.

A minute later, she walks back out onto the street with Mamma. They walk in silence to Santa Lucia Station, looking at the ground. She keeps imagining footsteps behind them, but she doesn't turn to check.

At the station, an announcement comes over the loudspeaker that the train to Rome is delayed by twenty minutes. The panic rises in Elena's throat. She looks at Alessandro, who's standing several metres away. He gestures for her to stay calm.

She mistakes every tall man that walks onto the platform for Christian. She can barely keep standing, her legs are shaking so hard. Mamma pulls white glass rosary beads from her pocket and prays the Apostles' Creed in a quiet voice. Elena joins her. They pray until the train arrives.

In the crowded carriage, they manage to find seats. The security cameras point down at them from every corner.

'Keep your head down,' she whispers to Mamma.

The northern Italian countryside flashes past Elena at high speed, but she sees none of it. She has no coherent thoughts; her brain is whitewashed with fear. Mamma produces a banana from her bag and offers it to her, but Elena's throat is too constricted to eat. Mamma sleeps on and off throughout the five-hour journey, while Elena stays on high alert. She makes eye contact with none of the other passengers. It's an eternity before the train finally pulls into their station in Rome.

Alessandro's waiting when they leave the platform. He ushers them to a black limousine. A short drive later, they reach the gates of Vatican City.

'I'm leaving, you know,' Alessandro whispers in Elena's ear in the back of the car.

'Leaving what?'

'Here. The Church. Everything.'

She whips her head around to look at him and he's smiling.

'I've only come back here to accompany you,' he says.

'Why are you quitting?'

'I love someone.' He blushes.

'Is that someone Marina?' She keeps her voice low so that Mamma can't hear.

He pulls her in close. 'That someone is.'

'I'm happy for you.' She leans her head on his shoulder.

'I'm happy for you too, puffetta,' he says, using the term of endearment he and Paolo had for her when they were young, and it's all she can do to keep it together.

She looks out the window as they're taken along paved roads, past manicured gardens, through parts of the Vatican she never saw on school trips to the city. The limousine comes to a halt outside an imposing brown brick building.

'We're here,' Alessandro says. 'The nuns will look after you well. I'll come and see you tonight.'

'Guarda, Elena.' Mamma points at the sky when they step out of the car.

Elena looks up. The clouds have parted; the sun's shining.

She and Mamma are bundled into the monastery by two waiting nuns dressed in ankle-length tan dresses. They're led through a grand ballroom and down wide hallways, whose walls are covered in gilded portraits of popes and saints and Jesus, to a small room furnished sparsely with twin beds and a wooden dresser. A smaller version of the painting of il Papa from Hotel Il Cuore hangs on the wall between their beds.

Elena and Mamma are given fresh clothes to change into and warm soup to eat. They're provided with toiletries and pyjamas and a Bible each. The nuns are kind and motherly, telling them they can stay as long as they need and that, in the meantime, the Vatican will arrange documents for them with new identities.

'You're safe now, Elena.' An older nun with a strikingly beautiful face, Suora Teresa, touches Elena's shoulder. 'The Lord has blessed you.'

Elena lets herself weep.

Gayle

Gayle watches Mike sleeping, his thick lips trembling with every snore. She lightly touches his arm, grateful that her husband is safe and sound and here with her, not in hospital like poor Signore Bianchi.

It's a rare occasion for Mike to be asleep by eight-thirty, but tonight he announced he was too worried about Noah to write his blog, so Gayle suggested an early night. She's happy to be in bed as well. The stress over Noah has worn her out. They've still heard nothing.

Mike startles himself awake with a particularly loud snore. 'You still awake, hon? How's your head?'

'Splitting.'

He scratches his beard. 'I'm fixing for something sweet. Wonder if there's any leftover cake downstairs?'

'Let me check for you, hon. You stay there. I just need the bathroom first.'

She's sitting on the toilet with her knickers around her ankles when there's a persistent knock on the door of their suite.

Her first thought is that it's the police bringing bad news about Noah. She thinks she might be sick. But how would the Italian police even know he's missing?

'Hold your horses!' Mike calls and she hears him open the door.

She emerges from the bathroom to find Christian Taylor looming large in their doorway.

His eyes are red-rimmed. He looks at Mike. 'Where the fuck is my wife?' His voice is so low she can hardly hear him.

Her gut clenches hard.

'I . . . I don't know what you're talking about.' Mike shakes his head.

'Don't lie to me, you old cunt.' Christian's tone is calm but the muscles around his jaw twitch. 'I found this in her mother's apartment.' He turns his palm up to show Mike what's in it.

Gayle sees then that Christian's holding a bright green sun visor. His fingers obscure the writing on the front, but she knows it says *They Fought For Us, We Walk For Them*. Her face goes numb.

'I . . . I swear I don't . . . I don't know where she is,' Mike stammers, stepping back from Christian.

Christian follows Mike into the room and closes the door behind him. Without speaking, he shoves Mike in the chest, who lands flat on his back with a thud.

Gayle screams.

'Call the police!' Mike turns to her. 'Quick!'

She lunges for her phone and her fingers shake as she types in the code to unlock it. She's three digits in when the phone is knocked out of her hand, slamming into the wall.

'You stay out of this.' Christian's face is next to hers. He pushes her and she tumbles sideways onto the bed.

'Get your hands off her!' Mike is on all fours.

Christian drives his knee into Mike's back, flattening him onto the floor again. Mike grunts as Christian grabs him by the shoulders and roughly rolls him over. Gayle flies off the bed and throws herself at Christian. He elbows her in the face so hard that she loses her balance again. Her head throbs from the blow.

Christian wraps his hands around Mike's throat. 'Tell me where she is,' he says in the same easy tone he could have used asking for directions. 'Tell me.'

Mike's eyes are frantic. He splutters and chokes.

Gayle picks herself up off the floor and throws herself onto Christian again. Try as she might, she can't loosen his grip on Mike's throat. 'Stop choking him!' she screams. 'You're killing him!'

Christian doesn't stop. He keeps his voice even, not taking his eyes off Mike. 'Tell me where my wife is.'

Gayle runs out into the hallway. 'Help!' she screams at the top of her lungs. 'Somebody help, please!'

She runs back into the suite and tries again to pull Christian off Mike but he's way too strong for her.

There's nothing she can do but watch as Christian chokes the life out of her husband.

Sophie

Sophie and Penelope lock eyes at the sound of a woman screaming for help. Sophie lets the tea towel in her hands drop to the floor as she runs out of the kitchen.

Oh God, oh God, oh God.

She takes the stairs as fast as she can with Penelope hot on her heels. Two guests stand unmoving in the hallway opposite the Dawsons' suite.

From the doorway, Sophie sees Mrs Dawson trying to fight off Christian, who's on the floor, straddling Mr Dawson.

'Tell me where she is,' Christian says over and over in a voice as monotone as an automated message. His hands are tight around the old man's throat.

Mr Dawson's blue in the face. He makes a strangled noise and shakes his head from side to side.

'Get off him!' Sophie screams. She tries to wrench Christian's fingers off Mr Dawson's neck. Penelope and Mrs Dawson are pulling at him as well, but Christian's somehow manifested into the Incredible fucking Hulk and maintains his iron grip, outpowering them all. He's repeating 'Tell me where she is' like he's in some kind of trance.

Mr Dawson thrashes around; his eyes are bulging.

Sophie looks for a weapon. The lamp! She pulls it off the bedside table but its cord is stuck in the wall socket behind the bed. She yanks hard but it doesn't budge. *Fuck.*

'He's dying! Look at him, he's dying!' Mrs Dawson screams.

Mr Dawson's just about passed out. Christian still hasn't let go of his throat. More unhelpful people have appeared in the doorway to stare.

'Call the police, for Christ's sake!' Sophie yells at them.

One of them does.

The silver blade of a letter opener on top of the chest of drawers catches Sophie's eye. She lunges for it and is about to bring it down onto Christian when it's forcefully ripped from her hand by her mother. Penelope plunges the letter opener deep into Christian's neck. He jerks his head up, a look of confusion crossing his face, and then he lets go of Mr Dawson and crumples beside him on the floor.

Sophie stands over Christian as he stares up at her, his hand reaching towards the blade lodged in his neck. Blood oozes onto the carpet in a thick red trail. She watches as he gurgles, and then he lets out a long low noise and his eyes glaze over. He's looking right at her when he dies.

'Oh, Jesus! Oh, God!' Penelope cries. 'He's dead. He's dead, isn't he? Oh my God!'

Sophie doesn't answer her mother. She doesn't even look at her.

'He's breathing! He's still breathing!' Mrs Dawson cries, cradling Mr Dawson's head in her arms.

'I'll call the police,' Sophie says. Calmly she steps over Christian's body and past the onlookers in the hallway, then just as calmly takes the stairs down to reception to make the call.

'Qual è l'emergenza?' the male operator says.

'I'm reporting a death at Hotel Il Cuore,' Sophie replies.

Elena

Alessandro is ushered by Suora Teresa into Elena and Anna-Maria's room at the monastery. His face is white. His phone shakes in his hand.

Elena feels the blood drain from her face. 'What is it? What's he done?'

He looks at her with a stricken expression. 'Elena, your husband is dead.'

'*What?*' She doesn't recognise her own voice. '*What?*'

'He was stabbed at the hotel. He died instantly.'

Elena's hand flies to her mouth. 'How? Why?'

'I don't have any details. That's all I know.'

'You're sure, Alessandro?' Mamma grabs his arm. 'You're sure he's dead?'

Alessandro nods. 'Rocco saw them take his body away with his own eyes. He's dead, Zia.'

'Santa Maria.' Mamma lets out a sob.

Elena's legs give way. She collapses onto the bed. Mamma sits next to her and rocks herself forwards and backwards as she chants, 'Ave o Maria, piena di grazia . . .'

Alessandro stands frozen in the doorway, with Suora Teresa behind him. He and Elena stare at each other while Mamma prays.

Outside, the cathedral bells ring.

LORETTA

Rocco calls Loretta at the hospital just before midnight. Sophie and her mother have been released from the police station after being taken in for interviewing. The lawyer Rocco hired has left, and Rocco's on his way back to the hotel with the two women.

'Their passports are suspended until the investigation's finished,' he tells Loretta. 'But il detective anziano is confident Sophie's mother won't be charged. He said it should only take a day, two at the most, until the case is closed. The Americans gave their statements, and their evidence matched up. He said it's looking like a clear case of self-defence.'

'Grazie a Dio.' Loretta exhales.

She's conflicted in her feelings about Christian Taylor. If it wasn't for him, Alberto would have lost his life twice in the last two weeks. But now Elena is free. Half of her grieves his death, while the other half rejoices in it.

'I asked about the hotel,' Rocco adds. 'He said they should be done by tomorrow night and then we can return to normal.'

'Return to normal? Nothing's normal any more.'

In the last twenty-four hours, one man has died in her hotel and two others, one of them her own Alberto, have escaped death by a whisker. When Rocco arrived at the hotel after Sophie called him, reporters were already camped outside, tipped off by the police. Her guests have all been evacuated, her beloved hotel is a crime scene. How can things ever be normal again?

The last she heard, Alessandro was being interviewed by police in Rome, and Elena and Anna-Maria were with police escorts on their way back to Venice. The whole thing is a mess.

'How's Papà?' Rocco asks.

'Sleeping peacefully since dinner. He complained about the food they served him. He wanted meat.'

Alberto's healing; at least there's that.

When Loretta ends the call with Rocco, she turns to Marina, who hasn't left her side for the last eighteen hours. 'Go home.' Loretta rubs her back. 'Get some rest.'

Marina shakes her head. 'I'm not leaving until he's out of intensive care.'

'That won't be until tomorrow. You need to sleep.'

'No more than you do. As long as you're here, I'm here,' Marina insists. 'I'll never forgive myself for not being there for you when Papà's heart attack happened. I'm so sorry, Mamma.'

'Child, you've apologised to me a million times.'

'I know, but I feel awful about it.' Marina speaks softly so as not to wake Alberto. 'It's just that it was my last night . . .' She gulps. 'My last night with Alessandro.'

Marina's honesty gives Loretta the courage to ask, 'Are you planning to marry him, vita mia?'

Marina sighs. 'I don't know. I believed him when he came home and said he was finally ready to commit to me. But something's changed this evening. I can feel it.'

'A lot has happened. Perhaps he's just distracted?'

Marina shrugs.

As if Alessandro is listening in on their conversation, Marina's phone pings. Marina reads the message with her hand over her mouth.

'What is it?' Loretta asks.

Marina passes her the phone. The lengthy message from Alessandro is essentially a break-up text, blaming his duty to the

Vatican. Apparently, once he had returned there, he couldn't bring himself to leave again.

It ends with *I have to put Christ first*.

Loretta passes the phone back to Marina. 'Come, cara.' She gathers Marina into her arms and holds on to her as Marina silently falls apart. 'At least you know this now, and not after you wasted even more years on him,' she tells her gently.

'Why did I have to fall for a priest?' Marina heaves.

'We can't help who we love. I know how you feel, tesoro, believe me.'

Marina frowns at her. 'How could you possibly know what this feels like?'

Since Loretta saw the way Alessandro and Marina looked at each other at Mass, she's been debating with herself whether or not she should share her story with Marina. Now she knows she has to.

'Marina, do you think I would have been a good catch when I was young?'

Marina looks surprised by the question. 'Of course. You were the most beautiful woman in Venice. And the heiress to a hotel.'

'Did you ever wonder why I didn't marry until I was thirty?'

'I suppose I thought you were being picky.'

'Picky? And I chose *him*?' She points at Alberto.

Right on cue Alberto lets out a long low fart in his sleep.

Marina smiles. 'What was the reason then, that you married late?'

Loretta takes a deep breath and tells her daughter everything.

Marina listens in stunned silence. 'Does Papà know?' she whispers when Loretta finishes.

'Of course he knows. He's always known.'

'Did you even love him, though?' Marina looks over at her sleeping father. 'Or did you just marry him to appease your parents? Do you regret your life with us, Mamma?'

'I love Alberto dearly and I wouldn't change a thing about how my life turned out. How can I have a single regret when Alberto gave me you and Rocco?'

Marina blows her nose. 'So you think I actually can get over Alessandro one day?'

'One day sooner than you think.' Loretta smiles as Luca walks into the room with a clipboard in his hand and a stethoscope hanging around his neck.

When he sees Marina, his face lights up.

On the
TWELFTH
DAY of
CHRISTMAS

Elena

Elena runs her hand along Papà's clothes, which line the wardrobe. She buries her face in the sweaters that still smell of him, before pulling out a favourite blue one and putting it on. It dwarfs her.

Mamma comes into the room, holding a cup of Earl Grey. 'One milk, no sugar. I made one for me too. I took one sip and poured it down the drain. It tastes like water from a hundred-year-old well.'

Elena smiles. 'Grazie, Mamma.' She takes the tea and follows Mamma into the lounge, wondering if there'll ever come a time when she'll be brave enough to leave the sanctuary of this apartment. It's hard to imagine it.

She tries not to think about Christian, because it makes her chest tight and her breath catch, but it's impossible to keep him out of her mind for more than a few seconds at a time.

The news is on the TV. His death made the headlines yesterday, but it was quickly replaced by stories of the acqua alta, the finale of the *Venice Rising* exhibition, and La Befana. There's too much going on in San Marco at the moment for the death of an Australian tourist to matter much to Venetians, even if it did happen in a famous hotel under unusual circumstances.

She's grateful that Mike and Gayle are safe. She owes them so much. She hasn't made contact with them yet, though. She hasn't spoken to Sophie either, or to Sophie's mother. The four of them will carry the trauma of Christian's death, of Mike's assault, of the police interrogations, for the rest of their lives on her account. One day, she'll have to reckon with that. But that day is not today. Reaching out to those who helped her, reading through the police report, dealing with the guilt – that will all come later.

For now, all she's going to do is sit on this couch in her childhood home, wrapped in the warmth of Papà's sweater, drink hot tea brewed by Mamma, and watch the happy faces of the children on TV as they show the reporter the stockings they've put up near the fireplace for La Befana to leave them gifts this evening.

Gayle

Gayle and Loretta keep each other company while their husbands nap at opposite ends of the same hospital room. It's warm on the ward and Gayle wipes the perspiration from her face with a tissue. She can just imagine how frizzy her hair is in this humidity. It amazes her how Loretta can still look so poised and elegant after everything she's been through. She doesn't have a hair out of place, and she sits tall and lithe with her legs and arms crossed. How can a woman who hasn't slept or showered still be this glamorous in a hospital ward, of all places?

Gayle's phone vibrates with a message and when she reads it, she almost forgets to breathe.

'What is it?' Loretta asks.

'It's Noah. He says he's safe. Oh, Loretta, Noah's okay! Thank God.'

'You see?' Loretta smiles.

'He says he needed time to sort out his thoughts when it became clear that Mike was still no closer to accepting Chris. He said it opened old wounds and he had to be alone for a while. He feels awful about scaring everyone the way he did, and Chris has made him promise to have some counselling, but at least he's home now. He's ever so concerned about Mike too, bless him. Despite everything, that boy still loves his pop.'

'This miracle happened because you attended the Mass,' Loretta says assuredly.

'I believe you might be right about that.' Gayle's hands shake in her lap.

'Maybe now that you know your son is safe, you will finally stop shaking,' Loretta says.

'I think it's because I can't get the image of Christian with Mike's knife in his neck out of my mind. Do you know what the policeman said? He said it was lucky for such a small blade to kill him. He said it got him right in the carotid artery. *Lucky*. That was his exact word.' She sighs. 'I've been praying over and over again for Christian's soul. Do you want to know why? It's because I'm ashamed at how happy I am about it. Loretta, I'm so happy I could dance. It's not right, is it? I know it's not right, but I can't help thinking that lucky is the perfect word for what happened.'

'You are praying for the soul of the man who tried to kill your husband. You are a good woman with a good heart,' Loretta replies.

The tea lady interrupts their conversation when she wheels in lunch. The second the squeaky trolley is pushed into the room, Mike's eyes are wide open and in a flash he's sitting up in bed, eyeing off the selection of sandwiches.

He winces as he eats. 'Hurts to swallow.' His voice is a hoarse whisper. The doctors say it should return to normal very soon.

Gayle holds his hand in hers.

'You have had an eventful stay at Il Cuore, signore,' Loretta says to Mike. 'Perhaps next year you would like to return and try again for a more peaceful vacation?'

Mike can't shake his head fast enough. 'Never coming back. Never, ever, ever.'

'On the house.' Loretta speaks over him. 'Two weeks' free accommodation and meals to thank you for being a hero. It is the least we can do.'

Mike's hand freezes with the sandwich halfway into his mouth, his eyes just about popping out of his head. 'Free?' he whispers.

'All free.' Loretta smiles. 'And we will even arrange a gondola ride with a different singer. What do you say?'

'Can't knock back such a generous offer.' Mike grins and Gayle's heart soars at the knowledge she'll see her dear friend Loretta once again.

When Loretta returns to the chair by Signore Bianchi's bedside, Mike whispers to Gayle, 'Hon, when that man was choking the life out of me, all I could think about was that I was gonna have to explain to the good Lord at the pearly gates why I turned my back on my own son.' He holds his throat, wincing again.

'Shh, rest your voice, hon,' she soothes. 'We can talk about this later.'

He shakes his head. 'I've got to tell Noah how sorry I am. I never should've made him dig that hole. I never should've made him feel bad about himself. I have to make it right. But what if it's too late? What if he's gone? It'll all be my fault.'

Gayle thinks her heart might just explode with love for him. The cancer in her marriage has been blasted to oblivion. 'It's not too late, hon. I heard from him just now while you were napping. He's fine.'

'Praise be! What happened to him? Why'd he disappear like that?'

'He disappeared because of us, hon.'

Mike's eyes fill with tears. 'Can I talk to him, do you think?'

She calls Noah, choosing the video option, and her beautiful child, perfect just the way God created him, appears on her screen.

'There he is!' Mike exclaims but it comes out as a whisper.

Noah looks so much like his dad, it's as if he actually is Mike from thirty years ago.

'So, you finally had some sense beaten into you or what, old man?' Noah grins.

Mike wipes his eyes. 'Son, how am I ever gonna make it up to you?'

For the first time in months, Gayle's headache is gone.

Sophie

Sophie sits on Penelope's bed, watching her pack. Christian's death has officially been classed as self-defence. Their passports were returned to them this afternoon. But Penelope isn't packing for Melbourne, she's headed to Switzerland. Sophie's booked her a room at the rehabilitation clinic Rocco went to years ago. The minimum stay is two weeks, but she imagines her mother will need significantly longer than that. Paying for this exclusive clinic is going to eat up most of Sophie's savings and she's okay with that.

Her phone pings with a message from Bec.

Penelope on that plane yet?

**Wish I could be there myself to make
sure she bloody well gets on it.**

Sophie snorts.
'What is it, darling?' Penelope looks up.
'Just a message from Bec.'
'Is she in a mood at you for leaving the magazine?'
'Not at all.'
When Rocco told Sophie that Loretta was scaling back her work in the restaurant to spend more time with Alberto, there was no question in her mind that Il Cuore was meant for her. She's enjoyed writing for *Foodie* but now she's ready to commit fully to her lifelong dream of running a restaurant.

Before all the trauma of last night, she'd had a successful debut with a dinner service that the guests raved about. It gave her a buzz like no other, and she's decided that people falling over themselves to compliment her cooking is just the kind of energy she wants for her life going forward. It feels pre-destined that her final feature for *Foodie* will be about Il Cuore. And what a feature it will be! The markets, the locals, the sights, the family, the *food* – she could write a whole essay on the gnocchi alone.

'You are going to be my boss in the kitchen,' Rocco said, grinning at her earlier today. 'I will have to do what you say.'

'Not just in the kitchen, Signore Bianchi.'

Rocco was at her side minutes after she called him in an almost catatonic state following Christian's death. With the hotel turned on its head, Rocco organised emergency accommodation for all the guests, and he was the spokesperson for the media and the contact person for the police. He even arranged for the carpet to be replaced in the Dawsons' suite today, all the while not leaving her alone for a minute. He's proven to her how dependable he can be in her lowest and most vulnerable moments.

The last two days have been the stuff of nightmares. The sight of Christian's body while he lay there bleeding out, Penelope's and Gayle's hysteria, the ambulance and the police storming the hotel – it all left her deeply shaken. And that was before she was manhandled into the police boat and taken to a stiflingly small room at the police station. There, she endured the ordeal of hours of interrogation by hostile detectives, with a language barrier complicating things further, and with a stone cold fear in her heart that they'd lock her mother up for good.

Sophie's spent more hours crying than not, and Rocco has been rock-solid through all of it. She's determined to be just as solid for him. She's found her person and she's going to support him as best she can in his efforts to stay sober. Because that's how Rocco deserves to be loved.

She's going home next month to get her little flat ready to rent out, then she's moving to San Marco, taking out a lease on an apartment on the top floor of Hotel Il Cuore and starting her life anew.

Penelope hands her a small plastic ornament of the Virgin Mary. 'Take this, Fee. Keep it in your room. Our Lady will watch over you.'

Sophie turns the ornament over in her hand. Its colour is odd. 'Does this thing glow in the dark?'

'Yes, dear, that way Our Lady can keep watch over you at night, keep you safe.'

'Mum!' she hoots. 'You can't honestly believe in the powers of a glow-in-the-dark Mary doll?'

Penelope purses her lips. 'It's a sin to mock the Blessed Virgin.'

Sophie straightens her face. 'Yes, right. Sorry.'

Her mother's lips tremble.

'Oh, Mum, it's all right, I'm sorry. I'll keep the ornament, I promise.'

'It's not that.' Penelope shakes her head. 'I can't get that man's face out of my head. The look in his eyes. It'll haunt me forever.'

Sophie's shoulders tense. She's haunted by it too. She keeps remembering how she stood above him while the air left his body in a low, final exhale. She never considered herself to be a violent person. In fact, she prized her gentleness. It made her feel superior. But that moral high ground collapsed beneath her when he died.

Now she's been forced to rethink what she's capable of. Murder, apparently. This new understanding is an epiphany of sorts, one that's come to her on the twelfth day of Christmas. Because life's funny like that.

Would her actions be the same if she had her time over? Unquestionably. She'd gleefully watch the canals of Venice run red with his blood, over and over again. That's who she is now.

All these years, Sophie's been judging her mother for what she did, but when it came down to it, she was no different. Her base instincts took over when it became a matter of survival, and she was fully prepared to kill another human being. Coming to terms with her own fallibility has made her accept Penelope's humanity for the first time. She truly understands why Penelope did what she did now.

'Can I ask you something, Mum?' she says. 'Why did you take the blade out of my hand yesterday? Why didn't you just let me do it?'

Penelope lets out a shaky sigh. 'Because I want you to go to heaven, Fee. I already have blood on my hands. But your soul's pure. I couldn't bear for you to tarnish it.'

Sophie freezes. 'What do you mean, you already have blood on your hands?'

Penelope looks her straight in the eye. 'You know exactly what I mean. There's no place in heaven for people like me.'

'So you *do* remember telling me what you did to Dad?'

'Of course I remember. Who can forget something like that?'

Sophie can almost feel the weight being lifted off her shoulders now that it's finally out in the open. 'Do you know what I'd love, Mum? When you come back from Switzerland, I'd love for us to start having some conversations about it and begin the healing process together.'

'We *can* talk about it, but, darling, it's too late for me to heal. My fate's sealed.'

'I don't think it can ever be too late.' Sophie turns the ornament of Mary over in her hands. 'But if that's what you really believe, then why do you keep up with all the praying? What's the point?'

'Do you think I pray to save *myself*?' Penelope laughs a small laugh. 'My dear girl, every prayer I've ever said has been for you and David. It's all for you.'

Sophie hugs Penelope tight. 'Come on, or you'll miss your flight.'

Rocco's waiting in the hallway, ready to escort Penelope to the airport. He adjusts his glasses and gives Sophie his megawatt smile when she emerges from Penelope's room.

'Pronta?'

Her heart leaps at the sight of him, this beautiful man who came into her life out of nowhere and made everything better.

'Sono pronta.' She smiles.

Loretta

Loretta steps out of the hospital a little over forty hours after Alberto was admitted. His drip and catheter were removed this morning when he was transferred from the ICU to the same ward as Signore Dawson.

She was shocked at how emotional she felt seeing the red marks around poor Signore Dawson's neck. Even though she'd heard what happened from Rocco, listening to Gayle's recap was heart-wrenching.

Once Alberto was settled in the new hospital room, Marina went home. There's something different about the way Marina's holding herself today, as if she's no longer afraid. Loretta's pride in her daughter knows no bounds.

Loretta stayed by Alberto's bedside until the physiotherapist came to take him for his first walk, which he managed while serenading the young man with a Julio Iglesias number, no less.

Now she's on her way home to shower and change before returning to the hospital. She's not in a rush because for once she's not needed at the hotel. Today is the first time in its history that Il Cuore is closed. The guests have all moved to new accommodation. San Marco's neighbouring hotels came to the rescue; the Venetian community knows how to rally. Alberto's coming home later in the week, and she smiles, remembering his face when she told him she was ready to start the process of handing over the running of the restaurant to Rocco.

'We'll have a good life together, Loretta,' Alberto promised her.

'I know we will.'

'As long as you don't go around kissing any more nuns.' He winked.

And just like that, she was forgiven.

What's surprising to her is that she has none of the panic she imagined would consume her at the idea of cutting back on work. All she feels is freedom. Glorious, liberating freedom. No more early morning alarms, no more scarfing down her lunch so she can rush back into the kitchen, no more debilitating fatigue and aches and pains all over her body from working it too hard.

Rocco told her last night that Sophie desperately wants to stay on at the hotel as a cook. In Sophie she has a woman she trusts, and whose passion for food rivals her own, to pass on her recipes to. And a son who loves that woman and will support her in the restaurant as much as he can. They'll make a formidable team, and Rocco's already put out feelers for extra staff to ease the load on them all. The future of Il Cuore is in good hands. Her nonna would be proud of her legacy.

Loretta holds her face up to the afternoon sun and shuts her eyes, feeling its winter warmth on her skin. The flood waters have drained, the boardwalks have been taken away and the ground is dry once more.

She walks past the beautiful gothic architecture of the palace and past the clock tower towards the basilica. Today, the crowds are back in Piazza San Marco and the square is decorated for La Befana tomorrow. A big wooden witch hangs from the lion statue near the basilica, flocked by tourists taking photos of it. The hawkers have set up stalls throughout the piazza, selling gaudy merchandise of witches, everything from helium balloons to cheap sweaters. Venice is abuzz and it warms her heart to see it. She's been ravaged, this magical city, facing every kind of adversary over her time: invasions, wars, plagues, environmental brutalising, and still here she stands. Beaten, battered, but standing nonetheless.

Loretta has stayed away from the piazza since her viral photo at the tank. Today, the tank is empty; Magdalena's gone. Floating in the dirty water is her white dress. The '*affogando*' sign in front of the tank has been replaced. The new sign reads '*fai qualcosa*'. Do something.

This morning the Prime Minister made an impassioned speech, vowing to hurry along the opening of the Mose Project, put an end to the big ships coming into port, limit the number of daily tourists to Venice and impose a tourist tax. He's even vowed to replace Venice's fuel-guzzling fleet of vaporettos with electric-powered ones.

All of these promises so soon after Loretta's photo went viral can't be coincidental. She knows, deep in her soul, that her tears weren't in vain. Those tears will help save Venice.

I did something, Magdalena.

Tomorrow is the big protest that Rocco and Salvatore are taking part in. Their sabotage of La Regata will undoubtedly garner even more worldwide attention for the cause. The Prime Minister and his government will have to follow through on the new promises or face scorn and ridicule from around the globe. Italians are proud people; they do not care for scorn and ridicule.

Turning away from the tank, Loretta walks across the piazza, past the orchestra playing Bach outside Florian, where the people are happy to pay a small fortune for a coffee just to feel a part of the wonder that is Venice.

Acknowledgements

Trigger warning: if effusive gushiness isn't your thing, please close the book now, we're done here.

Biggest thanks of all to my publisher, the one, the only, Ali Watts. Working with you has been a dream. Your vision, clarity, tenacity, instinct, intelligence, inherent loveliness and kindness, along with your wonderful sense of fun, all make me very grateful that I'm one of the lucky ones who get to be your author. I adore you!

A heartfelt thank you to my phenomenal literary agents, Jacinta di Mase and Danielle Binks. From the moment I said, 'So I had this idea . . .' you've both been the driving force behind me actually getting this story finished. It took me an age to get started on it, then an age to write and rewrite (and rewrite), and you were endlessly patient through it all.

Danielle, thank you for reading so many versions of the story that you're probably triggered for life at the mere mention of the word Venice now. Thank you for gently guiding and encouraging me, and then not so gently guiding and encouraging me by bringing out the CAPS LOCK and *italics* when I tried to chuck it in. How lucky I am to have you not only as my trusted agent, but as my much-loved friend.

Jacinta, thank you for plucking me from obscurity ten years ago, creating a career for me and having my back every single day since. Your unwavering loyalty and friendship mean everything to me, and I love you so much it borders on terrifying, tbh. Hooray to me for manifesting you!

Huge thanks to the brilliant team at Penguin Random House Australia:

Amanda Martin, your insightful, thoughtful edits rounded out the story beautifully, and you're just so lovely too.

Nikki Townsend, you're a creative genius. Thank you for painstakingly creating the cover to end all covers. I mean, LOOK AT IT!

Holly Toohey, thank you for being so lovely in welcoming me to the Penguin family. I feel very lucky to have someone as brilliant and warm as you in charge.

Hannah Ludbrook and Rebekah Chereshsky, thank you for being the most incredibly dedicated, hard-working publicity and marketing duo any author could wish for. You're both amazing in every way.

Natasha Solomun, you're my literary angel in sales. Thank you for believing in this story from the very first sentence. Jo Baker and Hannah Armstrong, thank you for leading the charge on sales with such enthusiasm and care. The wonderful national field sales team, thank you for your passion and generosity in taking this story out into stores. Special thanks to my rep here in Perth, gorgeous Jane Parkhill – for everything!

Bella Arnott-Hoare, Tina Gumnior, Jessica Malpass and all the other lovely publicists, thank you for keeping my little red street library bursting with new books.

Sarah McDuling, thank you for your faith in this story and for being so supportive of me ever since I was very first published. You're simply amazing!

Sonja Heijn, thank you for the thoughtful and careful proofread.

And thank you to the rest of the PRH team who helped bring this story to the shelves. I'm grateful to each and every one of you.

A special thank you to Mary Rennie, my wonderful first publisher, who still champions my writing. What a rare and precious person you are.

Writing is a lonely business, but it's made so much sunnier and funnier by beautiful friends going through the ups and downs of life with me. Thank you to my darling girlfriends, including my author friends, school mum friends, high school and university friends and my cousins who were my first besties and remain my besties now, for the support, kindness, love and many, many memes. I love too many of you to name but you all know who you are.

Now here are the people I *do* need to name:

Nina 'Pretty Ballerina' Casella, thank you for being my everything Italy person and for over twenty years of your beautiful friendship that I'd be lost without.

Sasha Wasley, Anthea Hodgson, Emma Cockman and Jennifer Ammoscato – thank you for the generous time you invested in reading drafts of this book. Thank you for the encouragement and belief and, above all, for your treasured friendships. And I'm forever thankful to you, Anth, for telling Ali I was a 'cool chick', which somehow miraculously led to the publication of this novel.

Rachael Johns, thank you for coming up with the perfect title, for the wonderful endorsement quote, for keeping the secret that I had started writing again and for always being just as curious as I am about the millions of things and people (most of them strangers to us) we feel the need to investigate online instead of actually getting our work done. I love you and our friendship so much!

Melina Marchetta, thank you for the amazing endorsement quote and for your steadfast friendship ever since I pounced on you like a crazed lunatic with my selfie stick when you were quietly minding your own business in Far North Queensland in 2018. That you didn't take out a restraining order on me but instead became one of my biggest supporters is a testament to your kindness and generosity.

Nicola Moriarty, thank you for the incredible endorsement quote and the even more incredible friendship across the miles for the last decade.

Holly Wainwright and Kate Eberlen, two other lovely talented authors who live far away who I'm grateful to have as dear friends and who were also kind enough to read and endorse this book. Thank you!

Lisa Ireland, thank you for keeping the faith even when I lost mine, for being an enabler of my rants no matter the topic, and for always being prepared to drive a million miles to see me, even if it's for half an hour in a crowd because that's just the kind of friend you are.

Greek goddess Spiri Tsintziras, thank you for the chocolate gold coins you gave me for good luck for 2023. They worked a charm and you're an angel!

Rebecca Sparrow, thank you for activating promo mode quite literally the second you found out I signed a new book contract, and for the gift of your beautiful friendship. Under 'kindness' in the dictionary, there should be a photo of you.

Back in 2016, I had lunch with Cheryl Akle. As we ate, looking at the sea, I shared a story with her. Cheryl looked me in the eye and said, 'This is the story you must tell. This is *the one*.' It took me five years to find the courage to write it, but Cheryl, I'll never forget your belief in this story from its inception on that day. Thank you also for remaining a truly loyal friend even though I make your life flash before your eyes when you're a passenger in my Mini.

Three brilliant Australian books inspired me greatly in writing *The Venice Hotel*. They are: *The Salt Madonna* by Catherine Noske, *Lapsed* by Monica Dux and *A Lifetime of Impossible Days* by Tabitha Bird. Thank you to these fiercely brave authors who (without knowing it) helped me to also try to be brave.

Booksellers, librarians, bookstagrammers and book bloggers – collectively you're my favourite people in the world, and I'm so grateful to call many of you my friends. Thank you, thank you, thank you.

Huge thanks to the best work wife ever, my receptionist Sally, for all the ten-hour days where you keep our clinic running like clockwork when I'm in edit mode and completely feral. There's nobody I'd rather laugh, complain and gossip through my workdays with than you.

The world will never know a bigger cheerleader than my mother. Love you so much, Mum, thank you for being the loudest, proudest and kindest always.

ACKNOWLEDGEMENTS

With every manuscript I write, my first two readers are always my husband, Paul, and my bestie, Daniella. Each time Paul is adamant that the very first draft is perfect in every way, and Dan points out the many, many parts that make her want to stick a hot poker in her eye. I appreciate and love you dearly for the adulation (Paul) and the reality check (Dan).

This time though, there was a new first reader before Paul or Dan, and that was my daughter, Lara, who turned out to be an insightful manuscript assessor and profoundly shaped the story. Thank you, my clever, hilarious girl with the biggest heart of anyone I know. I love you so deeply.

Thank you, Tommy, my lovely gentle son, for being so accommodating when you were unexpectedly called upon to snap my author photo (twice!). Thank you for understanding the assignment and getting the shots so quickly. You're the kindest 24-year-old man alive, and I love you with my whole heart.

And sweet Porsche, you're a shining light in my life too. I'm so happy you and Tommy found each other and that I found my book-loving/buying bestie/enabler in you too.

To the people of Venice, grazie per aver condiviso con me la tua bellissima citta. Thank you to the Venetians who were gracious and generous when I stopped them in the streets (and on the water) and who indulged me with their stories full of warmth, candour and humour. I hope I was able to do justice to your vibrancy and your urgency. Bella Venezia, you have my heart and soul, always and forever.

If you're a survivor of domestic violence, I send you my loving wishes for continued healing. And if you've been waiting for a sign to leave him, then I hope reading this book was your sign.

Finally, to you, dear reader, thank you for giving me your precious time. Come find me on social media and say hi. And here's some unsolicited advice for you, gorgeous reader (because I'm bossy like that): never ever say no to gelato.

Much love,

Tess x

Book Club Notes

1. Hotel Il Cuore sounds like a dream destination, but for which characters does it become more of a nightmare?
2. 'Loretta needs to work as much as she needs to breathe.' How does her work help and hinder her in life?
3. Do you understand why Sophie is so cautious about risking her heart on love?
4. In what ways does faith provide strength to the characters in the novel, and in what ways does it create obstacles?
5. Gayle believes Mike is 'smarter' than her, which is part of the reason she finds it troubling to be questioning his opinions lately. Do you agree with her assessment?
6. In what ways is Elena a victim and in what ways is she a heroine?
7. 'A parent will do anything for their child.' Discuss.
8. Do you agree with Sophie that 'Everything about Venice is magical'?
9. 'What is marriage for if not for rescuing each other?' How does this apply to the relationships in *The Venice Hotel*?
10. Discuss the significance of food in the novel.
11. Venice is a place many of the characters are escaping to, but it is suffering too. What did you learn about the environmental issues facing Venice presently?
12. Have you ever had holiday plans turned upside down?